The Ykx, [...]inged bipeds. It [...] [...]ilt the Gateway be[...] [...] who could make it open. But few now alive had ever seen them, fewer still could point Skeen along the trail they had taken. Yet if she could not find the Gate builders and win their secret from them, she would never be able to return to the spaceways again. She would never know the joy of claiming vengeance on the comrade who had stolen her spaceship—and with it, her life.

So Skeen vowed to search the entire world till she found her key to the Gateway. And she would let no one turn her from her path, no matter the price in gold—or blood!

SKEEN'S LEAP

Jo Clayton
has also written:

THE DIADEM SERIES

DIADEM FROM THE STARS
LAMARCHOS
IRSUD
MAEVE
STAR HUNTERS
THE NOWHERE HUNT
GHOSTHUNT
THE SNARES OF IBEX
QUESTER'S ENDGAME

THE DUEL OF SORCERY TRILOGY

MOONGATHER
MOONSCATTER
CHANGER'S MOON

THE SKEEN TRILOGY

SKEEN'S LEAP
SKEEN'S RETURN
   (forthcoming from DAW Books in Summer 1987)
SKEEN'S SEARCH
   (forthcoming from DAW Books in Winter 1987)

and

A BAIT OF DREAMS
DRINKER OF SOULS

SKEEN'S LEAP

JO CLAYTON

DAW BOOKS, INC.
DONALD A. WOLLHEIM, PUBLISHER

1633 Broadway, New York, NY 10019

DAW Book Collectors No. 692.

First Printing, December 1986

1 2 3 4 5 6 7 8 9

PRINTED IN THE U.S.A.

RUN, SKEEN, AND BLESS DJABO FOR LONG LEGS

or

THE WOMAN BETRAYED.

Toward sundown Skeen heard the howls of a saayungka pack and knew the P'jaa were after her.

Atsabani, you miserable snitch.

She had walked out of Chukunsa with a gaggle of low-level workers heading to their hovels for supper and a snuggle, she had left them behind, moving briskly along accessways until she reached the edge of the cultivated land; there she curled up for a few hours' sleep.

The Saayungka howls were getting closer.

Must have gone this way: Atsabani, promising silence, waited until she left, then went worming around to the Mye P'jit. Selling me. Selling me. Selling me.

She settled the pack more comfortably, heavy pack loaded with survival gear she'd bought blackmarket from that miserable worm; she stretched long legs into an easy lope, running through a sort of generic scraggle over ground that was sand-soft and slippery, with sprays of gravel put there to roll underfoot and wreck an ankle. Lousy nature—miseries leaping at you from every lousy bush. Give me city streets any day, any city.

The hills were getting steeper, the land rising around her, funneling her into a crack that turned swiftly from ravine to canyon. The trouble with country you don't know is all the things you can put your foot in, like a dead-ending canyon which this might well be. She shivered as the howls of the saayungkas pounded at her. Too easy to let that ugly sound prick her into panic. Easy and stupid. 'Twas said in Chukunsa that when saayungkas howl, someone is dead or caught. Not me, she told herself. Never. Not me. Fuckin' canyon, what now? Instinct and logic said keep to flat ground, easy ground, so she wouldn't run herself out; forget instinct and logic. She went scrambling up the side of the canyon, a steep slant of crumbling stone, cursing Tibo for running out on her, cursing Atsabani for selling her, cursing herself for being a blazing fool, jamming her fists into cracks in the stone and levering herself high.

TURN BACK TWELVE DAYS. WHAT MAKES A ROONER RUN?

"I don't believe it. . . ." She chopped off the words before she said something irretrievable. Had to be careful, her papers wouldn't stand a search. "Captain Fler you're talking about? We had an appointment tonight. What do you mean he's left?"

"Exactly what I said, vinde. There is nothing difficult about the words." Six of the little Honjiuk's tentacles played an irritable tattoo on the counter top. His three front eyes drooped shut and he exhaled a gust of sour spicy air, enough to make her gag. She waited. He cracked his eyes and was visibly annoyed to see her there. With exaggerated patience he said, "Three hours ago Captain Fler removed the ship called AngelBaby registered to the Jaggine Combine from the slot he was assigned in the orbitpark and departed. Filing destination papers is not required. Is there a question of a Complaint?'' He stopped squeaking at her (he was using his most formal mode of speech, an unsubtle insult in itself) and waited with a dozen tentacles poised to see if she'd have the gall to bother him further.

"No. I was only surprised.'' Mouth clamped shut and a hard hand on her temper, she left the shuttle registry and started back across the Gap to the city. No use throwing a snit. Honjiukum were like that. She couldn't afford to draw attention to herself. Bad papers and little money, a face and name tucked into too many files. She'd be lucky to make a work camp if the Honjiukum discovered who and what she was. Not that a work camp was anything to aspire to. You didn't live long there, you didn't live well, and who gave a damn? Not Honjiukum, that's sure. Tibo, Tibo, why'd you do it? How'd you do it? How'd you get my Picarefy to let you?

SHORT TREATISE ON KILDUN AALDA
or
WHY SKEEN HAS FALSE PAPERS.

Kildun Aalda is the only habitable planet in a star system sitting alone in a gap between two star arms, a strategic position that a number of starfaring species have found irresistible. There is vegetation and a wide variety of insects, but intelligent life has never developed, probably because Aalda's sun has a habit of flaring, the flares reducing to ash all life on the surface of the world.

Eight species have held control of Kildun Aalda (not counting the Honjiukum who are its present masters) and have left behind layer upon layer of ruins. Evidence (scanty) suggests lots of small smoldering wars among neighboring star systems with first one then another of the eight species gaining ascendancy until the smolders finally exploded into a conflagration that wiped away nearly all signs of who and what the eight were, except on Kildun Aalda. The planet is a treasure house of rare and priceless artifacts. When this was discovered, the Honjiukum were quick to lay claim to the system and brought a dozen family fleets to make that claim stick. Honjiukum are massive beings with horny skins, short stubby legs (six) and dozens of specialized tentacles. Presumably they find themselves cuddly and lovable, but few others do. Annoying them is impolitic; they squeeze a grudge tighter than a profit. Nothing annoys them more than a Rooner poking about.

Rooner: a specialized smuggler/thief/plunderer. A Rooner deals in artifacts from (mostly) dead civilizations, a thriving and lucrative quasi-legal professison. There are innumerable juicy ruins about and even more collectors avid for new acquisitions.

Skeen: a Rooner of considerable note, having been successful at the profession for more than forty years (antiaging shots keeping her fit and sassy.) Her ship and her name are widely known, which is why she has forged papers and her ship Picarefy has a new name (Picarefy was dryly sarcastic about the choice of AngelBaby) and why Tibo was registered as shipmaster Captain.

Skeen stumped scowling across the Gap and back into Chukunsa, winding from the more decorous streets near the Great Gate to the Warehouse District where life was more to her taste and her purse. Immersed in unhappy thoughts, she

stalked along, ignoring the noise and buffeting, slapping away
a pickpocket's hand, swerving automatically from a cutpurse's
slicer, glaring down at a stubby drunken spacer who seemed
to think that anything female was selling. He had to be very
drunk to come on to her, she wasn't the sort to attract this
kind of thing most days and especially not now. Thin and
dark, a nothing much face, about as much shape as a fence
rail, showing mad as a skinned tikal. What Tibo used to say
when she lost her temper at something: crazy as a skinned
tikal and half as sweet. Tibo you baster, I'm going to run you
down, she promised the air. You miserable lump of duplicity,
I'm going to carve your hide from your worthless carcass a
strip at a time and feed it to you raw.

BACK TO THE CANYON.

Skeen scrambled up the rotted stone, laying showers of
shards on the ground beneath, lunging up with nothing but
anger and desperation and the need to know WHY driving her
on. She grabbed roots poking through the stone and pulled
herself over the lip. Looking out over her backtrail, she saw
the pack coming up over the crest of a distant hillock, a low
dark swarm of lanky lurching bodies.

She fumbled in a pocket, stuck a stimtab in her mouth and
let it melt on her tongue. I'll grant you this, old Atsabani, you
may be a sniveling treacherous worm, but you give good
value for the money. On your feet, woman, long way to go
before you quit.

As darkness settled thick over the hill country, she slowed

to a swinging walk, annoyed by the mischance that chased her here, the Mala Fortuna in her slipstream—Mala, Mala, go haunt some other fool a while. Ruins, every inch of this maggotty world. The smell of them too rich, the challenge too ripe. Even Tibo that baster knew better—told me I was out of my mind to try fiddling the Junks. Galls me worse than tight pants to admit he was right.

Honjiukum didn't like competition.

Honjiukum kept all fifty tentacles squeezed tight about Kildun Aalda, Djabo send them itch-green in all fifty armpits. P'jaa hunters with their saayungka packs. Scanning satellites like lice in the sky. Bare countryside except for prey beasts and their food herds that the Junks imported to provide the P'jaa with amusement and keep their hunting skills sharp.

Tibo, Tibo, why? They catch me, start thumbing through their files, you know what's going to happen. He knew, rats gnaw his tight little gut, and still he ran out on her. Stole her ship. How'd you get round Picarefy, Tibo? Sweettalk her like . . . it was wrong somehow. Felt wrong. Unless she was denser than she thought. He wasn't that sort, not all surface and charm and steal your backteeth when you weren't looking. But she'd been wrong about men so often, how could she trust her instincts? Not wrong about things this serious. The other times it was fooling around with other women, or sneaky machismo slipping out, or selling little secrets that didn't seem worth more pains than kicking the baster tail over tap. This time it was her ship, her darling Picarefy, almost flesh of her flesh. Did Picarefy dump—no, Picarefy wouldn't betray her, but Picarefy was just a ship and a clever man with clever hands (she shivered at the memory of his small clever hands) could drop slave circuits on her before she knew what was happening. Tibo, Tibo, when I catch you, I'll roast those clever hands and feed them to you bone by bone.

TURN BACK ELEVEN DAYS.
FIDGETING IN CHUKUNSA.

Skeen moved out of the rooming house where she spent the night. Who slept in the streets of Chukunsa seldom woke again, but she had to hoard the little cash clinking in her purse; she'd left all but a taste of her working capital safe aboard Picarefy. Safe! If she had to, she could get some change by a little discreet burglary. She had her kit with her—never left that behind—cutters and lockpicks, pinlights and readers, other useful bits. Trouble was, what she picked up wouldn't be enough to get her off-world, that was sure. Merchants kept their places tighter than the royal vaults of Kinshaheer and there was no point taking anything but cash once she got inside. Who could she sell to anyhow if she went for other goods? They all knew each other's stock; they wouldn't bother the Mye P'jit, just erase the idiot and pass the stuff back to the original holder. She had nosed out a couple of licensed traders who had backrooms where they bought smuggled artifacts they euphemistically called *sourceless*. That was the answer, about the only answer: raise the passage fee by selling *sourceless* items. Easy enough to decide, tricky to accomplish. She strolled around the city, following the walls, inspecting the smallgates. Have to work out some way of getting transport past the guards; the ruins close enough to reach on foot were scraped clean to bedrock. Night. Have to find a hole. She drifted through the darken-

ing streets, searching for the right sort of Soak. Slipping
through the shadows, pushing against the curfew, watching,
watching, prying into cul-de-sacs, using skills she'd learned a
lot too young. She'd stopped being a child somewhere around
her sixth birthday. Her nose twitched. A gust of sour stink. A
stooped squarish gnome in the shadows ahead. She followed
him, staying well back, having learned respect for the instincts of these braindead Soaks; they smelled trouble before
it happened and reacted without having to think.

The Soak led her deep into the Warehouse District, in
among the smaller older structures, mostly abandoned, beginning to rot into the meager soil.

One minute he was walking along a wall belonging to one
of these, hand slipping over the wooden clapboard, the next
he'd vanished. She squatted in a doorway across the street
and waited.

A horn wailed. Curfew.

She didn't move. Let him get settled in. There was time, a
little, before the saayungkas were turned loose in the streets,
more time after that before they reached this part of the city.
She waited until she heard the howls a few streets over, then
unfolded slowly from the squat, tightened and loosened her
muscles a few times to work the kinks out, slipped across the
street and moved along the wall until she reached the area
where the Soak had disappeared.

The wall looked solid enough. She ran her fingertips along
the boards, applying an intermittent pressure until she came
on a section that gave a little. Wedged it during the day, most
likely, latched it at night. She continued testing the wall until
she located the spot where the latch was.

The saayungkas were getting closer, she could hear the
rattle of their harness, but she ignored them as she worked. A
hairfine cutting beam, a quick waggle, the stink of hot metal,
then a bit of the wall swung inward enough to let her
scramble through on hands and knees.

She crawled into a cubby made of piles of broken crates,
the dusty hole dimly visible in the pale gray light coming
through cobwebby glass in windowslits high up under the
eaves, clerestory effect. She listened, keeping her mind shut

down, her eyes closed. A heavy silence broken only by a few insect sounds and maybe something like a snore, too soft and distant to pin down, a sound just at the edge of her hearing.

Satisfied, she swung round and inspected the latch. It was a hook and eye, some cheap alloy she could bend with her thumbs. The cutter had sliced through the shank. One part hung down, rattling as the wind blew the door; the hook was still caught in the eye. She pushed the two parts back in place and used the little laser to weld them together. Impossible to hide all traces of her interference, there was a sway in the shank, an uneven knot about the weld that wasn't obvious to the eye but clear enough to the touch; she could only hope he was too far gone to notice. Well, the patch was good enough to hold the thing shut—that's all that mattered. Tomorrow, she'd arrange her own way in, once the Soak left for another day's drifting and caging. Right now, she'd better get busy fixing herself some place where she could sleep safe from interference.

COUNTING TO PRESENT, TENTH TO FOURTH NIGHT. A WILDLY IMPROBABLE WAY OUT.

For several nights the Soak was aroused and suspicious, prowling about the warehouse at odd hours and swinging an ancient torch that put out a yellow light dimmer than the gray glimmers the waning moon sneaked through the cobwebs of the clerestory windows. He never looked up, so he never discovered her. She'd made herself a sleeping platform among the rafters close to one of the windows. It was drafty up there and could be cold, but she gathered piles of shaving and flocking from the junk scattered about the floor (fire hazard of the finest kind) and made herself a cozy nest.

In spite of free lodging for the nights and care in spending, her money was dwindling rapidly; she fed herself on bread and sausage, adding to this meager diet apples plums oranges carrots celery, whatever she could filch without getting caught. Water was a problem. Getting enough to drink took considerable ingenuity; washing herself and her clothing was far down her list of priorities, though she had to keep herself neat enough to avoid the attentions of stray P'jaa looking for able-bodied vagrants to feed into the work camps. Djabo be blessed for eddersil, at least her tunic and trousers didn't need washing, she could shake them out, getting rid of accumulated grime and body oils with a few sharp snaps of the wrists, but she was beginning to acquire the odor of poverty, an effluvium that cried pauper pauper pauper to a discerning nose. Her undershirt and underpants were grimy and stiff with the exudates of her body, but eddersil was irritating against the tenderer parts of that body so she couldn't discard them. And she couldn't wash them so she never took them off; she knew she couldn't make herself put that filth back against her skin.

The Soak finally relaxed. No more snap searches of the littered warehouse looking for he didn't know what. That didn't mean he was any quieter. When he wasn't moving his bedding about, something he did two or three times a night, he was mumbling to himself, now and then yelping like a tortured pup, now and then belting out snatches of song. After the first few nights she found she could ignore this; sometimes she thought if this limbo-existence went on much longer his noises would be like lullabies singing her to sleep.

Toward dawn on her sixth night in the warehouse, she woke confused and a trifle disoriented. At first she didn't know what had jarred her out of her sleep, then she heard a scrabbling and a muttering beneath her and nearly gagged as a mixture of chigger fumes and human stink came gusting up at her. The Soak. He'd settled himself right beneath her. She cursed under her breath, then lay still, listening to mutters punctuated with the splash and gurgle of liquid.

"Roon." He giggled. "Roo-in roo-in roo-in. Bare and bu bu bu blasted." More chigger down his gullet. He giggled again and started singing, words swallowed by the mush his pickled brain made of his mouth; he finished his song with a long rolling fart that blended with his usual gamy stink and the fumes of the chigger to produce a stench so overwhelming she curled into a tight ball, pinched her nostrils shut and concentrated on not breathing for as long as she could manage. He started muttering again. She strained to hear, ruins, what about ruins.

"Gate. . . ." Something something something. "Shaunhaa. . . ." Probably saayungka. High-pitched titter. More sloshes. Scrapes and scrabblings. "Shtu pid junks. Shtu pid bal dies. Wor ked out. They say they say. Hoo hoo hoo." Slosh, spit, cough. Another fart. More coughs, juicy and strangling. Heels beating, muffled ragged drumming. "Tolchorok. Hee hee hee. Tol tol tol chor rok ok ok. Gon na gonna get back there. Gon gon gonna get back." Cough, belch, snuffle. "Roons roo ins my roo ins. Wor ked out they say they say they say. . . ." Something something something, she couldn't make out what he was saying and chewed on her thumb to hold back a hiss of frustration. "Hee hee hee Ol' Yoech he know he know bet ter. Tol tol tol chor rok rok rock. Treas sure rok rok rok. Yoech es treas sure. Tol tol tol chor rok ok." Coughing spasm, more muttering she couldn't make out. Clouds of stink, hot, sour-sweet; the acrid bite of urine, sudden, like a shout. She heard grunts and mushy sounds that might have been curses. The rustle of cloth as Yoech shucked his trousers, dragging sounds as he tore his bedding apart and moved the dry bits away. The sounds faded into the darkness and the stench began to dissipate.

She was on fire with possibility, trying to calm herself, telling herself it's a braindead's wet dream—you can't think of believing him—it's foolishness—you can't afford foolishness, but while she was telling herself all that, she was also thinking, I know Tol Chorok—first colony ruins—two, three days walk into the mountains—nothing there. They say. No, Skeen, don't be a fool, a Soak? You couldn't believe him if he said it was dark when the sun went down. Tol Chorok. Treasure?

BACK TO PRESENT TIME, SKEEN RUNNING THROUGH THE MOUNTAINS, KEEPING AHEAD OF THE SAAYUNGKAS BUT ONLY JUST.

Skeen heard the whine of a float and flung herself into a patch of brush, lying very still, willing it to go away. It hovered a moment. Heat seekers, she thought, and fought down a panic she'd kept off till now. A laser bolt stabbed into the brush a few paces downslope. A bull hijjik bellowed and went crashing away. The float whined on.

Hijjik. Where there's one. . . . Dawn was close. Clouds were gathering in the east, piling up over the worn peaks; there was that touch of heavy dampness in the air that meant rain. She started moving toward the clouds, working her way higher into the mountains. If she could keep loose until it rained, she was loose forever. Well, just about. Maybe jump a herd of hijjik cows and use them to cut her trail. She settled grimly to a slow grope through darkness the cloud cover made total, keeping her line as best she could with little faith in how well she was doing. Cities were her natural domain; in a city there was always something to measure against, every face a city showed you was different, not this eternal tree and rock, rock and tree, with one peak so much like the last it might have been cloned from it.

She broke out of trees into a marshy meadow, a large herd of hijjik cows and their calves in sleepstand out in the middle of the grass. She slithered to a stop, tested the wind, then went cautiously around the edge of the meadow, keeping in the thick shadow under the trees, moving as quietly as she could. When she reached the stream that ran along one edge of the meadow, she took off her boots, gathered small water-polished stones and filled them, then eased herself into the water. Stumbling, sliding, tottering, she began working her way upstream, jamming her toes, banging her ankles, scraping skin off, the cold intensifying the pain and at the same time numbing her feet until she could barely feel them; walking grew increasingly chancy and it certainly wasn't silent. She felt like a marching band. The herd took no notice of her and continued to doze placidly out there in the lush soggy meadow. The wind was still her friend. She stopped when she was a little past the herd, found relatively firm footing, dug into a boot, and brought out a handful of stones. All right, you cows, get ready. She let out a shrill warbling whoop and side-armed the stones at the nearest hijjik.

Yelling and hurling handfuls of stones she exploded the herd into a wild honking flight into the trees, tramping in a wide band across her backtrail, spraying the musk of their terror over her scent. Wiping out her traces. At least she hoped so.

Before the uproar of their flight faded, she started moving upstream, sliding, tottering, bruising every bone in foot and shin, shivering from the cold, cursing everything and every-one—the night, the world, Tibo, P'jaa, Atsabani, Honjiukum, Yoech, herself—as she plodded on.

After what felt like a hundred kilometers she climbed out of the creek and stood shivering on a flat stone, her teeth clicking together, her feet so numb she could not feel them at first, then shot with a thousand tiny pains that added up to one fuckin' huge hurt. The eddersil of her trousers shed the water caught in its fibers in an icy whoosh. She yelled and hopped around, then rubbed instep and sole on her pantleg and hoped about some more as she pulled her boots back on. She stomped her feet down in them and sighed with a combination of pleasure and pain. Hands warming in her armpits, she listened. Nothing but the usual night yammer. She moved her shoulders, took a few tentative steps, and decided her feet would hold her a while longer. She looked up. The cloud cover was too dense to let much light show through. Should be raining sometime soon. Just let me keep loose until then, hah! and the Junks can go suck a duck.

TURN BACK THREE DAYS.
PUTTING A FACE ON FANTASY.

Hunting Yoech in the dark, hypospray in hand charged with songbird jellies. Tracking by his smell, his mutters.

Prowling around him in the dusty dark, him nervous and jerking, wary as a hijjik calf with a pack of rii sniffing around the herd.

Working closer, closer, nozzle against the neck, songbird spraying through his skin.

"Sleep, old Yoech, sleep, no danger, no hurt, sleep, sleep, no need to fight, sleep, sleep ahhh. . . ."

She knelt beside him. "Friend am I, friend to Yoech. Who am I, Yoech? What's my name?"

"Sessi? Sessi-girl, coming for me?" Breath whined through

his awful nose, fighting with the snot. "Comin through the Gate?"

"Yes, it's Sessi. Sessi come to see my love. Where's the Gate, my Yoech? I've forgot. I'm frightened, my Yoech, I want to go home. Help me, tell me how to find the Gate."

"Tol Chorok, Sessi, I tol you and tol you, Tol Chorok."

"Where is Tol Chorok, my Yoech? This is Chukunsa, how do I get to Tol Chorok from here?"

"Everybody knows Tol Chorok." He wriggled under her hand and she wondered if she should shoot him again. She didn't want to; Djabo only knew how it'd mix with all that chigger in him. "Uh. Uh. Uh," he said. What he meant by it she had no idea. "Dry valley right up there under Chol Dachay, highest peak around with the tip bent over like it's broke." He giggled and started groping her. "I ain't broke, Sessi, I ain't broke, feel it." He fumbled at her arm trying to get hold of her hand. Before she had to decide what she'd do about that, he went vague and forgot what he was doing, and started mumbling to himself like he had last night. "Wouldn't believe me. Said I was cra zy said I was dream ming chig head dream ming. . . ." He went on muttering about pull and crazy and gate and this peculiar female named Sessi and going back to Somewhere.

She listened until she was convinced she'd learn nothing useful, bent over him, and tugged at his beard. "Yoech," she said, "my Yoech, tell me about the Gate."

"Running," he said, "Pack, uh, pack uh, there. Thing. Grabbed me. You know. Grabbed me just me, I fell through on you, you know." His eyes filmed over, and he no longer seemed aware that she was there with him. She listened to his mutterings. They were incoherent and wandering with almost no sense of time so he talked of things he'd seen yesterday in the street, events on the far side of the Gate, the accident that stranded him here on Kildun Aalda, running from the saayungkas, the words mushing up more and more until the time came when she couldn't understand a thing no matter how hard she listened. He grew restless. She stroked her hand over his matted hair trying not to think of what she was touching.

"I might be owing you a lot, old man. Mmm. With all that songbird mixing with all that chigger you're going to be sicker than a wert after beyrasco half-night. Food." She dug into her limp purse and pulled out a few coins. She looked at them a moment, then shrugged. "Not enough to do much outfitting—you might as well have it." She dropped the coins beside him. "You're going to be sick, nothing I can do about that, but food in the belly cuts the shakes. Food," she said firmly, making her voice soft as honey on velvet, something Tibo that baster said to her once when she coaxed him into doing something he called insane (right about that too, Djabo send him boils on his jutty little butt). "Food, sweet food, lovely food, comforting food, food to make the world look bright. When you wake, old Yoech, my Yoech, you're going to be hungry. Very hungry, my Yoech. Soon as you're awake, your belly says fill me. There's money in your blankets. Hunt it out and go eat yourself a fine hot meal. That's an order, Old Yoech, your Sessi orders you to eat. So what will you do when you wake?"

His mouth worked, he looked marginally more alert, rheumy eyes peering up at her, blinking slowly as he struggled to make out her face through nightshadows that were too thick for him. "Eat," he managed. "Eat b'fa. Sessi."

"And you're going to forget all this, old Yoech. It's only a dream, a dream that fades like mist in sunlight, only a dream."

"Duhreeem."

"Forget."

"Faa gaa."

"Sleep now, old Yoech. Sleep calm and wake rested. Sleeeep. . . ."

A snore.

She looked down at him with wry affection. Tough old buzzard. Didn't I think it'd hurt more than help, I'd try conditioning you to stop drinking. By Djabo's ivory overbite, I am tempted. Better not. You're getting along all right the way you are and sure wouldn't thank me for interfering. She got to her feet and strolled to the other end of the warehouse where she had her nest. She climbed wall beams and swung onto the slab, stretched out on a scavenged blanket and began making mental lists of what she'd need to go take a look at Tol Chorok. Fantasy maybe, but what the hell, what else did she have to do.

PRESENT TIME. DO OR DIE IN TOL CHOROK.

No rain. The clouds hung lower and lower but didn't let go.

The trick with the hijjiks and the creek didn't puzzle the saayungkas much. Not long after noon, when what shadow she had was puddled about her feet, she heard the howling behind her; the pack was closing fast.

She'd run out of hope and almost out of will but kept moving, drowning in that euphoric confusion that comes before collapse. Weaving, stumbling, sweat blinding her, she got down the last slope and moved onto the stony floor of a dessicated valley. No grass, no water, only dead rock with a thin layer of dust, dust that lifted at the lightest touch and hung about her. Looming over the valley (she kept seeing it through dust and sweat, losing it again as if it were a mirage teasing her) was a mountain peak, a peak that was leaner, more jagged, higher than the others, its point twisted sideways like a crumpled horn.

When she stumbled over the remnant of a wall and crashed onto hands and knees, she stayed down, dazed. Wall? She shook her head, trying to clear out some of the fatigue-trash clogging it, lifted it and saw the crumpled horn of Chol Dachay. Wall? She pushed up and back until she was sitting on her heels, rubbed at her eyes, stared at the lacerated palms of her hands, wiped them on her tunic.

Howling. Close. She looked over her shoulder and saw low dark beasts running at her. Minutes away. In a last desperate effort which she knew meant nothing but a little more time gained before the inevitable capture, she drove her body up and into a ragged run toward the center of that dry ghost of a city, toward a cluster of taller ruins where she could hole up and make them hurt before they got her.

Dust rose and circled about her. She thought it was her feet kicking it up, but it wheeled too high, whipped too vigorously about her. She thought it was the wind. But she couldn't feel any wind. The air was thin, dry, still.

She staggered through street-traces, her mind floating away from the beasts closing on her as she left the direct line to the center and began weaving a complex pattern through the ruins, body moving now at the hest of something else, the dust thickening and swirling closer, leaving a circle of clean air about her. Muffled by that enveloping dust she could hear snuffling and foot thuds of the saayungkas, the rattle of their harness; she thought she could feel the heat of their breath on her back; she caught glimpses of the dark forms circling her. For some reason they didn't seem able to get at her, couldn't break through the bubble. She couldn't make sense of any of this, she didn't want to try.

Pattern, Yoech said, there is a pattern. Her feet traced it until she reached a sketch of a doorway, two posts and a lintel, the lintel carved, the carving sand-scrubbed into anonymity. Gate. Subliminal humming. Other sounds muted, distanced.

Her ensorcelled feet danced her through the Gate.

SKEEN'S LEAP
or
I'M STANDING ON COOL GREEN GRASS THAT CAN'T POSSIBLY EXIST.

Skeen stepped into greenness and calm. Into humidity and hush. The thing that gripped her body lost most of its hold on her. Lost it suddenly. She staggered, crashed onto her knees, stayed there grasping in great gulps of the thick wet air, air that acted on her body like food and drink, recharging her. The thing that had yanked her through the Gate started tugging at her, felt as if it'd tied monofilament line about her arm and was trying to lead her about like a family pet. She ignored it and passed her tongue over her lips, like rubbing leather over leather. "Djabo's claws," she croaked. "He wasn't crazy after all."

She got slowly to her feet and moved closer to the Gate. On this side the posts and lintel were fresher, the carving was clearer—recognizable shapes—kites or flying squirrels, something like that. Some weathering, the shapes partly obscured by patches of dry lichen and damp moss. Dust swirled between the posts. She waited for it to settle so she could see what was happening on the other side. Why hadn't the saayungkas come through with her?

The dust didn't settle. It kept billowing and eddying, filling the space between the posts.

She listened, couldn't hear a thing.

"That's that, then." She used the tip of her knife to mark the stone of one of the posts. Djabo only knew how many of these things were scattered about, no point in taking chances, losing the way back. Nah nah, Tibo, you don't get away that easy. The SKA for Skeen, the PI for Picarefy. Neat not flashy, but quick ID when needed. Satisfied, she turned to inspect the glade. What was this place? Some kind of cemetery? The air hung still and silent, not a leaf was moving. No insect or bird noises. Trees like painted images. Short thick grass, not a blade moving. Weird. She moved her arm impatiently as the tugging on it increased in fervor and frequency. She turned, glared along the line of the pull. A short distance off, behind a thin screen of trees, she saw a shining white wall. For some reason that had nothing to do with logic she shivered as she scowled at it. Silly looking thing, a lot like a white-tiled bathroom wall, ridiculous out here in the middle of nowhere. The Wall or Something behind it reached out and tried to get a firmer hold on her; she began hearing music in her head, a soft summoning siren's song. Not fuckin' likely, she told the thing and swung around, fighting against the pull. One step. Another. Tiny change in the glade: a breath of air moved against her face, leaves rustled, small branches creaked. Through these small sounds she heard another, water falling, a liquid lovely music that drowned out the summons from the Wall. She tried swallowing but her throat was too dry, then she started walking toward the sound, tautly alert. She distrusted all this tranquility; life had taught her it was bound to change suddenly and violently. She pulled clear the holster flap and loosened her darter, engaged the lanyard that would keep the weapon tied to her even through spills and tumbles, moved on, laughing a little at herself, prowling through an embroidered garden. Dark feral figure, pale topaz eyes shifting, shifting, seeking, predator in Eden. She played with the idea but didn't lose her alertness even when she stepped into another sun-dappled glade and saw the fountain playing in the middle of it.

Water went up through a central pipe, rose a short distance beyond the pipe and fell in crystal showers into a cylindrical basin; the basin's wall stood knee-high covered with randomly shaped black and white tiles laid in a swirling abstract pattern; the outthrust lip was a solid black.

Cautiously she looked about her. The sky overhead was clear and cloudless, no sun visible. It felt more like late afternoon than morning, time would tell about that. Her throat felt like something with lots of quills had died there; the watermusic was cruelly lovely, enticing, but she didn't move. Nothing happened. She waited several breaths then moved a short way into the glade. There was neither dust nor moss on that shining tile. Hmm, who was the local char? Tongue between her teeth she frowned at the water, then she shrugged and walked to the fountain.

She touched the lip-tiles with a fingertip (little finger on her left hand, her least useful digit). No burn. Nothing jumped out at her. She straightened, touched that expendable finger to the falling water. Cool. Wet. Hah! of course wet. Touched her finger to her tongue. A hint of that wild green flavor that mountain water often had. She shrugged again. If it was poison, well, it'd be a quicker death than dessication.

After pulling off her boots, discarding toolbelt and backpack, with a joyful whoop she let herself fall back into the pool. A marvelous splash. Heavenly coolness. She pulled herself up so she could breathe, braced her head against the pipe, and lay languidly moving her hands in the crystalline water. After a moment she pushed away from the pipe, sat with her head tilted back so she could catch the falling water. She drank and drank until she was near foundering.

The clear blue of the sky acquired a faint violet tinge as she splashed happily about, stripping off her tunic and trousers, peeling off the filthy underpants and undershirt, scrubbing at them, getting the tough translucent cloth as clean as she could without soap. There was soap in her backpack but she was caught in the grip of an immense lethargy. She didn't want to get out of the basin. She tossed the underwear onto the grass beside the tunic and trousers and went back to paddling about in the water.

The darkening sky brought a cool wind with it and she started to shiver. Reluctantly she pulled herself out of the basin and stood dripping, her stomach cramping a little, the grass very soft under her bare feet. She wrung out her hair (short and straight, like a cat's fur), ran her fingers through it. Euphoria still bubbling in her blood, she kicked her clothing onto a dry patch of grass, stretched and laughed, danced wheeling about the glade, the exercise warming away the chills. She couldn't quite believe all this was true, but peeling off those underpants brought the realness close. She stopped dancing. So did hungerpains.

She dug a tube of hiprots out of her pack, about as tasty as eating rope, but adequate in providing energy and sustenance. After eating she got dressed again, feeling too vulnerable to stay naked though the underwear wasn't close to dry, then she curled up in what was left of the sunlight, intending only to doze a while as her head dried. But that lingering warmth was seductive and the drain from the stimtabs overwhelmed her and she plummeted into a heavy sleep.

DAY ONE ON THE FAR SIDE OF FANTASY.

Skeen woke stiff and sore with nausea threatening at the back of her throat. Creaky as an old board, she thought, and groaned up onto her feet. She hobbled to the fountain and eased down on the basin's lip. Blinking slowly she wiggled her toes, pushed her feet back and forth in the dew-wet grass. Here I am. Where's here? Good question. No good answers. She yawned, blinked some more. Where do I go from here?

No answer to that either. Pick a direction. She lifted a foot, bent her leg, rested her ankle on her knee and scratched lazily at her instep and between her toes. She stopped thinking about much of anything and sat slumped, relaxed, soaking up the fine morning.

After luxuriating in laziness a while longer, she sighed and reached for her boots.

She moved through the mountains all morning, going up around down, up around down, until she was dizzy with it, eating more of the hiprots paste as she moved so she wouldn't have to stop or think about what she ate; she was heartily sick of the glop and about at the end of her ability to choke it down. Up around down, up around down, glimpses of quick brown movement across a meadow, uparounddown, raptors riding the thermals in lazy loops, uparounddown, a stream with fish in it, looked much like fish on any world she visited, circumstances dictating form here as elsewhere, uparounddown, Sessi, Yoech's lost love, whatever, native? What would natives be like?

Late that afternoon, the violet haze darkening the sky, she came around a curve on a mountain and looked out across waves of foothills at a broad valley that vanished into haze on the far horizon. A wide river lazed along the length of the valley, a smaller one joined it a short distance south of where she was standing, a walled city sat in the curve near where the rivers joined. Boats on both rivers, their sails brilliant patches of crimson, emerald and gold, spread like butterfly wings to catch the wind. The plain was a patchwork of fields, with groves, orchards, vineyards, pastures with grazing beasts of several sorts too far to identify, dirt roads, dust clouds kicked up by riders, wagons pulled by oxen, smaller puffs from walkers, a long packtrain. Definitely pre-industrial. That meant handwork; lots of artisans making objects that would be uniques once she got them to the other side of the Gate. Yoech knows his treasure, that's sure. Scattered about in the middle of the fields were large walled houses, little huts snugging against the walls. Intensive cultivation but people seemed fairly thin on the ground. The groves interested her,

some of them out by themselves, actually in the middle of
row-crops, some of them in clusters like freckles on the back
of a hand. Two or three giant conifers amid thick stands of
shorter, broader trees, occasional glades, perhaps where a
conifer had died, been cut down, something. Placid scene.
She wrinkled her nose and slipped her darter from the snap-
flap holster, checked the charge and the paralevel, slipped it
back, hesitated a moment before snapping down the flap, but
did it because she didn't have anything immediate to worry
about. A small shy rustle behind her. She chuckled. Unless a
rabid mouse.

The darter was an ingenious weapon that would not run out
of ammunition as long as there was a puddle available.
Battery powered, recharged by sunlight, it used water to
make the darts, flash-froze them, forced them through a
concentrated paralyzer and sent them flying with pooshes of
compressed air, singly, or, with the slide of a switch, in a
tight cluster. No range, anything over twenty meters was
safe, but she trusted her wits more than the gun to get her
away from any danger beyond twenty meters off.

A deep breath, a shake of her body, then she started into
the foothills, determined to get as far as she could before
night dumped down on her. All her supplies were running
low; the sooner she got to that city, the better.

A DAY, A NIGHT, ANOTHER DAY OF DULL TRAVEL. WE'LL SKIP ALL THAT AND GET RIGHT TO THE NEXT EXCITING BIT.

The shadows were long when she reached the road, the sun half-gone behind the mountains. She walked along it a short distance but when she was following it round one of the groves, she heard hoofbeats, a rider coming up on her. Following instinct to keep out of sight as long as possible, she took a swift sidestep, then another, sliding into the shadow under the trees. The rider came around the bend, riding unhurried—a young man, sub-adult, thick brown hair, matte brown skin, standard issue humanoid. Loose shirt, pulled together at neck and wrists with drawstrings, the cloth some natural fiber like silk, trousers of a rough dark brown cloth tucked into finely made boots that reached almost to the knee. He rode a beast that looked too big and powerful for him, carried a short whip, a longer whip coiled and tied behind his leg, spurs with wicked rowels strapped to his boots. He rode with that arrogant I-am-the-lord-of-all-I-survey mien she'd met too often before—rich man's son, not old enough to hide his contempt for the rest of the world. She suppressed an impulse she'd never outgrown, a strong desire to stick pins in that kind of twerp, smiled at the thought of his rage if she darted the horse and dumped him in the dust, made him walk

where he was going like one of the common kind, but she let
him go on undisturbed.

She strolled along under the trees, content but tired, looking forward to a hot meal and a tankard of ale in a noisy
smoky tavern, maybe a little singing later on when the mood
was on her and she could bury her non-voice in the noise.
She glanced out at the road now and then, saw more young
men much like the first, alone or in small groups, riding their
tall horses with a total unconcern for the walkers they dusted
or forced off the road. Made her more determined than ever
to keep out of sight; this sort of society didn't tolerate inter-
lopers very well, at least the official part of it, though she
was fairly sure of finding a welcome among the outsiders. If
she was right about what she'd seen, there were a lot of
similarities here to the arrangement on the world where she
was born and raised.

The grove pinched out. There was another larger one directly ahead. She moved quickly across the intervening space
and plunged into the thickening darkness under the trees. The
way the travelers on the road were beginning to hurry could
mean that the city gates were closed at sundown or shortly
after. Maybe it'd be better to wait for morning before she
tried getting into the city.

When she was deep into the grove, coming up on one of
the small glades that peppered it, she heard loud crashing, the
tramping of hooves, wild whooping, all of it rushing toward
her. She jumped, caught hold of a limb curving overhead and
pulled herself into the tree, climbed higher, and found herself
looking down into the glade. She freed the darter, clipped the
lanyard to the butt.

A small figure burst into the open, stumbled, gasped,
angled across the glade heading straight for Skeen's tree.

Shit, Skeen thought; she took out the darter, rested it on
her knee.

A small woman with a mass of curly dark hair tumbling
about her shoulders, bunchy white blouse, a long dark skirt
with bands of embroidery about the hem. Her feet were bare,
her arms working; in spite of that damn skirt she ran like a
spooked kanchi. She'd almost reached the tree when a horse

and rider came galloping past it, knocking her off her feet.
She scrambled up again, tried to dart past him, but was cut
off by another whooping rider. Two more broke through the
brush into the glade, trapping her inside their ring. They were
boys, well into adolescence but far from adult. The woman's
head came up, she brushed a mass of curls out of her eyes,
and glared defiance at them. With a snap of her wrist, she
pulled loose a sleeve tie. One of the boys yelled something
and rode at her. Moving faster than Skeen thought possible,
she flung herself to one side, laughed shrill triumph, and
snatched loose the other sleeve tie.

A boy snapped a three-meter braided whip, caught her
around the ankle, and jerked her off her feet.

Skeen watched grimly. I should stay out of this, she told
herself. Whatever I do, I'll make enemies I probably can't
afford. The boy with the whip kept jerking the woman about,
the other three flung themselves off their mounts and circled
around her, slapping at her, kicking her, yelling things at her
Skeen didn't have to know the language to understand.

She darted all four of them, watched with satisfaction as
the whipboy fell off his horse and the others crumbled to the
leafy dirt.

The woman got to her feet, pushed her hair out of her face,
wrist strings dangling. She went from body to body, touching
each boy briefly. Skeen had a moment's uneasiness, wondering if she'd poisoned the brats instead of merely putting them
to sleep, then decided she didn't care all that much.

The woman straightened from the last body and turned to
gaze at the tree where Skeen was perched. She spoke, a flow
of sounds with a questioning intonation.

Get away from here, you nit. Skeen scowled through the
leaves at her. Go away before more trouble lands on us all.
Take the gift fate gave you. Bona Fortuna. Bona. Bona.

The woman spoke again, different words, different rhythm,
still a question.

Dead or not, those baby shits will be missed. Get away,
dammit, so I can cut out myself.

The woman thought for a moment, then she tugged loose
the neckstring, pulled the blouse over her head and threw it

down. She undid the lacing at the waist of the skirt and
kicked out of that. Naked (Skeen gaping, wondering what the
hell was going on) she ran out of the glade. Skeen blinked,
then settled herself to wait a while.

Time passed. She began to think about dropping to the
ground and heading straight for the river. Maybe she could
find an empty hut.

A flap of wings. Large bird close by. Skeen looked idly
about, shrugged. She slid the darter into the holster, unclipped
the spring lanyard, snapped the flap down, and reached for
the trunk.

A rustle overhead. She started to look up, caught a glimpse
of black fur, heard a snarl, then something soft and powerful
slammed her head into the trunk.

I ONLY WANTED A HOT
MEAL AND A BIT OF DRUNKEN
CHEER. HOW DO I GET MYSELF
INTO THESE MESSES?
or
THIS IS ONE HELL OF
A WEIRD WORLD.

Skeen woke belly down over a saddle, the stench of horse
thick in her nostrils, her head throbbing in time with every step.
Darkness around her thick as the horse stink. She suppressed
a groan and began testing the rope coiled around her arms.

The horse stopped walking. Sounds of creaking leather, the soft scuffle of feet. A warm hand flattened itself against Skeen's forehead. A force came suddenly from that hand, a blow that addled her brain without quite knocking her out again. Her nausea increased, her brain itched furiously, she struggled to move, to free herself. This was too much like the time she was really stupid and let the Widowmaker get hold of her and use a brainprobe on her. Terror flashed through her with that memory, she began struggling wildly.

The hand pulled away, but Skeen was barely conscious of that because funny things were still going on in her head. Her struggles were making the horse nervous; it was sliding about, snorting, jerking its head up and down. A voice. Speaking to the beast, soothing, gentling. "Hoosh ah hoosh, quiet now be quiet." Deep rich female voice, almost singing the words. She wasn't talking to Skeen but what she said reached through the panic and quieted her as well as the horse.

"Hang onto the stirrup," the woman said. "I'm cutting you loose. You don't want to fall on your head. It's had enough bangs for one day."

Another shock, a minor and welcome one. Language transfer, an organic version of sleep-learning, faster and a lot harder on the poor abused brain. Skeen went limp. The woman was right, her head was sore enough, no use trying for a record. The knife was briefly cold against her arm. The coils of rope fell away. She flexed her hands, then grabbed for the stirrup leather as footsteps went away, circled round the beast's tail. A moment later a small hand touched her leg—she felt the warmth of it through the eddersil—and the rest of the ropes slid off. Cautiously she walked her hands up the stirrup leather, pushing herself over and off the saddle. She caught hold of the cantle as her knees buckled, pulled herself upright; in spite of the pain shooting from her ankles to bang about her head, she was content to be in one piece, content to wait for the next thing to happen.

They were in the foothills somewhere, in a hollow between two grassy swells. Low in the east a gibbous moon was rising, a part-eaten round of mold-threaded cheese. Last night it'd been close to midnight before the moon appeared. Looked like they'd been traveling for hours. Djabo's horny toes, all that damn walking wasted.

"I couldn't leave you with the Pallah Chalapeer," the woman said. "They'd have put trackers on you, got you no matter where you went."

Skeen stepped away from the horse, stood rubbing at her wrists, angry and wary. "Chalapeer?"

"The boys. More importantly, their fathers."

"I take it I wouldn't like what happened when they caught me." She kept her voice cool and flat.

"Pallah aren't kind to strangers. Especially strangers who interfere with the pleasures of the highborn. Why did you?"

Skeen shrugged. "Enjoying themselves too much, creepy little gits. What now?"

The woman's face was unreadable. "Nothing. Go where you want. If you'll take a bit of advice, stay clear of Dum Besar. The city."

Silence. The woman didn't move. Skeen clasped her hands behind her back and watched the moon float up. She wants something from me. Good. Where there's a want, there's a price. I didn't get into this for the love of running.

The woman surrendered and broke the silence. "You can come with me if you want."

Skeen said nothing. She watched the moon.

"There's something I'd like to talk to you about."

Skeen smiled. "I've got no pressing engagements elsewhere." She thought a moment, decided she'd better make something clear. "And I'm open for hire." She swung into the saddle, looked over her shoulder. "My name is Skeen. Let's go."

"I am called Telka." The woman moved past Skeen and mounted the other horse, managing the long full skirt with an ease Skeen found impressive; she made a note to be wary round this one, her small size and delicacy was a snare and a delusion. Telka started out of the hollow after calling Skeen up beside her. "I am Min," she said. She spoke with a careful colorless precision, as if she were reading the words from a paper in front of her, as if she were afraid something about her would leak out with these words. "Those in Dum

Besar are Nemin. Not Min. I think you are a Pass-Through.
Most everyone speaks Trade-Min no matter what Wave he
belongs to.'' She glanced at Skeen but when she got no
response, went on talking in that neutral voice. ''The first
Nemin to Mistommerk were the Ykx; they made the Gate and
brought the Ever-Hunger. They came in streams and clots and
spread over the world; the Min were not alarmed because
they took land no one wanted and kept to themselves.'' She
sighed. ''But every hemicycle after that another Wave came
through the Gate, pushing Min off their own land, pushing
and pushing.'' Feeling crept into her voice then despite her
efforts to suppress it. ''Chalarosh. Balayar. Funor Ashon.
Nagamar. Aggitj. Skirrik. And the Pallah who were the last
wave, twenty hemicycles ago.'' She cleared her throat. ''Since
then only singlings have come through. Like you. No telling
when the next one.''

Hemicycle? Skeen thought. Mmm. Ah. Half a century.
Telka went on talking in that soft expressionless voice, but
Skeen stopped listening. She'd heard this tale a hundred times
before, more than that, heard it in beery mutters or drugged
mumbles, heard it from thieves and murderers and slummers
out on a tear, boasting the heritage that seemed their only
claim to self-respect. Ancient resentments cherished like only
children. She was bored with it the first time, she was bored
with it now. Folk who nursed ancient grudges and didn't get
on with living sounded like clones of each other no matter
how different the details of their stories or the shape of their
bodies. Mmm. Eight waves through the Gate, knocked back
to horsecart life when their tech wore out. The eightfold way
to treasure, ripe for plundering for one who knows how to
come and go. Which right now I know shit about. She smiled
at herself. But I'll learn, I guarantee. She tuned in to Telka
wondering if the Min was saying anything important, tuned
out again. Grudges, huh! What a waste of time and energy.
Either get rid of them or forget them. She grinned. Me, I
don't cuddle grudges. Tibo you baster, you'll find out once I
get some financing. If you've sold Picarefy to get your hide
out of hock, you'll find out how fast and definite I get rid of

grudges. She straightened her mouth and began listening to Telka again.

". . . it's only the Ykx who know how and why the Gate works, the few of them left—most are dust on the wind." Telka pressed full lips together, her rather heavy brows lowering into a frown. "I should tell you," she said finally, "there are many among the Min of Mintown who won't welcome you, even though I sponsor you."

Didn't expect they would, Skeen thought, and you'd be out of sight, lil darlin', didn't you need me. She patted a yawn, scratched at her palm, looked up. "Why?"

"You're Nemin. Where there's one, there might be many. Min fear another Wave."

"If my guess is right, that won't happen. Honjiukum are keeping a hot eye on the sun, it won't catch them sitting.

"What?"

"Timing. Hemicycles. Length of time since Kildun Aalda was last colonized. Looks to me like when Aalda's sun belches, the Gate opens."

"What?"

"Never mind. For what it's worth, I don't think you're likely to get another flood of refugees any time soon."

They had moved out of the foothills into the mountains and were riding along the bank of a creek, following a sketchy trail that gradually grew steeper and steeper until Skeen looking ahead began to wonder how the horses were going to negotiate it; about six lengths before a small and rather lovely waterfall, Telka turned into a dry ravine whose bottom sloped gently downhill, the crumbling stone walls rising higher and higher above their heads.

"We need your help," Telka said. She was riding half a length ahead of Skeen, her narrow back swaying easily with the motion of the horse.

Skeen thought about catching up so she could watch the little Min's face, but she was bored with these games and taking herself out of them as much as she could (or would have if her curiosity hadn't pricked her into responding). "Why me?"

"The Pallah don't know you."

"So?"

"They won't be laying traps for you."

"What about the trackers and those—what did you call them—Chalapeer brats?"

"Oh, they won't bother with me gone. They'll blame it all on me and make lives hard for Min a while. Without you there, they won't suspect outside help." Silence for several horselengths. Telka's back swayed as before; not many features to a back, what there were obscured by the thick flow of fine black hair twisted into flyaway helices and the bunchy white blouse. "Turn the Skirrik loose in Dum Besar, nosing out those not-placed, those without masters to speak for them. It'll die down in a day or so when the Casach discover they're getting nowhere."

All very nice, Skeen thought. "What am I supposed to do?" she said aloud.

"I have a sister. A twin. The Pallah have her. I was trying to get to her when the Chalapeer nits found me."

The hooves of their mounts, iron shod, struck bell sounds from the stone, those sounds echoing hollowly from the ravine walls. The moonlight was bright enough to show her a landscape of many grays, of texture and line, with an eerie compelling beauty. And something else. A flicker of movement along the top of the left-hand wall. She tried for more than a glimpse of the thing, giving half an ear to Telka. "She is a slave," Telka said, using that neutral monotone that seemed to leach the life out of her words; with Skeen's attention distracted to the ravine wall, a lot of those words were lost on the wind; when she tried to listen, she had to forget about the shadow up above. ". . . the Poet's concubine," Telka said, "until he tires of her, then. . . ." Cat, Skeen thought, a black hunter. ". . . because you can get into Dum Besar without alerting the Skirrik and through them the Casach, Dum Besar's ruling council keeps a strict watch on the gates." Skeen unsnapped the holster and engaged the lanyard; the cat was getting bolder. ". . . and bring her out to me, I am sick at the thought of her there, slave, used by him." The hairs stirred on the back of Skeen's neck; the

thing's watching me, hating me. "Think about it, please,"
Telka said.

They rounded a bulge in the left wall. The ravine opened
into a long narrow valley between the mountains.

A black mountain cat came bounding down the slope and
stood in the center of a rutted road, tail jerking back and
forth, a great dark creature with glowing pale eyes, mouth
gaping in a silent snarl. Skeen had the darter out and ready,
but Telka rode between them.

"No, Rijen." The Min's voice was sharp, commanding.

Skeen waited, darter held out of sight by her thigh.

The big cat took a step to one side, glared past Telka at
Skeen.

"This one is Pass-through, not Pallah," Telka said, anger
breaking her calm and shrilling her voice. She stood in the
stirrups, fury in her body like the fury in her voice. "Are you
challenging me, Holavish? I am Odats m'kuz. I am Z'naluvit.
What are you?"

Tail jerking, the beast sank into a crouch, snarled, the
angry sound increasing almost to a roar.

Skeen glanced from cat to Min, but didn't move to dart the
beast; Telka seemed very much in control. She relaxed enough
to puzzle over the titles the Min had claimed. Odats m'kuz.
Min(female) with seven skins. Huh? Holavish. Runner in the
high places. She thought about that some more. Appropriate
as it was to that snarling cat, there was something more,
word-fringes that suggested one(male) who walked alone,
throwing off the constraints of community life, one(male)
committed to the old ways. Z'naluvit. Speaker for Min(female, plural). Can you pick 'em, eh Skeen, hah! can you
pick 'em! She blinked. Talking to a beast. Huh. Don't be
parochial, woman. It's listening, Djabo bless.

Telka sank down into the saddle as the cat's tail stopped
twitching and drooped into a dejected arc. Submission. He
didn't quite roll onto his back and wave his paws in the air,
but there was that feel about him. He pushed back out of his
crouch and dissolved into a cat-shaped shimmer. Half a breath
later he was a naked man, dark and glowering.

Skeen gasped. "Which is impossible," she whispered.

Unconcerned about his nudity, the Min male took a step to one side, looked Skeen over with no softening of his scowl, then stalked off down the road. Handsome creature. Grinning, she watched his buttock muscles shift and clench; he had a rank maleness that made her stomach flutter. She giggled under her breath. From the expression on his face he wouldn't touch her with a ten-meter claw. Which was all right with her; for contact sports she preferred them little and agile and intelligent. Like Tibo that baster. But that didn't stop her from enjoying the view. She watched the Min disappear into the shadow under the trees. Formidable as you look, you handsome hunk, I'd bet my stash on Tibo, come to a fight between you.

Telka waited until he was out of sight, then clicked her tongue, urging her mount into a quick walk. She didn't attempt to explain any of that, she didn't look back, just started on and left Skeen to follow if she wished.

They rode along a dirt road through huge old trees, past glades where tree growth had been inhibited somehow. These garden plots were in various stages of growth, each glade planted with a single crop—pod plants, tuber vines, melons, a grain plant, leaf vegetables, fruiting bushes. No weeds, the sets planted semé, each plant the same distance from all those around it. Got the ground trained, looks like.

The trees ended abruptly, without that trickle-off most forests seemed to have. Fenced pastures surrounded by a new kind of plant, one she hadn't come across before, a mix between vine and bush twisted together to make open-work barriers. Large ruminants grazing in some of those fields, long, skinny, limber neck, twisted horns. Small ruminants in others, chunky, fine crimped hair shining softly in the moonlight. The fields grew progressively smaller, an arm of a long thin lake jutted dark and glittery past them. They rode straight ahead, passing thrice above lake water and narrow canals, the ironshod hooves ringing on the hard wood of the bridges. The road turned to follow the curve of the lake, heading toward a pair of giant conifers rising like watchtowers beside the open arch into a courtyard of a twisting humping structure that curved around the end of the lake, half a kilometer end to

end. It was very late, long after midnight, but there were
red-gold glows scattered the length of that dark mass. A
number of cowled figures came through the arch and stood
waiting, silent and hostile; Skeen wondered wearily just what
she was getting herself into.

Telka dismounted, tossed the reins to the shadow form that
came to meet her. "Get rid of these, the Chalapeer will be
hunting them." She walked away, leaving Skeen to dismount
and follow her as she chose.

IMAGES: a roundish court (nothing was built on the
square in this place and those rounds were irregular,
knotty and more than vaguely organic) with half-roofs
built out here and there from a noduled wall. Fire in the
middle of the flagging, burning in an oval basin made of
fieldstone, a huge inverted funnel of some pulpy material
suspended over it to catch the smoke and guide it away.
Faces, eyes following Skeen. Male and female, young
and old. An animal touch to all of them. All shapes and
shadings, even some parti-colored like the patches on a
calico cat. Eyes shining red, reflecting the fire. The dark
angry scowl of the Cat-man, Rijen. No one slept, not
even the children. No one said anything, though she
heard soft hisses and the scrape of claws on stone.

Skeen followed Telka across the court, then through another court with the same central fire and funnel, the same
mix of faces, the same silence and hostility. A dozen arches
led off from this second court and through them she saw more
Min, shadows in the glow from the open fires. This a house
or a cattle run? and don't they know about roofs? Must get
cold as a Chanker Hell come winter. And what do they do
when it rains? or snows? Well, easy enough to see the point of
half-roofs and open air sleeping if they're all shapechangers,
werebeasts. Djabo's ivory overbite, I have to be dead back in
those ruins and dreaming, that's more likely than this.

Telka pushed back a heavy curtain and stepped into the
corridor beyond. Skeen paused to inspect the curtain. Thin
strips of leather woven in a herringbone pattern. Two layers
of leather with a soft white substance like dandelion fluff

sandwiched between them. Ties dangling along the edge, staples on the wall. For windy days, no doubt. With the lead weights crimped along the bottom it was heavy enough to hang in place without flapping as long as the air was fairly quiet. Deft fingers fashioned this. She patted the curtain with pleasure, then followed Telka into a hole that was as knobby and twisted as if it were the inside of a root.

At intervals along the gnarly hall, below patches of glow globes, oval areas of wood were smoothed flat and embellished with stylized animal carvings, low relief, boxy abstractions imbued with the essence of the beast. Her trained eye recognized at least three different artists. Beautiful work. Her fingers itched, every acquisitive nerve in her body vibrated. Djabo gnaw their pointy heads for cutting such lovelies into the wood of the wall. One could hope, though, that more portable examples of Min work existed, waiting for her to get her hands on them. Talk about uniques!

A few more crooked turns, more than a few narrow escapes from tripping over gnarls, knobs, and rough spots or banging her head on ceiling dips, and she was sure of one other thing. The Min didn't build this place; they grew the damn thing, then made a few swipes at civilizing it.

Every third patch of glow globes there was another of the leather curtain-doors. Behind some Skeen heard voices, from behind one, a snore. Others hid silence.

Telka led her into a side branch, then into another, then into a third, this last one barely wide enough for her shoulders and low enough that she had to stoop or bash her head; one thing sure, she wasn't being taken to any grand guestroom. No carvings at all in this hole, even the glowglobes were scarce. Lucky I don't suffer from claustrophobia.

Telka stopped by one of leather curtains, swept it aside, and motioned to Skeen to go in.

Skeen wasn't overly enthusiastic about turning her back on the little Min, but she didn't hesitate—to hesitate would offer insult and make an enemy out of someone neutral and possibly a source of the Min work Skeen needed to buy her way off Kildun Aalda. She walked quickly through the doorway, crossed the room, and swung round to face Telka.

The little Min didn't leave the doorway. "You must be very tired," she said. "Sleep as long as you like and when you wake, pull the bell cord by the bed, there, that embroidered strip, good, that's right. Pull that and one of the firamayin will bring you something to eat. I have to ask; don't try finding your way about before I come for you, it wouldn't be safe." She made a throw-away gesture with her left hand. "I'm sure you understand." She pointed to a side wall where there was another of the woven leather curtains, this one with a flimsier look. "Water in there, void holes, a bathing basin. Are you hungry?"

"My stomach thinks my throat is cut."

Telka looked doubtfully at her then produced a brief pained smile. "None of the waves have had trouble eating our food—even the Skirrik who are the strangest. I will send a firamay with something. It will have to be cold food, I'm afraid. Will you drink cider or do you prefer something hot? That I can arrange."

"Cider will do."

"One other thing I must ask, though it is a discourtesy to a guest. Please do not speak to the firamay. She would find it very disturbing and I do not wish more difficulty spread before me. I hope you understand. My sister, my twin sister, is a slave, degraded nightly by that filthy Pallah who owns her. I cannot rest until she is free again."

"No talking. Fine with me."

"Sleep well, Skeen Pass-through. Don't worry, you're safe here." Telka stepped back, letting the door-curtain fall in place. A moment later Skeen heard the soft patter of her feet leaving.

"Djabo's loving toes, what a world." She looked around her. There were several glow globes set in clusters on the walls. "So we sleep with the light on." No corners, like everything else she'd seen so far. A squarish room like an ice cube with the corners melted off. A brick bed; even that wasn't square but a long oval, built over a firehole, nothing burning there this warm night. On top of the bricks was a thick quilted pad, on top of the pad, layer on layer of fleeces, on the fleeces two quilts made from some silky material that gave back rich glows where the globes' light touched the folds. She shook out the top quilt, inspected it with a sigh of appreciation. Birdshape, probably mythical, thunderbolts in one talon, a branch with green leaves in the other. All hand work, tiny even stiches; she coveted it mightily though it was old and faded, patched in two spots. Djabo bless, she told herself, I've got to come back when I haven't got this load on my mind.

She went into the bathroom, splashed cold water on her face, filled a ceramic mug she found there, then stretched out on the bed waiting for the food to arrive.

SKEEN IS HIRED WITH SOME CONSIDERABLE CEREMONY. I'M IMPRESSED, OH YES, WHEN DO YOU BRING ON THE ACROBATS?

Morning. Early. Light coming through an irregular opening above the broad end of the bed, a diffuse creamy glow through a skin scraped until it was translucent, then allowed to dry and harden on a frame. She could hear voices, laughter, the braying and blatting of beasts. Wonder if those are citizens or food? And how do they keep it straight? Skeen grinned, then she stretched and yawned, feeling rested and filled with renewed energy. The firamay, a bovine little creature, had brought her a tray filled with cold meats, cheeses, slices of a sweet yellow fruit in a tart sauce, crusty rolls, and a large goblet of cider. To think of hiprots paste in the same breath was blasphemy.

She wriggled between the quilts, enjoying the soft give of the fleeces under her. She was clean again, head to toe, and she'd have clean underwear, really clean this time, having washed undershirt and pants along with herself and hung them up to dry while she slept. She luxuriated a moment longer in that pleasure, then swung off the bed before it went stale on her.

She exercised vigorously for a while to work the knots out of her muscles, then padded into the washroom where she'd hung up her clothing.

She frowned at the skirt and blouse hung where her tunic and trousers had been. Came in while I was sleeping, maybe that cider was drugged, shit, I'm really past it if some idiot serving maid can creep in here and do all this without waking me. She went poking about, found her tunic and trousers neatly folded on shelves, her boots next to them. The boots had been cleaned and rubbed to a finer gloss than they'd seen in years.

She jerked the blouse and skirt off their pegs and threw them into the other room. Not fuckin' likely! I don't care if you have twenty fits, I'm not wearing that junk. She stomped back to the washbasin, pulled out the tap handles, and began splashing hot water over her face. Hot water had surprised her last night, but the taste, a faint hint of sulphur, explained its presence. Now she scrubbed at her eyes, splashed water along her arms and shook it off again, shaking off with it most of her anger at Telka's attempt to manipulate her. She was willing to hire out her services, but not her . . . well, call it soul; she'd stopped selling that a long time ago and wasn't about to start again. If they couldn't take her the way she was, too damn bad; there were other ways of getting hold of sellables, especially now she had a useful language and enough information to go on with. She dressed, stamped her feet into her boots, checked her hideout knife and the other bits she had tucked in hidden pockets. All there. She straightened Idiot! and strode into the other room.

Her backpack was in a heap by one end of the bed, close

enough to where she'd dropped it, but not how she'd dropped it, the folds were different. She had a special small gift, the ability to recognize patterns once glimpsed, and the ability to extrapolate from these memories to recognize similarities in other patterns. She went through the pack. Everything was still there. Some neat-fingered busybody had searched it, though. She didn't much like that, but she wasn't surprised; it was something she'd do herself given the opportunity. She clicked her tongue, dropped the pack, dug into the fleeces and found her darter. That, at least, no one had touched but her. She fished out the belt, swung it around her waist, and snapped the latch shut. After another moment's thought, she went into the washroom, dumped the old water in the darter's reservoir and refilled it at the cold tap. She strolled into the bedroom, sneered at the blouse and skirt, then yanked on the bell pull and settled back to wait for her breakfast.

Telka was annoyed when she saw what Skeen was wearing. Her heavy brows clamped down, her full lips compressed to a thin line—for an instant only—then her face cleared. She ignored the clothing tossed in a bunch on the floor. "The Synarc will see you."

Skeen fumed quietly. She'd lived in underclasses and among outcasts all her life and it took very little to wake resentment and rebellion in her. She sat without moving.

With barely restrained impatience Telka said, "Skeen Passthrough. Coming so far with me was a kind of promise. Do you renounce it? Do you treat Min like all the rest of your kind?"

"Not my kind," Skeen said firmly, "you've never seen my kind."

Telka's instant frown came back, instantly disappearing. She was a politician all right, knew when to push and when to leave off. The ones Skeen had come against before seemed born with the knack, even those chugging along at half-load. Which Telka definitely wasn't. Skeen wrestled her resentment down, got to her feet with a wide smile (I can play pol as well as you, see?). "Don't mind me. Does things to my temper, being closed in like this."

*   *   *

Telka led Skeen through a maze of gnarly corridors, moving so swiftly Skeen had no chance of ever finding her way through them again, then settled her in the arched exit of a tunnel, facing a court smaller and more intimate than the ones she'd passed through last night. The half-roof was almost complete, though there was a hole in the center large enough to let a condor through. The floor was paved with an elaborate mosaic made from bits of different kinds and colors of stones, incorporating differing surface textures that changed color and design with the changing angles of the sun. All around the court were other arches, the mouths of other passages. Trusting lot, Skeen thought. Bolt holes in case someone in the Synarc turns nasty. This place is a rat run, gives me strangulation of the brain.

"Sit here, Skeen Pass-through. And please, again, don't speak until I speak to you."

Skeen nodded, crossed her legs and settled herself as comfortably as she could. She felt herded in. Can't hurt to listen, she told herself. And repeated it several times as she waited for something, anything, to happen.

Shadowy figures moved into the arches and sat in what they meant to be intimidating silence, watching her. Screw you, she thought, as long as you pay me, I don't care how snotty you want to be.

Telka appeared in the arch and settled gracefully on the cushion waiting for her. Half a breath later a big golden male appeared beside her, so broad he filled the arch to bursting. When all the arches had occupants, Telka held out a hand. The big male was holding a short baton with bulging ends. He spun it so the larger end smacked into her palm. "Skeen Pass-through," she said, the neutral controlled tones back. "I Z'naluvit, have summoned the Synarc that we might inquire of you in what circumstances you will do a thing for us. I have a sister who knows our minds and hearts more fully than is comfortable to us because she languishes in the hands of the Pallah Nemin, a slave. Our hope ere this has been that the Nemin does not know who he has. Our hope has been that our sister has not so lost herself in her degradation that she

has told her master secrets of the Min. I will name the
Speakers of the Synarc. Think of what you desire from us,
say you will act for us.'' She waved her free hand at the arch
on Skeen's immediate left. ''Flet. P'takluvit.''

Speaker for those who wear wings and hunt from the sky.
Uh huh.

A little woman, smaller even than Telka, fine-boned and
fragile, with little flesh between those delicate bones and the
shimmergilt skin stretched over them—what Skeen could see
of it. Flet wore a loose robe made from cloth like canvas
whose angular folds concealed everything about her but long
nervous hands, a stretch of arm, and her taut and haughty
face. Wide dark pupils, the iris a shining gold rim. Her eyes
were fixed on Skeen with the shallow intentness of a predator
on its prey. When Telka named her, the golden woman
bowed her head, then went back to staring.

''Nerric P'shishulavit.''

Speaker for warriors/hunters.

A dark lithe man; hair, short and curly like the wool of a
black sheep, covered his head, chest, arms, grew down over
the back of his hands. He wore his fleece like a shirt. On his
lower half he wore tight-fitting leather breeches that creaked
when he moved. Bare feet, square and powerful—Skeen
could see the bottom of one; it had thick gray pads like a big
cat's. He reminded her a lot of the Cat-man Rijen, but wasn't
him. She suppressed a smile, Nerric didn't manifest much
humor. None of them did, so full of themselves and their
importance. He'd be horrified at what she was thinking; she
was amused by how vividly she remembered that naked man
strutting away from her. Nerric shifted restlessly on his cushion making it obvious he was there under duress. The gaze he
turned briefly but repeatedly on Skeen made the bird woman's almost friendly by contrast.

''Strazhha V'duluvit.''

Speaker for herds and herders. Uh huh. Who herds you.

A large, not-quite-fat woman with eyes round as copper
pennies and about the color of new-minted copper, a blunt
wide nose and a mouth of the width called generous by
flatterers, her thin lips a pale pale pink. Horn knobs, pointed,

slightly curved, about as long as the first joint of Skeen's forefinger, poking out through coarse hair that matched the color of her eyes. She wore a robe like Flet's but wore it carelessly, the hood pushed back, hands resting bare on bare broad knees, large hands to match the rest of her, shapely and well-cared-for. She watched Skeen with a detached amusement that was little kinder than the more overtly hostile gazes, made Skeen feel as if she was back on the line at the fish house. She'd spent some of the most miserable days of her teen years in a youth labor pool, swept off the streets with hundreds of others by a labor pressgang. Under that woman's measuring gaze she felt like a sub-standard fish fillet.

"Z'la. Chovluvit and V'klav."

Speaker for men, uh huh. Warchief, oh yes, no need to translate that one.

Massive muscles. So massive he looked fat. He wore a sleeveless leather jerkin, laced loosely across a chest that might have been carved from pale teak. His arms were bigger around than her thighs, his legs threatened to burst out of homespun trousers dyed a dark russet. He had a stiff mane of sunbleached coarse blond hair considerably longer than Skeen's. He watched her from mild, coolly curious yellow eyes. She'd never met anyone who exuded so much raw male power, such calm acceptance of himself, though she'd met quite a few men (Tibo that baster was one, damn his pointy ears) who didn't come close to matching his physical presence but were as comfortable as Z'la in their maleness, their knowledge of who and what they were, who weren't threatened by anyone, male or female, no matter how powerful. He saw her watching him, looking him over, and grinned at her. Hunh. This one might actually have a sense of humor. He returned her gaze, eyes moving over breasts and hips, then he was done with her, dismissing her as uninteresting. She was both amused and appalled by her reaction. Anger and despair at being rejected by a hunk of muscle who wasn't her type anyway. Well, hell with you too, hunk.

Telka touched her lips, her heart. "Telka. Z'naluvit." Right. Speaker for women. The way you share the middle with the hunk it looks like you two run this show. Sitting next to

that mountain of muscle Telka should have been diminished
to nothing, a nullity, a blackhole pinhead-sized. But it wasn't
so. She cut as large a space for herself as he did, dominating
by the force of personality and will.

"Sussaa. Kirushaluvit."

Speaker for earth, for rooted things and those who tend
them.

Sussaa, a secret man, huddled in robes stiffer and more
encompassing than Flet's. His hands were intermittently visible as he played with a string of worry beads, the sunlight
shimmering along the muted olive, ocher, and pale umber of
his delicately scaled skin. The beads clacked rhythmically
through unnaturally long unnaturally thin fingers, more of
them than the five the others exhibited; Skeen couldn't tell
just how many fingers he had but got the impression of a
flickering like spiderlegs. The cowl of his robe was pulled too
far forward for her to see anything of his face, but she
thought (from the angle of the folds) that he was looking
down at the beads, not at her. Always rather liked snakes,
even poisonous ones. Very polite creatures—leave them alone
and they reciprocated. Tibo made a lot of jokes about them
the time she had that baby constrictor wandering through
Picarefy's corridors, said it meant she was oversexed. Hah!
Old Lionface over there wouldn't agree with you. Maybe I
ought to haul you back here, you little worm, and feed you to
him. He looks like he doesn't mind tough meat. Long as it's
fresh. Huh, you'd give one hell of a bellyache—you're good
at that, damn you, damn you, damn you.

"Kladdin Delat'luvit." Speaker for artisans.

A little hairy gnome of a man who was far more interested
in the chunk of wood he was carving on than he was in what
was happening here. Artisans. Interesting. That's a lovely
little knife he's got there. Local work? Traded for? Wonder if
whoever made that makes swords. Always some dimwit willing to pay high for a hand-crafted sword. She looked back at
Z'la. He lifted a lip in a sort of smile, baring a pair of hefty
fangs. He wouldn't bother with swords. Not with those teeth.

Mmm. This place was grown here, I'm sure of that. Old
Snakehands or his granddaddy did it, no doubt. All right,

what do I ask for? Anything I can pick up getting this sister out? Hunh. That I don't ask for; that's my business, not theirs. I need information. Yeah, but not for payment. Gold? No way. Too heavy. Can't carry enough to make it worth while and it'd be kinda hard to outrun a saayungka pack hugging a hundredweight to my meager bosom. Gem stones or jewelry. Jewelry's best. Good old jewelry, artifact and gemstones combined, best price for the weight. And I get paid before I start. This bunch I wouldn't trust as far as I could throw the hunk.

YOU'RE RAMBLING THROUGH A DAMN FANTASY, SO RELAX AND ENJOY IT.
or
GETTING IN AND OUT OF DUM BESAR.

She walked along the dusty road, strolling through a warm golden morning, leading a neat little jennet, a genuine beast, one that wouldn't shed its skin and turn into a hostile Min. This beast was expendable as was everything it carried, part of her disguise as an Aggitj extra earning her living as a wandering peddler. Sussaa had overcome his distaste sufficiently to supervise the bleaching and dyeing of her hair until it was the color of moonsilver. She was wearing loose leather trousers that came to midleg, her own boots, a loose white shirt like those the chalapeer had been wearing, a long narrow vest ending at mid thigh, closed in the front with more lacing. She was moving away from a grove south of the city. Telka was perched somewhere in there with Skeen's backpack and the pouch of jewelry she refused to hand over before she got hold of her sister. No doubt she suspected Skeen would go in one gate and out another, scampering for the Gate, leaving the Min without their jewelry and their woman. I stay bought, she told them, but they wouldn't listen.

Sister. There was something they weren't saying about that. Skirrik or not, Timka was Telka's equal at shifting. No one had actually said so, in fact no one she talked with said much at all about Timka, that was interesting in itself; talk or not she got the strong impression Timka was Telka's equal in just about everything but ambition. So how come she was a slave? How come she was *still* a slave? Skeen couldn't imagine Telka enduring that state for a day, let alone a couple of years. Maybe Timka just got bored with all that stomach burning about lost land and took off. Djabo's hairy tail, it's not my problem. What she does after I fetch her out is up to her.

She started whistling as she walked along, sauntering contentedly toward the city. She couldn't sing worth a shit, but she could whistle. Little bird, Tibo that baster called her in one of his more drunken moments. Little—when she was a head and a half taller than him—ah well, it was nice to be cuddled and pampered a little. She was enjoying herself today, well-fed and well-rested, keyed up for the danger ahead but not imminent, her body humming like that sweet ship Tibo that baster choused her out of.

She always felt good when she was physically active. The long flights between worlds left her itchy and irritable and off her stride. One of the reasons she took up with partners. Sex was an exercise that didn't necessarily need much space and used up a lot of energy and continued to be interesting after a lot of repetition. She liked her men wiry and little with lots of stamina, jutting buttocks, knobby knees, small feet, small hands. And an intangible something else. Could call it imagination, if you wanted to be kind, slipperiness and a total lack of morals if you wanted to be snarky. Getting off with Picarefy, worms eat his poky arse. Five years with him, five years! May his liver rise up and choke him, may all his teeth fall out and boils afflict his butt. My taste in men is appalling. Death wish, that's what it is. She grimaced and went back to whistling, grimaced again when she heard what she was whistling and remembered where she learned that song. Tibo you little baster, why do I miss you so much, why does it still hurt like hell. . . .

She reached the Land Gate of Dum Besar around mid-afternoon. Tired, covered with dust, nothing about her to attract attention, even the fact that she was female concealed by the clothes she wore, she eased past the heat-dazed guards without being noticed. Eased past a Skirrik too, on guard at the Gate to sniff out uppish Min. Squatting beside the Gate on his powerful hinder legs, compound eyes glittering in the long light of the descending sun, green and brown chitin polished and waxed, set with patterns of jet, that semi-precious stone highly prized by the seventh Wave males. Feathery antennas—white—the color marking him as adolescent and virgin, still earning the jet for his marriage price, his senses at their keenest. He paid her no attention as far as she could tell, too busy grooming his antennas with the spurs at the back of his fore-wrists.

Skeen grinned and strolled into the littered streets, the jennet ambling lazily behind; she wrinkled her nose at the stench, signs were the Pallah had forgotten whatever they knew about sewers. The streets were narrow and twisty, houses several stories high, built oddly upside down so that the upper stories extended beyond the lower in a series of steps, the top stories so close a child could hop from one window to another, something she saw several times. Beggars crouched in corners, beside stairs, anywhere they could find a bit of shelter, displaying their injuries and deformities, shaking their begging clackers in a continual clamor that only ceased when someone dropped coins in a begging bowl, or a shop owner paid his cadre of beggars for their silence and their services keeping off others of their kind.

She found the hostel Telka told her about, close to one of the riverside walls, a small dingy place with a smell to it Skeen recognized instantly, a den similar to those she hung about in after she escaped from the labor pool. Kind recognized kind. She relaxed in one way and tightened in another, knowing from long experience just how little she could trust her kind.

She stabled the jennet and dumped her saddlebags and her packs in the room the clerk directed her to; he gave her a key for it and she locked the door behind her with no faith at all in the efficacy of that lock. If she lost her key, she could whistle the thing open. Whistle? A sigh might be enough.

Having dusted herself off, she went downstairs, hesitated a moment as she walked through the tavern. Dark and smelly, just what she liked, but there was no time for that now, not until she looked over the ground.

She left the hostel and began roving through the streets, ambling with apparent aimlessness toward the quarter where the wealthier folk lived, taking in the increase in house size and the size of the plots those houses occupied. Hard-eyed loiterers grew thicker on the scene, walking the tops of the walls, sitting in casual knots on benches outside the elaborate gates, eyeing her with increasing disfavor as the crowds in the streets thinned out and the garden walls grew higher and more imposing, the air fresher, the day quieter as it passed into the night. She slouched along, relaxed and unconcerned, with the invincible gawk of a sightseer determined to stick her nose everywhere. She located the house of Klikay the Poet (youngest and reputed to be the most useless of the brothers of the Byglave, the man and family who with a play of modesty told the Casach of Dum Besar how to govern the city and the domain). No one pays much attention to the Poet, Telka said. They don't guard him with any care because no one with the slightest pretense of a working mind would waste their time trying to kill or kidnap him.

There was a wall. Shabby. The plaster, insipid frescoes, covering the red brick was cracking and flaking away. She wrinkled her nose at the clumsy ugly scenes in dull pastel colors. No great loss if it all came off. Maybe he was a good poet, but his taste in art was gruesome. Probably spikes or broken glass on the top of that wall; she couldn't tell from where she stood, but it didn't matter. She could climb that wall easily enough using one of several trees growing out over it; from the look of the thing she wouldn't have to worry about leaving marks for guards to notice. Flet had sent one of her followers on several high flights over the city to give Skeen some idea about how the house was arranged, but once she was inside she was on her own. No Min except Timka had been inside that structure so the layout was anyone's guess. She didn't like going in blind but, Djabo's twitchy nose, no fancy traps in this jerkwater place. No sniffer alarms, no sorting ears or any of the thousand other things she'd had to neutralize or outwit before. She strolled on, scolding herself for her tendency to think she could walk in and out as if she was calling on the man. Carelessness like that could do her in faster than a fancy trap. You don't know this stinking world, woman. You don't know where the pitfalls are or what they are. Shapechangers, hah! What else is this place going to spring on you? Wizards shaking death rattles in your face? Witches yammering in the night? Tickled by the absurdities her imagination threw up, she walked along chuckling to herself, moving back into more plebeian realms, working her way next to the wall, walking along it, checking out possible escape routes.

The gates were closed at sunset, watched by Skirrik and squads of local guards. Herds of hungry massits were loosed on the parapet to discourage anyone stupid enough to try climbing over the wall; they'd strip this fool to the bone in less than a breath and a half. Telka said they had a special hatred of Min and a mass mind so powerful it overwhelmed the subtle control the Min exercised on most beasts. Thanks to Strazhha the V'duluvit she had something she thought might deal with that little problem, but she wasn't looking forward to using it.

Up close to the wall, the houses were elbow to elbow, narrow, hardly a room wide, each house jammed with people, with those who lived all the time in the city, with transients from all over, traders, tramp artisans, farmers, peasants, younger sons looking for adventure or work (which one depended on their family's wealth and status or lack of it). She started moving toward the market, passing through more visitors—rivermen off the boats that sailed up and down the Rekkah and the smaller Rioti, land traders with their stolid stumpy beasts, hordes of gawkers come to stare, come to buy or sell, come to complain about something, come as pilgrims to pay homage at the temple that was the tallest structure inside the walls. Lines of Blackrobes winding through the buyers and sellers in the market, solemn-faced children censing them and every one around with a pungent incense.

Skeen spent the narrow remnant of the day in the market, buying a few things that would be useful when she went over the wall—a large unworked hide, thick and supple, nicely tanned, several large iron nails and a wooden mallet, a few other odds and ends. She carried the leather rolled over her shoulder as she continued wandering among the tables and booths and heaps, excited by just about everything she saw around her. Everything crafted by hand. Swords, knives, mail shirts and other specimens of the smith's art. Bows of several sorts, arrow points (heavy multi-tanged hunting arrows meant for big game or armed men to small knobs meant to bring down birds). Reels of thread. Gold and silver wire. Papers of needles, papers of pins. Swaths of lace, ribbons. Wooden objects, from simple bowls to elaborate carvings. Glass mirrors and polished bronze mirrors. Lamps of horn and parchment, of glass and silver, the metalwork as fine as she'd seen anywhere, the silver inlaid with a delicate gold tracery in marvelous intricate whorls and webbing. Leather goods, saddles, harness, gloves, hats, boots, belts. A Rooner's dream, a whole world to be plundered, a world no one could reach but her—well, almost no one. Not that these were ruins. But Rooners are flexible, (oh yes we are, we take our artifacts where we find them). She thought about old Yeoch. Someone might finally believe him. Ah well, I can take care of that later, haul him here, maybe, and dump him, he might like to see his Sessi again. She grinned at the thought.

She nosed out a cookshop, got some meat pies and a mug of cider. When she finished eating, she went back to the room, stretched out on the bed and settled herself to sleep until it was time to go for the woman.

Skeen went over the wall three hours after midnight.

Flet and her fliers had mapped the routes the werehounds took as they prowled the city streets and tied their rounds to moon positions so Skeen could judge time by glancing at the sky. She couldn't complain about the back-up; the Min went all out for her once the bargain was struck. In spite of that her trek to the Poet's house was harrowing at times. She could hear howls a short distance away, once a chopped-off scream as a transient stupid enough to sleep in the street died under the jaws of werehounds. Worse than saayungkas, much worse. She shivered at the thought of deadly, intelligent beasts roaming the streets only a breath away from her, the senses and ferocity of the animals whose shapes they wore, the intelligence of a man directing that ferocity. But they had their patterns and ran them with a bored precision.

One guard on the wall, asleep in his shelter by the gate. More a porter than a guard despite his mail shirt and crossbow. His snores announced his presence a dozen meters away.

There were iron spikes and broken glass atop the wall. The spikes had once been sharpened to knife edges, now they were dulled by rust and long neglect; the glass had eroded to abrasive dust. She set the padded grapple on the spikes with a quiet ta-thunk, went up the rope with a few scrapes of boot soles against plaster, a rain of broken plaster to the pavement which she ignored, the sounds lost in the snores of the gateguard.

She ghosted through the garden alert for traps or prowling werebeasts but it was deserted; a wandering breeze rustled grass and leaves and rattled windows. She slipped the latch on a window and boosted herself inside, feeling as light-hearted as a kid trashing an obnoxious neighbor. It was impossible to treat this with any kind of care though she did keep telling herself not to underestimate them. He won't be guarded, Telka said, but this was ridiculous.

A large empty room filled with pale gray light from the

waxing moon. She prowled about, flashing a pinlight over any bit of shadow that seemed interesting. She slipped several small carvings and other bibelots into her shoulder bag, then went cautiously out the door.

After exploring a few more of the groundfloor rooms, she decided the bedrooms were upstairs somewhere and the woman was most likely in the Poet's bed. Telka said so, and she should know. Plenty more things down here she could pick up, but she had other business tonight. She left the tempting public rooms and started up the graceful free-floating spiral ramp that led to the next floor.

On the second floor she went more cautiously. The Poet had a family, though the Min knew little about them. So they said. Doesn't pay to be too mistrustful . . . they wanted Timka out of this place, the air in the court stank of it. She'd half expected the Synarc to add that she should kill the woman if she couldn't get her clear, but they didn't. Just as well, be a cold day on Vatra before she killed for hire.

She found Timka and the Poet in the third room she visited.

Big room, big bed in the middle of it. Lots of windows, the moon filled the huge room with its deceptive pearly light, giving her a good look at the sleeping Pallah once she crossed to the bed and stood gazing down at the man, walking ankle-deep in furs tossed about with a calculated abandon.

He was a lanky soft-looking man with a fringe of sandy hair about a freckled bald spot, a jutting nose that dominated a face with little else to recommend it, long, rather flabby arms, a pot belly that made him look like a stick doll who'd swallowed an orange. He lay curled up as tightly as he could with that pot, his back pushed against a slight figure that had to be Timka. She was darker, tauter, a flow of tangled curls spilled across her face. A close duplicate of Telka as far as Skeen could tell. The little Min lay on her back, snoring now and then, wavery squeaks that Skeen decided would get very irritating if you had to listen to them long. The snoring stopped. Timka moved her arm, made a shapeless grunting sound.

Hastily Skeen darted her, then the Poet. She clipped pinlights to her sleeves and began searching the room, taking her time, chuckling softly with pleasure as she scooped up brooches, rings for the fingers and ears, jeweled studs, coins, fancy pots and boxes—everything else that took her fancy, including three jeweled and embroidered cloaks. She grinned with satisfaction as she came across four swords with elaborately chased blades and jeweled hilts, four matching knives and sheaths. The blades were a fine steel with the wavy mottling that spoke of long patience and many folds, the kind of swords that brought premium prices at the submarkets. She looked over these prizes, glanced at the Poet. Vanity, ah vanity, where would I be without it. She grimaced. On that cannery line, packing fish and pregnant with some grunt's kid. Djabo bless all vanity. She pushed the blades gently back into their embroidered begemmed scabbards and set them on the bed. Different swords for different occasions, color coded to match your outfits no doubt. She sniffed as she examined the lanky body with its soft sagging flesh. You look like it tires you out to climb in bed. She looked at Timka. Obviously I'm underestimating your talents. She shrugged. The smell of sex was still strong in here, the coverlet was kicked onto the floor. Timka, little Min, I strongly doubt you want rescuing. Not my problem. Nobody asked me to pay you heed. Mmm. Better get busy, the dark won't last forever. She checked the ring chron. Couple of hours yet. No hurry.

Working briskly, she dressed Timka in the shirt and trousers she'd brought from Mintown. She set Timka on the floor by the bed, then began cutting up the coverlet, cursing the dullness of the ceremonial knife; she could have used her own but she felt a strong aversion to the idea and trusted her instincts. Been wrong before, but nobody laughed. She wrapped Timka and the swords in half of the coverlet, used strips of tough silk sliced from the other half to tie and gag her first, then bind the bundle together, knotting the ends to make an awkward sort of sling. She shrugged the sling onto her shoulder and started from the room, her darter in her hand, the lanyard engaged. In the doorway she hesitated, then went back to the bed. You're skinny enough, except for that pot, but the way my luck's been running recently. . . . She darted him again, resettled the Timka bundle and trotted into the corridor, intent on getting out of the place as fast and with as little fuss as she could.

Three strides down the hall. No warning except a low growl. With it, a weight slamming into her back, knocking her skidding along the polished wood. She crashed into a wall, cushioned by the small muscular body of the Min. The sword hilts digging into her side, she brought the darter up and around, more by instinct than will, then sprayed the hall with darts.

Her head cleared. She got shakily to her feet and stood blinking down at a slim, dark-haired youth sprawled naked on the floor. Tame Min, she thought, better tuck him out of sight. She shrugged out of the sling, dumped Timka on the floor, caught hold of the boy's ankle and began to drag him toward one of the rooms she'd looked into earlier and found empty. He slipped out of her grasp, turning to smoke that oozed between her fingers, reforming into a silver-shouldered wolf.

With a hiss of annoyance she darted him again. The wolf smoked into boy and the boy gathered himself to attack. For the third time she pumped a dart into him, thought a moment, then darted him once more just to be sure. She finished dragging him into the empty room, watched him until he started to stir, put another pair of darts into him. The shifting apparently flushed the drug from the Min system. Something I'd better remember. Handy for poisoning, I suppose. She watched a moment longer, nodded with satisfaction. They had to be minimally awake to shift, so he was out now until the stuff wore off naturally. She thought about tieing him, then laughed at herself. He'd just ooze out of whatever she used. She frowned. Timka? She went hastily back into the hallway.

The silk bundle moved a little. Shit. These Min and their impossible bodies. She pulled open the bundle, bared one of the Min's arms and put a pair of darts into it. That should hold you long enough, I hope I hope. She got the sling over her shoulder again, pressed up onto her feet and went on, moving quickly but a lot more warily now, her senses stretched wide, nose flaring, straining to catch a trace of a Min, musky and tart, ears straining for the click of claws on the polished wood, the pant of a hunting beast. Each shadow tightened her muscles and ratchetted her tension higher, but she came across no more guards and gradually began to relax. If there were supposed to be more guards, they'd hunted out a comfortable corner and curled up to sleep. She thought about the youth of that Min as she quickstepped through the darkness; his youth was probably the reason he stuck to his task. As it was the reason, for sure, that he hadn't called for help. His pride, his confidence in his strength and vigor kept him silent where an older, more seasoned guard would have howled alarm as he jumped her. But then, from what she'd seen, an older, more seasoned guard wouldn't have been there in the first place.

She maneuvered Timka through the window she'd entered by, hung her over the sill while she wriggled out herself, laid her on the grass while she pulled the window shut. That kid she'd laid out upstairs, he'd be quick to sniff out her trail so there was no point in being tricky. Shutting the window wasn't being tricky, just prudent. Even lazy guards stirred themselves occasionally, if just to take a leak; better to leave no stray drafts about to alert them.

Timka on her shoulder again, she loped across the garden and into the shadow of the tree where she'd left the rope dangling. Same wind. Same soothing night sounds. Same snores from the gateguard. Clumsy noisy business, hauling herself and her burden up the wall, grapple groaning under the weight. Heavy load—maybe she'd got a bit too greedy, weighed herself down—but she was in good shape and if it'd done nothing else, the run from the saayungkas had toned her leg muscles.

She crouched on the wall, hidden by the exuberantly leafy tree. If her reading of moonangle was right, a werepack was due past her right now. She scowled at the moon, chewed on her tongue, fidgeted impatiently. She wanted to get this job finished before luck turned sour on her. Hand on Timka's hip. Still out, thank Djabo. Skeen squatted on the folded hide and waited. And waited. And repeatedly checked moonheight.

She began to sweat. If those fuckin' weres didn't get by here soon, they were seriously off-pattern and her plans could easily go down the toilet.

Sound of soft yips, almost like a code, scrabbling claws, panting. She sat very still, waiting, listening. The pack trotted along, came past where she squatted, moved on without stopping or changing the rhythm of their trot. She started breathing again. She looked at her ringchron, glanced at the moon, settled herself to wait for another quarter hour to let them get well into their round. She tried not-thinking, tried being an emptiness in Skeen-shape, but found she was looking at the chron every two minutes. After a dozen minutes she decided not to wait any longer, got the sling over her shoulder, and slid down the rope.

She shook the grapple loose, started walking away, coiling the rope as she moved. Twice she heard howling, screams, shouts, then silence as a werepack ran down someone else. She started sweating, though the sounds were muted, distant, and the streets around her were empty and silent and stayed that way as she moved into the poor section, that thin ring of slum running around the whole city, pith to the wall's rind.

She found the alley she'd chosen during her earlier ramblings, dug out her climbing claws and started up the side of a corner house, nimble as a squirrel in spite of the awkward burden Timka made. The claws chunked into the soft wood with satisfying solidity, came out as they were supposed to. The world where that design originated was a long way from Kildun Aalda, but good ideas traveled far and fast in her circles. Kladdin delat'luvit took her to a brawny woman twice his size, Ellagin the Smith, and watched with interest as Skeen sketched what she wanted, then explained the sketch. While they watched Ellagin work, he asked her question after question about the folk who showed her how to make and use the claws, about all the different ways they used them, and when the claws were ready, he and Ellagin watched Skeen as she used them to climb one of the sentinel conifers.

She clawed her way onto the roof, unhappy with the noise she was making, sat a minute on the ridge pole, folding the claws into the soft leather protectors and tucking them away.

Afterward she moved from ridgepole to ridgepole, gliding with great care, making sure the flimsy structures would hold the double weight. The last house was squeezed against the wall, a tall thin anemic house that seemed to shudder with her every step. She heard howling again, a short distance off, and was happy to be up here where they weren't likely to spot her.

She balanced Timka's body across the ridgepole, dug into her shoulder bag and found a small round box. She took the lid off, poked at the grains inside to see if they were loose enough, then had to choke back sneezes that made her eyes water and her head feel ready to explode. Strazhha said it would drive off a starving wolf pack, Djabo grant it chases away the massit horde. Let them spot live meat, Telka said, and they'd jump ten times their height to sink their teeth in it. She set her balance, hefted the tin, careful not to spill any of the powder, put the top on again, lightly enough that it would fall off at a touch, tossed the tin up over the baffle that kept the massits on the parapet.

It hit with a loud rattle that made her wince. She heard squalls, high-pitched, pained, comfort to her soul, a scrabbling of clawed feet on the stone as the horde went rapidly away. She unclipped the rope from her belt, took the leather cover off the grapple, swung it in a wide loop, and let the rope slide through her hands as the iron claw soared up and over the baffle. She heard it land, jerked lightly on the rope, and felt it catch. She pulled harder. The grapple came loose and flew over the edge of the wooden wall. Hastily she pulled it to her, catching it before it hit the roof. She felt the points, mourned the steel from her universe. The claw was blunted and a little sprung. She scowled at it, rubbed her hands along the wall. If it wouldn't catch in wood, no way would it hold on the granite. Well, try again. She whirled the grapple and loosed it. Again it seemed to catch, again it came loose when she put weight on the line.

She stood very still a moment, her hands and forehead pressed against the cold stone, her eyes shut, calming herself. Then she moved back a pace, stood balancing on the ridgepole, frowning at the wall. A moment later she lowered

herself and sat pulling the rope through her hands, figuring its
length against the height and width of the wall. Obviously the
baffle was no good; she was going to have to get the grapple
all the way over and hook it under the outside overhang of the
parapet. She coiled the rope again. It has to work. I am not
going to be sitting here come the dawn. She got slowly to her
feet, set herself as solidly as she could, whirled the hook
round and round until the rope was singing through the air;
then with all the strength and skill she had in her, she set the
grapple arching up and over the wall, letting the rope flow
freely, not touching it but ready to catch it if it seemed about
to flop out of reach. Up and up it went. Arching over.

A large nighthawk caught the hook in its talons, dropped
with it behind the wall.

Skeen heard a muted cheer, glanced around. Folk in the
house across the narrow alley were looking out the window
watching her, applauding, not about to interfere. She grinned,
sketched a bow, then forgot about them as she settled the
bulging sling over her shoulder and began the difficult climb.

She dropped to the ground with a grunt of relief, stood
shaking her arms. Telka waited with two horses. She started
to speak, but Skeen ignored her. She slung the Timka bundle
across the withers of the riderless horse, swung into the
saddle, snatched the reins from Telka, and kicked the beast
into a run. When Telka caught up with her a moment later, a
hundred questions in her mouth that Skeen didn't want to
hear, she lied swiftly, instinctively, "Werepack. Chased me
onto the roofs. Got to get under cover."

They rode north to fool the Pallah who'd expect them to
head directly for Mintown and most likely would chase that
way, wasting time. The plan they'd worked out, sitting beside the lake watching Min-dolphins play, called for them to
cut across the fields to the foothills and circle south through
the mountains. The Pallah wouldn't follow them into the
mountains.

A DAY, A NIGHT, AND PART OF ANOTHER DAY OF TEDIOUS TRAVEL. IMAGINE TIMKA KEPT DRUGGED AND DRAPED UNCONSCIOUS ACROSS SKEEN'S SADDLE, SKEEN AND TELKA RIDING IN UNFRIENDLY SILENCE, NEITHER TRUSTING THE OTHER, DOZING IN THE SADDLE, STOPPING ONLY TO GRAIN AND WATER THE HORSES.

or

IT'S PAYOFF TIME IN THE MOUNTAINS.

The fountain glade.

Skeen swung down, lifted the dreaming Min from the saddle and put her down beside the fountain. She straightened, started to turn. Warned by something, she was never sure what, she flung herself aside, plunged into the fountain basin and somersaulted out the other side as a black snarling fury leaped at her, slammed into the central pipe and slid round it into the water, yowled, gathered herself to leap again.

Skeen darted her. Then did it again to make sure the drug would hold.

Skeen stepped back from the fountain and contemplated the two Min propped against the basin wall. Both women were tied with strips sliced from the coverlet. Not that that would hold them if they shifted. Have to watch them both. Neither one I'd trust outside a Jinki slaver's holding cell. Stubborn, hard-headed, grudge-holding. . . . She yawned. Djabo! do I want sleep. She settled herself with sandwiches and water from the fountain, eating a leisurely meal and struggling to keep awake while she waited for them to surface.

"Buy you," Telka spat at her. "And you stay bought." She twisted her hands against the silk bonds, closed her eyes, apparently having forgotten entirely her attack on Skeen.

"Try shifting, Min, and I dart you again."

Telka's eyes popped open, rage making her teeth chatter so she couldn't talk. Skeen watched, putting on an expression of polite interest she meant to be as infuriating as it was. She'd practiced it on Tibo and men before him. When she thought Telka was about ready to listen, she said, "Sure I stay bought. Did what you hired me to, didn't I?" She waggled the nose of the darter at Timka. "Which is a lot more than you can say. You think you might explain that little exercise just now?"

Telka looked at her with contempt and loathing. "Nemin," she said, no more than a whisper but loaded with everything she'd kept suppressed till now. "Twisting us for treasure. Our ancient glories." Then her discipline clamped down on her emotions. "What now?"

"Wait till your sister joins us. I'm too lazy to explain twice."

Telka dug her elbow into the sleeper's ribs. Timka groaned. Another jab and she muttered, blinked, tugged at her bonds. Her form began to shimmer.

"Shift, Min, and out you go."

Timka frowned as she solidified once more. "What?" Her voice sounded thick, she was flushed and her eyes looked dull, though that dullness was rapidly vanishing. She turned her head, worked dry lips into a smile when she saw the strips of coverlet around Telka's wrists and ankles. "So you finally met someone else you couldn't fool." Her voice was hoarse, breaking twice in midsyllable, but the satisfaction in it made Skeen laugh silently.

Timka turned bright green eyes on Skeen. Coming more and more awake, her persona taking command of her flesh, the likeness between the two Min diminished considerably. She cleared her throat, coughed, said, "I know this place. You're a Pass-through."

Skeen nodded absently. She contemplated the silently smoldering Telka. "You understand, Min, attacking me tore up the contract." She bent her leg, flattened it and inspected the small pulls where the werecat's claws had glanced off her leg, weren't for the eddersil she'd 've got to the bone. She straightened the leg out, scowled at Telka. "Doesn't matter, it's finished anyway. You really want her, don't you, and not to kiss and make up."

Telka stared at her, saying nothing, her lips almost disappearing as she screwed down her emotions and withdrew into herself.

Skeen smiled. She turned to Timka. "Timka," she said. "Listen a minute, then I'll cut you loose." She kept the darter on Telka and made sure the Min knew she was keeping an eye on her. "Seems to me you've got yourself a couple of choices. You can try for the city, doubt you'd make it, though, and unless you're hooked on the Poet, I don't see why you'd do that. Or you can head for Mintown, but me, I wouldn't go near that hanging mob waiting for you. You know your folk better than me, you know what your chances are. Up to you. Or you can come through the Stranger's Gate with me." She grinned at the fuming Telka. "I owe your sister a kick in the butt, why not take advantage of that. Take a chance on my world. I'll show you how to go on, then it'll be up to you to keep yourself. Shouldn't be too hard with your talents. Think about it, but don't take too long. You Min make me nervous."

Timka lifted her bound hands, rubbed them across her face. "What did she do?"

"Jumped me. Tried it anyway. Didn't work out the way she thought."

"You'd have sold me to her without that?"

"Yes."

"Why?"

"Why not? Didn't know you."

"What stops you from selling me again?"

"Me telling you I won't."

"Why should I believe you?"

"Throw the dice. And ask yourself what you've got here that's so great."

Timka held up her bound wrists. "What about cutting me loose?"

Skeen slipped the knife from her boot; watching Telka with additional care, she flipped the knife into the ground within Timka's reach but on the side away from her sister.

As Timka began the awkward job cutting herself loose, Skeen got to her feet and backed off a few steps so she could watch both more easily, trusting neither of them.

Timka got to her feet, stood rubbing her wrists as she gazed down at her sister. "Hanging mob. That's right, isn't it, Telk. Don't bother answering. Brain-burn me, won't they, Telk. With you goosing them on if their enthusiasm flags, yes sister?" She ran her hand through her hair, grimacing at the greasy feel, struggling to bring some order to the matted mass. "I wonder how much control you'd have over them if I really decided to fight? I'm the oldest, remember? I could always beat you when I had to. Oh, don't tense up so, I won't. You were quite sure of that, weren't you. Well, you're right. I'm not going back to be caged in until I die of boredom. And you bore me worse than any of them."

"Whore," Telka whispered, hate so thick around her it shivered the air like heat waves. "You like eating Nemin dirt."

"Same old song, Telk. Boring, Telk. Booorrriiing." Timka turned her back on Telka, making a production of it, crossed the glade to stand in front of Skeen, making a production of that also, a graceful sway in her walk, exaggerated to intrigue Skeen and infuriate Telka. "Free woman?"

"Free by me. You watch yourself cleverly enough, you can stay free. But don't expect me or anyone else to pay your way forever."

Timka tapped the black compo handle of the knife against her cheek, then swung round to glare at her sister. "How long before you got tired of trying to fish me out and sent one of your dupes to cut my throat?"

Telka glared back, said nothing.

Timka started for her.

"Nope, not that way." Skeen tapped the Min's shoulder with the darter. "Give me the knife."

Timka hesitated as if wondering whether she could successfully defy Skeen, then turned with a brilliant smile, a flutter of her hand in graceful surrender, offered the knife over her arm, hilt forward. "You'll be sorry you didn't let me finish this. I don't know how she'll manage it, but she'll make you sorry you left her alive."

Skeen shrugged. "I'll take my chances. Where I come from, cutting the throat of an ex-employer is bad for business. Makes the rest hesitate to hire you."

"This isn't there. She tried. . . ."

"Doesn't matter what she tried—up to me to see she loses out. Which I did. Forget . . . no, you don't, shifter." She put a dart in Telka as the Min began to blur at the edges, then darted her again.

Telka fought the drug, struggled to shift before it took her, but she lost the race and slumped against the basin.

Skeen frowned at the two horses, stripped of gear, cropping languidly at the grass, then she shook her head, holstered the darter, caught up the pack and dipped her arms through the straps.

"Why not take them?" Timka scowled. "Leave them for her? Why?"

"No water, bad footing, too noisy. We go quiet-quiet like a mouse."

Timka sighed. "I hope you know I'm all over bruises and my head isn't that steady."

"Exercise will work the kinks out and food will take care of the swim in the head. Let's go."

OH SHIT!

The gate looked different. The woods were full of noises. Buzz of insects, rustle of leaves. The white wall had lost some of its shimmer and menace.

Skeen stepped to the gate and looked into it.

And looked through it.

Saw the trees on the far side of the glade.

She looked over her shoulder, saw the despair dragging down Timka's face, so it didn't surprise her much when she walked between the posts, walked around the Gate and came back to where she'd started. "Gate's closed," she said. "How come?"

Timka sighed. "Who knows.'

Skeen closed her eyes, chewed her tongue. At that moment, she had a strong impulse to dart the Min and toss her back to her bonesucker sister. She cleared her throat. "You aren't surprised."

"I was hoping you knew what you were doing."

Skeen lost her outrage in a sputtering laugh. "Now who's the fool. Djabo!" She giggled some more. "Both, I suppose. All right. The Gate is closed. Not much I can do about that. When will it open again?"

"When someone comes through from the far side, I suppose."

"Not helpful. Any way of working it from this side?"

Timka gazed at her, mouth open, face blank.

Skeen narrowed her eyes, read the laughter and the tension behind that blankness. "Come off it, sweetie."

Timka gave her a quick nervous grin. "The only folk who know that would be the Ykx." She glanced over her shoulder toward the fountain glade, looked down at her feet, glanced very rapidly at Skeen and away. "Ykx. . . . I don't really know anything. Not know. Just a place you could find out. Pass-through, let's get out of here, I don't want to stay so close to Telka. Believe me, you don't know what she can do when she's driven by fury."

"In a minute. A place, you said, where I could look for information about the Ykx."

"Rumors, something someone said at one of the Poet's dinners."

Skeen thrust her fingers through her hair until it stood in short pale spikes about her head, swallowed irritation like a mouthful of burrs and nearly choked on it. "You say go away from here. Where do we go? Where do . . . we . . . go?"

"I've never been beyond Dum Besar. Why don't we just go back there? The Poet has a big library. . . ."

"And he'll bow politely and say oh yes forget that little contretemps, I've got plenty of pretty things, I'll never miss what you took. Hunh!" She rubbed at her nose. "Library, hmmm. Where does the Poet get his books?"

"That's it, you've got it. The Tanul Lumat, most of them. Let's get the horses and get away before Telka wakes up, or . . . or something happens."

"She will know the Gate wasn't open for us."

"Yes."

"She'll come after us?"

"Yes, yes. But if we can break away, lose ourselves . . . she can't be away from Mintown too long or she'll have to step down from the Synarc. She won't do that, but she has got a lot of influence with the holavish and holavay; they're the war party, they want to raid in the valley and kill every Pallah they come across; there aren't a lot of them, bless lifefire; the Mountain Min want nothing to do with Nemin, but aren't hot to kill them; these Min just want to be left alone to live like they always have." This was spoken slowly, softly, with considerable reluctance, a reluctance Skeen didn't understand, but didn't question, no time for that; at least Timka didn't use that lifeless neutral tone Telka favored.

"Whatever we discover, we have to come back here."

"Yes."

"And if she doesn't catch us first, she'll be waiting."

"Yes. Not alone."

"Sheeit." Skeen walked over to the gate, kicked at one of the posts, lightly so she wouldn't break her toe or scratch her boot. "Fuckin' useless. . . ." She swung around, set her shoulders against the post. "Little more information before we move anywhere. Where's the Tanul Lumat and what is it?"

"The Rekkah passes through a pair of lakes southwest of Dum Besar. There's a city, Oruda, on the first lake. The Tanul Lumat's there, too. A place where scholars gather, a library, a place for things forgot elsewhere." She made a brokenwing, aborted gesture, said nothing more . . . just waited.

Skeen walked away from the Gate, started for the fountain glade. "The thing behind that wall. What's that? It's behaving itself today."

Timka was trotting beside her, having to hurry to keep up with her, three steps to her one. "The Ever-Hunger." She was panting a little, speaking in quick bursts. "Must be asleep or some thing." She managed a shudder without breaking stride. "It's more dangerous when the Gate's shut down."

In the fountain glade, Timka pulled in the two horses, sat on the basin lip a short distance from the limp, comatose Telka while Skeen saddled and bridled the beasts. "The Poet was always having visitors," she said. "They came from all over, but most of all they came from the Lakes. Dinners. Went on for hours. Booorriinng, you wouldn't believe. Talk about things like the third poetic cycle of the fifth wave gonheleurs in Dipsy Dor. Whatever. Argue for hours over if a word meant jewel or toadshit. All the time the food getting cold and no one paying any attention to the singers and musicians right there. All they could talk about were ones long dust. And after the meal, they'd read at each other and the Poet would read his scribblings and they'd talk about them as if they were really important. Well, he wasn't bad, but it was all pretty words, nothing real. Maybe if he had to go out and earn his keep with his songs he might have been more than good; sometimes he even wanted to do that, but his family leaned on him when he was young and he didn't like being hungry and dirty and tired, so he caved.''

Skeen came over and stood looking down at Telka. After a minute, she took out the darter, held it up. "Put your finger here if you need to shoot. I've got some things to do before we leave; among other things I want another look at the Gate."

"Be careful of the Hunger."

"How?"

"Well . . . I don't know. Stories say you feel it when you come through, that it is always more dangerous when the Gate is closed."

"Why?"

"I don't know, something about the Gate, I suppose. The Wall shines more, it feels different, or so the stories go. Min keep away. Too close and we get called in and eaten."

"Hm. Let me think about that a while. Oh yes, how long is the Wall?"

"It makes a square around the Hunger, a side is somewhere around four days' ride."

"Four days. If Telka looks like coming out of it, dart her twice. And you could be filling the waterskins while you wait." She caught up a bulky bundle resting beside the limp skins. "I'll be back in a little."

Skeen toed over a flat section of shale, part of the tumbled rock piled against the posts. She dropped to her knees and began shifting stones, smiled when she uncovered a neat hollow lined with dried grasses and bits of fur. Some small rodent was about to lose its home. Maybe had already lost it, the place smelled old and musty. She undid the bundle and began tucking away the rings, broaches, necklets and other items from the Min, adding some of the smaller items she'd picked up in the Poet's house, as much as she could fit into the hollow. She set the stones back in place as carefully as

she could, scraped up a handful of dust and scattered it over
the pile, got to her feet, and looked over her work. She
couldn't see any signs of tampering; that didn't reassure her
much, these rural types were quick to pick up on the smallest
hints. She took her boot knife and scratched obscenities from
a dozen languages onto the stone of that left-hand post, then
threw a minor fit, kicking at the stone piles, gouging up
clumps of grass and kicking these over the stone, having
herself a fine and furious tantrum that not only eased her
anger and frustration, but provided an adequate explanation
for the disturbance of the stones. She stood back, hands on
hips. "Djabo bless," she said. "You might even be there
when I get back." She caught up the swords and capes and the
heavier items from the Poet's house and stood holding the
loose bundle, wondering how she could hide the things so the
Min wouldn't find them.

She rewrapped the bundle, tied it shut with the increasingly
raveled silk strips and started walking slowly back to the
fountain glade. Werebeast noses would track her if she left
the patch she'd beaten into the soft soil going back and forth
between the Gate glade and the Fountain glade. A limb
arched low over that path. Leaves brushed against her face.
She stopped, blinked. "I see," she said. She slipped her arm
under one of the strips, jumped, caught hold of the limb and
pulled herself up onto it, then ran along it to the trunk. That
trunk split into six smaller ones, with a dark and rather smelly
hollow between them; smells wouldn't hurt anything, and she
hoped to be back before the damp was too damaging. She
eased the bundle into the hollow, moved back out along the
broad limb. Even before she reached the path, she could no
longer see the things. She swung down and went on to the
fountain glade.

Timka was sitting on the basin lip, the darter in her lap.
Telka was curled up on the grass in a slightly different
position. "She started waking," Timka said. "I put half a
dozen darts in her."

Skeen took the darter, slipped it into the holster, snapped
the flap down. "That won't kill her. Won't do her much
good. She'll wake with a sore head, that's all."

"Well I know," Timka said, rubbed at her temple. "How long will she be out?"

"Five, six hours."

"It's something, I suppose. Too bad it's not five, six years."

Skeen swung into the saddle. "Offer's still open," she said. She leaned forward, then back, settling herself as comfortably as she could. "Or you can take off, go where you want, hope she chases me not you."

Timka got to her feet, stretched, patted a yawn. "Lifefire, I'm tired." She bent to the falling water, splashed a handful on her face, drank. She straightened, wiped her mouth. "Do you want to get rid of me that much?"

Damn right, I do, Skeen thought. Aloud, she said. "All I'm saying is it's up to you."

Timka swung into the saddle. "I stick with you."

"Hm. You know the land. What direction's the Lakes?"

Timka glanced at the sky, pointed. "That way."

"Djabo's weepy eyes, so's Mintown, unless I'm turned around. You sure?"

"Yes. Oruda's ten days' ride from Dum Besar, three days by riverboat, given a good wind."

Skeen clicked her tongue at the horse, nudged him into an easy walk, heading south. When Timka came up beside her, she said, "And from here to Oruda. How long?"

"On a straight line, a guess, maybe twelve, thirteen, fourteen days, depending on the going."

They moved under the trees, into the growing shadow of the late afternoon, riding side by side, unhurried, Skeen thinking, Timka content to leave the planning to her.

"Direct line is out," Skeen said.

Timka looked drowsily at her, nodded.

"Soon as she wakes, your sister will have scouts searching for us."

Timka yawned, nodded. "Fliers," she said.

"That complicates things. We'd have a good start on any other low tech world, but we can't outrun wings. Your sister could trace us and set up ambushes just about anywhere she wanted."

"Told you. Should have let me use the knife."

"Call me squeamish. How can we break out of this trap?"

Timka raised her brows. "Me?" She shook her head. "You're the Pass-Through, the fighter. I float. What happens, happens; the less fuss I make, the less pain there is."

Skeen grimaced. "Better change your mind about coming with me. You must have kin in these mountains who'd take you in and keep you safe."

"No."

Silence for a long while. The sound of hooves on forest mold, of leaves rustling, a web of insect, animal and bird noises—a kind of white noise, soothing and restful. Skeen forced herself to go on worrying at the problem, her thoughts had leaden feet, didn't want to move at all. More than anything else she needed to sleep. She was in that state when mistakes were fatally easy and unusually fatal.

"The Ever-Hunger," she said.

Timka glanced at her, startled, straightened her back. "What?"

"What is it?"

"Hungry."

Skeen frowned, made a brushing motion as if to wipe away feeble attempts at humor. "I mean, what does it look like?"

"Don't know. Anyone who got close enough to see it got eaten." She shivered. "Mostly it lives on deer and bear; sometimes in winter, we can feel it there . . . hungry, beating against the wall, reaching for us." Again she shivered, looked sick. "It sings. You go close enough, it sings to you and you go closer and it crawls inside your head and you climb the wall. In the winter, we lose a lot of children to the Hunger."

"Why stay then?"

"Where can we go? This is our land."

"Hm. Given a choice you wouldn't go near the Wall, even on wings."

"Lifefire, no!"

"Nor any other Min, even on wings?"

"You don't mean. . . ."

"Why not? Listen, I've got an idea. This damp, the clouds, smells like rain."

"Before morning. It's the season. But rain won't stop the Hunger."

"Didn't think it would. What it will do is wipe out our spoor, nose and eyes neither one any good. Give us a day loose after that and Telka will be biting her own tail because that's all she can find."

"You don't know what you're talking about."

"When you said it sings, you told me all I needed to know. Besides, I had a taste of that song when I came through the Gate."

"You're not thinking of stuffing wax in our ears. A Min tried that a few generations back when her children got caught and she went after them. It didn't work."

"No, not my idea. You're more sensitive to the thing than I am. How far is the Wall from here?"

"Oh, about a stad, maybe a little more."

"And what's a stad?"

"The distance a horse can cover at a quick walk in one hour."

"Sounds rather indefinite."

"The edges blur; it's not important."

"How close do we have to be before the Hunger gets dangerous?"

Timka scowled down at hands clenched about the reins. "Half a stad. After that, the calling . . . the singing . . . you can't break away."

"How good are you at estimating time and distance?"

"Not bad. I'm almost afraid to ask why."

"Hour. I'm fairly sure what that means to you isn't close to what it means to me." She showed Timka the ring chron. "This is set to ship standard time. My hours. Up till now I haven't bothered with yours—haven't had to and it was just too much trouble. But your day is a little longer than our arbitrary ship standard, so I expect your time divisions are quite different. They usually are, planetside. So if I'm to have some general idea of what a stad is, I need your help."

"I see . . . I think."

"Right. Suppose I give you a start, then you tell me when you think we've been moving for an hour."

"Yes, I can do that."

"Right." She looked at the chron, waited a few breaths. "Now."

"Got it."

"Good." Skeen yawned, rubbed at the nape of her neck. "Djabo! Can you listen and count time? I need to keep talking or I'm going to fall out and it'll take a jolt of lightning to wake me."

"Talk. It won't bother me."

"This is something that happened to me when I was a lot younger and a whole lot rasher, before I had Picarefy—oh Tibo you baster, I hope she fries your liver. . . ."

"What?"

"Never mind. Habit I've got into, meaning nothing. Where was I . . . yes. What with one thing and another I was stranded on this crazy world, a place called Dragons Fart. Vulcanism like you wouldn't believe. What land there was changed shape day to day, mountain into swamp, swamp into desert, desert to mountain . . . well, it was not a place you went for fun. The south pole had the biggest hunk of land and was fairly stable, warm enough so there was some plant life. The seas were a real soup, walking on water was no miracle there, and the stink! Your nose gave out after ten minutes of breathing that air. As air goes it was reasonable stuff, but the stink would make you swear off living, it was that bad. How I don't know, but someone found out that one of the plants on the fringes of the ocean produced a juice that could be refined into one of the dandiest aphrodisiacs ever, good for all live-bearing oxygen breathers with iron-based fluid in their veins. Which made for one hell of a huge market, especially when the bosses did a little gengineering on it. You couldn't get that plant to grow anywhere else, and believe me, lots of types tried it. Which the bosses didn't mind all that much since it gave them a stranglehold on the stuff.

"A while before I got there, two refinery jocks got in a fight where one of them was killed. I heard the story in a dozen versions, no one was quite sure what actually happened. Some said it was over one of the sporting women working the barracks; some said it was because Erb was a tittuppy, acerbic type designed to provoke the worst in Dolf who was from a rabidly patriarchal world and neurotic about his masculinity, that Dolf kept riding Erb until Erb exploded; some said it was Erb's pet responsible for the nesh, that he bit a hunk out of Dolf and Dolf tried to stomp him and Erb jumped Dolf. Whatever started it, they cut each other up till it was hard to find enough pieces to pray over. When it was done, no one could find that pet.

"The beastie was a singing swamp lizard the length of your forearm, tail included. Carnivorous little worm—Erb used to feed it baby rats, always rats wherever there are men. It must have lived on garbage and rats, plenty of both around. A couple of men and a woman said they saw it scuttling about. Problem was, it grew. Oh how it grew. When it got big enough, it needed something more substantial than rats and developed a taste for biped . . . large live wriggling meals. It grew cunning, too, as it got bigger and bigger, never set pinky in any of the traps. Soon enough, things reached the point when either someone took out the Whistler, that's what everyone called it, or all flesh was going to have to get off-world and wait for the lizard to starve. The bossmen didn't care for that idea, they needed men down there. Androids rotted out and were a lot more expensive than your basic flesh machines, so they put a bounty on the Whistler's head and armed any fool who thought he was a great hunter. What that did was get Whistler a lot of easy meals.

"When it wasn't dining on hunter, it'd sit outside the settlement and whistle its meat. Soft and natural so not many heard it. Someone always did. Someone would go out and for all we knew walk right down Whistler's throat.

"There I was, landed in the middle and broke to my toenails. Living with a Hulk and a Snake and working in the Gummery to pay my food bill, all of us were and likely to spend the rest of our lives at it, since the pay was a hair above slave comp. When the bounty was doubled, Yamchik, that was the snake, he had a bright idea. The Hulk and me and him, we'd go hunting old Whistler. I thought it was one of his better ideas; Dragons Fart was wearing on me hard. What I didn't know was he planned to use me for bait. Come the dawn, there I was tied to a shaved fern on one of the few dry spots outside town. I did not appreciate the compliment, no way. Yamchik and the Hulk were in separate patches of bracken trying to keep leeches out of their shorts, clutching pellet rifles Yamchik had liberated from Stores. I'll say this for Yamchik, he had the hands of an artist when it came to locks. Taught me a lot, but that's nothing for now.

"So picture the scene. Gray slime in all directions. Some sour murky water standing in hollows of the slime. Hummocks of decayed leaves and fern. Air thick enough to chew with swarms of gnats and sapsuckers who were turned on by blood. After a couple of hours with those bugs crawling over me and I couldn't scratch or slap, I was praying for Ol' Whistler to show. Dead would be a change for the better. Uhhh! Makes me itch just thinking about it. The only thing that took my mind off was planning what I was going to do to those . . . those . . . well, Telka didn't supply those kind of words, you supply your own . . . anyway, what I was going to do to them when I got my hands on them.

"It got to be noon, turned steamy hot, really unbearable. Us rejects stuck on Fart didn't much go outside during the midday heat. Ol' Whistler did. The sound came curling through the stink and the bugs, saying come come to me, come to me, come, come, come. Djabo bless, I would've done it if I wasn't tied to that fern tree. The Hulk and Yamchik, they heard it and they weren't tied. They came walking out of the bracken, left their guns behind. Yamchik's plan had this little flaw in it. I was going crazy trying to pull loose. When Yamchik walked past me he sort of absent-minded slashed at the ropes of my arms, dropped the knife by my feet. Don't know why he did that. Maybe Ol' Whistler didn't like part of his lunch being kept away from him, he was a twisty old lizard.

"I broke the last threads of the ropes around my arms and started cutting my feet loose. I was late for dinner where I was the dinner. Whistler went quiet a minute, Hulk, I suppose, going down hard. The bugs were swarming round me, making their own keening, and that broke the fading dream. Soon as I was loose, I went diving for the rifles. By that time

Whistler had finished off the Snake and was wanting dessert which was me, so the whistling started again. But I'd got the idea from the humming bugs and I started whistling myself. Uh huh. We had quite a concert out there. Irritated him a lot when his meat talked back. He reared up out the mud. Yeee, that sucker was big. You see that tree over there, the top of it'd stand hip high on him. Puny pellet rifle looked like a mistake. Nothing I could do but try it. Yamchik had his weak points, but he wasn't always dumb. Somewhere he'd got hold of boomers. First shot hit that lizard in the eye and just about tore the top of his head off. Got him in the chest and belly and one more time in the head. He went down, and I almost drowned in the mud tide he sent up.

"No way I could cart him back to the post, so I settled for a couple of teeth, a finger, and a patch of skin. I collected the bonus and got off that world like my tail was on fire. For almost a year after, I was taking a couple of baths every day trying to wash away the memory of that stink." Skeen rubbed at her eyes, straightened her back. She was starting to feel every muscle she had. She turned her head. "Hour yet?"

"A while to go."

Skeen glanced at the ring chron, sighed. "The reason all that came to mind," she said, "your Ever-Hunger is a bit like Ol' Whistler, uses a kind of sound to seduce. What sound makes, sound can break. You said plugging the ears didn't work. That figures. Vibrations act through headbones too, can't plug those. What you want to do is set up a counter vibration. I've got a thing. . . ." She shrugged out of her backpack and began fishing around in it. After a moment of muttering and scowling, she brought up a battered case, opened it and took out an equally battered silver shepherd's pipe with an odd-looking mouthpiece. "Hold this a moment, will you?" She handed the pipe to Timka, returned the case to the pack, buckled down the flap, and swung the pack into place.

She took the pipe back, shook it out, blew into it lightly to get rid of some bits of fluff. No sound. "I ran across this not long after I left Dragons Fart, collected it on my way through . . . well never mind that. I figured what happened once could happen again and I was going to be prepared.'' She grinned. ''When I'm right, hey, I'm right. Might take forty years. . . .'' She blew into the mouthpiece again, slapped the pipe against her palm.

''Hour now,'' Timka said.

''Nice timing. Hm. Say you're reasonably accurate, one of yours equals one of mine plus, mmm, a dozen minutes. What do you think about this? We've got about an hour—your hour—clear ahead of us before Telka wakes. Actually, it's nearer two hours but I don't want to take chances. We keep riding along like we are now, no strain, for that clear hour, you keeping watch for a Min overflying us though we'll hope that doesn't happen, ride Bona Fortuna just a little. Then we head for the Wall, moving well inside the danger area, me playing my pipe like a demented jongleur. If it stirs up the Ever-Hunger, all the better. Your sister's Minions,'' she grinned at the feeble pun, ''they'll keep well away.''

''I don't like it, but I suppose it's the best chance. Will you listen to me if I tell you the pipe isn't working?''

''Oh, definitely. I've no wish to decorate the inside of that one's belly.''

CONCERT FOR THE
INSIDE OF THE HEAD.
or
SKEEN ACQUIRES A COUGH
AND LARYNGITIS.

Skeen turned her mount away from the direct line south and started riding toward the wall, glancing continually at the ring chron to make sure she didn't get too close; the trees were thick and there was a lot of brush—she'd be on the thing before she saw it.

After about fifteen chron-minutes, she turned to Timka. "We should be in the danger zone."

"You can't feel it?"

"Not a twitch."

"It's there. Awake now. Trying for me."

"Why didn't you say something?" Skeen knotted the reins, dropped them on her mount's neck, took out the pipe. "How are you doing?"

"Holding off. But it's getting louder."

Skeen searched within, shook her head. "Not a tickle." She scratched along her nose with the pipe's mouthpiece. "Maybe you and I vibrate so far apart, it can't do us both at the same time." Thunder had been rolling about them for several minutes, now a large drop landed on Skeen's nose. She grimaced. "Wet, too. I'll be lucky I don't come down with pneumonia."

Timka managed a weary smile. "I thought you wanted rain to wash away our trail."

"Sure, but that doesn't mean I can't bitch about it, too." She frowned at Timka. The little Min had a glazed inward look; she was struggling with a force Skeen couldn't even feel.

She tried turning her horse; it resisted her briefly, but she managed to pull its head around and shoulder Timka's mount about. Knee and heel keeping the gelding heading south, she began playing a nearly inaudible song on the pipe, feeling a tickle suddenly flourish in her own brain a breath or two after she started playing. A breath more and her mount shook his head, repeatedly, shuddering and snorting as if ants were crawling up his nostrils and into his ears.

She glanced at Timka. The strain was melting out of the little Min's face. She caught Skeen watching her and mimed flying with her hands, then pursed her lips and whistled a version of the tune Skeen was playing.

They rode south, the rain falling in earnest about them, Skeen lowering the pipe only to spit or snatch a drink from the waterskin Timka held for her. She found she had to change the tune every stad or so, the sly creature behind the Wall found a way to alter its siren song. As soon as her mount began heading toward the wall, Skeen switched songs. Hour after hour, stad after stad. The rain finally stopped. The sun rose. They rode on, the horses reduced to a slow walk. Hour after hour. Skeen no longer bothered being fussy about her playing, just kept pushing air through the pipe.

By mid afternoon, her lips felt swollen and her head was swimming so badly it was hard for her to keep her balance on the horse. Finally she turned her back on the sun and moved away from the wall, glancing often at the ring chron so she'd have a clue when she could stop the playing without being sucked in by the Hunger. She was so tired she wouldn't have will enough to blow out a match that was burning her.

Timka touched her arm. "You can stop," she said.

Skeen lowered the pipe, drew the back of her hand across her mouth. "Ga' t' sleep."

They were riding south in a long skinny valley between

two sets of peaks with the Wall somewhere to their left and a small noisy stream on their right. The sun was tilted into the west, the shadows were growing toward night. Skeen's head throbbed from the concentration though her dizziness gradually diminished. She slipped the cork of her waterskin and drank for a long time, letting a trickle of water slide down her aching throat. Finally she lowered the skin, tapped in the cork. "Less stob." Her mouth was so sore, she had trouble articulating the words, sounded mushier than Old Yoech the Soak.

Timka frowned at the sky intermittently visible through the thin screen of leaves. "I haven't seen any searchers, but we should stay in thicker cover than this."

"Wha' 'bout unner those?" She lifted a two-ton arm and pointed at three ancients with high round crowns that spread out over a grassy space, mottled light and shadows shifting and shifting.

Timka sighed. "Why not."

HERE IT IS AGAIN, THAT OLD QUEST STORY, HERO TREKKING ACROSS A GOOD PART OF THE WORLD CHASING DOWN A MAGIC OBJECT MEANT TO RESTORE HER TO HER SEAT OF POWER.
or
SKEEN WAKES UP.

A large brindled bird swooped under the trees, dropped the wet flopping fish on Skeen's head, went powering away with cackles like human laughter. Skeen laughed, shook the fish at the bird. "Crazy Min." She crossed to a tree-shaded flat rock that pushed a little way into the stream, knelt, and began gutting the fish. Timka had got scathing about lighting fires to cook fish when likely every Min in the mountains was hunting them, but Skeen just grinned and told her to wait and see. She dug a firehole while Timka was out fishing, lining it with small stones she collected from the stream.

She took the gutted fish, dusted a few spices in the cavity, then plastered a thick layer of mud over the outside and set the fish aside as Timka-bird came back with a smaller fish. Skeen glared at her and the bird dropped it neatly by her knee. Another cackle and it was gone.

Skeen cleaned this fish, fixed it like the other, carried them to the hole. Using the small flamer from her toolkit, beam spread to a fan, she heated the rocks red-hot, dropped the two fish in, covered them with more stones, heated those, pushed dirt over them . . . then settled back to wait.

Timka-bird came back with a fish in each clawed foot. She dropped them onto a slab of stone, lit beside them, and proceeded to devour them with a neat efficiency that left little debris behind. Skeen found she preferred not to watch. When the bird was finished, her form smoked and changed into a naked Timka who had lost any trace of blood or muck in the shift. She moved to her clothes and began pulling them back on.

Skeen watched, fascinated. "Shouldn't you have waited until you digested that a little?"

Timka pulled the neckstring to the proper tightness, tied the ends. "Why?"

"I don't know. It just seems. . . ." Skeen dropped it, no point in fussing about something she wouldn't understand if Timka tried to explain. Besides, there was a question she found more interesting. "Hm. Things being the way they are, how do you know friend from food?"

"Tie these things for me, will you?" Timka extended her arms. As Skeen tied the drawstrings about the delicate wrists (looked like Skeen could break them with a snap of thumb and forefinger, but she had a strong suspicion that was illusion), Timka said softly, "Min knows Min, doesn't matter the shape. I've got seven basic shapes—bird, hunting cat, swimmer, deer for running, rock-leaper for climbing, and this one I've got now. But I couldn't hide from another Min in any of them." She shook her sleeves until the folds pleased her, bent for her vest. "I found them because Telka did, she was always pushing ahead of me and Carema my mother's sister made me catch her, but I haven't practiced them much; except for the bird, I don't really know them." She slipped her arms into the vest, began threading the thong through the grommets. "Most Min have two base forms, no more— this . . ." she waved a hand at herself, "and one other." She tied off the thong, settled herself away from the rock she'd used for a table, on the grass where a bit of sun came through the leaves and painted warmth over her.

Seven skins, Skeen thought, what a world. She went to dig up her fish, mouth watering, anticipating the hot white flesh flaking in her hands.

They rode cautiously south, keeping to the mountains until they were several days beyond Mintown, resting in the day-time, sleeping, eating, letting the horses graze, riding at night, with Timka in her owl-form scouting ahead, making sure they didn't accidentally stumble over a Min holding or a hunter out about his or her business.

There were small holdings scattered through the mountains, three or four families that might or might not be related. Timka told her that most Min got nervous where there were numbers of Min around. The crowds at Mintown were there for a few days only, come to petition the Synarc for this and that. At times there were large gathers. Timka mentioned them in passing, almost by accident, but wouldn't say any more about what happened at them. Skeen had some pictures in her head of what a whirly chaos of form and shift those meetings must be. She was intensely curious about them and about the Min, tried to get Timka to talk about herself.

Timka seemed quite willing to talk and did a lot of chatting and it was several days before Skeen put things together and realized that beyond the few snippets of information she wrung out of her with questions about dangers they could face as they moved through the mountains, the little Min evaded any probing into her own childhood or into Min life with vague statements and a smooth transition into stories about her life with the Poet. Skeen found the Pallah boringly like a lot of other regressed societies she had dropped in on to track down rumors of ruins. By the time they reached the valley floor she was tired of prodding at a pillow; Timka could keep her hoarded secrets. She was free enough with information about the land ahead, that was all Skeen really needed.

"Spalit. The river divides there. One branch goes west to the Lakes, the other goes south to the Wetlands, gets lost in

the swamps. And those swamps are full of Nagamar who
don't want to see, hear, or smell outsiders. Spalit is about
half the size of Dum Besar. There's a palisade around it, but
nothing like Besar's wall. Rumor says every second person is
a thief and every sixth is available for anything including
murder if the price is right. And they don't pay proper taxes.
The Byglave used to get very exercised about them around
tax time and the Poet had to soothe him down and remind
him tactfully about what happened the last time the Casach
decided to discipline the Splitters by collecting back taxes and
fines out of their hides.''

''What happened?''

''The Casach sent a hundred armed men. By ship, so
warning wouldn't run ahead of them, leaving on Black Night
when there wasn't even a moon to light them. Ship ran into
cables stretched across the Rekkah about twenty stads north
of Spalit. Anyone not drowned had his throat slit by a collection of thugs wearing bags over their heads. Two did manage
to escape, though wounded. When they stumbled into Spalit
come the morning, the town Mozeed was appalled and indig-
nant; he told them so, then launched himself into a diatribe
about the failure of the Casach to protect their people against
such outrages. If I'd known you were coming, he told the
sore and weary men, I would have sent my patrollers out to
meet you and keep you safe. He went on about that for some
time, the story goes, and repeated it to the emissary from the
Casach. The point was taken and the experiment was not
repeated.

Skeen heard distaste in the quiet voice, but no reluctance to
speak about these things; Timka responded to her questions
about the Pallah with an odd docility that she didn't understand. But was it really docility? Timka was like water yield-
ing to everything, yet in the end going her own way.
Remembering all her attempts to find out about Min life,
Skeen had to acknowledge (ruefully but honestly) that the
Min was smarter than she was and a lot better at manipulating
people. Timka frustrated her, made her angry, and fascinated
her. She tried to break through the soft slippery surface and
make Timka see that she didn't have to be that defensive any

longer, then she'd find herself ordering the Min about, tacitly acquiescing in the role Timka seemed to demand of her. She would run her hand through her hair, curse under her breath, then try to come to terms with this impossible situation so she could do something to save her self-respect. Timka acted as her personal slave whether she wanted a slave or not. She'd taken on this companion as a kick at Telka, acting on impulse. Tibo that little snake, he told her one time that she seemed to have a valve that popped whenever she'd been cautious and prudent overlong, and anything she did then was almost guaranteed to turn out a disaster. I took you on impulse, you baster, and you prove your prediction right.

They rode across rich dark soil heavy with planting. The air was humid and still. Skeen felt if she set a foot down too long it would take root. She sweated and the sweat stayed on her skin, laying over her body like a sheath. The saddle was wet where her legs and buttocks pressed against the leather; the eddersil let sweat through it without absorbing any, so she didn't have to worry about soggy clothing. Though she washed her face and hands as often as there was water to do it, dirt seemed to grow beneath her nails and in the creases of her hands. And she could almost feel her hair growing. Salt sweat beaded on her eyelashes and rolled into her eyes. She wiped her face again and again with a handkerchief that had been soaked so long it was speckled with mildew and smelled strong enough to scare off a garbage dump rat.

Three days. Four. A handful of days. Nights as warm and even damper than the days. The horses were restless, as uncomfortable as Skeen, their tempers worsening by the day. They needed grain. There wasn't enough forage outside the fields and Skeen was still avoiding notice, so she didn't stop at any of the tiny villages. So, no grain.

Six days. Seven. A double handful. On the tenth day they rode round a grove and came out behind a packtrain of Ygga, short-legged stolid beasts with great ivorine horns reaching out a meter on each side of long skinny heads, the nose a trunk of sorts slightly longer than a big man's handspan, these noses swaying like pendulums of wrinkled flesh. Goods were piled so high on their broad backs, they looked like traveling tents under the protecting tarps. They brushed the bushy growths on both sides of the narrow track and Skeen was compelled to eat their dust if she wanted to keep to the road and that she did want. The packtrain was as good a cover as any for going into Spalit and the dust, however irritating, was as good as a mask. Well, better than a mask. A mask carried mystery and provoked curiosity. Dust was just dust, cast up by the clawed feet of the Ygga and deposited on ten days' worth of sweat. Fine red dust as slippery as chalk that got into the eyes, nose, mouth, and more private crevices of the body, that flew out from the eddersil with every move she made. She giggled silently to think how peculiar she'd look, perfectly neat black trousers and tunic, boots that looked like someone painted dust on them, a dust mask runnelled with sweat, dyed hair gone a dull red with that same dust— like she'd put on clean clothes for town but hadn't bothered to clean herself.

When they reached the gate, she roughened and deepened her voice, tossed a bronze coin to one of the gate guards. "Eh-vakkit, what's a place we can get a tun of wine to cut the dust and a hot bath to chase it altogether?"

The Watch looked at the coin in his hand, grinned at her. "The Spittin Split will do yo all that. Turn riverside where yo see a house with a red door." He flicked a long thumb at the end of a long nose, winked at Timka. "She look like she ull clean up fine, but yo want a change, Red Door they got some lively ass. Go twar River till you see a big shup with a wall 'bout it, 'n a signboard swing over an arch, two-head fish, one spittin water t' other spittin wine. 'N hey, tell ol' Nossik that Tiddin sent you by."

"I'll do it." She gave him a two-finger wave, heeled the weary horse into a walk, and started along the shell-spread street. The shells kept the dust down, but did little for the stench from the sewer ditches on both sides of the broad street. The stillness of the air was beginning to break with the coming of night and made the smell inescapable. Timka caught up with Skeen and rode beside her. "How did you know what to say to him and how?"

"You told me what the town is like."

"But I didn't know. . . ."

"There's always a town like this and a Watch like that. And he's generally the one on duty late in the day like this because that's when travelers want steering the most and are most willing to pay for it. He gets a commission for everyone he sends to Nossik or the Red Door. He knows I know it and will be sure to mention his name. It's all part of the rules and because I know the rules, I slide in easy. Folks round here will know I'm a stranger but not really a stranger because I've got the mark on me."

"I don't understand any of that."

"Thief's mark, Timmy."

"Don't call me that. My name is Timka."

Skeen shrugged, rather pleased to get that much reaction out of her. It'd been building for days, Timka was tired and dirty and surrounded by folk she distrusted, even feared, so it was no wonder she allowed herself to get a bit grumpy.

"Are you really going there?" Timka said.

"Why not. I want a bath so bad I'd stomp a tiger for it. If you're fussy after the last dozen days, Djabo's asshole, you'll never be satisfied."

"Won't it be . . . dangerous. And . . . and not clean."

"Clean as anything we can afford here. Old saying a line-boss used to beat into me and kids like me. Cut your cloth to fit your purse."

"The price you got for me. . . ."

"Never mind what I got for you." Skeen grinned at her, mud splitting and flaking off her face. "It's coin I picked up from your Poet that's going to feed us and pay for our baths and get us across this river." She stopped her mount, sat contemplating the cleverly carved Innboard. The wine-spitting fish had a silly grin on its face and a wicked gleam in its eye, the water-spitter had a look of fine disgust. She slid down and led the horse through the broad arch into a tidy paved court-yard. "If you want to do something, take these horses round to the stable and see they are fed and curried while I see how little I can pay ol' Nossik for room with bath."

*   *   *

Skeen took a long pull at the tankard, sighed with pleasure. "Ah," she said, "that cuts the dust."

The taproom was dark and shadowy, the front half of the ground floor, with huge fireplaces at each end and smoky lamps dangling from heavy iron chains spiked into beams running the length of the room. Around each hearth, in a ragged arc, the host had placed wooden wingchairs with one arm broadened into small tables for the convenience of the patrons. And there was a low rail where those patrons could put their feet up for toasting on inclement days. Between the two semicircles, tables were scattered about, light backless seats pushed in around them. Only one of the fires was lit, more a token than a source of heat. The men sitting by it were talking in low voices, continuing conversations begun weeks or months ago.

Nossik laced his fingers over the short leather apron wrapped round his ample middle. "Plenty dust."

"Could have plowed and planted me and reaped enough to pass a winter. I like your sign."

Nossik chuckled. "Water has its uses."

"Exteriorally." She thought it over and decided she'd said it right.

"Wouldn't argue with that, my profession being what it is." He was puzzled by her, aware she was female, but uncertain how to treat her. Females dressing, talking, acting like her weren't something he saw every day. He tended to hover, but she didn't mind. Happy to have someone to talk to she didn't have to make allowances for. Timka was upstairs, too nervous to come down; her edginess had got worse instead of better after a bath and a meal. Skeen wrapped long thin fingers about the tankard and sighed; it was a good fat drinking cup, they knew something about life's little pleasures here in the Spittin Split. "Hot," she said.

Nossik mopped at the bar, a universal gesture, a matter of marking territory and attracting the eye to meaningless motions while the shrewd measuring eye of the man behind the bar assessed his customers. "Oh, it's not so bad. Now last year . . ." he paused, folded his wipe into a neat square, "last year it was really hot. Got so your taties came out of the

ground already baked. Generally, folk waited till dark to eat
'em, you could burn your back teeth otherwise. Talking o
teeth, you want another?''

She pushed the tankard across to him. ''Why not. Have
one yourself, friend. Ale this good goes best in company.''

''Now I wouldn't say no to that. My Yenna has so deft a
touch at brewing, it's a temptation to drink up my profits.''

While he was gone, Skeen swung round and looked lazily
about the room. The Pallah by the fire were bent over a
complicated game involving numbered sticks, flat stones, and
a board marked with squares. A trio of Skirrik males squatted
in a padded niche sipping something through metal straws
and skritching at each other, looking as relaxed and contented
as she was feeling right now. Their antennas had an orange
tinge and they glittered with jet; most likely they were heading home to dance for a bride. Four tall thin types, very
young, pushed the door open and came strolling in, all bone
and gristle and immense drunken dignity. Very very young. I
never was that young, she thought and sighed. Silky pale
not-hair, beaky noses, very small mouths. Aggitj extras.
What Sussaa tried to make her; she ran her fingers through
fake-blonde hair, caught the boys looking at her, polite but
puzzled. And was retrospectively annoyed (considering that
excess of nose and near absence of chin) at Telka's insistence
she'd pass for a perfect Aggitj. Nossik's daughter went over
to them, got them settled, took their orders. Their voices
were high and soft, a touch androgynous. I'm getting a little
sloshed, she thought and swung back around as Nossik brought
her refill and his. She pushed a pair of coppers across to him.

''Praise the Lifefire,'' he said.

''Praise the Lifefire and drink to good living.''

Nossik drank, licked his lips, put the tankard down. ''You're
right, he said gravely, ''it is a touch warm these days, but I
still say, nothing like last year. Yooo, that was hot! I had to
buy ice from the mountains to put in my henhouse just so I'd
have eggs for nogs; 'thout that, they were laying 'em
hardboiled.''

''Know what you mean. Where I grew up, we had a lot of
days like that. I remember one time, we had this old dog.

Smartest dog I ever saw. Of course, it was never so bad as you get here; desert country, lot of sand about, dry heat."

He nodded. "It's not the heat, it's the humidity gets you down."

"Uh huh. This dog I was talking about, he had tender feet; come midsummer he stopped moving unless he had to. He slept a lot like old dogs do and sometimes he was forgetful. One day what he forgot was that shade moves with the sun; he woke with one hellaceous thirst and all the shade on the far side of the tent. It was a little after noon and the sun was beating down and the sand was sending up heatwaves tall as houses and twisty as a born liar. Old dog started for the well trough to get him a drink, took one step, and let out a yell you could hear over the horizon. I heard the noise and stuck my head out. I was just a kid then, this high, I was supposed to be sleeping but I was sweating too much. Like I said, I heard the yelp, then some funny scritching sounds, and I looked to see what was happening. There was Old Dog, stomping on those heat waves like they were springs, bouncing along, kaboing kaboing kaboing, until he ran out of waves because it was enough cooler by the well to turn the waves into flimsy little shivers. Never hold him and he knew it. I saw he knew it because he stayed on the last big wave and went bouncing up and down up and down, higher and higher. I saw him eyeing the well with a considering look, then he went up a last time, came down slanting, and took off, sproinggg, like a chizzit with its tail on fire. He missed the water trough, though, and went splashing down the well. Took us a day and a half to get him out. He sure didn't want to leave all that cool, but he got hungry and he couldn't abide fish or frogs and that was all there was to eat down there."

"You're right there. Most dogs don't like fish. Could be the bones, too many of 'em. There was this cousin of mine though, he had this kogla dog that really loved fish stew. Got so he wouldn't eat anything else and he'd sit around the house whimpering and whining when there wasn't any fish. One day Sturrik couldn't stand it any longer; he'd got better things to do than spend all his time fishing for dogfood, so he took the kogla out and showed him the net and showed him

the river and said, "You want fish stew, you catch the fish."
He was maybe a bit drunk at the time. He's my cousin, but I
have to say he can't hold his liquor worth a shot. He dropped
the net by the dog, took a couple more swallows of his
homebrew, and went to sleep. Next thing he knew there was
a slimy feel all over him. He woke up half covered with fish
and an eel or two, one of which started crawling up his
breeches which sobered him fast. He shook the eel loose and
kicked it into the river—he can't abide eels. Then he saw that
kogla swimming toward the little broke-down jetty he built
himself, dog's head sort of canted back. He's hauling in
another net full of fish.

For a time there Sturrik had a good thing going. Dog
couldn't count. Long as he had all the stew he wanted, he
was happy. Sturrik sold the leftover. He spent that whole six
months it lasted half-drunk and happier 'n a barrel of rutting
dinkos. Then the kerrash migration started. Those eels get
longer than one of those Aggitj over there, with sour tempers
and a mouthful of teeth that'd scare a pickpocket honest. The
kogla ran into a bunch of them and had just about enough
sense to get out of there with no waiting and no fussing. Lost
the last three inches of his tail, too. Put him right off fish.
And Sturrik never found a way to make him go back in that
river."

More stories—Pallah, Skirrik, and Aggitj as the others in
the taproom joined them at the bar. Skeen drank a lot more
than she'd planned on, spent a lot more of her coin trading
rounds for those stories, though she gathered a lot of information about the local situation—what the going was like on the
far side of the river, funny stories about the ferryman, the
name of Nossik's cousin's Inn in Oruda and a message to take
to him. News from Dum Besar (which tickled the locals until
they could hardly swallow their ale). The Poet's favorite
concubine had run off, taking a lot of junk with her just to
rub in the insult; Poet was steaming, Byglave was shouting,
Besar was like an anthill some fool put the boot to. Aggitj in
the Boot in the middle of a Yilsa war, the young blonds
passing the stories from one to another, telling it in a tonal

prose that had a touch of poetry to it. The Skirrik trio, gently sozzled, did a dance song very late on, at least a fragment of one; they collapsed in giggles, legs tangled or waving in the air. Skeen lifted a tankard to two legs when she saw what happened to six, joined by the grinning locals, while the Aggitj boys struggled to right the Skirrik. She finally ran out of push and realized she was about three breaths from curling up in front of the fire and spending the night there.

She went cautiously up the ramp that swung against the wall in a graceful spiral with squared corners. Her feet were a trifle uncooperative, but she held onto the rail and took her time, thinking that they were very sensible on this world preferring ramps to stairs, nothing to catch the shaky toe.

The room was colder than the ramp. Draftier. For a minute all that ale stirred at the back of her throat, but she shoved it down again. A matter of pride. Moving slowly slowly slowly she lowered herself onto the edge of the bed and sat pulling off her boots. She held each one a while staring at it, then set it very carefully beside the bed. Sat a while, just breathing and swallowing, then slid out of her trousers, held them up, waved them about, giggling softly, tossed them into the dark. She did the same with her tunic, then rooted into the bed which Timka had got nice and warm, stretched out with a sigh of pleasure, and lay scratching at her stomach through the fine slippery material of her underpants.

"You're drunk. And your feet are cold."

"Uh huh. And I'm gon sleep. Now." Skeen closed her eyes, yawned, began breathing slowly and steadily, using imitation sleep to tease herself into real sleep. Dimly she heard Timka going on about something, but didn't bother paying attention. Then she heard nothing at all until Timka shook her awake after what seemed three seconds later.

"Come on. Come on. Wake up, will you."

Skeen groaned and rolled onto her back. Her lashes were stuck together and her mouth felt like something had died and rotted there. She rubbed at her eyes, licked dry lips, forced herself up. "Wha . . ."

Timka started pacing fretfully about the room, alternating

bursts of energy with slumps. "Min," she said. "Min flying over. Min circling round. Getting closer. I can feel them."

Skeen grunted, fumbled back the covers, and swung her legs over the side of the bed. She didn't feel up to coping with this right now. She sighed and blinked, looked vaguely around. "Telka?"

"No no, not till they pin us. It's her Holavish."

Trying to ignore the upheaval below her ribs, the throbbing of her head, Skeen pushed onto her feet. "We located yet?" She looked around for her clothing, saw her trousers and walked slowly, carefully to them, squatted beside them. "How much time if we aren't?"

"No, not yet. I don't know."

Skeen reached for her trousers, grunted as she nearly overbalanced. With an exclamation of disgust, Timka darted over to her, picked up the trousers, shook them off, tossed them on the bed. Hands on hips she turned round looking for Skeen's tunic, saw it crumpled in one corner, darted to it, shook it out too, and tossed it beside the trousers. She shoved her shoulder under Skeen's arm, muscled her back to the bed, left her sitting while she poured some water in a basin and slopped a washrag in it. She slapped the dripping rag onto Skeen's face, scrubbed the remnants of sleep from her eyes, then pushed the rag into Skeen's hand. "This is so boorring. You. The Poet. Making fools of yourselves." She fetched a towel, tossed it to Skeen. "Get yourself dressed and do the packing while I see to the horses." She sniffed and went out, slamming the door behind her.

"No need to yell," Skeen muttered.

Saddlebags and pack thumping against her legs, Skeen walked out the door. A heavy fog filled the court; condensation dripped from every edge, adding to the melancholy of the pale gray light. The damp crept into every crevice, started runnels through her hair; she swiped at her face, her head throbbing; the thought of getting on a horse and galloping off made her bones ache. The clop of ironshod hooves, dark forms looming in the fog. Timka came up with the horses, her eyes huge in a pinched face, almost in a panic. "Circling in," she whispered.

Skeen sighed, rubbed at her temple, trying to think. "No Hunger to keep them off us, hmm, confuse them. Maybe the river—any water-Min there?" She slung the bags behind the saddles, tied them down, strapped on the pack. "Or can you tell?"

Timka didn't answer until they were leading the horses through the arch. "No," she said. "The river is empty."

Her mount clopping behind her, Skeen started off through the fog toward the ferry landing south of town. "Five days to Oruda," she said. "From what I picked up last night, it's open country, savannah." She wiped at her face, drawing the back of her hand across her mouth, sighed, and kept her eyes on the bit of ground visible around her feet. "Might diddle them some if you swam the river to Oruda. I'll take your clothes with me, meet you there."

Timka was a blurred shape in the fog, her expression veiled, the color of her eyes not green but a shadowy gray. She walked along gazing at Skeen, saying nothing.

"I will meet you," Skeen said patiently, "my word on it. Besides, I've got to go there. You can depend on that if you don't trust me."

Timka continued to gaze at her, saying nothing. The ferryhouse was a gray blur ahead, more of a stain set deep in the fog than a solid form. Then she nodded and began pulling loose the ties at wrist and neck. She tossed blouse and skirt to Skeen, shifted to a large cat-form and went bounding off into the fog.

Skeen rolled the clothing up, strapped the roll into Timka's saddlebag, clipped a rope lead to the bridle on Timka's mount, then started on, not altogether sure she'd see the Min again, and regretting the possible loss of her companion more keenly than she'd expected. Timka was a puzzle she was only beginning to unravel, showing interesting possibilities as travel and trouble abraded away that irritating surface.

She woke the ferryman, argued him into taking her across, then rode along a rutted road between two hedges, the faint rose flush of the morning sun directly head of her. Already the nightcool was dissipating, though the heat seemed to thicken rather than melt away the fog. She rode without hurry, feeling relieved of pressure now that Timka had gone off on her own for a little, amused at the contradiction she held within herself, missing the Min yet glad to be free of her and her problems . . . at least for a while. She thought about whistling, she felt so good, but she was enjoying the distant hollowness of the sounds around her—the steady clip-clop of the horses' hooves, the jingle from the bridles, the creaking of the leather, and farther off a birdcall, the honking low of a large beast, an occasional splash. Every sound separate and entire, framed by a narrow line of silence. The aches and debilities of a morning-after melting out of her, she settled into the saddle, her body moving in easy unison with the horse until she felt adrift and unconcerned about it.

The sun floated higher and the fog began to lift. The water dripping from branches, leaves, gathered on grass blades disappeared—not so much drying up as being sucked back into the air and into whatever it was clinging to. The hedges broke apart into separate bushes, then vanished, giving way to open grasslands with trees scattered about, singly and in small groves. The horses were well-fed, rested, and inclined to run, making rough going for a while before she got them settled to a steady walk. She was early on the road and had it to herself. The ferryman had groused continually from the moment she routed him out of bed, cursing her and all her kind, not repeating himself once the entire time it took to cross the Rekkah. Entertained by his fluency and versatility, she'd handed him a silver bit instead of the three coppers that was his usual fee. It pleased her to think Timka would have been disgusted with her for the waste.

By noon she'd sweated a skin of water around her body and was back to breathing through her mouth; every time she glanced toward the river, she felt a pang of envy at the thought of Timka gliding through the cool green depths.

For a long time she rode alone. Nothing but grass and trees on a gently rolling land stretching horizon to horizon on both sides of the river, but around midafternoon she started catching glimpses of riders in loose white robes and herds of slab-sided, long legged-beasts. None of them near the road. Nothing to disturb her from this slow easy respite from danger and excitement and the need to stay alert, nothing until near sundown when her mount's shadow jerked long and angular in front of her. A wing of large birds flew over her, curled away, came back flying lower. There was a squawking exchange over her head as they circled round and round. Annoyed by this recall of things she wanted to forget, she rode with her hand on the holster, fingers near the edge so she could rip up the flap and get the weapon out, but the danger didn't materialize; the birds flew off, heading back toward Spalit. She didn't relax until they were out of sight and never regained that earlier contentment.

Another crew of robed riders almost lost in the dusty haze along the southern horizon. Funor Ashon. Leave Funor alone and they'll leave you alone, Krigli had said. Short dark man working the river, in the Spittin Split with a pair of local contacts. Small black mole at the corner of his mouth that vanished into a crease whenever he smiled or frowned or drew his mouth down in a mime of extreme disgust. And lifefire make it you don't ever hurt a cow, he said. Unless you like pain. Safe enough to live round them if you understand the way they feel about their herds and family honor. Time you got to watch out is when a young buck is out to blood his horns and you get in his way, or he thinks you did. Say you whomp the pest, but don't hurt him, just try discouraging him. First thing you know, his whole family is on your tail, gonna play the tens on you. You made the youngster lose face, you're gonna be made to look ten times the fool. Got any smart in you, you'll let them do it, too. One of them dead, nine of your family is dead with you. So if you spot a shorthorn snorting, you get the hell out of his way. Another thing to remember is every goddam Funor is related some way to every other one, so if you get a bloodfeud going, you're damnwell gonna have to exterminate the whole damn species. Last thing—they've still got most of their tech, got coms that reach around the world so there's no place you can run if you think about getting away.

Couldn't be that bad, Skeen thought, just not practical.

There's probably some sort of blood-money arrangement to shut off the spread. Who knows what another species is going to consider practical? Leave them way alone, Krigli's right about that.

The violet haze that presaged sundown was spreading across the sky; Skeen was tired and starting to look for a place to camp for the night. A pair of fliers came back, swooped down to land in the dust in front of her, shaking off their feathers to show themselves slim young males—very young, crotch hair barely sprouted. One stepped a bit ahead of the other. "Where is Timka?"

"She smelled trouble and took off." Skeen raised a brow. "You two?"

"Where did she go?"

"Took off in the fog. You could find her faster'n me. I'm not looking." She looked down her long nose at them. "I'm tired of this nonsense." She shook the reins, clicked her tongue to urge the horse forward. He stood like he'd grown roots. She cursed under her breath because she'd forgotten what Min could do to ordinary beasts when they had time to work on them. She smiled at the boys, a tight stretching of the lips that showed her teeth and ignored her eyes. "Funny aren't you. Real clowns. Well, clowns, maybe Telka told you about this?" She lifted the darter. "Maybe you're tired and ought to take a rest."

They stepped back, moving together, identical expressions on faces that were somewhat alike, though it was a kinship of kind rather than blood. Min-fliers. Together they shifted into bird shapes and powered into the air. The horses snorted and sidled nervously as they were released from the thrall of the Min. The birds circled overhead. She heard two screeches, then felt two wet gooey splotches landing on her hair and forehead. She gasped and scraped most of the glop off her.

Still cursing, she turned the horses toward the river, climbed down the bank, and used handfuls of sand to scrub her hair and face. She stopped cursing because it was wholly inadequate. Skinning would be inadequate. After she was reasonably clean, though, slogging up the bank toward the horses, a giggle tickled the back of her throat. Godlost little twerps. If I had wings . . . hah! Once again she felt a pang of jealousy. It'd be marvelous to fly like that. She swung into the saddle and started on, humming a droning tune, musing over memories of soar-bubbles in assorted Pit Stops.

She began to pass camps. Individuals with dung fires. A packtrain, maybe even the one she followed into Spalit. She rode on into the dark until a voice came from a few dark figures silhouetted against a small fire. "Skeen, Skeen, come join us." She rode closer. The Aggitj boys from the Spitting Split. She turned the horses off the road and rode to the grove where they had their camp.

"How did you four get so far ahead of me?"

"We didn't waste time sleeping."

"We couldn't afford Nossik's prices."

"Either beer or bed. Who'd ever pick bed over beer?"

"We can sleep anywhere anyhow, but Nossik's ale is only in Nossik's kegs."

"We hauled the Ferryman out of bed."

"Oh he was mad, oh mad."

"Got a real educated tongue, never repeated himself, not once."

"Once we got over, well, it was a nice night, a little fog settling in, but that'd keep the roadlice off us."

"So we just kept going."

"But the horses needed to rest and graze."

"So we made a camp, caught some fish, they cooking now. And broached a keg of Nossik's ale."

"And we saw you riding by and we said hey there's a one who knows a story to two to pass the time. And we thought that one she might like a taste of fish and a touch of ale and maybe would tell us maybe huh a story or two about what it's like now on the other side of the Gate."

Four pairs of hazel eyes watched her from under four thatches of moonsilver not-hair that stirred restlessly in the warm thick air.

Skeen chuckled. "Feed me and water me, and yes I'll tell you a tale or two."

A TALE OF TIBO'S YOUTH.
or
THE FIRST TIME I
SAW THAT SNAKE.

"A story about the other side. Hm. When you're a traveler, after a while you begin learning to slide into new folkways like a frog sliding into a new pond. It's all around you and you take part of it into you but only that part nearest you and when you leave again, that part slides away and is mostly forgotten, though it leaves its mark on you one way or another. Dip, splash, move on, adding a few words and sounds to the store of languages in your head and after a few more dips you forget where you got them and what was the larger context where they took their meaning. There are many kinds of travelers. Company folk whose home is not the ship but the corporation in whose mothering arms they are born and live until they lose their usefulness and are discarded. Free trader families living in the belly of a world ship that sails between the stars and never ever touches earth. To touch down for them is to die. Travelers, yes—mercenaries, gamblers, smugglers, thieves, assassins working or looking for work, players of all kind, dancers, singers, entertainers who do things it would take a month to describe and still you wouldn't understand. I've seen them and I don't understand. Pilgrims and missionaries from a thousand and one religions, going where they're going, doing what they're doing for reasons only they comprehend and sometimes even they don't really know why they are where they are. Colonists, explorers, marginals who drift because that's the way they're made; if there's a place to go they have to go there, if there isn't a place they haven't seen, they'll find one. I suppose you know fairly well what I'm talking about—you're travelers, too. You have your reasons for moving along just as I do. And like Nossik's Inn, there are places that most travelers know, places where they can stop a while, rest, meet their kind, buy and sell according to their needs and desires, get high or drunk or absent to this plane, chat with friends they haven't seen for a handful of years and won't see again for as many more years, pass on things they've heard and seen . . . rumor and fact, speculation and explanation. We call these places Pit Stops. Don't ask why, I don't know.

"Some years back I nosed in at a place called the Nymph's Navel. I'd been rambling about doing this and that for over a year, alone most of the time because my last Companion had turned out to be a macho jerk, so I was wanting company pretty bad. Nymph's Navel is a place you can relax and not worry about your back or who's got his hand in your credit belt. I don't say there aren't fights and folk getting killed and plundered there; stupidity is its own reward, if you know what I mean. But if you took reasonable care, you didn't have to worry about phluxes jumping you to feed their habit, or Noses landing on you for something they think you might have done. Even blood feuds are parked outside a Pit Stop.

"I got in about midday local time, spent most of the afternoon unloading my cargo. Already had buyers waiting for the biggest part of the load; the rest I passed on to the local jobbers on consignment, so by nightfall I was awash with gelt and ready to celebrate. Picarefy was wanting to redecorate, so I arranged a credit line for her, Picarefy is my ship. She's technically not alive, eh, how do I explain it, say it's like a sailing ship that could talk to you, never mind how it's done. I stashed most of the gelt with Picarefy so I'd have going away money; Picarefy would scold me sober before she let me get my hands on that stash. I caught the syncline to the Juwell bubble and proceeded to have myself a fine time in the

Glass Madonna's house of varied pleasures. I won't sully your innocent young ears with what I did. Huh? You want to be sullied? Forget it, kid, that's another story. Anyway, round the fifth cycle I was feeling a bit tired and about ready to take off again. I was sitting in a fingerbowl, getting some of the kinks out of my spine and other assorted parts when a really odd match-up came strolling in.

"I've led what you might call a varied life, which by the way is a lot more entertaining to look back on then to live through. And I've seen a thing or two, but that was just about the funniest pair I've ever chanced across. You expect weirdness when the pair or set or whatever is a cross-species mix. I mean, once you've seen a Kombui eight-legs with a Yokapoe no-legs and a Pavchid all-mother all three dancing a tango, mixes don't surprise you much. But same-species weirdness is something else, makes you go ukk! and huh? and how do they manage and I'll leave it at that. This pair. Male and female. She was . . . tall. Yes. Tall. The essence of tall. Two and a half meters. Say you set Hal on Hart's shoulders, about that tall. And thin! You could fold her up and pass her twice through the eye of a needle. She wore this red thing that fit like it was painted on her. You could count every rib and dive in her navel. Her breasts were like oranges cut in half, her nipples were cherries perched atop the orange halves. She had a long thin face with a long thin nose and a tiny pink mouth and huge, really huge no-colored eyes. Though it doesn't sound like it, she was pretty in an austere way. Marvelous skin—even from as far off as I was, I could tell it was velvet soft and flawless. She had a shock of butter yellow hair. It stood out from her face like dandelion fluff. Looking at it you'd think you could put your hand on it and your hand would sink and sink through its softness. That was the woman. Her name was Alelo. One other thing. Her voice. It was deep and warm and honey on the ears, fit to enchant even an argebost than which there are few things nastier not human.

"The man was short. Next to Alelo he looked a dwarf. Ders, if he stood looking at you, his eyes would maybe clear your navel. A meter and a half, if he stood toe-tip. Bald. No

eyebrows. He was the color of Nossik's dark ale, eyes the
bluest of any blue you ever saw, the blue of the sky on a
summer day when you lie flat on your back and stare up and
up into the bluest part. He had small hands and feet, was
well-muscled in his upper half though he was wiry rather than
a little bull. Limber and neat. Pointed ears. Handsome. A
grin to charm the rings off a matriarch. A tongue hinged in
the middle and oiled with glamour-glow, able to charm you
even when you knew very well he was a scheming little prick
who hadn't meant a word he said since he popped from his
mother's womb. Tibo he was. Tibo whose name was anath-
ema on so many worlds he couldn't count them, not having
learned numbers that high, or so he always claimed. He wore
a gold lamé shirt and gold shimmersilk pants with Barunda
leather boots, the dark crimson leather that cost a fortune and
a half for a single skin. And diamond and ruby earrings and
firestones on four fingers. On the hoof that first time I saw
him he was worth a ship's ransom and then some. Tibo the
Slide, master of his trade, riding a streak of luck a lightyear
wide.

"I crawled out of the fingerbowl into a party to end all
parties and forgot I was tired.

"A lot of cycles later, I lost count in the middle somewhere, Tibo, Alelo, me, a gyoser named udJian, a mixed pair
of dancers from Kemur named Beeba and Beeka, and a
yumrick Gefurn named Squeeze, we landed finally in a
slumbabounce, half-asleep half-awake, and altogether out of
touch with whatever passed for reality round there. I don't
know who started, but after a while, one by one, we were
telling stories, things that happened to us when we were
children. You want a story from beyond the Stranger's Gate,
here's Tibo tale. I do not guarantee the truth in it.

"Tibo was a naked little man, drifting from pouf to pouf.
His voice came to us here there, rambling on until we forgot
the teller in the telling."

We were contract players on a Gancha worldship, a
wide-bind family, my bodyfather and bodymother, my teaching mothers and training fathers, my sisters and half-

sisters and line sisters, my brothers and half-brothers and line brothers, the cross cousins and parallel cousins, the adopted affiliates and so on. We were one of the oldest and largest wide-bind families living in the ships. I was born and suckled on ship Samal Haran, learned the family trade in ship Eyasta Hus, and left the world ships forever after what happened in ship Chiar Frawa. Let me tell you about world ships. The travelers buying transport, the traders buying space, they know the upper levels, those around the garden of shipheart where even the poorest of passengers could roam where he pleased for an endless round of delights, among them the Player families dancing, tumbling, performing in playlets, juggling, jesting, all the things Player families do. That passenger might even have got a little deeper out, into the outer edge of crew quarters. But he'd never make it all the way to us. We would not permit that. Though we had little clout with the Family that owned the Ship or the Captains in their aeries, that they granted us, treating us Contract Families like their own people. If a passenger visited crew, it was outsider crew—hire-meat, the pursers and stewards, the clerks in shops when they weren't part of a Family, waitresses, cleaners, scut workers— not the real Crew that ran the Ship and had shares in her.

My bodyfather was a tumbler and an acrobat and that was what I was taught. We had actors and seers of all kinds, read anything for you, dancers, singers, gamers, and others. We were a family rich in talent and passions, a noisy brawling close—ah close—family.

When I was fourteen I fell desperately in love with an affiliate, a girl we adopted in not long after we changed ships, she came from hire-crew, the bodydaughter of a food designer who doubled in a pleasure house, the daughter being destined to follow her in both, something she hated the thought of. She auditioned for us and we adopted her. She was a little older than me, a dark small creature, agile as a newt on a hot wall, and she had more courage and spirit than a dozen ordinary folk. From the time she came into the family, she was thirteen then and I was seven, I was her slave, followed her everywhere. She was good-natured about it. She liked to talk and I was a willing audience. She liked to do crazy things and she needed an audience for that, too. I adored her like a sistermother when I was seven and when I was fourteen I wanted her for lovemate.

A worldship's skin isn't solid or smooth, even on the outside. Costs being what they are, the ships grew as the Family could afford to build on more space. Chiar Frawa was a hundred generations old and immense. And the rind was so complicated even shipmind didn't know all the ins and outs. Works like this. There's the outshell, the sealerskin, then a space filled with metal sponge, then layers of air, then more sponge alternating with air filled with crawlways and springbeams. Then the meddashell, then the serviceways in a very wide airspace filled with beams and braces, ducts and boards—every three steps off the catwalks you're in a hole with a whole new shape. An endlessly permuting mazeway. The walkways were kept cleared because the crew used them just about every day, and even if they didn't the children of the Worao Crew Families spent part of each day in there keeping the fungus off them. In the offspaces though, the fungus grew thick and strange. Other things grew in there, too. They are damp places, warm. There are orchids and other epiphytes, even small trees in catch-pockets, vines, exotics from a hundred worlds, passengers bringing in spores on their clothing, sometimes even seed. Rats, birds, lizards, worms of all sorts. Other things, dangerous things. The cleaning children were generally under guard by an armed adult in some sections, specially where the ways were narrow and seldom used. The light didn't go far from the walks, but there were clusters of luminescent fungi that produced almost as much light as a glowstrip, so there were a lot of temptations for imaginative children. The guard was there as much to keep them herded on the ways as to protect them from rat swarms and other things.

Though we were Player Family and not required to

work on the ways, my love Qessara and I often volunteered to join clean-gangs. It was scut work but it got us out of scutwork for the Family that was a lot more boring; besides, more often than not, we could sneak off and explore that marvelously complex jungle. It was deadly dangerous out there; children and adults both had got lost before in that maze and were never seen again. Qessara knew it and looked on the danger as spice to the pleasure of exploring, but she wasn't stupid. We both carried mark-sprays to leave a trail that would take us out again and well-sharpened knives to discourage attack. She needed those brushes with danger more than any drug, every brush with horror a reaffirmation of her worth; she never talked about her life before the Family, but I'd learned enough about her to make guesses that got me hot and sick and furious at my helplessness before her pain. She was a dancer who could madden a crowd, men and women alike. I watched her dancing once and I hurt so much for her I never went again. That dance was a cry for help so desperate, so hopeless . . . ah well, she used to say she didn't know what all the fuss was about and she certainly came back into the Family space so cool and unconcerned I never got it straight in my head whether she was just performing or she'd learned like most of us to deny the thing that hurts.

We went running through the jungle like large gray rats. The Law Mother knew well enough what we were up to when we volunteered and scolded us apart and together for playing the fool with our lives, lives that belonged to the Family and weren't ours to squander, but we earned pay-points for the Family and favored status among the Contractors and much good will, so she never forbid us our games. There was something else. More than once we brought back rare and beautiful orchids. The Worao claimed half the price for them, since it was their fields we raided, but even with that the Family had gelt to buy luxuries undreamed of before our games, so no one cried foul and forbid us. But certainly no one encouraged us—quite the opposite. My bodyfather

reddened my butt each time I got home late and glared
unhappily at Qesarra who led me astray and my uncle-
father who taught me juggling and games of chance
scolded me for endangering myself and my auntmother
who taught me my letters tried to reason with me and
with Qesarra. But reason and pain and shame have little
effect on the crazy and I had that infection from Qesarra.
And nothing serious had ever happened and like all
children who are tenderly raised, I had a bone-deep
conviction that nothing bad would happen.

This went on until I was fifteen and Qesarra past
twenty. During that year the disappearances began to
increase in tempo until it was a loud staccato thrum,
staccato from the empty spaces where Crew, hire-crew,
and Contract Crew used to stand. The edict came down,
bristling with dire punishments for those who ignored it.
No more children on the service ways, not for any reason. Something prowled the jungle out there, a demon
with an everdemanding gut. Only the passengers knew
nothing of the fear that tightened around the rest of us. I
heard the whispered stories and was afraid, not so much
for myself as for Qesarra.

There was a Sound. It was a sigh like wind through
grass, seeping into crew quarters and ours. It first it
seemed such a harmless even rather pleasant sound. It
teased at us, seemed to whisper secrets just beyond our
ability to hear. The Worao Captains sent SP crew into
the ways, armed with laser snappers and flamethrowers,
but the Sound was everywhere; the ways wound for
stads and stads. Those that came back saw nothing but
plants too soggy to burn. Those that didn't come back—
who knows what they saw. The High Captain withdrew
with the Worao Elders to see if they could worry out a
way of clearing the Insul without crippling the ship. There
things stayed while the Worao argued.

Skeen interrupted the story. "To appreciate the problem
the Gancha Family Worao faced, you should know that were
the ship Chiar Frawa set down on top of us, it would not fit

between the mountains, not half of it, not a tenth of it. Were
you to ride across it at twenty stads a day, trading horses
every ten stads to keep up the pace, it would take a thousand
days to ride across the widest part of it. Just to clear a small
segment of the Insul, that area between the meddashell and
the serviceways, would be like trying to sweep all the dirt off
the plain. You see? Right. So back to Tibo and his story.''

On the fifth day of the Sound, Qesarra was so jittery she
couldn't sleep or eat. I watched her closely because I
was afraid she'd do something even I knew was stupid. I
followed her to the dance space. I hated all the folk who
came to see her, hated them for sucking at her terror
and desperation; it was like they were one huge beast
feeding on her. When her dance was done, they called
her back and back to dance some more until she was
exhausted. Abla and Jerron, two of our cousins, had to
carry her back to the Family space. I went to do my part
of the Family Act and forgot about her for a short while
because the brother and sisters who worked with me
would make my life unlivable if I messed up. Besides, I
was the best tumbler of them all outside my bodyfather. I
had my pride.

When our part was done, I hurried to Qesarra's cubby.
She wasn't there. I stood by her mussed bed and wondered what to do. The Sound went on and on. We were
all used to it by now, we tuned it out, but I started
listening to it because it was somehow different. Focused. I began to feel it working inside me, looking for a
hold on me. And then I knew where Qesarra was. All the
grishes to the serviceways were warded now, those anyone knew about, with alarms to bring Worao SP running
if anyone tripped them. I let the Sound catch me and
lead me. There had to be a grish no one knew about or
why did folk keep disappearing. I tried to close off everything but the will to follow. I didn't want the Sound to
dump me or take me somewhere Qesarra wasn't. I was
frantic not knowing how long Qesarra had been gone,
but I tried to look casual as I moved through the family

cubbies and the Green Space, where the Families grew vegetables, where children played among the waterbins. There were some younguns there with an Amamother keeping an eye on them; she frowned and looked worried when she saw me. I grinned at her, waved, and hurried on. Old Amamothers were apt to have intuits at the most inconvenient times and I cursed chance for letting one get a look at me now. As anger flared in me, the Sound seemed to retreat like I burned it. I forced the anger back and tried to calm myself. I succeeded enough that the Sound grew complacent and teased me along faster. It was a grish close to the Green Space, hidden when a new waterbin was moved in. There was just enough room to squeeze around the bin and slide the panel back.

There was a dukkurbox by the grish, dusty and old but it had to have what I needed. I closed my eyes and let my hands work the latch; there was an alarm here too, it'd sound on the bridge, but I didn't care now. Inside there were emergency stores and other supplies. And a flame thrower. I worked as fast as I could, though it seemed like years before I got the flamer and the aid kit tucked into my shirt. I suppose it only took a second or two; I know the Sound didn't seem to notice. I let it take me faster and faster along the ways. Every time I passed a dukkurbox I jerked it open, laying a trail as long as I could. I collected two more aid kits just in case. The Sound got louder and louder. I took out one of the kits and opened it without looking at it or thinking what I was doing. Closed my hand about the anahastic spray. I fumbled the kit closed, shoved it back in my shirt and ran along the way clutching the small can.

When the Sound finally pulled me off the walk into the jungle maze, I shot a gout of anahastic at the wall and marked my trail with it every tenth swing of my arms, getting this into muscle knowledge so if the Sound got so strong it canceled brain-think, body-think would keep laying down the splotches of spray. Anahastic flouresced under torchlight; anyone following me—and I hoped (down deep, not letting myself think about it) that half the SP's on the ship were after me by now—would see it.

The Sound pulled me deep into the jungle until I finally came to one of the larger spaces and saw IT. A monster fungus that had hundreds of small holes all over its orange and green body. It moved all the time, like a cloud of smoke in a gentle breeze. I saw later it had grown up over one of the fan holes that kept the air moving in the Insul. At the moment all I knew was that the thing was singing to me from a hundred mouths while long ropy tendrils that grew in explosion patterns about several such sphincters were wrapped loosely about Qesarra, that fibers along these arms were punched into Qesarra—into her eyes, her mouth, into her skin. That thousands of tiny red spiders swarmed over her, liquifying her so the fungus could suck her dry. There were other husks of skin and bone scattered about the space, rustling dryly like fly bodies about a spiderweb.

The sound called me closer and closer. More swarms of red spiders were pouring out of the singing holes. I couldn't have broken free if I tried. I didn't try. I saw Qesarra being drained by that thing and I went berserk, running at it. The tendrils brushed at me, trying to get a hold of me, but I was doing a dance more desperate than any of Qesarra's and they only brushed at me. I didn't feel the jolts that were supposed to paralyze me. I got the flamer out and turned it on Qesarra. Her arms went black, her sleep robe caught fire, her hair burned. The tendrils smoldered, then burned. The torch that was Qesarra fell against the thing and it screamed. The sound blew me back, addled my head worse than it already was, but my body knew its work. I held the flamer on the thing, held it there flaring full out, held it even after I'd exhausted its fuel.

I would have died like Qesarra because the wetness in it kept quenching the worst of the fires. The tendrils charred and flaked and fell away, but the nubs were still there. Parts of the surface boiled and dripped down, but one flamer would never have killed the thing. It was huge—filled up that space and flowed into other spaces—half a kilometer around. I did minor damage, made it hurt, but ten men with flamers wouldn't have dented the thing.

I didn't die. The Worao acted fast when the dukkur alarms started sounding. An SP team went into the ways, followed the line of alarms, then found and followed the anahastic trail I'd laid down. They came charging to the rescue with more flamers and a pair of sonic disrupters. They blew that horror into fragments and fried the fragments, then spent the next several cycles flushing the most powerful fungicides they had through the Insul. I didn't know anything about that until a lot later. When I came out of what it'd done to me, turned out I couldn't stay in a world ship any longer. The hurt had gone too deep and there was the thing about Qesarra. The Worao were grateful enough to put me in therapy on Feyurnsha and leave enough credit for my treatment and re-education, though that didn't work out quite the way they planned, I didn't turn into a docile productive Feyurnit. But from the day they landed me to this, I've never gone back on a world ship and I never will.

AFTER A BUSY NIGHT, SKEEN COLLECTS A FOLLOWING.

Skeen woke the next morning in a warm and sweaty tangle of flesh with Hal suckling at one nipple and Hart playing with the other. Hart laughed when he saw her awake, yelped when her fingers found his not-hair and tugged. He swung over her and began raking his fingers along her ribs. She bucked vigorously, slithered away, slippery with sweat though weak from giggling. She was ticklish all over and the four Aggitj youths had discovered that with much glee, which she repaid in kind when she found that fooling with their not-hair sense organs drove them even wilder.

Much later they swam in the river, ducking and diving, splashing each other. The Aggitj were seals in the water— agile ivory, rose, and gold seals—narrow limber bodies beautiful in their watery arabesques.

She came out of the water sputtering and laughing, half drowned, feeling lazy and scrubbed clean inside and out and full of energy and languid as a worm three days dead. She rubbed herself dry with one of the blankets, pulled on her wet underwear, shook out the eddersil, and got dressed.

Breakfast. Bread, cheese, a handful of plums, the last of the ale. Clean-up. Bury the coals, shovel dirt in the craphole, scatter leaves where their night-wrestling had messed the ground and grass. The Aggitj did the work. Their movements had the flavor of ritual and they sang a droning song while they worked.

Skeen sat in the saddle watching all this activity with interest and some impatient. She couldn't see they'd made any great mess, but the Aggitj were very serious about what they were doing. Timka had been much the same way about their camps, eyeing Skeen with disfavor when she started to leave before the place was put back close to what it'd been before they came. Skeen wanted to leave now, but she owed them more courtesy. Good kids, limber and loving and sexy as hell. She felt like their mother, well, maybe not their mother, considering the games they'd got up to last night. She had enjoyed herself to the max last night, but she didn't want to repeat it. When she dived into a Pit Stop, she seldom spent two nights in the same place with the same person. It felt better to say it's been great, guys, see you.

The Aggitj finished their fussing, huddled together a moment to sing a short wordless song, a kind of celebration, maybe of a happy night and a joyful morning. They moved

apart, chattering cheerfully in their own tongue, swung into
the saddle, chattering on in Trade-Min, so persistently they
canceled each other out until Hal who was the oldest put two
fingers in his mouth and blasted the other three with an
ear-shattering whistle.

He waved Hart, Ders, and Domi back, then maneuvered his
mount beside Skeen.

Skeen started on at an easy walk, Timka's horse ambling
patiently behind. They rode in silence for half a stad, then
Hal said, "We want to come with you, Skeen ka Pass-
Through."

"You don't know where I'm going."

"Doesn't matter. We got no place we need to be."

"I've trouble on my tail. You could get killed."

"So? We're extras, Skeen ka. We can't go home without
an army behind us. We don't want to settle yet with an
otherwave woman and start grubbing a living. If one gets
killed, the others will mourn him and skin the killer. If we all
get killed, our troubles are over."

"I've got other commitments."

"So so, the Min. We know."

"You seem to know a lot."

He grinned at her.

"If you're thinking every night will be like last night, you
can forget it. I don't repeat myself. One is fun, more's a
chore."

"Never?"

"Well, I never say never, but don't count on it."

"We travel hopefully and make do."

"And you must feel free to leave whenever you get a better
offer." She saw that he wanted to protest and stopped him
with a lifted hand. "You won't lay the burden of oaths on my
shoulders, you cheerful young con artist. No way. The arrangement is you travel the same road I do until you're bored
with it. No strings on me, none on you" She frowned at him,
slapped her hand on her thigh. "And no fuckin' secret oaths
either. I get a smell of something like that and I'll shove all
four of you off the nearest mountain."

He laughed at her and started to sing, the other three joining him in some happily complex polyphonic music.

The day passed pleasantly, calmly; Skeen enjoyed having the Aggitj with her. They distracted her from fussing over the miseries bound to happen to her. A number of birds flew by overhead, some of them large enough to be Min; not being Min herself there was no way for her to tell if those were temporary shapes or the ones they'd hatched with. No more gooey bombs. After a while she relaxed; didn't matter if they were or if they weren't, they couldn't do anything but watch. She began to appreciate the limitations of the shape shifters. Couldn't carry much, no money since all the gelt on this world was metal coin, much too heavy. Couldn't take clothing along. Weapons, maybe, but on this world arms wouldn't be much more than a neat little knife or a dram of poison. She grinned, remembering the tin of powder provided by Strazhha. Sneezing powder. She stopped smiling. If she half tried, Strazhha could come up with something really nasty.

They camped again beside the river, cast nets for their super, drank pots of tea with triangles of waybread, swapped songs for a while, then scattered for the night. A polite hint or two politely turned aside and Skeen slept alone.

The next day they began meeting travelers coming away from Oruda and catching up with slower packtrains, threading through the humpy proboscidate beasts, loaded like the hairy, flat-footed nodders who had dusted her and Timka outside Spalit. The Aggitj knew half the guards and the trainmaster, trading jokes with them, answering questions, passing a flask around, generally enjoying themselves. Silent and apart, Skeen rode along the edge of the road feeling as conspicuous as a crow in a flock of doves. She caught a few curious stares, but no one asked questions. After shouting out messages to be dropped along the way, the boys came swirling around her.

"Kondu Yoa. He's a summer-ender. Balayar.

"Kamachi Yoa. She's a winter-ender. Kondu's sister.

"They know EVERYONE."

"Yoa Kondu, he's going into the Boot. He'll tell our sisters we have a patron."

"Sorta patron."

"No difference, the look's enough."

"Tell Chor Yitsa we looking good."

"Got prospects."

"A place we're going, not just fooling around."

Skeen laughed at their exuberance, but she started to feel uncomfortable again, not quite sure what she'd got herself into.

On the fifth day the land began to change its nature. More trees, water in the ditches, not just mud. The river broadened and acquired marshy fringes. The road moved farther from it onto higher ground to catch what wind there was and avoid the sullen stench of the wetlands. On the slopes to the south of the road were neat vineyards and orchards—small, two or three rows of vines in one place then a clipped hedge, half a dozen trees showing fruit mostly green, here and there rows of berry vines. Another tiny vineyard. Then the pattern repeated. "Pallah farms," Hal said. "Runaway serfs, outcasts, whoever can't get along the other side of the river. Funor Ashon sold them the land to make a screen between Funor lands and the road."

They rode into Oruda as the sun was writing rubrics on the dimpled dark water of the lake. Tepa Hapak the Funor Ashon called it. Tepa Vattak was the second lake, half a stad beyond Hapak. The city was long and thin, clinging to the edge of the lake, separated into two parts by the marsh where the river ran into the lake. The two sections of the city were not only separate but looked very different. The South Branch was open and jumbled, buildings plunked down wherever it suited the builder. What streets existed were wildly eccentric scrawls liable to stop and start without much concession to logic or plan. The North Branch was closed and secret, hidden behind high walls. No streets there either, at least none visible to the casual observer.

Skeen sorted through hazy memories from the night at Nossik's Tavern, retrieved his instructions and rode deeper into the city, threading through crowds out to enjoy the balmy evening or get some last minute shopping done in those market stalls that weren't closed down. She found the Grinning Eel in a reasonably uncongested area, a large walled establishment much like Nossik's, torchlit now, the flickering red light making the Grinning Eel look like he was flexing his loops and laughing at whoever rode through the arch beneath his swinging sign.

In the stable, Hal touched her arm before she could begin negotiations with the hostler. "We'll leave you now, Skeen ka, and find a place to snug in for the night." Behind him, the other three nodded solemn agreement.

"I'm like to be in Oruda for a while," she said. "If you plan to go on with me, then I'll pay your shot here until you can find work. Pay me back when you can."

"Skeen ka, what if we can't? Better we do as we been doing and forage for ourselves."

"You been here before?"

"No. Nor you either, remember?"

"True enough, but I'm not going to be sleeping rough. I was warned about the Funor. Too easy to stray on land where you don't belong and get shortened by a head."

"Oh, Funor. We know about Funor."

"Oh, do you." She turned to the hostler who was listening with polite interest. A small dark man with eyes like brushed black tar. A heavy earring of dark smooth wood and beaten silver hung from one lobe. He grinned at her, showing elongated, fangish eye-teeth. "Tell these idiots."

"Ya-true, Paksha-wat. You push your toe over the line, chop." A swift down blow of his bladed hand. "Where t'ain't no fences, it be them that say the line it be here. Chop chop." He turned to the Aggitj. "You won't have no trouble finding work. They like the extras here, got an extra on t' council, I send you to him, he puts you to work."

Hal worked his mouth; with a quick twist of his hand, he asked a moment's grace then retreated to a corner of the stable with the other three. They began talking in earnest whispers.

Skeen smiled affectionately at them, then turned to the Hostler. "You're a long way from home." She looked thoughtfully at the earring. "Seems to me I could put a name to that home."

"Ah now, could you, then you've come a long way your-self." He grinned at her. "Sometimes it takes one helluva long way from troubles to get the teeth off ya tail."

"So I know."

"So we both know."

"Gate jumper?"

"How else."

"Here long?"

"Twenty-three years local come first snowfall. Junks still got their tentacles on Aalda?"

"Take more than me to pry them loose."

" 'Nother wave's due, think it's likely?"

"No. Already some rumors of evacuation when I was in Chukunsa. Less than a month ago."

He clicked his tongue against his teeth. "Bai! Damn world too crowded now."

"Ever think of going back?"

"No. This suits me fine, bought me a sweet pair of femmes from the Snake Lady, going shares here with Portakil, had all the jumping about I ever want. You?"

"I've got some scores to settle the other side. Anyway I like my life a bit more spiced and a lot looser than I'd have it here."

Hal came back. "We pay you soon's we get work. We'll go looking in the morning, yes?"

"Fine with me." She turned to the hostler and began the tussle to set a reasonable fee for housing their horses.

Declining from full, the moon was still bright enough to kill the light from all but the most aggressive stars. Much (though not all) of the night noise had died away, the narrow crooked ways were mostly empty, even the cutpurses had opted for bed. Skeen walked warily down the middle of those open spaces between those dark silent structures, head up, eyes moving side to side, holster flap tucked back, the lan-yard buttoned on in case she had to roll. A few furtive shadows flickered across eye-corners, but no one came close enough to threaten.

When she reached the waterfront, she strolled out to the edge of a wharf and settled on a squat snubbing post.

The lake stretched out to the horizon, dark and secret, lapping lightly at the piles beneath the wharf. Behind her she could hear voices and snatches of music from a tinny lute, a bit of revelry still going on in a lakeside tavern. Long torches were burning at intervals along the curve of the shore suggesting there was a watch band that patrolled the wharves. For now there was no sign of them and she hoped they'd stay away a while longer; she was enjoying the night, comfortably tired, comfortably full of good food and tart cider, comfortable with her solitude and reluctant to break it by whistling for Timka and calling her in. She swung her legs, watched the dark water lift and fall. Finally she sighed and whistled the agreed-on signal, waited, whistled it again, waited, repeated the tune a third time.

She waited, kicking at the hard wood of the bitt, listening to her boot heels thunk. The lake was big and Timka could be anywhere in it, though she was quite able to count even in her water form and would probably be close in tonight. If she wanted to keep traveling with Skeen. Skeen didn't understand why Timka stayed with her; if she'd been the little Min, once she hit the lake, she would have kept on swimming and found someplace on the far side of the world where Telka would have fits trying to find her. Ah well, Timka was a good traveler, she didn't bitch or complain, did her share of the work (sometimes more than her share because she'd done all the hunting and gathering), though she was quite willing to let Skeen do all the cleaning and cooking. A comfortable division of labor. And it was quite handy having a winged scout smelling out troubles ahead.

A splash, a flurry in the water some distance from the shore. A dolphin leaped high, blurred in mid-air into a wide-winged owl. The owl glided in to shore, circled Skeen's head, and went sweeping high to drift in wider circles.

Skeen got to her feet and strolled back to the Grinning Eel.

When she was in her room, she opened the window and stood back.

The owl tucked her wings in, slipped through the unglazed

opening, popped her wings wide, and landed with a faint thud on the braided rug beside the double bed. A moment later Timka was standing on the rug; she looked around, saw a belted robe spread waiting for her on the bed. She raised her brows.

Skeen nodded. "Bought it in the market this evening.

"Thank you." Timka pulled on the robe, tied the belt about her, then sat on the bed, her eyes on Skeen. "Any trouble?"

"Nothing to speak of. You?"

"No. I'm tired of fish."

Skeen chuckled. "Portakil's cook will cure that." She stretched, groaned, leaned against the wall, her hands laced behind her in the shallow curve where her buttocks pushed her backbone from the flat. "Two boys showed up in feathers, annoyed because you weren't with me. I told them you got a whiff of Min and took off in the fog. Doubt if they believed me. Oh, and I acquired some companions, four Aggitj extras. Nice boys."

A shadow passed across Timka's face. "Do they know it could be dangerous?"

"I told them. They nodded like they were treasuring every word and I'm sure they didn't listen to anything I said." She sighed. "Djabo's tickling toes, what happens is on their heads now, not mine. I suppose they'll be useful sometimes and they're good company."

Timka gazed down at a hand pleating smoothing pleating the cloth of the robe. "Have you visited the Tanul Lumat?" Her voice was soft and submissive, made Skeen want to slap her.

"No time yet. We rode in around sunset today." She yawned.

"Tomorrow?"

"Do my best. Any suggestions?"

"There was a scholar who used to talk to me, most of the others ignored me like they did the musicians who played at dinner. Pegwai Dih. Balayar. Didn't pat my bottom either. He was . . . was interested in me. Yes, that's it. He was interested in everything. Little man, wide as he is tall, so alive you don't see how he can hold all that energy inside his skin." Warmth, unexpected and pleasant to hear, in the Min's voice; a small smile teased at the edges of her mouth. She smoothed her hand along her thigh, looked up. "The Aggitj. Why are they riding with you?"

Skeen thought of saying because they like me, but she didn't believe that herself. "They think they want to cross the Gate with me. Didn't say so, but I'm sure of it. Didn't know I won't let that happen."

"Why?"

"They're good kids. I like them. My worlds would chew them up."

"You're taking me through."

"Hunh you! You'd take on the sharks, chew them up, and spit them out. You're a survivor like me, know to trust folk about as far as you can throw 'em."

"How do you know that?"

"Judgment call. But I'd back it with cash."

"The shifting?"

"Part. Part seeing you and your sister together. Said you could beat her at anything she tried. It showed. I wouldn't take her. Look, Timmy, I'm easily twice your age. Maybe more. I'm still alive because I learned about people, well, most of them. Tibo that baster, he suckered me good. Never mind that. In fact forget the whole thing. What do you want to do?"

"Want? What do I want?" Timka closed her hands into fists, beat those fists on her thighs. "Want?" The repeated word had a whispered intensity. "I want to be left alone. I want a man who will keep me comfortable and treat me well when he's tired of me. I want silk against my skin and scented oils in my bathwater. I want clean sheets on my bed and fine food and finer wines. I want each day to be like the day just past, with a little variety but no jolts. Don't tell me I'd get bored because I'm the one living inside this skin. The years I spent with the Poet were the best I've known. But I can't go back to him. Telka can't stand the thought I'm alive somewhere; she's persuaded herself that I can't be trusted and persuaded the rest of the Synarc I'm a dozen times traitor to the Min. As long as I'm alive she'd never let me be. Never. Never. Nev . . . er. . . . '' Her voice trailed off, a dying groan with a click at the end. She looked down at her fists. With visible effort she uncramped her fingers and flattened her hands on her thighs. ''Which is why I have to go where she can't follow me.''

Early next morning Skeen left Timka to do what she wanted with her day and went out to find the Tanul Lumat. She stopped by the stable to check on the horses and the hostler told her the Aggitj boys had already found work. Aggitj extras, especially fours like her friends, were prized by the local employers. The Aggitj were cheerful, honest, and hard workers, not given to ambition and generally handsome in their long skinny way. There were a number of communities of extras outside the Boot and the Backland who gathered in and helped the stream of new extras as they were forced away from their homes. Even those whose clans were feuding in Boot or Backland set those differences aside while they were beyond the Distergas, the mountain range that cut Aggitj lands from the rest of the continent.

Pleased with the boys' success, Skeen strolled out and found herself caught up in the bustle of morning in Oruda. The fish market was in full cry, noisy and damp, with the faint mossy smell of fresh fish. Fish, eels, shrimp spread in wriggling glistening piles. Clams and oysters in buckets. Lobsters and crabs scuttling in slat boxes, clattering and clanking as carapace knocked into carapace. Other crustaceans of wild aspect and violent color swimming in vats and tanks. All vanishing into buckets and baskets of motley appearance, carried by a motley assortment of types male and female, even Funor Ashon in their enveloping robes, gloved hands passing over coins for fish their gloved fingers pointed to. Chalarosh from the desert—folk gave them all the room they needed because of the poison they could spit from pouches in their necks. Balayar from the Spray—square and brown, ebullient, arms waving, full of laughter and shrewd bargaining. Aggitj from Boot and Backland—old and young, few women among them. Skirrik of all ages—from the dewiest youths (antennas just budding, the only jet they had the hatchday triangle set between their triune eyes) to ancient females, their burnished exoskeletons a deep purple with scarlet glows. At least half the buyers and sellers were Pallah, most of them refugees from the feudal villages on the Plain where they were little better than slaves.

Skeen ambled through the busy noisy bustle, enjoying the sights and smells, the crowds surging around her, alert to cutpurses and snatch artists, in no hurry to get anywhere, feeling sentimental about being in a city again, though she knew how silly that was, mooning over garbage two-legged and otherwise.

She made her way eventually to the wharves and moved along these, careful to keep out the way of those working where ships were unloading; she waved to Ders and Domi who were hauling timber off a barge, and wandered on. She passed an old man sitting beside a fishing pole propped into a brace and whittling at a chunk of wood. The whittlers of the world, like the old man who took care of her when she ran away from the uncle who alternately beat and raped her. Whittlers. Elusive, dealers in anything that required no great effort, ears pricking for every rumor going, sometimes drunks, seldom druggers, sometimes burnt out, sometimes disaffected, subversive in a passive way. They generally knew everything about everyone and passed on rumor among themselves and those few they trusted. Nothing ever to anyone remotely connected to those in authority. Under coercion they were instantly senile—confused, drooling, rheumy old cacklers about a breath and a half from turning vegetable. Her old whittler taught her to read and write and when she showed some aptitude how to tickle open locks. He'd given her enough training to show her how much she didn't know when the whole section of slum was bulldozed clean and those who lived there were pressed into the labor cadres.

She walked the length of the lakefront, saw several more whittlers, walked to the edge of the marsh, the intricate lacery of channels when the river flowed through reeds and water-weeds into the lake. All the early morning bustle seemed concentrated on the south side. Here by this miniature swamp, away from the noise of the shops and the wharves, she could almost feel the silence oozing from the north side. A pier or two, some small boats tied to them or nosed in on the sand, pleasurecraft or transportation, not working boats. As she watched, several small robed forms came through breaks in the massive walls and began using long-handled rakes to comb neat patterns into the broad sandy shore between the walls and the water, removing every trace of debris, even the smallest feather.

She watched a while, learning little except that those who lived behind the walls wanted no contact with outsiders, then started slowly back toward the busy lakefront.

She ambled out to the edge of a wharf, lowered herself to the planks and sat with her feet dangling overside, a double arm-length from a whittler. He had a pole anchored to a snubbing post with a double twist of rope and a slip-knot, the line dangling into the water below. While he waited for a bite he was whittling at a smallish block of wood, carving something, but he hadn't got far enough into it for her to tell what it was. He was one of the Oruda Pallah, a solid old man with heavy shoulders and a soft sunken belly that rested on his thighs. He wore a wool jerkin over a sleeveless shirt, brown homespun trousers with frayed hems brushing at his ankles. Worn leather sandals on horny, gnarled feet. The nail on the great toe on his left foot was thick and bruised black. His feet were dusty with old gray dirt ground into the calluses, but otherwise he was a very clean old man. His clothing looked and smelled fresh, his bony hands were scrubbed pink. Some time in the past he'd injured the tendon on his left forefinger; he held it stiffly straight, away from the wood he was working on. He glanced at her when she sat down, pale blue eyes under tangled gray-brown brows, and went back to his carving.

Skeen swung her feet and thought about him, amusing herself by making up a life history about him based on things the Aggitj and Timka had told her about the Pallah.

A land-fasted who ran from his fief. A younger son with less than nothing to expect from life there but endless back-breaking labor and a maybe-wife without a dower. No trade but working in the fields and no love for that work. Perhaps more brains than was good for him—more than the usual run, making him restless, not letting him forget the misery and the hopelessness around him which was what waited for him, too. So one day he looked around and saw an uncle or a cousin old and worn and mute as a beast and he said to himself, not me. So he waited till the night and slipped away to join other restless, kinless wanderers.

The water slapped gently against the piles, curled chips of wood made tiny ticks when they fell into a tin plate set between his legs. A lakebird let out a mournful cry. Farther down the wharves the noise of unlanding made a curiously peaceful background to the silence around them. Without looking at the whittler, Skeen said, "Catching much?"

"Some." His voice was deep, gravelly, sounded rusty from lack of use.

She let a new silence lengthen and fill itself with the sounds of the morning.

The float jerked. With no hurry he set aside knife and wood, jerked the knot loose and took the pole from the loosened rope. He set the hook with an expert snap of the pole. Another measured twitch and the fish flew up, slapped into his free hand. With a smooth redirection of the fish's motion, he slammed its head against the snubbing post. He set the pole down. With neat-fingered care to avoid the spines about the mouth, he worked the hook loose and tossed the fish into a bucket. When he had the pole tied in place again, he rebaited the hook and tossed the line out.

Skeen kicked a foot out at the quiet stretch of city on the far side of the lake. "They like their privacy over there."

"They do." He turned the chunk of wood over and over in his hands, examining it with slow care.

"Tanul Lumat," she said.

"Ah." He ran his thumb over the side that was taking on a complex curve.

"I hear they answer questions."

"Ah." He began smoothing the knife over the most pronounced part of the curve, taking off tiny peelings fine as hairs. "Say you got the price."

"Costish?"

"Some." He turned the block over and began flicking off small chips from the unworked side. "Depends on the question."

"Slides, then."

"Ah."

A fish struck and was hauled in, hook rebaited and tossed back.

Skeen watched the whittler pick up his knife and start work on the block. "Got into town yesternight."

"Ah."

"Big place this. Say you wanted to get to the Tanul Lumat, how'd you go about it?"

"Be needin a boat."

"Hm. Hire?"

"Grandson's got a boat. Hauls things here and there. Might haul a passenger, price was right."

"There and back."

"Long way to swim otherhow."

Skeen kicked her feet and watched the float bob up and down a while, listened to the tink of the chips as they hit the pan. She sighed. "Where? When? How much?"

"Here. Straight up noon. Settle price with m' grandson Langgo."

"I hear." She sat a bit longer, watching the play of light on the water, the hypnotic dance of colors on the restless surface, then she got to her feet. "Noon," she said. "I'll be here."

THE QUESTER'S OBLIGATORY VISIT TO THE SACRED ORACLE.
or
SKEEN AT THE TANUL LUMAT: HOW TO EMPTY YOUR PURSE IN ONE SHORT AFTERNOON.

With a helpful boost from the rear, Skeen climbed onto the stubby landing; she turned to look down at the skinny brown boy in the ancient boat hardly larger than a rowboat though it had a large sail that was so new it shone a blinding white and creaked with every slight shift of the wind. His sun-bleached light brown hair blew about his tanned face, his light hazel eyes were squeezed into wrinkled slits. "Pick me up an hour before sundown," she said. "I'll add an extra copper if you have to wait long."

"Hour before sundown. Got it." He pushed off, scrambled to the stern and swung the sail so it would fill. By the time she stepped onto dirt he was sliding swiftly alongshore, heading for a small knot of hooded and robed Funor about halfway back to the rivermouth.

Skeen followed a flagstone path that dipped between huge wrinkled trees with stiff scalloped leaves and bark like badly tarnished pewter, cracked and folded, rough as weathered granite. The trees had a pleasant earthy smell with a tang to it that caught her at the back of her nose whenever she took a deep breath. Not unpleasant, just very noticeable. She shortened her stride, enjoying the peace and solitude. This was tamed land; the ground under the trees was planted with a lush dark green grass and small beds of flowers, all of them in bloom.

The ground swelled into little hillocks, the trees thinned and drew back from the path. She stopped at the crest of a hillock and gazed with interest and surprise at the Tanul Lumat.

Gray domes bunched together like a cluster of dirty soap bubbles. A short distance beyond these, huge round towers with crenellated tops like stone teeth biting at the sky. Swung in a shallow arc beyond these, the peaks of giant stone tents, their outlines graceful catenaries sculpted in a white stone that glared like snow in the summer sun. Farther along that gentle arc, long tunnels of woven reeds, like two-story worm-castings pressed together, a rich warm golden brown. Curving back toward her, several adobe houses, white-washed with sod on the roof, gardens with small shrubs, flowers, grass. The far cusp of the lune, long wooden houses built on piles, roofs of tile, the flat tiles a deep warm brown, bright red tiles in half-barrel shape riding the ridge pole, the eaves glittering with mirrors and the one wall she could see so intensely decorated with so much jewel color it made her eyes ache and her mouth grow dry with reawakened greed. In the center of the arc a series of stone buildings, graceful in their heavy way, with flying buttresses and cloister walks, cascades of arches around half-seen courts. It seemed reasonable that those extremely varied structures in the shallow arc were the living quarters of the scholars and the central complex housed the meeting rooms, the library Timka had mentioned, whatever else they had there, of course the administrative offices.

She followed the path to that central complex, walked through an arch into a broad tiled hallway. It was dark in there after the glare outside. She stood blinking about her, waiting for her eyes to adjust. There were doors in twin rows down both sides of the hallway, heavy wooden doors with bronze latchhooks hip high on the left side of each door. No way to tell what any of them led to. She started walking. The silence was profound, only deepened by the grate of her bootsoles on the tiles. Annoyed but controlling it—anger was a loss all round in a bargaining contest—she walked to the end of the hall and found another door, this one marked with the glyphs for enter.

She pulled the hook down; the door opened with a heavy silence and a gliding ease that spoke of careful balance and oiled hinges. She stepped inside and shut the door behind her. A long narrow room, the entrance in one of the short sides, cut in two sections by a broad counter, the greater part behind the counter. Lit by a pair of roof windows and an efficient array of curved mirrors that multiplied the light until the room was filled with it. Backless benches along the walls. No one at the counter, though three robed youths bent over tables some distance behind it, working with such concentration they had no idea that anyone had come in and might want some attention. Skeen had a strong suspicion they were playing games with her, but she'd long ago learned how futile it was to complain. She crossed to the counter. A small wooden mallet lay beside a polished wooden block, both attached to the counter with exquisitely chased bronze chains, each link slightly different from all the others, a clever variation on a theme, something a master craftsman had tossed off once upon a rest time, just to show he could. She touched the chain and briefly coveted it, but there was no point in that right now, so she lifted the mallet and rapped on the block, startling herself with the amount of noise she produced.

Three heads popped up. One of the robed figures rose and came to the counter. "How many I serve you, Maneke?"

"I have questions. Would it be possible to speak to a scholar named Pegwai Dih?"

His round young face went solemn. "Maneke, a scholar's time is very expensive and you'd be wasting your coin to ask him something a novice could answer."

"I appreciate the courtesy, Manoush. What are the charges for answers you can provide me?"

"If I know the answer and don't need to search, one copper. If it requires consulting a readout, five coppers. If it requires extensive file search, that will be one silver. Is that enough to go on with, Maneke?''

"Let's try it, Manoush." She fished in her belt pouch, put a copper on the counter. "Question: Have you maps of this world, all or part?''

"Some maps we have. The Rivers Rekkah and Rioti from source to end. The Boot and the Backland. The north coast of Rood Meol. The Islands of the Spray. A few sections of the coast of Suur Yarrik across the sea. Some of the coast of Rood Saekol." He swept the copper into a worn wooden box. "Someday we'll have the whole, but not yet."

Skeen put another copper on the counter. "Do you sell copies of maps or let outsiders see them?''

"No cost for this answer. A silver for each page you buy, a copper for each master you look at.''

Skeen frowned at the counter. It was waxed and caressed to the kind of deep glow only time and loving care could produce. She didn't want the world and his brother to know her business, but if she didn't ask, she'd never get answers. "Do you have a brief history of the eight waves and where they ended up, with some idea of the present distribution of the species?''

The boy collected the copper. "We have such a book, but it's at least a generation out of date. We have Seekers out now gathering information and scholars working on updating the book, but the new edition won't be completed for several more years." He cleared his throat. "For one copper you could look through our lending copy. If you decide you want a take-away copy, we will print one for you for two silver. I think you will find it useful, Maneke. It was written for singling pass-throughs." There was a hint of question about the last words, but Skeen let the hint lie untouched. She had a sinking feeling that the book however interesting and useful would have little information about the present location of the Ykx, the one thing she really had to know.

"I've an afternoon free. How much if I take the book to one of the courts around here and read it there?''

The young man smiled. "That I'd better ask about, give me a minute. . . ." He glided away, went round behind

some ceiling-high bookshelves. Skeen heard a subdued hum
and the soft clacking of an antique keyboard and had to
discipline her face into placidity. Computer? Likely. She
thought about several xenologists she knew who'd go into
ecstacies over this world and plan a dozen lifetimes of pro-
jects. She thought about old Yoech and frowned; any day,
any hour, any minute some other fool Rooner could hear him
and believe him. It didn't bear thinking about.

The clerk came back with a battered old book; he set it on
the counter in front of her. "For five coppers you may take
the book into the Cirincha garden. If you wish, in about an
hour, someone can bring you a light snack, say bread, jam,
cheese, and a pot of tea. Four coppers. One copper for the
use of the garden, that would make ten. Only if you wish."

"Sounds good to me, Manoush." She counted out the ten
coppers, picked up the book. "How do I find the Cirincha
garden?"

"A pledge will be waiting outside the door. He will show
you, Maneke."

A young boy, a pre-pubescent Aggitj in a short robe that
barely reached his rather grimy knees, led her around the
main building into one of the pleasant arcades. He shook his
head when she tried to question him, though he smiled politely all the while. He laid a forefinger across his lips and she
understood he was bound to silence, at least in the presence
of outsiders. Obviously he found the required muteness ag-
gravating in the extreme and had to jerk himself up several
times as speech bubbled up in him. He was a gangly child,
with hands and feet much too big for sticklike arms and legs,
but he had the same kind of cheerful acceptance of the
world's difficulties and his own shortcomings that she'd found
in the four extras. In the short distance between the hallway
and the arcade, without saying a word, just by the bounce of
his walk, the insouciance of his grin, the happiness of his
tea-colored eyes, he gave her a good feeling about the place.
He was where he wanted to be and willing to endure the little
difficulties they made for him as long as they let him stay. He
left her in the court and bounced away with a farewell flicker

of his fingers. She settled on the grass beneath a blooming Cirincha tree and began reading, picking up speed as she grew more accustomed to the syllabary of Trade-Min.

YKX: Frail in appearance, stronger than they look. Covered with a thick plushy fur. Color ranges from a dark cream to an umber almost black. Gossamer flight skins, also much tougher than they look, attached along the bottoms of long thin arms and the outside of long thin legs. Ykx do not fly, but they are skilled and agile gliders and could stay aloft for hours if conditions are right. Three fingers and an opposable thumb, claws, tough arcs of horn with needle points that add an extra dexterity to the long fingers and thumbs. The powerful eyesight of a flying predator, though the Ykx have never been known to kill anything without extreme provocation. Irises like molten copper. A curious assemblage of secondary eyelids which aid in the shift in focus from distance to extreme close work. Face mostly eyes. Knife blade of a nose. Unable to survive for long periods if separated from their kind. Long-lived and apparently slow breeding though very little is known about the more intimate aspects of their lives. Preferred dwelling—caves carved into tall, vertical cliffs. Their assemblages are called Gathers. Closest comparison is to nest domes of the Skirrik.

Beyond the physical description and some speculation about their social habits, there was very little solid information about the Ykx in the book. Nothing she could use, nothing to help her find them, nothing to help her bargain with them. Something stirred briefly in her head, then was gone. Bargain she'd have to; no one gave away something as valuable as the key to The Stranger's Gate. And talking of value, best check her purse. The Poet's money was going fast. Nossik's hadn't been cheap. The Grinning Eel was making the coin vanish just as fast even with the Aggitj paying their way. She didn't want to mess her backtrail by running out on the rent. Chances were she'd have to come back this way to reach the Gate again. She looked at the pile of coins by her knee; no problem yet. She yawned, glanced at the sun, then dumped the coins back in the pouch and tied the pouch back on her belt. Busy port city, bound to be a House worth nightwalking. But that was for later. She yawned again, got to her feet. It was warm and quiet in the court, making her sleepy. After a few stretching bending exercises to let air into her brain, she started back for the office.

A bang with the mallet brought the same clerk to the counter. She pushed the book across to him. "Seems I must speak with the Scholar Pegwai Dih. Would that be possible this afternoon? And how much will it cost me?"

"One moment and I will check the roster, Maneke. One gold to speak with a scholar of Pegwai Dih's rank." He waited until she nodded her consent, then went back around to the concealed readout. A few clacks, silence, a few more. The clerk came back. "Scholar Dih agrees to see you, Maneke. One gold, if you please."

He took the coin, weighed it on a small scale, dropped it into an iron-lipped slot beside the mallet. Taking a small rectangle of paper, he dipped a steel-nibbed pin into a stone bottle of ink and scrawled a few glyphs. This crazy world, she thought, computers and steel nibs in wooden holders, turgid ink in old stone bottles. He held out the slip. "Show this to the Scholar Dih, Maneke. A pledge waits outside to take you to him."

"Many thanks, Manoush, you have been most kind."

The girl waiting for her was small and dark and quiet. In the shadowy hall she thought the child was Balayar, but when they passed one of the few windows cut through the stone, she saw the tracery of scales on her skin and the odd crinkled hair; it'd looked black but was really a dark green. This quiet shadow girl was a Nagamar up from the marshes along the coast. Where the Aggitj pledge had to struggle with his nature to keep the silence, this pledge walked in silence as her natural right. She brought Skeen into a vast room heavy with age and books.

A broad solid man sat in an armchair in the midst of a

clutter of paper and books, inkpots and pens. There was a metal box on wheels beside his chair, a thick black flex snaking from it to vanish under the shelves.

The pledge left, quiet shadow with a pensive abstracted air, dignified and self-contained little person. Skeen watched her a moment, smiled, then turned and held out the slip of paper.

Pegwai Dih took it, glanced at it, dropped it among the others cluttering the table; he looked her over, his face alive with interest and a brisk enjoyment she didn't know how to read. "Sit, Maneke, sit. You give me a crick in the neck standing like that." He had a deep bass voice, rich and warm, that made her feel folded in affection and liking, that sent an answering flush of warmth through her.

Fighting against the charm of the man, Skeen pulled a chair away from the table so her legs wouldn't be encumbered if she had to move fast. The arms blocked easy access to the darter so she slid forward until she was sitting on the edge of the seat.

He watched her maneuverings with considerable amusement. "The Poet sent word to watch for someone like you."

"What does that mean?"

"Nothing at all, just a comment. He can send all he wants, what answer he gets is another thing."

"I didn't pay a gold for natter natter about things that mean nothing to me."

"Games, games, always games. You've nothing to fear from me, Maneke. Had I my way, slavers would be hanged and slave owners made to disgorge."

"Your way." She tapped the fingers of her left hand on the chairarm. "Talk's easy."

"So is silence when it's called for."

"As you say." But she relaxed, slid back in the chair, crossed her legs, and waited for what he'd say next.

"Gate closed on you? No answer? No need for one, I suppose. Let me see. . . ." He searched among the papers and found a long strip of papertape about the width of his thumb. He ran this through his fingers. "Dum Besar is boiling. The Poet's pulling any strings he can get his hands on—seems he's rather more important than people thought;

he wants the Min back and he wants the hide of the thief who took her. Spies told him the thief was a Pass-Through female hired by some Mountain Min to steal his slave. He was making half-serious plans to take an army into the mountains and erase Mintown when he discovered they didn't have her either, same spies. Mintown is in a ferment to match that in Dum Besar. Quite a trick breaking free of the Min. Some day you'll have to tell me how you did it. The favored notion is you brought some device through the Gate, something that makes you invisible perhaps. Poet wants to get his hands on that almost as bad." He set the tape down and watched it curl into an irregular coil. "I'll put the rest together, shall I. You're here. The Gate shut on you. You want to get away from the storm you stirred up; perhaps the Min woman is still with you. The chances are strong you want to cross back through the Gate. You inquired about a document giving the current location of all representatives of the eight Waves, then spent the afternoon reading it. After all that you still wished to speak to a scholar. Me. I suppose you got my name from Timka. Odd little thing. Slippery as a bead of mercury. I wonder if you got more out of her than I could. No matter. My conclusion: you are trying to locate an Ykx so you can persuade him to re-open the Gate. No no, let me finish, you can add or amend later. Timka is in Oruda with you; she has even more reason than you to get away from Mistommerk. You can't stay in Oruda long or the Poet's spies will report to him and the Min searchers will report to Mintown. Distances and travel times considered, you've got a sennight clear before you need to start worrying about trouble on your tail. So. Say your say, Maneke. I'll answer how I can."

"Hm. You don't leave me much to say."

He chuckled. "I pander to my vanity throwing all that at you. Given time and need, it's possible to find out quite a lot about visitors to Oruda." He opened wide his black eyes, pulled a comical face. "Unless they're Funor who strangle intruders without bothering why they've come." He chuckled again. "It amuses me, Maneke, that you've come here using the Poet's coin to buy what will take you beyond the Poet's reach. No no, say nothing. I really mustn't know for sure. If I did more than play at guessing, I'd have to act. Harmless speculation to pass an old man's long days—that's nothing to take seriously. Well well, folk here say my tongue's hinged in the middle and my pledge time did serious mischief to my feeble brain. So ask. I listen."

Skeen scratched at her cheek and contemplated the smiling Balayar. Not so old as he was claiming, probably not more than a year or two older than her although that was a bit misleading considering her ananile shots. His body looked solid if a bit portly, his hands and wrists were firm and well-muscled; running a pen wasn't the only thing he did with them. Neck and jowls were plump but taut, nothing flabby about him. And his eyes had the gleam of a mischievous child, would probably keep that till the day he died. A bit chunkier than she preferred, but otherwise he was just the sort of man she fell hard for, a brainy little rogue, soul-brother, she'd swear it, to Tibo that rat. She looked away from him, flooded momentarily with the grief and pain she'd kept pushing away from the moment she walked out of the shuttle register. Tibo you baster . . . the words came mechanically, none of the wry energy they'd had before . . . wait till I get my hands on you, you. . . . She passed her hand across her face. "Very well, I will put into words what you expect me to say. Where can I find the Ykx?"

"The honest answer is I don't know. Even rumors of Ykx are scarce these days." He fished among the papers and found another long coil of tape. "I ran a search for my own curiosity while you were reading. Disappointing. Only two reasonably plausible sightings in the past century."

"Century!" Skeen leaned forward, scowled at the tape he was pulling through broad fingers. "That's not a whole helluva lot of help."

"Shall I go on?"

"Yes, at least it's something."

"Good. South of Suur Tanzik, that's the continent you're on right now, on the far side of the sea called Tenga Bourhh is the subcontinent Rood Meol. Chalarosh land. Mostly desert except for two fertile strips, north coast along the Tenga Bourhh, and a loop about a large freshwater lake the Chalarosh call the Coraish Sea. Could swallow both the lakes here and not notice them. Unfortunately, we've got no detailed maps of the interior; the Chalarosh are second only to the Funor in their unfriendly ways. Happily for your purposes, the sedentary Chalarosh in the fertile belts are more inclined to be reasonable and they control access to the interior. I'll gather what information we have about dealing with them and give it to you in a bit." He cleared his throat, consulted the tape; Skeen got the impression he didn't really have to, but was buying time for some reason. It bothered her she couldn't decide what that reason was.

"There's supposed to be an Ykx Gather near the northwestern curve of the Coraish, in the mountains between the lake and the western desert. I must tell you, the last reasonably reliable sighting was over fifty years ago. Before my time here. A Lumat Seeker was given leave to map the coastline of the lake. An Aggitj extra named Doegri who did some fine mapping of the delta of the lower Rekkan. He had with him a small computer with direction and distance capacity, which had come into his hands in a regrettably irregular way. Rather beside the point, but it explains what he was doing and why he was alone (he wanted no company watching and coveting the computer while he was using it) when he came across a juvenile Ykx out on his first free soarings. The cub had pulled a muscle and had difficulty walking and with Chalarosh swarming around as they were right then, his lifespan was about a minute and a half. They're tough, but they're light, the Ykx, so Doegri had no trouble packing the cub back to his people. He was invited into the Gather and given a fine welcome, fed, loaded down with gifts, especially from the cub's family. He also got some good recordings of Ykx speech and enough translations into Trade-Min to give scholars here pleasant work since inquiring into the constituents of that language and how it reflects Ykx social life, but you're not interested in that. I'll call up a précis of what we've learned and the phrase book we've developed; you probably won't need it, most of the Ykx Doegri met were fluent in Trade-Min. That's the closest Gather site. The other is on the far side of the world, somewhere round the middle of Suur Yarrik, Lake Sydo area. It is not quite so . . . so reliable.'' He looked away, tapped his fingers on the papers, making them rustle. ''It comes from one Perinpar Dih, a cousin of mine with a well-deserved reputation for stretching the truth out of shape. He swore grand oaths that what he said happened really did happen and even Perinpar wouldn't foreswear himself on the hearthstone of his mother. He said he pulled a wounded male Ykx out of the Halijara Sea. He owns a two-master and is too restless to stick to ordinary trade routes. Which is why he was poking around in the Halijara, not a healthy place for an outsider. He took the Ykx up the Shemu River through Plains Min territory all the way to Lake Sydo and left him on the isle in the middle of the lake. He said it swarmed with Ykx. More Ykx on the cliffs around the lake. They gave him some gems and metalwork to pay him for his time and effort, then told him to get out and not come back. Plains Min were hanging about, looking hostile. He might not have made it to the Halijara without his escort, four Ykx soaring overhead until he got clear of the Min. If the Gather at Coraish is gone, the Lake Sydo gather is about your only alternative.''

Skeen nodded. ''I see. Or I would if I knew more about this . . . world. I really need maps. Wouldn't mind a skimmer to cut the distance down.'' A smile twitched her mouth. ''Any idea what I can use to entice a favor? From that last, it seems they aren't eager for trade.''

''No, I'm afraid . . . no, we know very little about the Ykx. Should know more. We don't. Never seemed the right time to send a Seeker. Never enough to do all we want done. Never enough money. Or people. The right people. Maybe it's too late. . . .''

''Hm. Something you didn't say—how long ago did your cousin pick up the Ykx?''

He looked startled, then nodded. ''Not quite ten years.'' He spread his hands flat on the papers. ''Shall we do a deal, Maneke Pass-Through?''

''I thought we had, Scholar Dih.''

''The gold bought you time, Maneke, nothing more. No

answers but the ones I choose to give, no impedimenta but those I choose to pass on.''

"You've got a sweet racket here, I see that, but find my appreciation of it somewhat limited.''

"So is the scope; you understand, if we disappoint too many too often, we lose our funding.''

"Why do I have difficulty visualizing you as a huckster?''

He chuckled. "The innate sensitivity of your soul, Maneke. Timka told you about my visits to the Poet. What do you think I was doing there, enjoying his verse?''

"She didn't think it was so bad.''

"Oh, he has a certain flair with words and a nice taste in images, but nothing to say. And we praise his tropes and chide him for the times he's taken too easy a way out of a difficulty and we milk him for the money to provide a living for better poets than he'll ever be.''

Skeen glanced at her ring chron, mentally adjusting the reading to tell her how much time she had before sundown. An hour and a little over, say an hour to be on the safe side. No need to push, the boy would wait and what was a meeshy copper in the mega flow out of her purse. "Lay it out, Scholar.''

The black eyes beamed at her, guileless as a friendly puppy, warning her to hang tight to everything she owned including her skin. "Let me tell you about the Tanul Lumat,'' he said. "We were established by the Funor Ashon. You look skeptical; fair enough, from what you've heard about the Funor they don't seem exactly like benevolent benefactors. They aren't. They had a much more practical reason for donating the land and the funds to get us started. They were the most organized and supplied of all the waves and they had the advantage of seeing what had happened to Nagamar and Balayar, how rapidly we lost the ability to repair and reproduce the spotty technology we brought through with us and they were determined not to follow our example. They were considerably better off than we'd been, plunging in a panic through the Gate as we did, but an assessment of their situation showed them that they had problems ahead and not so far ahead. No machines to make the machines and no one who knew how to make the plans to make the machines that made the machines, if you see what I mean. Thus the Tanul Lumat. Though they are fanatic about the purity of their bloodlines and the bloodlines of their cattle, they are as firmly convinced of the value of mongrelizing ideas. Put a clutch of idea makers together and let the ideas breed like fury. Thus the Tanul Lumat. And they aren't fussy about disciplines; a historian is as welcome as a chemist and a good glassblower is worth both put together. Thus the Tanul Lumat. Part university, part factory, part museum, part . . . well, I suppose you could call it boarding school and orphanage, part refuge for persons who fit nowhere else. . . ."

"A lot of parts."

"And even so not near the whole. I haven't mentioned the Seekers and the mapmaking, the navigating instruments of all sorts we produce, the experiments with metals, the medicines, the surgeons and physicians—well, the list could go on for a while yet, but that's sufficient to give you some idea what the Tanul Lumat is. Knowledge is the reason we exist and in large part, knowledge is the commodity we sell. We have to eat. We go on begging rounds like the dinners with the Poet. The Funor Ashon continue to subsidize us but only provide sufficient to underwrite food and drink and the maintenence of the buildings. The children we train, the Seekers we send out, most of our experiments—all these things we have to fund ourselves. Sometimes the families or communities that send children to us pay fees, but a gifted child without resources is welcome also and we must provide for our old. Fees such as you paid are a very small almost infinitesimal part of our income. We beg; we make mirrors, goblets, windowpanes, what have you in our glassery; we forge fancy swords . . ." he grinned suddenly, "like those you stole from the Poet." He held out a hand, showed her several burn scars on his palm and forearm. "I've spent more than a few hours in the forges. Our looms are famous for the quality of their weave and the woven patterns; the Skirrik Scholars are especially adept at weaving. We are busy busy busy— there's never enough time for the work that brought us here. Never enough Seekers out mapping and noting the changes in the way folk are living, the impact the waves are having on each other, the impact of the occasional Pass-Through, well, you must see what I'm saying. Each century a little more is saved, but lifefire alone knows what is lost. The Ykx could be gone tomorrow and we know nothing—NOTHING—about them.'' He sighed and leaned back. ''That really is enough. I wanted you to understand how strongly I feel about what I'm going to ask you.'' Another smile, rueful and self-deprecating. ''A sorry huckster I am, giving you all the advantages. First, my part of the bargain. I will see you accredited to the Tanul Lumat as a Seeker. That will give you sufficient background to keep folk comfortable around you and explain why you are traveling. The Lumat has a lot of goodwill to call on in a lot of places. No funding. Things are too tight, they're always too tight. It's you who'll have to provide . . . well, that later. I'll get you the best maps we have, some that aren't available to the being who walks into the office. I'll get you a précis of the latest information we have about the state of the world. Much more current than that in the book you read. I will arrange your passage on a trader that'll take you down river and across the Tenga Bourhh. I will get you an introduction to the authorities in Atsila Vana who can give you permission to travel into the interior of Rood Meol.''

''And what do I do for all that?''

''Two things.'' He leaned forward again, his eyes fixed on hers. ''Before you leave, you spend as long as it takes to tell us everything you know about the Stranger's Gate and tell us everything you know or have guessed about the Min.''

She nodded. ''Reasonable.''

He flattened his hands on the table. ''And when you leave Oruda, you must take a real Seeker with you. We must know about the Ykx.''

She choked down a laugh. One more beast for her menagerie. Funny, he really seemed to think she'd balk at this. Maybe she would have yelled and kicked and spouted platitudes about she traveling fastest who traveled lightest, but she already had four Aggitj and a Min, what was one more? The magic goose, she thought. How many fools will glue themselves onto me before I leave this crazy world? Still, best be cautious, he could stick you with a real loser. "Agreed," she said, and was hard put to swallow a giggle as he relaxed, "provided we get along. I'm not going to travel with some git who irritates me just by breathing."

"Me," Pegwai said, with a nervous grimace meant to be a smile.

"What?"

"I've been a Seeker many times before, young woman. I have friends and acquaintances that will be useful to both of us. I'm healthy and not stupid. Why not me?"

"Why not indeed. Fine with me, given two qualifications. I like things loose and easy, but in a pinch, I'm the boss. I say hop, you turn into a twitchy flea."

"She who pays the fiddler calls the tune. The second condition?"

"I see what you meant about the funding. Would you feel morally outraged at traveling with a working thief? That's the second condition. No preaching or prying." She laughed at the expression on his face. "How did you think I was going to provide for six besides myself? I'd far rather steal than whore and preference aside, I haven't the temperament or physical qualities for that line of work."

He ran bright eyes over her face and form. "I wouldn't say that. There are men who like their woman lean and fiesty. Not enough, I suppose. And there's always the matter of that temperament." Laughter in his voice, then a question. "Six?"

"Count 'em. You. Timka the Min. The Aggitj extras, Hal, Hart, Ders, and Domi. Last time round my fingers that makes six."

"You couldn't talk some of them into waiting here for us to come back?"

"No."

"It's a caravan."

"Isn't it."

"I can see why you didn't object to adding one more."

"A bit late for that."

"Expensive."

"Now that you're part of the expense, you might throw in

another dollop of information. Some names to be considered as our involuntary patrons."

"Tactfully put." He fidgeted nervously with the coil of tape. "It's pleasant outside from the look of the light." A quick wave at the light shining down from high narrow windows.

She got to her feet. "Why don't you give me a quick tour of the grounds. I need to be back at the landing by sundown, but I'm free till then."

Pegwai Dih pushed his chair back and came to his feet with the lightness she'd seen before in men of his build. Showing off a little. She rather approved of that. He knew what he was doing, shared his understanding with a sudden smile, a wink of complicity. Not ashamed, amused at his own antics, the scholar standing back and watching the natural man be himself. A lot like Tibo, oh Tibo you baster, you jackal, you bloodworm, lost your own ship in that crazy business with the Heeren, you had to take mine, oh you slipt in the nod, you. . . . He knew what the Junks would do to her once they ran her down, he knew, he had to know, he knew how to hurt her, how could she have misread him so completely? Nothing to tell her what . . . should have known . . . I should have I should have known . . . how could I know . . . what was there to tell me he would steal my ship, strand me? The uncertainty about her perceptions had shaken her badly, like standing on earth that shifted suddenly under her feet, that opened up and swallowed her.

She stopped thinking and looked at Pegwai Dih. His head was shoulder high on her, about where Tibo's came, but he was near two of Tibo wide. His hands were clasped behind him, hiking the robe up a little over his solid rump. The jut of his solid little rear was the one part of his body Tibo was self-conscious about, the one thing he wouldn't let her tease him about. And he didn't want to hear her tell him how it excited her. Ai-eee, Djabo, stop this, woman, stop it stop it stop it, there has to be an explanation, some reason. . . . Pegwai was strolling along, square shapely feet appearing and disappearing beneath his homespun robe, the afternoon sun glistening off his square shaved head. All this time since the

Junk had squeaked the news at her, she'd been playing games with her hurt and anger. There's no need, she kept telling herself, no need to face these wounds as long as I'm in fair control of my life. As long as she had directions she could move in where she didn't have to trust someone. Now there was Pegwai, proposing to come with her. Maybe it was all right, maybe if she didn't depend on him for more than a moment's aid and not at all if there was trouble, maybe she still had maneuvering room. She emerged from her self-absorption and looked around.

They were strolling in an open woodland, probably that between the lake and the Lumat grounds; a slight breeze stirred the humid heavy air, smells that were hot and thick, afternoon smells, a little stale from being around all day. She was tired, felt like she'd been wrestling alligators the past few hours. "Know much about the other side of Oruda?"

"We're not cloistered here, Maneke, and I'm a man who likes homebrew when he's got coins to rattle in his pocket. And there's a cookshop near the Eastend where they make a telazera to dream on." He slanted a glance up at her, sly laughter in his eyes, knowing very well why she'd asked the question, taking pleasure in verbose sidetracks. "That's a dish of cheese and breadcrumbs and lazzo. Lazzo being those small purple lake spiders, the ones with the pointed spiral shells."

"Good?"

"The smell alone would raise the dead."

She eyed him speculatively, then decided to follow his lead. "How do I find it?"

"Prozzi Loe's place up near marsh edge. You're in the Grinning Eel, come out under the arch and turn right. . . ." He ambled along giving her more precise instructions about how to find the cookshop, chatting on about the man who ran it, Prozzi Loe, a friend of his, a Balayar come north to leave behind some tangles he'd knotted about himself on his home island. Pegwai kept up a gentle flow of genial chatter until he led her from the trees to a rustic bench beside a small noisy stream that tumbled down a shallow declivity and boiled past their feet.

"Skeen," she said. "My name." She propped her boot heel on a rock and crossed her ankles. The bench back creaked under her shoulders, but held her comfortably. Her hair was starting to kink up as sweat popped out and began trickling down her neck and the side of her face. She drew the back of her hand across her brow, grimaced at the muddy smear on the skin. A yawn caught her by surprise. She coughed and blinked. "Running all day is easier than this poking about."

"You wouldn't find many who'd see it that way." Pegwai loosened the robe about his neck, pushed the sleeves up past his elbows. He was sweating very little, a few drops on his brows, on the smooth tight skin of his arms. The muscles of his arms were long and sleek and powerful, just enough fat to keep from looking ropy. Thick wrists. Strong hands, long tapering fingers, a useful look to them, that aura of competence and skill that clung to the hands of artists and artisans and made her wonder what they'd feel like touching her. She lingered a moment on the thought. I'm getting horny as hell, must be getting close on my period. Djabo, I've lost track of days in all this mess. Lousy timing and there's probably nothing like a tampon on this whole lousy world. Hm. I wonder if any of the waves are offshoots of the cousin races? Too late to check that out now. No problem with the Aggitj, no fertile mix there. Pegwai, now, he even smells like a relative, not that he's making any show of noticing the signals I'm putting out. Well, soon as this month's leak is finished, I'd better check my implant, the way my luck's running, I'll end up pregnant. Djabo's nimble tail, who'd be a woman. Well, none of that, you're just depressed, old girl, because Pegwai's treating you like his favorite sister. She sighed, then was annoyed with herself for doing it. "Can we talk now?"

He flushed, leaned forward and gazed at the water. "Perhaps I was exaggerating the difficulty." He straightened. "But I must live here, I want to live here."

"Fair enough."

The wind freshened and began blowing spray at them, a

cooling mist that touched away the stickiness from the heat and beaded on her hair.

"I'm tired of improvising this jaunt," she said after a short silence. "You know country and cost. Give me some idea of the gear we'll need and the expenses of traveling. No, not now, make some notes. I can pick them up when I come to do my chat." She stretched her legs, crossed them the opposite way. "I have to do some prospecting before I do any buying." She turned her head, raised her brows. "I asked this before. Perhaps I can get an answer out here. You happen to know any very rich and morally scabby types? The kind that folk around here would enjoy seeing dumped in a mudhole?"

"Let me think about this a little. You're asking me to make a large alteration in the way I think about myself." He gave her a rueful laughing look, then swiveled around to stare at the stream, his back to her. He wasn't happy about turning fingerman, but he'd come around. Before long he'd be justifying himself by concentrating on the flaws in those she planned to rob. As long as she stole the ill-gotten gains of evil folk (she grinned at the thought), he'd talk himself around. It wasn't so different from what he did on his begging rounds—flattering bigots and tyrants, licking the feet of pretentious would-be literateurs, snobs, and slavers and other parasites. His nimble-footed capers about his own integrity and his tongue play were a sort of whoring (he had no business teasing her about her tastes), doing indirectly what she proposed to do a lot more directly and effectively. So it took him a while to readjust his thinking, so he should get on with it. She kicked her feet out, drew them back, wriggled on the bench, rubbed at the nape of her neck. Well, he was intelligent, not a bad trait, and even better, seemed to have a fair fund of common sense, and he could laugh at himself. She was rather looking forward to sharing laughter with him, to enjoying the absurdities of the world with him. The Aggitj boys were fine and fun, but they thought with their bodies. Timka was intelligent and capable of saying interesting things, had even laughed a time or two, but there wasn't much fun in her, at least none that Skeen had discovered thus far.

A scrape and a chuckle broke into her musing. Pegwai had swung back around and was gazing at his linked hands, enjoying some private vision.

"Funny?"

"I was visualizing Kerakevaladam floundering in a juicy mudhole. He's one you might tap to the cheers and encouragement of most in Oruda. Renegade Chalarosh. Calls himself a spice merchant; rumor is he controls the flow of tersk which is a particularly nasty addictive drug. One of these days some father or sister or whatever is going to put a knife in him. And there's the slaver Duppra Mallat. Nagamar. She trades in slaves, runs whorehouses in every fair-sized city on the Plain, stocks them with her own merchandise, mostly women and children. Those two are the richest, the most despicable, and, my dear Skeen, the most dangerous pair in Oruda. Kevaladam keeps samchaks, nasty little vermin, poisonous, miserable dispositions, attack any thing that moves, go after your ankles, drop on your head from the rafters. Nagamar are rather good with the poisons also, and Mallat has a stable of guards with noses so sharp they could track a moth on its mating flight." He frowned, looked anxious, as if he already regretted mentioning either of them.

Skeen got to her feet. "I've a lot of thinking to do before I go hunting. Time I was heading for the landing and my ride across the Lake."

Pegwai nodded and walked beside her as she started into the trees. "A year ago one of my students thought up a project; she's going out Seeking in a year or so. Methodical little thing. Skirrik, so she's very good at translating three dimensions into two, chart-making, I mean. For practice, she made a complete scale map of South Oruda, the drawing alone is beautiful work, but she went a lot further and named every major structure in the city. I'll have a copy made for you. You can pick it up tomorrow." He grinned at her, a nervous twitch of his full lips that left his eyes unhappy. "I'll look it over tonight and mark some other possibilities for you. Oruda has a healthy clutch of folk needing a moral lesson or two."

He was still uneasy; she could hear it in his voice, see it in the set of his body. Though he'd object strenuously to the characterization, he was very much an innocent, sheltered most of his life in a way Skeen knew she couldn't comprehend. Tibo was like that too, what he told her about himself, it was like a fable in a child's book; she couldn't believe in it. Tibo . . . no. Pegwai had convinced himself that he was acting in a good cause, but everything he'd been taught warred with that feeble conviction. Sheltered. Yes. Her own first memories were of her uncle, her mother's brother, who took her and her sister in when their parents were killed, memories that still surfaced as nightmares when she was under stress, memories of pain and fear and sick rage. No shelter for her. Pegwai had a solid thereness to him that told her a lot about his family; there was love back then and acceptance. And he had a place here in the Tanul Lumat which he wasn't really afraid of losing no matter what he said. No, he wasn't afraid. It was that web of beliefs and truths he learned in that warm and happy family. Thou shalt not steal. All right to lie and trick and flatter money from pockets not your own, but not all right to reach in your hand and take. Well, she'd never been against such teachings; in fact she quite approved of them when her own possessions were involved. She recognized the inconsistency in her attitudes and was amused by the capacity in her for righteous indignation when someone did to her what she'd made a habit of doing to others.

Though she didn't share them, she liked Pegwai for his scruples, liked him all the more because he didn't bray about them or try pushing them on her. She liked the way he struggled with an alien viewpoint and gave it its due. There were some who'd say he was struggling to corrupt himself, that he was being tempted from the path of righteousness by the Evil One, cloaked as usual in the lust-rotted filth of female flesh. She knew that Voice. She had it recorded in the bones her uncle had broken, in the scars on her back and buttocks, heard that Voice in her uncle's mouth when he shut her in a room with him, preached that Sermon to her, ranted to her about her sins—her evil nature, her corrupt flesh—

ranted at her, then buggered her, then beat her for seducing him. Everything that happened between them, it was her fault, always her fault. Her uncle told her it was her fault. Her aunt told her she was a liar and filth and beat her, too. But the worst thing, the worst thing in her whole life, the very worst day came when she was nine, the day her uncle took her into the center of the city to register her for trade school, the worst day came when she caught a glimpse of her uncle standing beside her in a long mirror, no, not a mirror, it was a plate glass window with blackness behind it that made an imaging glass that was too accurate for her comfort. They stood by a streetlight waiting for a robocab to take them back to the grim suburb where her uncle clung to the rags of respectability. By that light she saw herself beside her uncle, saw too a likeness that struck deep into her, turning her deathly ill, though she had to conceal the sickness behind the bland baby mask she'd learned to paste over pain almost before she learned to talk, when she saw that his face and his body were stamped into her bones and into her flesh and she'd never be rid of him, not as long as she dared look into a mirror. Nine years old and visited with a doom like no other doom she knew. She fled two months later after killing him and chopping his face into hamburger, but it was another ten years before she managed to reclaim her body as her own and not a wretched surrogate of her wretched uncle.

Langgo's boat was snubbed to the landing, two robed forms sitting silent in the bow. He handed her down, disclaimed any long wait, pushed off and sent the boat skimming across the lake.

Timka was curled up in the bed, snoring a little, that squeaking whistle she made sometimes. Skeen didn't bother tiptoeing about; once the little Min relaxed and let herself sleep, a mountain could fall on her and she'd not bother waking. She dropped onto the bench at the foot of the bed and pulled her boots off. She stretched her legs out, wiggled her toes, flexed her arches, sighed with the pleasure of free movements. Pegwai, Pegwai, Djabo chew your ears for you, you stirred up things I've worked to forget. She stretched, groaned, got to her feet. She'd ordered hot water this morning, ready at sundown in the bathing room. Get a move on, woman, your bath is getting cold.

She stripped off tunic and trousers, shook them clean and hung them on wall hooks, then slid into the robe she'd bought in the market that morning. A last glance at Timka—she hadn't stirred—and Skeen went padding out.

Along the hall, down a dark ramp, in a narrow door. Cans of cold water, cans of hot water steaming up the small windows. Glazed windows courtesy of the Tanul Lumat. Underfoot, well-scrubbed planks set with small gaps between them to vent overflow from the tub. That tub was round, metal hoops binding plank sides set at an angle to the base; it was scrubbed clean and smelled faintly antiseptic. Several oil lamps in wall brackets smelled of pine and cast a soft amber glow over the room. Those, too, she'd paid for; the only luxuries that came free were song and talk and even those had to be supported by passing the bottle round.

She hung the robe on a hook, stepped out of her underpants and shirt and tossed them into the tub. I am going to have to get some spares made before these rot off me. She began pouring the cans into the tub, hot first, cold to adjust, more hot, until the tub was full enough. She stepped in, danced a little from the heat, then lowered herself gradually until she was sitting with the nape of her neck hooked over the edge, water lapping over her breasts. She closed her eyes and luxuriated in the warmth seeping into her bones and the prospect of being clean again, hair to heels. After a short while, though, she sat up, scooped soft soap from a bowl and began scrubbing off several days' accumulation of sweat and grime. This bath was costing her more than a week's room and board and worth every copper. She rubbed soap into her hair until her scalp stung, then dunked herself under the water, shook her head about, came sputtering up to dump dipper after dipper full of water over her head until she was dizzy with it, laughing and filled with energy and soaked to her back teeth. She dipped more hot water into the tub until it was steaming again, then she settled back, head over the edge, the water up to her shoulders now, her arms floating under water crossed loosely over her ribs, her mind drifting with the slow currents of heat that grazed her body each time she moved. She was getting involved with this world in a way she'd been careful to avoid other times. Diving in to raid some ruins, sliding around patrols, ignoring natives if any, in and out smooth and slick, her only contacts would be hirelings who did the more delicate work her androids couldn't handle. Nothing like here. Damn this place, it was seductive, this impossible crazy world. She smiled drowsily as she thought of Pegwai though she had a suspicion the strong attraction she felt was not reciprocated. The targets he'd offered her were both of them not Balayar; probably none of the others he was selecting for her would be Balayar. The waves here in Oruda seemed to mix amicably enough on the streets, in the markets, in taverns like this, but from what she'd seen so far the permanent residents of the city lived in small enclaves that fit into each other like the pieces of a picture puzzle—Pallah living with other Pallah, Nagamar with other Nagamar, Chalarosh with Chalarosh, and so on. Except for a few comments dropped by the hostler and Pegwai, she knew little about the way the Orudish governed themselves, a free city with a council, generally ignoring both Pallah and Funor Ashon attempts to claim them, she didn't care to learn more—except about the local cops, if any. How good they were and what they were authorized to do. Probably they operated by knocking a cutpurse or two on the head and if he died, too bad; no one asked questions about corpses. A system probably well-abused, but weren't they all, and you just walked tippy-toe around the gunmen, took them out first if you had to. The system was the system, whatever system it was and for folk like her, no system was much good. Or maybe those with goods to protect hired their own cops. Better ask Pegwai tomorrow. She moved her hands, rubbed her neck along the tub rim, yawned. She thought about the Aggitj boys and wondered briefly where they were. Wouldn't mind another bit of friction with them, wouldn't mind hahaha, if it wouldn't be starting something I don't want to go on with. . . . Tibo Tibo Tibo. Why? She cried a little, sniffled, stirred herself to splash some cooling water onto her face. The back of her neck was starting to hurt. Reluctantly she sat up, wriggled her shoulders, pulled herself out of the water.

She stood dripping, stretching, yawning, rinsed herself off with the last of the lukewarm water in the hot cans, stepped out onto the planks and began rubbing herself dry. She felt good. All over good. Work ahead, a definite goal, the means to achieve it. She was clean and relaxed and ready for a large and tasty meal, then some singing and stories. And sex if she could manage it. She hung the towel up, started to reach for the robe. Shit, washing to do still. She groped in the soapy water, found her underthings and began scrubbing them between her fisted hands. *I am definitely definitely definitely going to have to get some spares.*

Timka was sitting on the bed staring at the glass in the small window. She didn't turn until Skeen was draping her underpants over a wall peg and shaking out the shirt. "Did you get what you needed?"

Skeen slid the shoulder straps of the undershirt over a pair of hooks, twitched the front loose from the back. "Hm. Got a start at it. We're going to be here a few more days. Any smell of Min poking about?"

"No."

"Supped yet?"

"Yes. I don't want to go down again."

"Well, I'm hungry enough to chew a leg off a horse." She poked through her pack and found her comb, dragged it through her wet hair. Djabo bless, it was growing out fast, the bleaching turned it into straw that tangled at a breath. "After I eat, I'm going to be wandering about, picking up what I can. You want to come along?"

"No." A short silence, then Timka spoke again, reluctantly amplifying her answer. "The Poet will have spies here. The less I'm seen, the safer we both will be."

"I suppose so, but it sounds boring as. . . ." Skeen tossed the robe onto the bench and began pulling on tunic and trousers; the chafing wouldn't be too bad for a few hours. "You sure you don't want to come along? What's life worth if you don't take a few chances?"

"I might fly a little if I feel like it. Later."

Shaking her head, Skeen left the room. I'd be banging my head on the wall before an hour passed. Well, we can't all be itchy and bless Djabo it's so.

ORDEAL BY POISON BREATH.
or
AFTER FIVE DAYS' NOSING ABOUT, SKEEN IS FINALLY ON THE JOB.

The reed structure was big enough to house an army if that army didn't mind wet feet and bug swarms. Two-story wormcastings pressed up against each other, others penetrating these and each other, twists and turns and rooms common to two or three or four of the castings, the center marked by twin towers rising twice the height of the rest. According to Pegwai, that was where she'd find Duppra Mallat and where she found Mallat, she'd find Mallat's gold. Plays with it every night before she goes to bed, he said.

The house was built on the edge of the Nagamar enclave near the southernmost reach of the lake where lake water had been drawn off into a hollow within a ring of grassy hillocks to form a shallow lagoon. A number of footbridges zagged irregularly from the hillocks to the platform the house sat on. No cover on the hillocks except a few lacy low-crowned trees. No cover on the walkways either, though the shallow water was thick with reeds and lilies; long sinuous mostly unseen things swam there—hints of motion, oily slides, opaline mucus staining the water, a vee from a wedge-shaped head. Not a wading pool. A number of large raptors swung in wide loops over house and lagoon, dropping down at intervals onto the perches installed for them on the tops of the towers.

No one knew how many lived inside the complex or exactly how it was arranged, but Pegwai made his peace with his conscience and threw himself into the planning with a zest that appalled Skeen; she had all she could do to keep him from tagging along when she went in. He got her some sketches of similar queenhouses built in a number of marsh settlements. That made her nervous because there was no way he'd be careful to keep himself clean, he didn't have that kind of mind. If Mallat had a way into the Lumat. . . .

Timka with her, silently disapproving, Skeen left the tavern quarter and went to a cozy little hollow surounded by prickly brush. She stripped and gave her old clothing to the Min who, still silent, went gliding away to conceal the things beside the lake. She was waiting now in the lake, swimming nervously back and forth, keeping watch on the shore though it wasn't likely she could do anything to help if Skeen got into trouble.

Skeen whipped up a frothy mixture of oil and vinegar and assorted spices, the most pungent she could lay hands on, added a raw egg for body, then slathered it over her body, into her ears, between her toes and fingers, into armpits and pubic hair. When she was basted to her satisfaction and disgust, she pulled on the clothes she'd bought for the occasion. Everything from the skin out was new—fine leather gloves, boots that laced to her knees, loose shirt, knee-breeches, the black silk stocking with the holes cut in it she was going to use for a mask, the cloth lootbag. Before she left the hollow, she scattered ignebebet powder copiously about, making sure not to breath it in. Her nose wasn't as sensitive as a Virgin Guard's, but the ignebebet would ream it out and stun her sense of smell, something she'd rather not have happen. She carried away the pot with the odorous mixture, spread more of the ignebebet, throwing it into the night breeze and letting it float away as she took a rambling looping path toward the lake shore. She threw pot and powder into the water, then started her prowl for the Duppra's house, the bag carefully slung onto her back to keep the shells from crushing. She couldn't take the darter, it was far too distinctive. Might as well sign her name on the front door, Skeen the Pass-Through, your friendly neighborhood thief. With the para-jellies for the darter, glass floats and wax and her tool kit, she contrived some neat little gas bombs. With Pegwai's help she'd tried some of that gas on a Nagamar scholar's pet waterlizard. Worked fast and produced no ill effects except the lizard was uproariously drunk and staggered about the room eeping and chasing its own tail. Be a nice touch if Duppra and her guards woke higher than the guardian raptors.

She lay on a hillock inspecting the house. There was no way to avoid those jagways and whatever traps they concealed, no way to tell which was the least dangerous, so she left it to chance. A little amateur divining with four coppers pointed to the jagway closest to the lake and she worried no more about it. The raptors soared over the house in wide slow circles, crossing and recrossing the waning crescent of the moon. Time slid past. One settled. Then another. And another. Finally they were all down. Too many years since Duppra Mallat faced any sort of threat in her own house, she'd grown complacent and let her defenses go slack.

Skeen moved quietly up the jagway, the soft-soled boots making no sound. Moving swiftly, touching down only the balls of her feet, she kept as close to the edge as she could manage, balancing as if she walked a highwire, running along it with the speed and sureness Tibo had trained into her.

Her cutter bit through the bar that pinned the door shut; she slipped the cutter into a pocket of the cloth workbelt that held her shirt tight to her waist, pulled out a pinlight and snagged it onto her sleeve, then pushed at the door. It opened with a heavy silence. The darkness inside was full of rustles and whispers and thick with lizard stink, sharp and musty and clinging to everything. She stood without moving until her eyes adjusted, then began gliding toward the center of the structure where the towers were. After a few turns the gloom lightened. A strip of fungus growing along the ceiling gave off a faint blue-white glow, enough light to show her that this corridor was empty. She saw nothing, no one, but the rustles grew louder. The stench of the lizard spray grew stronger. They're in the walls, she thought, and didn't like it at all.

She ghosted along, close to the wall, listening to the loudening rustles, stifling in the stench of the lizard spit; her feet made no sound on the floor, her clothing was loose and made moving easy, soft enough so it made no sounds either. She was excited and cool, moving at a stretch, shoulder bag around front now, one hand inside, closed about a glass float, ready to act.

The stench acquired a sharper bite, the rustles grew louder, more complex. Must be papered with lizards inside those reeds. She began to feel odd, a familiar oddity, an old memory from a period in her life she didn't like to remember, when she was screwing up everything, trying to kill her inadequacies with larger and larger intakes of pilpil. The moment she placed that memory she stopped, dug into a pouch of the toolbelt and brought out a tube of noseplugs. She pushed up the bottom of the stocking on her head, eased a plug into each of her nostrils, pulled the stocking back down and put the tube away, doing these things with careful deliberation meant to calm her revved-up body. The shaking slowed and finally went away. She hated the feel of the plugs and knew they were only a partial protection, but the lizard spit would take longer to affect her going through the skin. She monitored her sensations as she started on again, pressing inward toward the househeart. A lot of the spit already in her bloodstream, but not enough to incapacitate. Hallucinogen of some sort. She grinned a bit tipsily as a huge silently snarling saayungka leaped at her from the darkness. Hello, old anxiety, she thought at the beast and it dissolved as she walked through it. Nagamar males came down a side vault; she started and pressed herself against the wall until she realized this was a replay of a procession she'd watched two days before. Adult male Nagamar, crooked legs gave them a waddling gait that was quick and smooth in spite of its ungainliness. They carried a pole chair with a powerful ease that Skeen found uncomfortably impressive. Duppra Mallat half seen inside the chair, a massive form, a curve of cheek, a mound of arm, long and sweeping, the flesh smooth and solid as polished stone. Long-fingered hand, three fingers and a thumb, resting on the topshelf of the door. Elaborately detailed serpent painted onto that arm, scaled skin of the serpent a brighter mockery of the scaled skin of the woman. The procession stopped a short distance from her and Duppra Mallat descended from her chair. Solid as a sea idol carved from stone, polished goldstone. Dressed in paint and little else, a snakeskin belt and brief lizard kilt. Hair braided into elaborate loops, stiffened with strands of gold wire. A pet lizard curled about her neck. Old miser kept her treasure for private fondling, needing no bedizening to give her status in alien eyes.

The replay faded and Skeen moved on.

Moved deeper into the horrors stored in her mind.

Her uncle coming at her, over and over, hand raised and mouth working in a soundless rant.

Running silent with herds of children scrambling away from the labor pressgangs.

Fighting in the pits, clawing other phluxes bloody for a dose of pilpil, the watchers screaming for blood and maiming.

Her uncle coming at her. . . .

Because she'd gone through this before, gone deep into her head and faced the demons that lived there, they didn't throw her now; she knew what was happening and ignored the horrors that swam at her out of that fetid fecund darkness. Yet they were getting to her, the mix in the air, the mess in her blood, disorienting and disturbing her. Tibo came again and again. Go with the flow, let it flow, keep on keeping on. Tibo came, mocking her, sneering laughter she couldn't hear but heard anyway. Tibo came with her uncle. It went on and on and the worst was knowing she was doing it to herself. She kept walking, soft soles coming down soundless on a floor she couldn't see. Couldn't see the walls either, in spite of the fungus and the pinlight clipped to her sleeve. They melted and ran like mush boiling over the sides of a pot. The rustles and creaks were sometimes inaudible and sometimes roared at her, confusing her even more.

The pinlight touched a shimmer of scarlet, the acrid stench was suddenly thick enough to chew. Clicking sounds, high warbling shrieks. Glitters of crimson, emerald, gold darting at her. Out with gas egg. She threw it ahead of her, pinched her lips together and ran through the wisps of paragree, laughing to herself because she already had the plugs in place, threw another globe into the writhing mass of lizards. Seemed to be thousands of them, but the spray they spat at her could be multiplying them as if she saw them with a fly's multifaceted gaze. Might not be there, all illusion, delusion, part of Nagamar magic. She threw more of the pressurized globes, stopping only when the stillness about her convinced her, vision or not, the lizards were out of it. She moved carefully through the bodies, cursing because she had to use the globes, the crashes as they broke like thunder in her ears.

The Nagamar behind the heavy reed doors swept peacefully on; the corridors stayed empty.

She reached a corner where a different light spilled round the bend, a flickering red-gold, playing over floor tiles and woven reeds. On her knees she eased closer, listened. No sound, but a feeling of tension, an intangible almost nothing that brought the hairs erect along her spine. She felt in the bag and cursed her drugged recklessness, only three globes left. She held one cuddled in her hand, gathered herself, threw herself around the corner, keeping low, almost on her belly, flung the globe at the tiles in front of the two guards as they started for her, curled onto her feet and stood waiting, knife ready.

They ran into the cloud of gas, took another two steps, faces gone slack, bodies driven by will and impetus, then crumpled to the floor, spears clattering beside them.

She reached for another egg, changed her mind, let it click back against its mate. Using strips cut off their kilts and their leather gear, she bound the guards' hands and feet and gagged them, then she hauled them into a corner and left them facing the walls. As she straightened, the bodies swelled and seemed

to be trying to change into large lizards; for a moment she
was fooled, jumped back gasping, swaying, stumbling into a
strong current of air that flooded over her, flushing away
some of the confusion in her head. The guards were Nagamar
again, unconscious, tied, laid like logs against the wall. She
looked up. She was under one of the towers and it was
funneling air and moonlight down to her, a yawning emptiness overhead. Made sense. No point in having woozy unrelia-
ble guards. The air felt marvelous on her skin. She thought of
taking the plugs out, then thought it would be really stupid to
be caught by her own gas. Head not working too well,
woman. Get a move on, will you, the night won't last
forever.

She turned to the massive door the armed females (the
Duppra's notorious virgin guards) were protecting. The first
wooden door she'd seen here, a massive slab of light colored
wood with an intricate glyph carved in it. A torch burned at
the left of the door, turning the glyph into a twisty, snaky
thing that oozed menace at her. She rubbed at her eyes.
Damn lizard spit. With slow care, using hands and ears as
well as eyes, she examined that door, remembering what
Pegwai said. You don't steal from Duppra Mallat and you
don't try cheating her. Cheats paid her back with an arm or a
leg or both depending on how much they owed her; thieves
she ate whole. She'd got a taste for exotic flesh and had
roasted her share of every species in Oruda during the five
years it had taken to establish herself in Oruda. That was over
three decades ago, but the stories still went the rounds, with
the speculation that some of her more succulent slaves left the
pens for the stewpots of Mallat House.

The door was too solid to yield under the small pressure
she could apply with her fingertips and the hinges were on the
inside. No latch visible. The other door was hinged on the
left, probably have to do both sides anyway if there's a bar.
More than one bar, yes. If the rumors are true and she keeps
her hoard in there. Djabo grant they're true or I've wasted a
lot of time tonight. She slid the cutter down the slit between
door and jamb, starting with the right side. Acrid stench from
the charred wood. She pushed at the door. It gave a little but

wouldn't open. At least one bar. She moved swiftly to the other side, started the cutter at shoulder height and brought it to her waist, pushed again. This time the door swung open with a heavy silence. She listened a moment, then slipped inside.

A number of lamps burned about the room, horn and alabaster, providing a dim and tranquil light, faintly orange, very restful on the eyes, but tricky, making you think you saw a lot more than you actually did. Faint lizard stink, not enough to bother. Skeen pulled the door shut.

Steady even breathing from the big bed. Djabo, that thing's huge. Longer than it was broad and broad enough to bed Skeen, Pegwai, the four Aggitj boys, a girl for each of them, leaving space for Timka, Telka, and Z'la. Tall, too, the top was higher than her head; she might be able to hook fingers over it if she stretched. Elaborately carved sides, four mighty posts like piles holding up a wharf, also carved in deep relief. A glistery canopy draping in graceful curves between the posts. The breathing suggested Mallat was in her bed, but there was no way Skeen could tell without climbing up and looking.

Another heavy breather, lower and closer. An ancient Nagamar female, hair a dirty off-white in this faint light, sleeping on a pallet spread over a huge chest with sides carved as elaborately as the bed. A quilt pulled up to her shoulders. A small pile of carved wooden adornments on a table beside the chest—beads, bracelets, earrings that looked massive enough to drag her ear lobes down to her waist. Shaman for sure. Skeen looked covetously at the adornments, sighed, and took out one of the grenades. She sucked air through the nose plugs, not clogged yet. Good. She took careful aim and broke the globe against one of the bedposts, threw the last one against the chest near the sleeping shaman's head. The shattering of the first globe jerked the shaman out of sleep just in time for her to get a good lungful from the second.

Skeen stepped beside the comatose shaman and began climbing the nearest bedpost then swung atop the footboard. She clutched at the post and stared down at the bulk in the nest of silken coverlets. She felt a flash of satisfaction, then grinned at herself. Taking all this too seriously, woman, stop gloating and get busy. She slashed strips from the coverlet and bound the huge woman's wrists and ankles. No wonder her chair bearers had crooked legs, she must be a ton of muscle on the hoof. Skeen stuffed some of the coverlet into her mouth and bound it in place. I hope you're not a mouth-breather, dead I don't want. Weren't snoring, so that's not likely. Not that I'd weep terrible tears if you popped off. She sliced more strips from the coverlet, then swung off the end of the bed onto the chest. She tied the shaman and rolled her onto the floor, kicked pallet and quilts after her. She started to move the table aside, stopped, and frowned down at the shaman's regalia. She lifted one of the bracelets, ran her thumb over the carving. There was a man on Sekkur-nakala who'd drool. . . . Reluctantly, she put the bracelet back and shifted the table. Taking that regalia would put smellers on her trail forever. Chances were good they'd off everyone they even suspected might have done this thing. Can't have that. She stepped back and scowled at the chest. Bound with hoops of sword steel and a bulky lock. She ran her fingers along the belt, fingered the cutter's tube for a moment, then shook her head and took out one of her larger lock picks. She knelt by the chest and began working. Brute force, very little skill. She sighed at the crudity of the lock and had it open in a breath and a half, didn't even have to strip off her gloves. She turned back the lid and nodded. Right. Miser like they said. Coins, jewels, like a pirate's treasure chest in a child's adventure book, the ones that glittered with heaps of gold and ropes of pearl and dangling diamonds and amber beads, all dripping in extravagant excess over the sides. She sighed at the jewelry but left it as she had left the shaman's regalia, and began filling her lootbag with gold and silver coins; she wanted nothing that could be easily identified. Handfuls of silver and gold shoved into the bag, gold was worth more but silver was easier to spend. Struck by a sudden thought, she took some necklaces and brooches, stuffed them down the front of her shirt. Let Duppra Mallat waste time looking for those, they'd be sunk in the mud on the bottom of the lake.

Confusion to you, old witch, may you be stuck with the taste of it for a long long time. To make a little more confusion, she stirred the coins up, then snapped the lock and turned the wards. Confusion, confusion, oh lovely confusion. She spread the pallet on the chest, muscled the shaman onto it, stretched her out and smoothed the quilt over her.

She retraced her steps, moving swiftly, her feet a soft pad-pad on the tiles; the resident lizards were sleeping off the gas so the air was clearer. And her head was clearer. Ten minutes, less, and she was easing out the door. The raptors were dozing on their perches. And sweetest dreams to you, Djabo bless. She ran the jagwalk and jumped onto the grass, her head swimming with a euphoria that was a mix of the lingering effects of the lizard spit, the intense satisfaction of bringing off a very neat little caper and the possibilities it opened for her. She sucked in a long breath, exploded it out, and reminded herself the night was far from over. She had to break the trail first, wipe away all scent connection between her and Mallat House. She started running toward the lake.

When she reached the water, she tipped her tools onto the grass, then waded out until the water reached her waist. She whistled a fragment of tune, slapped the water in time with it. A sleek black dolphin broke the surface, swam over to her. She wriggled her shoulders, slid the bag free. Timka-dolphin creaked at her and she laughed. "Here, my fish, dump it deep," she said. She let the bag down so Timka could get her teeth into the strap. With a flirt of her tail flukes, the dolpin submerged and was gone.

Skeen laughed again, reached her into her shirt and pulled out the jewelry. "Look hard, Mallat." She flung it out as far as she could, watched it plop into the water, then started stripping. When she was down to her skin, she tied every-thing, boots, mask, gloves and all, into a compact bundle. Using her feet she kicked a shallow hole in the lake bottom, tromped the bundle into the hole, scraped mud, rocks, gravel back over it until she couldn't feel cloth underfoot any longer. She swam out into the lake, submerged several times, scrap-ing at her skin; didn't do much good, the oily mess clung to her and refused to wash off. Closer to the shore, she brought up handfuls of mud and plastered it over her, rubbed it into her skin. When she was finished with that, she could still smell the stink of that salad dressing. A nudge. Timka floating beside her. The Min shifted, waded to a small pile of scummy rocks, took from a crevice a bowl of soap.

"Thought you might need this, so I went owling back for it. Your clothes are half a stad along the lake. There." she pointed. "Where there's a deep bite out of the shore. I put a scrap of cloth on a bush to mark the place. Yellow." She shifted back to dolphin and went flashing away.

Skeen wrinkled her nose at the soap. Cheap oversweet perfume strong enough to turn her stomach. Ah well, it was soap. She scrubbed herself all over again, hair to toenails, then did another mudrub to get rid of the soap stink. She heaved the soap bowl into the lake. "Sorry, fish, but what can I do." She collected her tools, rinsed off the picks and the knife, sealed the cutter and swished it through the water, then swam slowly steadily until she reached the inlet where the cloth fluttered in the rising wind.

She was rubbed dry as she could manage and getting dressed when Timka came back. She spat two fish onto the sand, shifted to biped form and began poking in the bushes. "Any problems I should know about?"

"No. Lizard spray got to me a bit, but I don't think I dropped any stitches; two guards got a glimpse of me, nothing to worry either of us. What about you, any trouble with the bag?"

Timka worked a fishcreel loose and put the two fish in with others already there. "No difficulties, but raising that weight will be harder than sinking it. What was it like in there?"

Skeen smoothed the fly shut, pulled the tunic over her head. "Stink and dark." She ran a comb through her hair, pulled on a knitted cap, tucked hair ends carefully under it. "Lizards like lice in the walls, local watchdogs I suppose." She'd taken to wearing the cap the past several nights so no one would think it odd if they saw her with it now. She looked around. Dawn was so close she could smell it on the wind. "We'd better get back."

Timka nodded, handed Skeen the creel and a fishing pole.

"Not we," she said. "You. I told Portakil you were going fishing for kopija so the cook would make you butter-backed kopj; I said it was stupid to spend half a night chasing a handful of idiot fish; I said, me, I was going to enjoy my warm bed all the more thinking about you sitting in the mud dipping a hook in the water. There's nine kopija in there," she nodded at the creel, "packed in waterweeds. From what everyone says, you couldn't catch those in less than five hours. He promised you a memorable feast to celebrate your last night in Oruda if you managed to get enough kopija."

You continue to surprise me, Skeen thought. "Thanks," she said. "A clever play." She grinned, lifted the creel in a kind of salute. "Confusion to Mallat."

Timka grinned back at her. "Confusion to all of them after us." She shifted to owl and powered off.

Skeen watched her vanish into the dark. "Well," she said. She shook her head and started for Oruda.

LAST ACT IN ORUDA.

A tall Nagamar female, one of Mallat's virgin guard, stepped into the common room of the Grinning Eel. She said nothing, just stood looking around. Pegwai, the four Aggitj, Timka, Portakil, and the head cook sat with Skeen at two tables shoved together near the fire. A few minutes after the Nagamar's arrival, the cook's assistant came marching in, bearing a steaming tureen whose enticing odors filled the room. Behind him came kitchen boys with platters of hot crusty rolls, slices of gaudy yellow cheese, bowls of greens lightly cooked in flavored oil, and plates of creamy tubers sliced and cooked in milk and cheese, then toasted under a hot flame. The Nagamar touched a regular on the arm, bent down, murmured to him, listened to his answer, gave an impatient jerk of her head and went out. Skeen relaxed with a suppressed sigh, then caught Timka watching her, lifted a corner of her mouth in a quick wry smile, a tribute to Timka's foresight. She sniffed delicately at the bowl the cook handed her, tasted it, set the spoon down, lifted her hands high and clapped them in tribute. More clapping, laughter, then talk went general, mixed with the sounds of appreciative eating.

Pegwai's captain, Terwel Mo, came in a few minutes later. Balayar, something Skeen expected, young to have his own ship. He looked almost as new and tender as the Aggitj boys and was a lot more beautiful. His skin was burnt dark by wind and sun, yet soft and supple, so fine-grained it seemed poreless. Large mouth with full lips sharply defined as if carved by a sculptor given to excessive emphasis on line, bold jutting nose, a beak with flaring nostrils, that mixture of vulgar elegance which Skeen found aesthetically pleasing. She could look at Pegwai's Captain with the same sort of detached appreciation and enjoyment she felt with Z'la the Min without being at all aroused by him while Pegwai's blurred, almost comic version of those features put a heat in her groin and a tingle in her nipples when she looked at him or brushed against him. Terwel Mo was so young. Shrewd, no doubt, intelligent, forceful, maybe even charismatic, but sooo young, so many certainties and jutting corners to him that time had not yet broken off or rubbed smooth.

The Captain's long black eyes roamed the table as he came up, settled on Timka, and began to glow. Skeen watched with amusement and appreciation as he maneuvered himself into the space next to the little Min and focused intently on her. Timka looked a bit startled at first, then settled into a slashing exchange with him that she seemed to enjoy as much as he did. The Min saw her watching, winked at her, and went back to the thrust and parry with the Captain.

The dinner wound on, fragrant with grand food and grander laughter, a complex of crosstalk, wine, ale, mulled ciders, the kopj and side dishes of small crunchy deep-fried crustaceans, and finished with a great mound of salad and pots of tea. Four hours of eating, drinking, and talking reduced the feast to shreds and the feasters to a comfortable torpor.

After a long whispered colloquy with Timka, Captain Terwel pushed back his chair and stood. "Tide turns an hour before dawn. The Meyeberri is bound to leave with it. Those sailing with her should be there at least an hour beforehand so we can get you settled in and, if you'll pardon the terms, out of the way of my crew." He nodded at them, exchanged a long smoldering glance with Timka, then went sauntering out.

Pegwai sighed and got to his feet. "My baggage is already stowed," he said. "It would take a dozen men and a vat of icewater to get me out of bed that early; I'll be sleeping on board. See you sometime after sunrise."

The Aggitj conferred in low voices, waved a hasty farewell, and hurried out to spend some of their wages on a last night celebration through the tavern quarter of Oruda. Timka laughed as she watched them clatter through the door. "My turn, Skeen. I'll see you on the ship." She got gracefully to her feet and strolled to the door, grinned over her shoulder at Skeen, then went out.

Left alone, Skeen moved to a chair by one of the fires, a glass of Portakil's own plum brandy in one hand. She sat staring into the small fire while his daughter and the hired girls cleaned away the tattered remnants of the feast. She'd got away clean. Enough time had passed to make that fairly clear. She sipped at the brandy, feeling warm and floaty, and thought about hunting some company for the night, but she didn't move. She was too lazy, too comfortable where she was. Feet up on the fender, the warmth of the fire washing over her, the warmth of the brandy spreading to meet it, she drowsed and dreamed.

The Nagamar came into the mostly empty room and crossed to the fireplace. Skeen glanced up, then away, doing her best to seem indifferent. She set the glass down on the chair arm and let her hand fall close to the darter.

Greenish copper eyes shimmering in the firelight, the

Nagamar gazed at her without blinking, translucent membranes sliding over her eyes and away.

"You'll know me again," Skeen said, giving the Nagamar a sleepy guileless smile.

"Yes," the Nagamar said. "I will know you." She came closer, reached toward Skeen's arm but stopped her hand before she touched the skin. "Permit me, vovo."

Skeen bought time with a yawn, worked her mouth, blinked up at the guard. "Not gon bite?"

"No, I will not bite." The Nagamar took hold of Skeen's wrist, lifted it, turned her hand over and sniffed daintily at the palm.

Skeen tried not to sweat; she kept her arm limp and reminded herself that abandoning the clothes she wore, scrubbing every inch of her with soap and mud and a hot bath since in the Grinning Eel's bathing chamber, disassembling the cutter and cleaning every surface, polishing the lockpicks and the knife, the only things to come back to the Inn with her and even those were wrapped in parchment sealed with wax.

The Nagamar set her hand gently back on the chairarm. "What species are you, strange one? Are you male or female?"

Sitting ruthlessly on her relief, Skeen smiled with lazy amiablity. "A species too courteous to intrude in another's private concerns. By what right, by what authority do you ask me anything?" She thought it time to wake a bit and let some indignation show. She sat up, swaying a little, playing drunker than she was, though she wasn't all that sober. The Virgin was young with the stern, pinched look of the moral autocrat.

After staring at her a moment longer, the Nagamar moved around the chair with the stalking silent power of a highly successful predator. She looked back once again, then passed out the door into the heavily overcast night.

Skeen looked at the quarter inch of brandy left in the glass and decided it was a little too sweet for her now. She got heavily to her feet, threaded through the tables and chairs, ignoring the locals seated at them who paid her no notice either, being too involved with their own business. She waved to the sleepy nephew behind the bar and started up the spiral ramp, wincing when a foot slipped or a toe stubbed into a shadow.

DEPARTURE BEFORE DAWN.
or
THREE HOURS' SLEEP! HOW HOW HOW DO I GET MYSELF INTO THESE THINGS.

Despite a hangover that banged behind her eyeballs and a brain still dead asleep, Skeen was almost dancing as she walked down the ramp. Somehow, in spite of the miseries of her childhood, she had acquired a hope, almost an expectation, that one day the fabric of the universe would crack open and magic would shine through. She didn't know what the magic would be, but she associated its glow with the shivery happiness she felt when a sudden touch of light or color turned familiar things strange and wonderful. That instant after a rainstorm when colors had power. The moments during storms when lightning walked around her and thunder rumbled in her bones and she felt like a giant striding across the cityscape. Through all the scrambling she did and the hammering she took as she worked her way into a ship and a profession of sorts, she'd never lost that quiver of hope, that subliminal glow of expectation that came each time she started a new project. There'd never been any magic in the things that she did, no magic in her lovers even when she was free to choose them, no magic in the worlds she raided or the Pit Stops where she played. The closest thing to it was her feeling the first time she took Picarefy out; it was the casting off of shackles, the throwing off her clothing to swim naked between the stars.

Now she walked down a curving ramp lit by oil lamps newly filled and still smoky, their odor stronger with the pressure of a dawn still two hours off, and she felt that quiver of expectation again, laughed a little at it and let herself enjoy it. Another beginning ahead of her, another crack opening for wonder; more than anything else it was this feeling that made her jump at the mumblings of an ancient Soak. A Gate between universes. What could be more magical? More fundamentally absurd? She'd done it before, this leap into the dark grabbing for the flickering vanishing tail of a dream, sometimes connecting, sometimes missing and falling on her face.

She paid her bill with the last of the Poet's gold and went into the dark silent streets with the holster flap tucked back and the lanyard engaged. If Mallat decided to act without proof, she was going to get a fight she wouldn't forget.

There were dark silent forms slipping after her; she didn't try to challenge them and they stayed a steady distance behind her. She reached the wharves without incident and ran lightly up the Meyeberri's gangplank, went along the rail until she was out of the ordered confusion on the deck; Terwel Mo's crew knew their work so well that they needed no instruction, accomplishing an enormous amount in a very short time. The Captain stood on the quarterdeck watching with a relaxed alertness. When he saw her, he waved her up to him.

"Duppra Mallat sent to ask about you, where you were going, who was traveling with you, and how you paid your fare."

"She say why?"

"She never says, only asks. Do I have to look for trouble?"

"You'd have to ask her that, not me. I've never met the woman, just saw her a couple of times when she came into town."

He raised a brow, but had obviously expected such an answer and had asked for form's sake only. "The messenger seemed most interested in the fare and disappointed when I told her you were accredited Seeker and the Scholar Pegwai Dih was paying for the whole party.'' He bent over the rail, called a crewman up and ordered him to take Skeen to her cabin. ''Timka Min is there already,'' he said and looked complacent. Skeen left without saying anything, telling herself he was, after all, very young.

Timka sat on one of the narrow bunks in the closet-sized cabin, perched on the end nearest the small square window. The parchment hole-cover was rolled into a tight cylinder at the bottom, the laces were twin coils tied with decorative bows. The storm plug was lifted flat against the wall above the opening, held in place by a pair of spring clips. She was looking out at the spread of dark water with its small curls of mist. Skeen swung the door shut, dropped the latch. ''Got the bag up? Pegwai has to pay the Captain before we pass the locks.''

''I know.'' She pushed her feet out, sat looking down at them. ''It's under the bed.''

''Any problems?''

''No. No problems. It was just complicated. Juggling shifts and that weight. Just complicated.''

''Anyone see you?''

''I thought not, but who knows.''

''See any Nagamar about?''

''Not while I was diving. A short while ago there was a Nagamar on the wharf watching the ship. I think the one who came in last night when we were eating. Have they found some way to link you to the gold?''

''I doubt it. I was followed coming here, but no one interfered with me in the streets or tried to stop me coming on board.'' She shrugged out of the backpack, swung it onto the upper bunk. ''Come up with me and watch the departure.''

''There's no lock on the door.''

''Djabo, Timmy, who knows what's under your bed? Pegwai and he's asleep and wouldn't touch it anyway. Nagamar might guess, but there's none of them on board. And even if it's stolen, remember how I got it; I'd just have to go to work again.'' She slapped at the holster, ran fingers through her tousled hair, tugged her tunic down. ''Well, I won't argue. Sit here if that's what pleases you. Me, I want to watch the sails go up. I've never seen an ocean sailer leaving port, but I'm told it's a pretty thing.''

In the light from smoky torches and lanterns strung about the ship where they'd be out of the way, she saw that the organized chaos on the deck and the wharf had settled to a low hum. The Captain shouted orders that turned the bustle into a dance of straining muscles and shifting bodies, a syncopated ballet of strength and skill. The heavy fibrous cables came away from the snubbing posts, the sails rose with snaps and creaks and fluttering hooms. The ship moved away from the wharf with a massive delicacy that reminded Skeen of a mid-sized spacer backing off from an umbilical.

She glanced at the wharf. The young Virgin stood on the wharf watching the ship leave, her strong features cut out of darkness by the torch burning above her. She wants me to see her, she wants me to be a little afraid. Skeen pushed her hip onto the rail and watched the slice of water widen between the ship and the wharf. Idiot, doesn't she see that she's showing me I've got nothing to worry about. No one believes her suspicions or she'd be standing beside me now. Skeen wriggled about until she was comfortable, sucked in a breath, and let it out in a silent whoomph of relief. She went back to feeling good.

The Meyeberri passed across Tepa Hapak at an easy ten stads an hour, speaking several other ships on the way, reaching the locks by mid-afternoon. Computer driven, finely machined, the locks were built and operated by Funor who'd lost the least in their leap through the Gate. Despite their smooth operation, the day was finished by the time Meyeberri emerged from them into Tepa Vattak. The Captain hung lamps with red horn sides to the bow and stern and the top of the mainmast and kept on going. They met more ships, red lamps showing, who meant to heave to by the locks so they could get an early start on the passage through them. Terwel Mo also kept close watch for lake barges; these were low in the water and tricky to spot.

Skeen stayed on deck for a long time, watching the rise of the diminished moon, thinking about the two-score days she'd been stranded on Mistommerk, watching the lurid glow from the mast lamp drip like blood down the taut canvas, listening to the web of sound. She had imagined that anything powered by wind alone would glide silently and magically through the water, but there were the shouts of the watch, snores and groans from the deck passengers, and all the body noises of the ship—hums, creaks, long groans, a mix of smaller sounds. The ship flexed and complained and muttered like a live thing. Picarefy, who had her own sweet voice, her subliminal sounds that Skeen knew like the throb of her heart, Picarefy rode thunder up and down the gravity wells of a thousand worlds, but inside her walls her voice was a gossamer whisper alongside the cries of the Meyeberri. Skeen sat with her back against the rail trying to deal with the things stirring in her. Not knowing, that was the worst irritation. Tibo, Tibo . . . Djabo's claws, thinking of him reminded her of the hurt and rage she kept suppressing, but it also brought an aching itch to her groin. She told herself it was as much habit as need. She was always hot on journeys and usually had company to help cool her down. There were the Aggitj; no, she didn't want them—thinking of them turned her off. Almost. They were too young. Too what? Dumb? No, not dumb exactly, but tracked, yes, they were already what they'd be if they lived to die of old age. Put them back in Aggitj lands and they'd be what their fathers were, everything acquired outside Boot and Backland sloughed off like an old dead skin. They'd never betray her like Tibo had, they'd never delight her like Tibo had. Twisty as they came, he was capable of immense generosity—she'd seen it a thousand times. Never mean. She'd owned a part of him, at least that's what she thought, but never the whole and that was the way she liked it. Always the edge of danger, of uncertainty, the possibility of pain that made pleasure so much greater. She expected him to run out on her some day, but steal from his kind? She rubbed at her breasts again, glanced at the Captain standing on the quarterdeck still, looking out over the ship with a pride in his stance she could read from where she sat.

No. Like the Aggitj, he was too damn young. Besides, the way he looked at Timka, Skeen was too old, too angular, too assertive for him. He'd shy like a startled horse if she propositioned him. He'd be polite and tell her how honored he was and turn her down gently and carefully, even tactfully, but oh so definitely. In her mind's ear she could hear him when he was home on his island and relaxed and maybe a little drunk, telling friends and cousins how he was hit on once by this gaunt crow of a woman, old enough to be—a wink and a poke of the elbow—his auntee-in-law, do yourself a mischief on the potong's hip bones. That wasn't anything she wanted to think about. What she needed now was sleep, what she *really* needed was sex and sleep, and if not sex some cuddling. She shook her head and went below.

She stopped, her hand on the latch to her cabin door, stood staring at the panels, Why not, what can he do but turn me down. She moved to the next door over, hesitated a moment, then knocked lightly at a panel. Maybe he's already asleep, she thought, but she waited without moving, her stomach in knots.

The door opened. Pegwai looked up at her. "Skeen?"

"Peg, could I talk to you?"

He looked uncertain, then stepped back, pulling the door open wider. "Shall I light a lamp?"

"No." She sat down on one end of the lower bunk and watched as he pushed the door shut and settled at the other end of the bunk, his face in shadows. "Peg," she said softly, "I know . . . I know you don't want me." She saw his hands move on his thighs, then go still; she spoke again, more hastily than she'd planned. "What I'm saying so clumsily is . . . is this, I suppose. Where you love and where you desire is no business of mine and has nothing to do with this moment. At this moment I am driven by urgencies that have . . . that don't require either from you. What I'm saying is will you please, my friend, will you hold me and caress me and help quiet the heat in me?" She looked at his hands, they clenched, opened. She thought of saying more, but did not.

A tense silence. A long sigh. Pegwai pulled his face deeper

into shadow, lifted a hand, let it fall. "Why me, Skeen? The Aggitj, a deck passenger, any of the sailors could give you what . . . what I more than likely cannot." Before she could say anything, his voice came again, squeezed and filled with pain. "Should not. Must not."

She made a brushing gesture with a hand. "I don't want them."

He abandoned the shadow, leaning forward to stare at her. "Me, but I'm. . . ."

"Ah well, I didn't ask you where your fancies flew, don't ask me to explain mine."

"You don't understand. I don't want to start something I can't handle. I. . . ."

"Handling is all you'll have to do, dear friend, unless you find the thought of touching me distasteful."

"Not distasteful. Merely rather . . . frightening. Skeen, listen. . . ."

She got to her feet, crossed to the window opening and laced the cover in place, shutting out the moonlight, plunging the cabin into a deeper darkness. "Tell me nothing, my friend, unless it's to leave you. That I'll do, if you ask it." She heard him moving, heard the bed creak, waited for an answer, but he said nothing. "Then I'll stay." She stripped, folding her clothing and putting the things on the upper bunk, pulled off her boots and set them beside her belt and holster. He was moving, too. When she sat beside him and took his hands she discovered he'd removed his robe and tossed it away. His arms were stiff; she could feel the tension in him. "We'll neither of us break," she murmured, then frowned; for some reason that was the wrong thing to say. He tried to pull away. "Peg, is it that bad? Tell me to go." She felt him shudder, but still he said nothing. Maybe she should have listened to him before, but if she left now, what would that mean to him? "Let's take this slow," she said, keeping her voice soft and easy. "Lie down, my friend, stretch out and relax, on your stomach if that would make you more comfortable."

When he was stretched out, she straddled his back and began working on the knots in his shoulder muscles, doing

some silent crying because she remembered all too vividly
doing this for Tibo and what happened afterward. She began
working down his spine. He was plump but not sloppy,
without Tibo's well-defined musculature. She kneaded and
smoothed and worked over him until he was deeply relaxed
and almost purring, not aroused by her efforts (to her considerable disappointment, she'd had hopes) though she could
feel the deep pleasure he got from the handling. Finally she
stretched out beside him, put her hand flat on his chest
between the spring of his ribs. "Do for me now, my friend,
please. When the time comes, I'll show you what else I need."

His fingers dug into her buttocks pulling a grunt out of her.
"Skeen!" Her name groaned out of him and he wrenched his
hand around hard. She gasped and tried to twist away. His
weight came down heavy on her, pinning her to the pad. "I
tried . . ." he whispered, "I tried to tell you. . . ."

"You're bleeding." A whisper in the darkness. "I tore
you." A whisper filled with remorse and wretched pleasure.
The weight moved off her back. She heard him stumbling to
the commode, heard the sound of water pouring and a moment later the coolness of that water as he sponged away the
blood. His hands shook and he sobbed.

Skeen lay limp, the pain answering some deep need in her
she'd never known was there, easing that other pain she
carried with her. She reached out, long arm adequate when
she bent a little at the waist, and stroked Pegwai's smooth
flank, drew her hand across his hard belly and down. His
short thick penis was standing high and hard again. Without
thought or intent, not knowing why she did it, she jabbed her
thumbnail into his testicles, hard, pointed nail, weapons Tibo
called her claws, thinking of him she raked those claws hard
down Pegwai's flesh. He shrieked and wrenched her hand
loose, twisted her arm high up her back until she was fighting
him, hissing with pain, then he threw himself on her. . . .

She woke pressed up against Pegwai, half on him. Carefully not-thinking, she eased away from him and off the bed.

She unwound part of the lacing on the windowcover, letting
some of the dawn light into the cabin, then went to stand
frowning down at him. He looked like she felt, bruises
starting to show, blood crusted on long ragged gashes from
her nails, livid tooth marks, some deep enough to draw
blood. His mouth hung open, the cheek she could see looked
sunken; he lay on his stomach, face turned to the wall. She
dressed as quietly as she could, wanting rather desperately to
get away from this room before he woke. Carrying her boots,
she padded to the door.

One hand curled about the door's edge, she looked back. A
certain stiffness about the outline of his body suggested that
he was awake, that he was pretending to sleep because he
wanted her gone as much as she wanted to be gone. The
thought depressed her yet more. She pulled the door shut and
almost ran the few steps to the cabin she shared with Timka.

The little Min was curled in a tidy knot, producing her
high-pitched, breathy snore. Skeen set her boots down carefully, then stripped again. She poured cold water into the
basin, began scrubbing her body, teeth sunk into her lower lip
to stifle her groans, yearning for a hot bath but making do
with the washcloth and contortions. She was sore all over,
her hide in worse shape than Pegwai's. When it came to
washing her pubic area, she took extra care, dabbing at
herself, breath snuffing hard through her nostrils. Not going
to use those parts until she healed a bit. She hadn't hurt so
much or felt such a nauseating mix of excitement and self-
disgust since the time with her uncle. She still couldn't
believe how savage the thing had got, as if each woke in the
other a beast that found pleasure in hurting and being hurt.
I'm not like that, she told herself. I know plenty who are, but
I am not. I never have been. She shuddered, then struggled to
stop thinking while she did a few isometrics and some
bends to work out the worst of the stiffness, repressing groans
and gasps because she did not want to wake Timka and
exhibit her battered carcass. She turned to the bed to get out a
set of the spare underwear she'd had made by a seamstress in
Oruda.

Timka was awake, staring at her with appalled curiosity.

When the little Min met Skeen's eyes, her own went blank. She yawned and turned onto her side, pretending to sink back into sleep.

Grateful for the diplomatic pretense, Skeen finished dressing and went out.

Only the tip of the sun was up, slanting red light across the deck, sailors busy with rigging and wheel, moving through the long shadows like game pieces on a changing board. The deck passengers were wrapped in their blankets asleep, though here and there a man or a woman was crouched over a brazier, coaxing a tiny heap of coals alight. The smells of the countryside were heavy on the wind—fresh mown hay, damp earth, the acrid tang of urine, fugitive sweetness from unseen flowers, a blend of other odors, none of them identifiable. During the night they'd passed out of Tepa Vattak and were gliding down a broad river that looped in elaborate meanders through heavily settled farm country. Funor Ashon. She saw robed figures running the water wheels that dumped river water into irrigation ditches, others driving milk herds toward distant barns, more already at work in the fields, a few on the banks watching the ship move past.

She was suddenly very hungry and sighed to think it would be another hour at least before breakfast was served. A glance at her ring chron verified that. She leaned against the rail and watched the water slide past. A nice little cuddle to chase away the jimjams, hah! She was appalled by the events of the night, didn't want to think about them, name them, yet. . . . The intensity of the experience, the . . . she couldn't call it pleasure, but what else was it? She loathed how it made her feel, how it took control of her, but. . . . It was like the time in her early twenties when she was kicking off the hold of pilpil; she knew what the drug did to her, she knew she was destroying herself by using it, she'd fought against being someone else's slave, fought for control of her body, her life, and was losing all that to pilpil, yet there was in her a powerful urge to go back under, to regain that numbness when she felt nothing at all except a warm and gentle peace. She rubbed her thumb along a scratch on her neck, dipped her hand inside her tunic to smooth her fingers over the bruised

flesh where his teeth had worried her breast. Last night's
pain/sex mix could turn out to be as addicting as pilpil and as
debilitating. The warning sighs were there; she knew them
too well to be fooled by her rationalizing mind. She closed
her eyes and swore to herself *never again*, then cursed softly,
remembering how many times in withdrawal she'd sworn that
never again, and how many times she forgot the oath. An
unhappy laugh and she went back to watching the water slide
past. Not to worry, woman, Pegwai won't come near you.
Shit. If he was feeling anything like her, there went a friendship she was beginning to value. She scowled at the clear
green water as the sounds of stirring increased behind her.
The ship was waking. Have to work out some way of going
on. We're not children, far from it. With a little luck, maybe
we can keep the friendship. A little luck, a little time. Smells
of cooking drifted to her, her stomach growled. She sighed,
glanced at her ring chron, and went below to breakfast.

Day flowed into day with peaceful memory as the ship
moved down the river. For a while Pegwai was uncomfortable when Skeen was around; he would not even look at her,
but as the calm days slid past, they began warily working
their way back to the friendship they'd shared before. For a
while they avoided any circumstances that would present them
with the temptation to explore again that kinship in pain at
once so lethal and so unbearably intimate, then they began
setting tests for each other and smiling at each other in
righteous complicity when they withstood those self-imposed
trials. One night there was apple brandy with the supper. The
ship was tied up at one of the larger rivertowns, the last
before they went into the canyon the river had cut through the
mountains, and Pegwai bought a skin of homebrew from one
of the new deckers and Skeen went with him to his cabin to
share it and ended up sharing a good deal more before the
night was out. Both woke with the clear knowledge that more
of this meant one of them would quite likely kill the other.
Pegwai had a broken rib, a deep gouge on his neck uncomfortably close to a carotid, Skeen had fingermarks on her
neck and a memory of a black moment when she was sure

she was dead. They helped each other clean up and went to sit on the bunk.

"We've got no boundaries," Skeen said.

"No stopping points." He reached over and ran his hand down her arm; she shuddered with fear and desire and groaned when he took his hand away. "It's impossible," he said. "I want . . . lifefire, Skeen, look at me, you'd think I'd be drained after. . . ."

"I know, I know," she whispered. "I'm a rag, but I'd start again, do everything again, even if it meant . . . Djabo, Peg, I don't understand any of this. I don't understand me, I've never. . . . I'm not like this. And you—you're a kind, gentle . . . don't shake your head, it's true."

He sat pushing his hands down his thighs, pulling them back, pushing them down. "Skeen. . . ."

"Peg?"

"I . . . you . . . I've thought about you, I've thought . . . it's like I wake in you the need to punish yourself for something I don't . . . something that makes you feel less . . . less worthy than . . . than you should." He looked past her at the gray light coming through the parchment window-cover. "It's my fault. I tried to tell you, I should have let you . . . made you go when you offered to. It's what I am, Skeen. I walked the manfire and became a man in name, in deed was something else. I played the man with a girl or two, my cousins, a night or two, much drunk, and with one. . . I woke on a morning like this, Skeen, gray light around me, gray in heart and soul. It's the sin we don't forgive. Hurting. . . . If my family knew . . . the girl didn't guess what I did was . . . I left the Spray and came to the Tanul Lumat. Except for a few times when I went to Mallat's women, when I couldn't push . . . the need off any longer, I've lived a celibate life. It got easier as I got older, wasn't ever all that hard to abstain. Sex for me, my friend, means a lot less than learning, and as I said, the older I got, the easier it was to . . ." sudden grin, "handle the urges. They stayed shut inside me. Women were like the reformed drunk's full bottle of brandy, sealed and intact, a challenge and a reminder. Until you tempted me to drink. Lifefire, no! Forget that. No! You couldn't know, I could have sent you away, not your fault. Help me, Skeen. Help. Me.''

She drew her hand down the side of his face, tenderly along his shoulder, down his arm, closed her fingers about his wrist. "I love the feel of you, the taste of you, Mala Fortuna, Mala, Mala, why?" She lifted his arm, let it drop and pushed onto her feet. "Do you want to stop here, go back to the Lumat?''

"I should . . . no!''

"I suppose I shouldn't be, but I am pleased. I'd miss you, Peg." She sighed and started pulling on her clothes. "At least we've learned how stupid we can be. Maybe that will serve to keep us straight.''

From the first day the Aggitj tetrad (who had insisted on traveling as deck passengers) made themselves useful about the ship, helping with the myriad small tasks that kept a sailing ship in prime condition, helping to load and off-load cargo when they stopped at open towns along the river. They were friendly, easy-going; they liked to keep busy, were as willing to listen to wild tales as they were to tell their own. And they were the most unaggressive young men Skeen had seen in all her travels. They never quarreled and smoothed over quarrels among other men with a supple skill more instinctive than learned. Not dull-witted or slow in any real sense, they were inclined to drift rather than plan, had little interest in the why or how of things. They were curious about other lives because it amused them to listen, but they seldom bothered probing beneath the surface. In Skeen's experience such mild and amiable youths would have been victims a hundred times over, but the Balayar sailors gave friendliness in return for friendliness and always treated the boys with respect, even the worst-tempered among them. As did the deck passengers, and the other cabin passengers, one of them a perpetually angry Chalarosh.

As the ship moved into the canyon, Skeen stood leaning on the rail of the quarterdeck looking down at the swarm on the deck, watching a game of bones and tiles. Hal and Hart were playing a pair of deck passengers, Ders and Domi kneeling behind them. Skeen glanced at the Captain, snapped thumb against finger. "I've watched that game a dozen times, a dozen different combinations of players, some bold and fancy cheating, but no one ever cheats the Aggitj."

"You don't know much about Extras."

"True."

"Obviously you haven't hurt or cheated an Aggitj."

"What? They're nice boys. I like them."

"Oh I agree. Speaks well of you." He smiled at her, his teeth very white in his handsome sunburnt face. "This is how it goes. Anyone can cheat an Aggitj once; like you said, they're nice boys, they're all nice boys, slow to believe someone is doing what it seems obvious he is doing. Try it twice, his heart is roasting over a fire, the Aggitj have themselves a feast. That's when they stop being nice. You might have noticed, they don't have much imagination. Got just the one penalty—two coppers, twenty gold, all the same. Not so nice."

Skeen looked at the animated faces below, shook her head. "No, I don't know much about Extras."

Timka was a center of disturbance among the male passengers and the crew for the first two days on the river, then she moved her body and bags into the Captain's quarters. She took the bag of gold with her; she couldn't be as casual about it as Skeen. The Captain's cabin had a door that locked.

Day flowed into day, the river meandered eventually into a winding canyon that took them through a mountain range and out into another broad plain. They left Funor Ashon cities behind as they left the Ashon savannahs and the river wandered now among the Skirrik domes, great gray humps like wasps' nests surrounded by gardens and fields that merged into complex growths of vegetable and flower, some of the blooms larger than a man's head. Skeen stood at the rail and enjoyed the living tapestry spread out before her. Impossible to tell which plants were ornaments and which were food, or where the thready streams ended and the land began. The chitinous forms of the Skirrik swarmed through these fields

and like the exotic plants they grew, seemed to have pushed
all native life far from the river. No Min about, at least, none
she could identify. She thought of asking Timka but the Min
spent most of her time in the Captain's quarters, especially
since Skirrik started coming on board. The Meyeberri slipped
along, stopping at the domed settlements, loading, off-loading,
staying a few hours, starting on again, until they came to a
collection of domes a dozen times larger than the others.
When they were tied to the wharf, the Captain came out and
announced they were staying for three days. The deck passengers would have to go ashore and find accommodation there,
but should be back on board by dawn three days hence.

"As cabin passengers you and Pegwai are free to stay
aboard," the Captain told Skeen, "but you might be more
comfortable in one of the Wayfarer's Domes. Timka will stay
with me."

Pegwai and Skeen wandered through the crowded spaces
between the Nests. Small black Skirrik darted everywhere,
the size of large dogs; their constant chatter made an ache in
Skeen's head though she could hear very little of it.

"Neuters," Pegwai said. "Do most of the scut work. Not
very intelligent, but lots of energy."

A huge old male, his carapace glittering with jet, its greenish brown darkened to old bronze, sat in one of the larger
commons, playing an intricate stringed instrument, using three
of his forelimbs to produce a strong rhythmic music that
served as background to the words he declaimed. Off to one
side four young females were ignoring his words but dancing
to the music. A fifth was tapping against her chitin and
improvising a pattersong that had the dancers and the young-
sters (a mix of male and female) gathered about them giggling and clicking their grippers in appreciation. Pegwai led
Skeen through a market where a thin scatter of Balayar and
Chalarosh mixed with the Skirrik and did their bargaining in
Trade-Min. He ambled along at Skeen's side, amused by her
fascination with everything around her, particularly some
free-form wood sculptures whose tight grain had been rubbed

and waxed until it had a wonderful luster. "They grow those," he said, "not a touch of a chisel anywhere."

"I know two men and a sinalure, any one of them would pay the price of Terwel's ship for that. Djabo! To see all this and take nothing away. . . ."

"Dissarahnet is a Skirrik scholar at the Lumat. A good friend. I talked to her about finding Ykx. No, no, she won't chatter. Not outside the Lumat, and what's so secret about a Scholar hunting Ykx? Her bodymother is one of the High Mothers in the Nests here at Istryamozhe. If Ramanarrahnet chooses to listen to her daughter, she can give us an introduction into Atsila Vana that will make a large difference in how we are received."

SKIRRIK: Their nest domes are made of macerated wood treated with a hardener to waterproof them; they are bunched together like clusters of soapbubbles, each cluster a separate Nest. They are light and airy inside, with drafts that move gently but constantly through the complex structure, carrying with them the fresh green smells from the many small gardens and fountains scattered about the knobby complex of openface rooms and the walkways that are made from a lacy webbing that looks fragile but is capable of supporting the weight of the oldest and heaviest females. Plants grow everywhere, some throwing out blooms, some producing brilliantly colored galls, pods, nodules, or seeds. Except around the fountains, these plants are gathered in clusters like highly colored abstract tapestries, living tapestries that change day by day as parts grow, mature, die, are removed, and replaced. The changes are coaxed and guided by individuals who live near the clusters. Skirrik see no need for privacy, though each has territorial rights to specific corners of the Nest and each spends time and effort making his or her corner both recognizably separate from the nearby areas and recognizably his or hers. The neuters have their own separate society and customs that rarely agree with or impinge on those

of the males, the breeding females, or the non-breeding
females who act as neuters but are not—their state
being a choice usually taken because they are too busy
and interested in what they occupy themselves with to
take time out for the debilitating process of producing
eggs. Also they tend to lack ambition; the road to power
among the Skirrik is motherhood. Female minds shut
down when the body is gravid, female bodies go into a
torpor that lasts until the eggs are expelled. But the
breeding female is a nexus of relationships that give her
constituencies that make the sacrifice worth while; the
greater the number of males mated with, the wider her
net is thrown. An average laying produces five fertile
females, two fertile males, eight or ten neuters. A special
cadre of neuters, the elite among them, tend the brooding mothers, wash and wipe them, feed them, give them
drink, treat them like mindless infants for the six months
the brooding lasts.

Pegwai and Skeen followed the immature female through
the complex interior of the nest to an airy chamber near the
apex of the largest dome. The room swam with sunlight. A
huge female sat in the sac-like open space, her carapace a
purple so dark it was nearly black, only the sliding highlights
as she moved testifying to the true color. The chitin on her
upper body was elaborately inlaid with amethyst and ivory
until it seemed she wore jeweled armor. Like all mated
females, her antennas were a matte black, rising over her
head in graceful arcs, so fine at the tips they were more like
stiff thread. They swayed as she moved her great head,
swayed when she was still, touched by the circling air currents. The walls of the chamber were a mosaic of mosses,
greens and ochers, winding threads of vermilion and garnet.
A subtle varying of textures wove a secondary pattern across
the pattern of the colors. The old female (High Mother
Ramanarrahnet) was working on more of the mosses, using
tools with points so fine she wore magnifying lenses over her
triune eyes. Ferns swayed about her head, providing a lacy
sweet-smelling shade.

Their guide scurried over to the High Mother and skritched at her, more than half of what she said inaudible to the visitors. Ramanarrahnet took off the goggles and turned to gaze at Pegwai. When she spoke, her voice was full and rich though she had a little trouble with her plosives, but her Trade-Min was clear and easily understood. "Pegwai Dih, young Helsi tells me you bring news of Daughter Scholar Dissarahnet."

Pegwai bowed low, held out with both hands the thick packet he'd brought from the ship.

High Mother Ramanarrahnet took the packet and slit it open with the claw at the end of one of her grippers and scanned the looping scrawl that made bold patterns on the shiny surface of the pale gray sheet. When she was finished, she eased herself about, settled her large stiff body more comfortably for talking. A number of the small black neuters came rushing in, helped her shift her legs, moved her worktable out of the way, brought cushions to tuck around her until they were satisfied she was settled properly, then they vanished as quickly as they'd arrived.

"Daughter Scholar Dissarahnet tells me you go on a long and difficult journey and solicits my easing your way by whatever means I can. We will speak of this in a nush or so. Tell me Scholar Dih, my daughter writes that she is well, but she'd never worry an aged parent. Is she content and healthy?"

"High Mother, the Scholar Dissarahnet sings when she rises and pursues her studies with the enthusiasm I am sure you remember. She has an ache or two in the joints on cold damp days, but so do I. It's merely a question of advancing age and bodies starting to wear out, nothing more. The Nest at the Tanul Lumat is well cared for, the nidlings you send to serve the Nest and the Scholars do their work well and without fuss. You may rest easy, High Mother, the Daughter Scholar Dissarahnet is healthy for her age and content with her life."

"You reassure me, Scholar Dih, for which I give you many thanks. Lifefire send you success in all you do. What can the Skirrik of Istryamozhe do to forward your journey?"

"Your kind wishes, High Mother, and perhaps a letter of introduction to a High Mother in Atsila Vana, asking for her favor and reassuring her that my companion and I will do our best not to disturb or bring harm to them.''

"Yes. What this one can do, Scholar Dih, this one is happy to do." She turned her head with a spate of Skirrik speech sent young Helsi scurrying out. She turned back, bent her soft triune gaze on Pegwai. "The Ykx, Scholar Dih? You seek them in Atsila Vana?''

"There's a report of a Gather on the shores of the Coraish Sea.''

"I have heard that said; I have also heard that the Gather is empty, but that is a rumor of a rumor. I will not say don't go, I will say go prepared for disappointment.''

"Even an empty Gather is worth seeing.''

Skeen stopped listening as Pegwai and the High Mother began talking about matters she had no interest in. She moved a step to one side and began examining the nearest of the moss mosaics, discovering that the mosaic had a double pattern, the abstract flow of the colors and the figurative arrangement of the textures. If she looked very carefully and endeavored to blot out the play of color, she could make out the image of a male Skirrik, a full-body portrait. She coveted that living tapestry with a passion all the more powerful because it was so impossible to buy or steal.

The return of the young Skirrik woke her from her frustrated contemplation of the mosses. She looked around to find the High Mother watching her with complacent interest, wondered briefly if she was expected to say something, but in the end kept her silence and waited. It was a fairly safe rule that the powerful of whatever species considered it their prerogative to begin and end all conversations.

"What you see there, Seeker, is a twenty-summer tapestry. My final mate.''

"What I see there, High Mother, is a marvel that would grace an emperor's walls. I sigh because such a wonder will never be mine.''

"If you wish instructions for the making of your own, Seeker, I will be pleased to give them.''

"Alas, High Mother, I never stay in one place long enough for such a work to root.''

"It seems it's often so among your kind, Seeker." A deep chuckle that sent the ferns to quivering. A gesture of a forearm, sweeping along her massive form. "I am far too unwieldly to engage in such dartings about." She turned to Helsi and spoke briskly for a short time. The young Skirrik produced a pad and stylus and began writing rapidly as the High Mother dictated to her; when the letter was finished, she knelt and held it out. Ramanarrahnet took it, read it over, reached out and took the stylus a neuter was holding up. Skeen blinked—the little Skirrik appeared so suddenly it seemed to materialize out of the air. The High Mother signed the letter, folded it into a small packet, reached out again, received a moistened wafer, and used it to seal the packet. A flicker, a faint rustle, and the neuter vanished again. The High Mother held the packet lightly, looked from Skeen to Pegwai, a pensive tilt to her head. After a brisk nod in answer to whatever question she was considering she shot an order at the guide, moved restlessly in her cushions. The neuter popped in again, this time with a glass globe filled with a transparent liquid; it held the globe up while the High Mother sipped at a long bent glass straw. Skeen glanced at Pegwai; he was standing with his hands clasped behind him, looking sleepy and endlessly patient. She sighed and reached for her own patience.

Sounds from outside the chamber. The High Mother pushed away the globe, straigtened up a little. "Scholar Dih, I have a favor to ask."

Three young Skirrik came in, the immature female and two even younger males, antennas milk white, their only jet the birth gift triangle that one wore set in the chitin of his head, the other on a silver chain about his neck.

"Milgara Rahneese," the High Mother said, "daughter's son, her final brood." The male with the jet on his head bowed, said nothing. "Chulji Sipor, rahnaffiliate honored friend Sanasa." The male with the jet on a chain bowed, said nothing. "As a service for a service I ask you Scholar Dih to take these youths with you to the Nests at Atsila Vana. It's time they started earning jet. In return for their passage and your care of them, I offer this," she held up the packet, "a letter to Demmirrmar, High Mother of Nest Irrmar, with a request that she tell you all she can discover about the Gather on the Ykx on the Coraish coast and facilitate your visiting that Gather whether it be occupied or empty.''

Pegwai glanced at Skeen. She grinned and nodded, amused by collecting another brace of stragglers to add to her companions. ''One can bunk with me,'' she said, ''the other with you.''

The lands changed, the fields became woodlands, the woodlands gradually turned to wetlands as the meanders of the river grew broader and more frequent; the only times it ran fairly straight were when it cut across oxbows. Pools of water glinted among the trees; after a while water spread in sheets deep into the forest. The air thickened, clouds of small biting insects swarmed everywhere, what breeze there was carried the stench of ancient mud and rotting water. The deck passengers were subdued, they burned piles of ashishin leaves on the braziers and produced clouds of pungent smoke that gave some relief from the biters and almost none for the lungs. After three days of stifling claustrophobic creep along that green-brown flood, the woodland began thinning, replaced by vast stretches of reeds, open water, scrub, giantfern, scattered hummocks of low many-trunked twisty trees, with fragments of other life appearing and vanishing among them, the rutted backs of large reptiles, fish and eels leaping to catch a breath from water thick enough to walk on.

The main current began to split and diverge. The Captain sent two crew out ahead in a small boat with sounding lines and edged along behind them, holding the Meyeberri back with drag anchors. ''The bottom here changes almost hour to hour,'' he told Skeen. ''We'll be picking up Nagamar pilots soon, when we make the first village.''

The village was built on large and small islands of matted reed, some of the islands with smaller less complex versions of Duppra Mallat's reed palace, other islands with small somnolent cattle, dogs, tamed reptiles, other livestock. The Nagamar poled from island to island, kneeling in shallow reed boats, darting about like waterbugs skating over a pond

surface. Children splashed in and out of the water, agile as
their pets, looking half fish with the water gleaming on their
softly scaled skin. Not a word or shout or laugh out of them.
Skeen was amazed until she saw the flashing wiggles of
fingers, hands, arms, the eloquent twisting of faces, a silent
language to maintain their privacy before strangers. The Captain called the sounders back, and began bargaining with the
Nagamar who scooted toward the ship in their kneelboats,
shouting names, offers.

The pilot he closed with brought on board four others;
Terwel Mo was annoyed—two was customary, four was an
imposition, but he didn't argue. He knew better. The Nagamar
were touchy and if his pilot refused to guide him, no other
would take her place; more than that—he'd be jeopardizing
his access to the Rekkah for several years, perhaps forever,
depending on the influence of this pilot and the degree of her
vindictiveness.

The extra two were tall tough females. The moment Skeen
saw them, she knew why they'd come aboard; if she'd had a
hope otherwise, the way they looked at her would have
erased it. Cool, calm, measuring, giving nothing away. She
gave them back the same with an additional touch of bland
and beaming vacancy, and was quietly delighted that the
Skirrik male had his pallet in her cabin, that Timka slept with
the Captain and kept the stolen gold under the Captain's bed
behind a door that locked. Maybe I should borrow your
crystal diviner, little Seer. Caution does have its points.

When she strolled to her cabin on the second night after
they picked up the pilots, she caught one of the Nagamar
searching her cabin, mimed anger and ordered the woman
out. A long insolent inspection, hair to heels, then the Nagamar
left.

In the morning, Skeen warned Timka to be sure the gold
was well hid, in case the Nagamar managed to get into the
Captain's quarters. Not likely but they certainly had the gall
to try.

With one Nagamar swimming ahead, the second at the
wheel, the ship moved swiftly through the wetlands; other
reed villages were visible at some distance, but the Captain

called for no stops until he reached the mouth of the river and
the largest of the marsh settlements, a city not a village.
Standing at the rail, the Aggitj crowded around her, Skeen
saw her second queenhouse, a huge edifice of reeds woven,
bound, braided, compacted. The Captain dropped anchor,
the deck passengers scurried about, the evil-tempered Chalarosh and other cabin passengers had their goods on deck,
there since first light that morning. As soon as the sails
came down, the waters swarmed with reed boats loaded
with:

  perfume, essences, drugs, pearls, feathers, live birds, furs,
  reptile skins, meat, dried seeds, liqueurs, lengths of cloth,
  art objects.

their paddlers seeking:

  blades, axes, machetes, spear heads, cooking pots, char-
  coal braziers, beads, glassware, bottles, mirrors, silk from
  desert looms, damasks from the Lumat, batiks from the
  Balayar.

The pilots and the spares stayed below out of sight until
dark, continued to linger as long as they could push it,
left reluctantly. Skeen hunted them out and made sure the
Captain knew they were aboard; they ignored his annoyed
questions, went over the side with silent ease, no protest
but resentful last looks at Skeen. They'd found no evidence
she was the one who invaded Duppra's House. She watched
them drop into empty kneelboats, sighed with relief and
exasperation as they paddled off. And decided she'd better
spend the night patrolling the rails to make sure they didn't
come back.

Shortly before dawn she stood close to the mainmast,
hidden in the shadow there, the moon still up but just barely.
She heard a soft chunk, not enough to alert the two sailors
standing guard, one on the quarterdeck, the other in the bow,
or the sleeping deck passengers. Bona Fortuna touching her

on the shoulder for once, Skeen happened to be looking in the direction the sound came from and saw the small grapnel bite into the wood. A shaggy head followed almost immediately. Before the intruder was high enough to swing over the rail, Skeen called out, "Come farther, whoever you are, and I'll drop you before you get one foot on deck."

At her first word, the form went still, by the time she finished the sentence, it disappeared. She heard two very faint splashes, then nothing more.

"What is it?" The guard on the quarterdeck called down to her.

"Nothing now. Stickyfingers, most like, not waiting to explain."

"Fuckin' frogs."

There was more stirring, muttered complaints as peddlers and small merchants riding the Meyeberri's deck roused themselves to guard their goods from any return of the rousted thieves. Skeen looked around and decided she could leave angry traders to keep the watch and get some sleep herself. She was tired and bored, the edge gone off her alertness because she was reasonably certain the Nagamar wouldn't be back.

With dawn's first stain, the Captain upped anchor and started across the Tenga Bourhh, heading for Rood Meol and the multi-city Atsila Vana.

THESE MIN, THESE MIN!
or
NEXT TIME I LEAN AGAINST
A TREE I'M GOING TO PINCH
IT TO SEE IF IT SQUEAKS.

Tenga Bourhh. The Mother of Storms the Balayar called the
stretch of water straddling the equator. It lived up to its name.
They ran into one of the Tenga's offspring a little after
sundown. The crew fought the wind to tie the stormnets over
the passengerwell and the Captain chased all his cabin
passengers off the deck, ordered them to lock down the storm
plugs and stay put, keeping out of his hair until they passed
out of the storm.

The ship began leaping and cavorting like a drunken mountain goat, the movement sending Skeen's stomach into uneasy
knots. By the time she staggered into her cabin and forced the
door shut, the young Skirrik had tucked himself into the
upper bunk and was very quiet, even managing to look a bit
limp despite his rigid exoskeleton. Poor little nit, looks like
he feels worse than me—and me, I feel like the ash-end of a
three-day drunk. She jerked the plug from its spring clamps
and slammed it into the windowhole, but not before she got a
face full of icy spray. Working by touch, she brought the
hasps around and clanked home the pins that locked them in
place. Slammed from wall to wall, floor dropping on her

then threatening to slam into her chin, she staggered to the
bunk and sat clutching the end post and contemplating the
fuzzy blackness about her. Wonder how long this lasts. She
swallowed experimentally, then swallowed again. Djabo, dry
land for me. Can't believe I was complaining so much about
a silly little thing like humidity. At least the ground was
steady under me.

She heard a groan. Poor kid, he sounds bad. Wonder if
Skirrik vomit? Djabo, his head's this end, maybe I better take
a look. No looking in this mess, where's that fuckin' lamp.
Ah. She used her cutter to light the lamp, being in no mood
to fuss about with wet matches even if she could find them,
turned the wick way down, uncertain about the wisdom of a
fire in these conditions, then staggered back to the bunk.

The Skirrik was gathered into a miserable knot, his six
limbs tucked up tight against his segmented body; he was
being slammed from sideboard to wall, rolling helplessly,
groaning, the breath whistling painfully through his spiracles.
Every time he hit, it sounded to Skeen like the times she'd
used a small wooden mallet to break lobster claws; she
winced, then eased herself down and pulled off all the blankets from her bunk. With a great deal of difficulty, she
managed to get a little padding between him and the wall,
then between him and the sideboard that kept him from
rolling completely out of the bunk. He still rocked and groaned,
but the ominous crashing sounds were gone. She put her hand
on his thorax, tried to steady him. "Chulji, Chulji Sipor,
what do you need, how can I help you?"

He heard her. The sound of her voice triggered a shout,
then he convulsed. And shifted. Min. What the. . . . He
began shuddering and shifting from shape to shape to grotesque blends of the basic forms he could take. The changes
quickly became so violent, the groans so wrenching that
Skeen was afraid he was dying. She chewed on her lip.
Nothing she tried helped him. Bathing his face or whatever it
was showed up in the convulsions. Talking to him. Holding
him. He just got worse. Cursing under her breath, she hauled
herself along the bed, got the door open and fought her way

to the Captain's quarters. She beat on the door, praying to a hundred gods that Timka wasn't sick, too.

Timka looked a bit pale, but she was on her feet and her shape was holding steady. "Skeen, what. . . ."

"Chulji. I just found out he's Min. He's really sick, Timmy. Shifting all over the place, like he's tearing himself apart. I don't know what to do."

Timka frowned. "I think I know what . . . go on back, I'll be with you in a minute."

Timka looked at the convulsing boy for a moment and touched him, her hand twitching in time with his shifts. She bought out a metal object like a small tuning fork, struck it against the bed post and put the stem against his head when the boy went through a momentary and partial Skirrik phase. He shuddered and became mostly Skirrik though his extremities kept mutating through stranger and stranger shapes. She talked to him with voice and whatever else it was Min used to communicate voicelessly with Min, striking the fork over and over again, touching him over and over with its stem. Gradually the convulsions slowed, gradually the violence of the changes lessened, gradually the groans quieted; the boy calmed. Sweating, her weariness showing after an hour of this, Timka brought the boy into his Skirrik shape and kept him in it until the ship left the storm behind.

She collapsed against Skeen when the boy finally threw off his seasickness and slipped into a deep sleep. Shuddering, limp and exhausted, she let Skeen ease her down onto the lower bunk and bring her cup after cup of water. Finally she sighed, dipped her fingers into the cup and splashed a few drops of the lukewarm water onto her face. She smiled wearily. "Now you'll know what to do if it happens to me."

"That likely?"

"No. He doesn't have a waterform yet, when he does he won't have to worry about sea Choriyn."

"You've a dolphin shape, why'd you say what you did?"

"There are many Chorinyas. A Min never knows what will provoke a Choriyn until it happens." She smoothed her small hand across Skeen's brow, wiping away the scowl. "No, my

Pass-Through friend, the past doesn't count, each Min has different sensibilities." She yawned, got heavily to her feet. "Time I was getting back."

"What do I do when he wakes?"

"Send him to me." Timka moved her shoulders, passed her hand over her sweaty hair. "The main thing is to get food into him, to replace the flesh he lost. He'll be rattling inside the shell for a day or so."

"Got you." After Timka left, pulling the door shut with a weary thunk, Skeen swung her booted feet onto the bunk and stretched out on the denuded pallet. She punched the pillow into the proper shape and considered getting undressed. It didn't seem worth the trouble. Before she finished that thought, she was asleep.

HERE WE ARE IN ATSILA VANA, ANOTHER LEG OF THE QUEST COMPLETED. DON'T EXPECT MUCH, THESE THINGS ARE ALWAYS MORE COMPLICATED THAN THEY FIRST SEEM.

Seven days and two storms later, the Meyeberri dipped around the lefthand wing of a massive seawall and dropped anchor at the walled-off Freeport section of Atsila Vana. The two parts of the sea wall were built several millennia before

by Skirrik, Aggitj, and Balayar under the direction of Funor
engineers hired by the Chalarosh; in partial payment for their
labor the four Waves were given freehold rights to sections of
land about the bay. As she walked off the Meyeberri, Skeen
saw Funor garden roofs rising over Funor walls, Aggitj
castles, Balayar stilt houses, their extravagant colors glittering in the sunlight, tight packed Skirrik domes, and across the
bay, the white peaks of Chalarosh stone tents.

She waited on the wharf while the Captain argued in
mutters with Timka. He wanted her to stay with him, had
been spending the last two days working on her, growing
more and more hostile to Skeen as Timka smiled and patted
him and agreed with everything he said but would not commit
to stay. Now he was waving his arms about, struggling to
keep his dignity intact but on the verge of exploding.

Pegwai left the Aggitj and the Skirrik boys, strolled over to
her. "She could do worse. Has done. The Poet."

Skeen grunted.

"You think she won't stay with him."

"She likes him."

"Then why. . . ."

"If she stays, he'll likely be killed. At least hurt."

"The Poet? You're beyond his reach. Way beyond."

"Hm. No. Mintown."

"Why?"

"Craziness. Hate. Ask Timka."

Timka gave up trying to soothe him and walked away,
moving quickly so he wouldn't put his hands on her and try
to hold her with them since his words couldn't. She'd got
fond of him, but she was Min, he Nemin; get him into his
home islands and see how loving he'd be. When she ran
from Telka's spite, she learned painfully and early just how
much Nemin promises meant, especially the ones men made
to her. No matter how much good will there was in the homes
where she stayed, and there was good will though she forgot
that often enough in the depths of rage, she was never
accepted with the unthinking freedom of the born Nemin; she
was always the outsider, always the one the others made

allowances for, always the one who made them feel uncomfortable when some local bigot got up on his hoofs and held forth on the disgusting and possibly dangerous habits of those animals the Min.

Skeen nodded to her, and started off, following Pegwai who was walking beside the two Skirrik boys, talking quietly to them. Timka stepped in behind Skeen, the tail of the parade, watching the narrow back of the tall Pass-Through. Muscles like wire, about as feminine as a sword. Odd woman. Interesting. Answered to no one. Timka thought back to her outburst in Oruda, wrinkled her nose. I'm going with her—she promised to take me and I'm going to hold her to that.

The Min-Skirrik boy troubled her, shook the steadiness of her intent because he offered her the kind of sanctuary she was ranting about back there. Among the Skirrik, far as she could tell from that brief visit, there was no Min-Nemin jangling. Min-Skirrik were everywhere, all ages, deeply involved in nest life. If she found a Skirrik-form, maybe Telka would let her be. No. No. No. She knew Telka's will, strong as sword-steel and more lasting, knew it because she shared it, as she shared most everything else Telka was. There was no place on Mistommerk, no matter how far she ran, where Telka would leave her in peace. She didn't understand Telka's hatred; why was her sister so adamant about erasing her? Timka didn't care that she had a duplicate with her abilities, almost her mind, who could match her form for form, each form as identical as the shape they were budded in. She'd never liked Telka much, knew the feeling was reciprocated, but there was plenty of room in the mountains, they didn't have to come near each other. The budding; perhaps that was what did it, that twin budding, that splitting in half of the primal bud. Twins were rare among the Min and always trouble; Timka ripened in the normal way and broke from their mother with no problem, but Telka clung and sucked life from her weeks beyond her time, nearly killed her, had to be separated by surgery, had fought the separation with a violence incredible in such a tiny, wholly instinctual being. Sucking and sucking and sucking substance from their mother until the knife did what the midwife couldn't.

Telka was a whiny difficult baby, Timka started enjoying life the moment she was a separate being. Their mother loathed them both. By the time they were old enough to understand a few things, both children knew that their mother wouldn't stay in the same room with them beyond the time needed for her to secrete the gel that they needed to grow and be strong. Their father was indifferent until their talents began to manifest, then he began planning how to use them in his drive for power. Telka's obsession was equal to his, that too manifested early. He preferred her to the sunnier and more indolent Timka, kept Telka with him most of the time. They liked the same tricks, they had the same skewed outlook, they had the same ambition to control every aspect of life about them. Timka rebelled against their attempts to control her, despised their attitudes and goals. And showed that all too often when she was young. She endured spite from Telka and disdain from her father, but he didn't mistreat her and if he caught Telka tormenting her, he scolded his favorite, even punished her. Both Timka and Telka understood that it wasn't the malice he was punishing so much as Telka's carelessness in letting the malice show.

Timka hated most of the things her father and her sister made her do, so she did them badly and lied when she was given tasks she found repugnant, things mean to intimidate and frighten people. After a while her father gave up on her, telling her with cold scorn that she was lazy and weak, too stupid to understand the uses of power. He called her ignorant and sly and ungrateful. And he stopped bothering with her. He was not a cruel man. He never beat her or tore her apart in company even when she'd been particularly stupid and incompetent, but he was a cold man. Being around him snuffed her, stifled her spirit, made her act and speak more stupidly than she really was. Her self-esteem sank lower and lower. She couldn't gather enough sense of worth to be angry with him. Telka was different. Telka she could fight and did. Usually with a fair measure of success when her father and his minions weren't around to interfere. Gradually she learned that she was a hair smarter, stronger, and quicker than Telka. More creative. Telka was cold like their father, calculating, rigid in her thought patterns. She had a superb memory, was shrewd enough to compensate for her lack of empathy when she wanted to manipulate people. They meant nothing to her, less than dead leaves, even her father; there was only one person in existence as far as she was concerned—her. When she saw loving gestures, when she saw other folk exhibiting their affections, she thought it was all acting, people using each other. There were a few times when she wondered whether she might be missing something, a few times when she had a tepid wish for some tenderness from someone, but that never lasted more than a breath or two; she thought of it as fools' dreams and worthless.

After her father gave up on her, Timka moved in with Carema, the nurse-midwife-brewer who took care of the twins once they didn't need their mother; she divided her time between learning herb-lore with Carema and running wild in the woods, playing kissy/touchy games with boys from the steadings deep in the mountains. She lagged behind Telka in the finding of her different shapes and the various mind skills Min practiced. Though she had greater natural stamina and scope than her sister, she lacked the will that drove Telka to excel, the vanity that demanded that everyone take note of how much she did excel. If Telka had left her alone, Timka would have vegetated happily in the woods, no rival, no danger to her ambitions, forgotten by everyone except Carema and a few young males. But she was like a sore tooth in Telka's jaw. Telka wouldn't, couldn't, leave her alone. Again and again she forced Timka to act or react, again and again Timka pulled out of her depths resources that turned aside her sister's attacks and taught them both that Timka would always be just that infinitesimal degree better, faster, more capable than Telka.

When she was just past puberty, working contentedly in Carema's compound, Telka tried for the first time to kill her. Timka survived because the attack was so secret it gave her too much room to maneuver, because Telka was forced to use the largest part of her power in concealment, letting Timka scramble free and shield herself. The attack was over in a few breaths, almost a dream. But Timka had tasted the bitter hatred that flavored the fringes of the mindblow and knew who had set at her. Telka's power frightened her; her sister had almost managed to trigger a massive stroke.

Timka said nothing. What could she say? My sister tried to kill me. Why? What did you do to make her act like that? I don't understand it, I don't know why, I think she hates me merely because I exist in the same world with her. No one would believe her. Telka might be cold, but she was admired, she'd learned that a little kindness brought a large return, as long as that kindness was seen but not paraded. She was calm, polite, a model child and young girl, almost (that unfortunate coldness) the daughter that any Min family would pray to have. Timka was careless, passionate, with a temper she too often didn't try to control, she was lazy and wild and had a lot of bad habits with little respect for the authority of her elders. Those who liked her championed her, but she offended more than she charmed and charmed only those wild like her—outsiders, powerless, or the healers and singers, equally powerless. Telka had spent several years sighing over the estrangement between her and her sister, had carefully put about the idea that Timka hated her, had provoked Timka into attacks that appeared to arise from spite and jealousy. Very few would believe Timka if she claimed Telka had tried to murder her.

She went deep into the woodland that night, waking no one, not waiting for dawn or telling anyone where she was going, running on the four feet of her cat form. She curled up in one of her secret nests and tried to think what she could do. Tell Carema, yes, that was the first thing; she shivered and whined in the thick darkness of the lair. No, not the first thing, the last, keep Carema free as long as possible from Telka's menace, tell her because she'd have to fight against rumor and scandal meant to strip respect from her. Telka would have a hard time with that, Carema was tied too deeply into too many lives, but that wouldn't stop her from trying. As long as I'm here, as long as Carema protects me. By dawn all her thinking and squirming was reduced to a single choice: either I stay and die and drag my friends down with me, or I take my chances with the Nemin.

Telka hated and feared Nemin with a fervor she had learned from their father; neither was likely to come after her. Timka thought briefly of trying to find their mother; she had her own fears of Nemin, but Tyamtok Twin-bearer had left the mountains long ago and from what Timka remembered of her she wouldn't welcome either daughter. No, it's Nemin for me.

She woke Carema just before dawn, told her about the attack and what she planned to do. Carema didn't try to talk her around, just dug into her chest and gave Timka a small bag of Pallah coins and a Pallah skirt and blouse, then shifted into horse shape and carried Timka down to the Pallah Plain.

And all that was a score of years ago. Timka looked around her at the noisy melange of types, even wild Funor shorthorns without their robes and cowls, making nuisances of themselves stamping up and down the streets in herds of four or five; a score of years to make her way to Dum Besar, huh. And following Skeen the Pass-Through, she'd made ten times that far in a pair of months. She laughed and felt free again for the first time since she left the mountains, free and wild as those crazy shorthorns.

High mother Demmirrmar was wading about a shallow pool, tending the lilies and reeds growing there. When her cousin's great grandniece brought the visitors, she settled herself on the sandy bottom of the pond and watched them approach, a pair of overblown lilies draped about her neck, muck trailing from the roots at the end of long limp stems, stains meandering through the amethysts and ivory set into her thorax. Her lambent lavender gaze passed mildy over all of them, then she took the packet young Wanasi was thrusting at her, broke it open, and read what Ramanarrahnet had written. When she had finished, she clicked her mouth parts impatiently, tore the paper into long strips, swished them through the water until the ink was blurred into illegibility, handed the strips back to Wanasi. "Put that in the compost heap." She pulled one of the lilies from around her neck, looked at it with a hint of surprise in the set of her head and threw it onto the grass. "Migara Rahneese, Chulji Sipor, be welcome to Atsila Vana." She snapped her grippers and a

dozen neuters trotted up, sank flat to the grass in front of her.
"These will take you to your quarters, show you how to get
on. We have called in a lot of youths this month, you won't
be lonely."

Chulji dropped hastily in a submission crouch. "High
Mother."

She moved her mouth parts in astonishment, arched her
neck. "Eh?"

"With your blessing, High Mother, I would like to continue on with Scholar Dih and the Seeker Skeen. They will
allow this if you consent."

The water rippled and splashed as Demmirrmar jiggled in a
continuing astonishment. "What what, go on with these?
You allow this, Scholar Dih?"

"With your blessing yes, High Mother, without it no.
Chulji Sipor finds our quest something the poets will sing
about, or so he has said to us, and he wishes to find the forms
to conquer the Choriyn that shook him on the way here. For
our part, we find him an amiable youth with talents that could
be useful."

"Hunting Ykx is not the safest of occupations."

"So we said. And he said, outside the Nest what work is
ever safe?"

"His family sent him to me. How can I say to them your
child has died because I let him tie himself to some lika-
brained nonsense like this?"

Chulji quivered impatiently, but had the sense to say nothing. The High Mother arched her neck again and eyed him
skeptically. Pegwai waited in silence. Skeen crossed her arms
over her breasts and watched the clouds float by. The Aggitj
fidgeted nervously; when Chulji felt healthy enough to go on
deck he'd proved a fine listener to their tales and a soul-mate
in some pranks he thought up with them for the time after
they got off the ship, but they'd been trained from birth to
respect their elders and speak when spoken to and not otherwise. Timka watched them all, detached but inclined to sym-
pathize with the young Min. He reminded her a lot of the
boys she'd played games with in the woods what seemed
such a very long time ago.

"Tssssst-tsssst," the High Mother said. "Young idiot, more trouble than he's worth, but if you want him, he's yours. Bring him back whole if you can, no doubt his family will miss him." She stretched over, tapped Chulji's hard exoskull. "Behave yourself and don't bring disgrace on the Nests. Now get out of here and let adults talk in peace." She turned her eyes on the Aggitj. "This will bore you also, Aggitj; why don't you go with these nidlings and plot mischief to make your elders sorry they gave in and hauled you along."

Hal turned to Skeen, she nodded, he grinned, made a graceful deep bow. "With pleasure, Oh Mightiness." The small black neuters fussing about them, the six youths went bouncing out of the garden. As soon as they were hidden by trees and shrubbery, their voices came back with snatches of laughter. Skeen couldn't hear what they were saying, but she suspected they were taking the High Mother's instructions quite happily and planning something she emphatically wanted to know nothing about.

Demmirrmar pulled the second lily from about her neck and tossed it away. "It's hard to break the ties, but necessary." The air whistled through her spiracles in the Skirrik version of a sigh. "Rama tells me you hope to find Ykx in the Coraish Gather; she tells me she warned you the Gather might might be empty. It is. Two tribes of the desert Chalarosh made an arashin-gey against them, a purification sweep, and managed to exterminate all the Ykx left there. They were dying out anyway, don't know why, so the place has been empty the past twenty some years. Looted. Picked over. Anything with a pretense of value has been carried off."

Pegwai moved his feet impatiently. "It's not loot we want, but knowledge. That's even more important now. How long before all the Ykx are gone? What do we know about them? Nothing." He glanced at Skeen, his face red with the passion in him on this subject. She moved close to him, put her hand on his shoulder, squeezed lightly. He calmed, took a deep breath. "I brought an imager with me; even ruins can give us a lot about the Ykx and my companion is learned in the interpretation of such things. Will you help us, High Mother?"

Demirrmar contemplated Timka. "The Min can't go with you. The Chalarosh will never permit that."

Timka chuckled. "Nor am I all that interested in turning over stones in a ruin. I will quite happily remain behind."

Skeen frowned. "Timmy. . . ."

Timka wrinkled her nose, but she'd given up long ago on Skeen's habit with nicknames. "What the Seeker means, High Mother, is that I have bitter enemies among the Mountain Min, particularly one, who would be delighted to catch me alone and undefended."

"Mountain Min," the High Mother said thoughtfully. "We have no commerce with them. Would they really follow you across the Tenga Bourhh?"

"Might. Might not. Depends."

"On what?"

"On how desperate my enemy is. Time works for her if she can wait. We have to go back when the quest is done."

"The Stranger's Gate."

"Yes."

"You won't be particularly comfortable, young Min, but you will be safe staying here. My Nest is yours."

"I thank you, High Mother and accept with pleasure. Chulji and I might teach each other while we wait. He can find the dolphin and I can find the Skirrik."

"Good idea. You can keep that imp out of my webs. On your head not mine, young Min." She turned to Skeen and Pegwai. "Are you weary, must you rest? I would like to hear the tale of the Gate and the Pass-Through and the Ykx; there is no point trying to gain a hearing with the Cadda Kana today, or the Doferethapanad. It's one of their eternal feast days, something to do with a war or a miracle of a well going dry. I've heard explanations of all this todo a thousand times and I still don't understand a word. If it were some sort of carnival and a lot of loud fun, I could begin to understand but the Chalarosh take all of this nonsense so seriously; I hope you are not seriously religious, it gets so tiring trying to grasp the ungraspable." She hauled herself out of the water and stood dripping while a cadre of neuters bustled about her, washing, wiping, polishing. When they were done, she

skritched orders at a handful who darted away while the rest
scurried to their waiting places in the bushes. "I've sent for
some cold ale; story-tellers from other Waves find it oils their
tongues nicely. And there's a pleasant sittage just beyond
where there are benches your kind seem to find comfortable."

Coming before the Cadda Kana. Questions. Interminable
and annoying. Keep your temper, Skeen, you know these
types, outwait them. Permission given to proceed into the
interior. Scholar Pegwai Dih, Lumat Seeker Skeen. Provided
Scholar and Seeker take along a guide and an inlal of klazits
to protect them from the dangers of the countryside. To
protect the countryside from us, Skeen thought. The Aggitj
argument. The boys insisted on going along. Skeen was their
patron, they said; they were oath-fasted to her, bound to
protect her, to fetch and carry for her, to do whatever she
wanted or needed. Muttering among the veiled men behind
the long table on the dais. Permission given. Too easy, Skeen
thought, an inlal of klazits (whatever those are) and a guide;
are we cover for spies? She wasn't happy about the possibility.
The nomads were nasty to intruders. No, she wasn't happy
at all. This could get them all killed; she had no faith in the
understanding or abilities of those fuckin' gits planning to
use them, yes, she was sure of it.

Timka the Min they wanted to put in preventive detention,
but agreed to leave her with the High Mother Demmirrmar
provided she was available for inspection every second day.

Chulji Sipor started to argue he was part of the team now,
but was instantly suppressed by the High Mother. The Kana
didn't know he was Min and she wanted to keep their ignorance intact. You've got studies, she told him. Put your ener-
gies into them.

Petitioners dismissed. Hand on Skeen's arm, holding her
back, escort separating her from the others. There are questions, her detainer said (eyes cold above the veil, voice calm
and unthreatening), as a courtesy to the Cadda Kana, stay and
answer them.

*   *   *

Shortly after dawn on the sixth day after Skeen arrived in Atsila Vana (third day of her interrogation) she was escorted to join Pegwai and the Aggitj and rode with them out the Gamta Telet (the Lake Gate), sitting in a large and remarkably uncomfortable wagon. Pegwai swallowed his questions and dozed beside her, the Aggitj chattered theirs but desisted when they got no answers and occupied themselves with a noisy game of stones and tiles. Two veiled klazits rode on each side of the wagon, a fifth rode ahead of the praks pulling the wagon. Stolid beasts, curlicued horns bent upward in a graceful lyre shape, big brown eyes, massive shoulders, ears that twitched incessantly. It was a splendid day, a little nippy because this was below the equator and the end of winter instead of the end of summer.

An hour later they were herded onto the boat that the Cadda Kana had authorized (though Pegwai had to pay the hire out of Skeen's gold hoard). The guide spoke Trade-Min but not the sailors or the klazits. Chosen for that reason, Skeen thought, so we can't ask dangerous questions or tamper with their loyalties. Wonder if Pegwai speaks Chala, he hasn't shown signs of it so far . . . just as well. Eh, old woman, stop fussing. He's done this before, he knows the pits set for his feet. You're not the only devious bitch around. The Aggitj tucked away their game and looked about with considerable interest, switching from Agga to Trade-Min so they could pester the guide with innumerable questions about the boat and its day to day operation. They had grown up along the coast of the Boot and were on the water before they could walk; they were delighted to be back in a working boat, disregarded the guide's scowls, got his name out of him (Lakin Machimim), and prodded him into translating their questions and the monosyllabic answers they pestered out of the ship's master and his men. Impervious within their calm good nature, caring nothing for opinion outside the Boot, they ignored the hostility of the Chalarosh and by the time the crossing was completed were on easy terms with the boatmen. Even the sullen suspicious guards relaxed a little whenever Machimim took his eyes off them.

They landed near a small village. The men and boys were

out fishing while the women, girls, and youngest children tended water wheels and worked in fields and gardens. "Stay here," Machimim said, "talk to no one. He strode off the shaky dock and went into conference with a self-important type who looked annoyed at first, then obsequious as an oil machine once he got a look at the metal plaque Machimim thrust under his nose.

The ship left, the master glad to rid himself of foreign taint. The Aggitj went back to their game. Skeen and Pegwai strolled to the end of the dock, glanced over their shoulders. The klazits were some distance away, gathered about the Aggitj, watching the play. "All this cooperation," Skeen said, "stinks."

"Worse than a week-old fish." He touched her arm. "I was beginning to worry."

"Oh they were marvelous hosts—very tasty food and plenty of it, gave me privacy, talked soft, but talked all the time. Wanted to know what the hell I was, then when I came through. Lost interest a bit when I told them the Gate was shut. Asked about the other side. I lied a lot." She grinned. "Enjoyed myself, feeding those prickheads that drivel. Wanted to know what the Lumat was doing. Figured I'd better stick with the truth there. Sort of. Said the Lumat was afraid there weren't any more Ykx about and wanted to collect as much data as possible before it was lost. That was so logical they had a hard time believing it. Still, I think they did in the end. Hard to say with those damn veils."

"The High Mother had little Wanasi running all six legs off carrying letters of protest."

"Have to thank her. Even if they didn't bust me loose, I got good food and those vacuum brains didn't go physical on me."

Machimim twisted what they needed out of the headman— five tall ponies for himself and the klazits and two carts, one loaded with water barrels, blankets, and other supplies for their trek through the mountains. The other was empty except for a number of coarsely woven sacks that rustled dryly. The women had vanished with the children, the fields were empty, the waterwheels swayed idly. The oleaginous headman kept

looking at Skeen and the others from the corner of his eyes as
he protested the guide's demands, his pointed ears twitching
as spastically as those of the praks hitched to the carts.
Machimim sent him off with a snapped command, waved the
others into the cart, then mounted the beast one of the klazits
held for him and started off down the rutted single street of
the small village. Two klazits arranged themselves with the
carts between them, spare ponies on a long lead. The other
two climbed to the plank seats of the carts and slapped
ticklers into the rumps of the offside praks, starting the teams
forward, following Machimim through the village.

Skeen, Pegwai, and the Aggitj settled with their personal
gear onto the sacks; they were marginally better than the
stinking planks of the cartbed, but the fiber they were woven
from felt as if it'd been stripped whole off nettle stems; it had
millions of tiny prickles that raised red welts even through a
layer of cloth. By the time they'd left the village behind, Hal
had had enough. When he couldn't make Machimim listen,
he argued the klazits into providing blankets enough to cover
the sacks, using passion and gesture to make up for lack of
language. Pegwai sighed with pleasure and stretched his legs
out; as her burning shins cooled off, Skeen promised herself
she'd find out what Hal wanted most and see he got it.

The road degenerated to a track as the afternoon turned
toward night. Weed-grown and punishing. Not much traffic
here, not for a long time. In spite of the slow jolting progress,
they reached the lower slops of the foothills before the sun
went down and made camp beside a smallish stream. After
the meal, plain but filling, Skeen, Pegwai, and the Aggitj
passed a wineskin around, sang and told stories, watched
from outside the circle of light by the suspicious and grumpy
klazits (with Machimim's eye on them, they didn't dare take
the cups the Aggitj tried to pass to them).

The next day was spent negotiating an impossible track that
the winter storms had eroded into something like a series of
animal traps, potholes that threatened to swallow up one or
both of the carts along with the riders and anything else that
came along. There was a little patchy snow in places where
shadow lingered most of the day but none on the track, and

rockfalls where snow melt had weakened the soil. Klazits and Aggitj labored to clear these, exchanging curses as they wrestled the stones out of the way until Aggitj were mouthing elaborate Chalarosh anathemas and the klazits were tossing rocks aside in tune with staccato Agga obscenities. And while they were riding between the falls, the Aggitj began coaxing names and small phrases out of the guards, at least while Machimim wasn't watching them.

They camped in a barren pass, a cold camp because there was nothing to burn; they chewed on jerky and honeyed nuts, drank sparingly from the wine skin, even more sparingly from the water sacs, most of the water they carried being for the beasts, and rolled quickly into their blankets to escape the bite of the wind that swept without ceasing along the pass. Skeen wanted to sleep in the cart, but Machimim wouldn't permit that, he was enjoying their discomfort, the worm; no, he was going to sleep in the cart alongside the watch so he'd be available in case of trouble. Think of the watch, he said, the poor man will have to stay awake in the cold and the dark, how can you grudge him that miniscule shelter? I can, Skeen thought, oh yes I can. But she didn't argue, not wanting to breathe out the last threads of warmth in her.

The next day was like the last, only worse. Rumbling downhill on a precarious track with inadequate brakes and drivers whose lack of experience was dangerously evident. More rockfalls. And the supply cart got one wheel over the side of a pothole. But they reached the foothills on the far side of the range still intact, though much shaken, and made camp at sundown in a dessicated wadi, a camp as dry as the one in the pass but a lot warmer. The klazits joined their charges at the fire after supper and helped them kill off a wineskin. Pegwai told a Balayar ghost story (which the guide condescended to translate), Skeen dug out her flute and played an accompaniment to a Chala song after she'd caught the gist of it. The Aggitj came to their feet as soon as the song was done and beat a rhythm for her, then did a leaping, stamping dance while she played for them. That night, for the first time (leaving out Machimim who had his responsibilities) the whole party went to sleep wallowing in good feeling for each other.

The next day they left the low hills for a land of gently rolling swells, a brown land, brown up the sides of the mountains to the stony peaks, brown up close, gray-brown, red-brown, hazel, bright brown, dull brown, yellow-brown haze at the horizon blending brown sky and brown earth so that it was impossible to see where one ended and the other began. Around noon they hit a tiny area of living green as refreshing to the eyes as the water of the spring was to their gullets. They refilled the waterskins and the stock barrels, considered camping, but the greater part of the day was ahead of them and Pegwai didn't want to waste a moment of the short exploration time given him, so they went on. More brown—a plethora of browns in a monochromatic landscape. There was plenty of growth, but everything from the patches of brush to the flat succulents were sundried to some sort of brown, most of it a dull beige. What leaves the vegetation sported were smaller than the last joint on a man's little finger, with slick shiny surfaces as if painted with a gray-brown varnish. Lots of long thorns everywhere, thickly set, changing their slant with the change in the altitude of the sun.

Midday on their fourth brown day Machimim led them back into the hills and around the side of a mountain to a narrow wadi by a cliff that rose a steep four hundred meters, its glossy glassy surface, though ancient, still visibly the result of a power cutter sweeping down through the mountain. Interesting, Skeen thought, lost it all? If not, what's the problem? Why couldn't you tromp a bunch of barbarians? A scratchtrail switched back and forth up the slope south of the cliff to meet a horizontal wrinkle drawn across the face around three hundred meters up. Front door? Looks like it. What it'd be to have wings right now.

They stopped at a crude stone fort near the base of the cut. No roof, a head-high circle of stone laid on stone, built by the sedentaries from Atsila Vana when they heard the Gather was empty and came to see if there was anything valuable to be found in the ruins. There was a well inside, a wobbly corral for draft and riding animals, water troughs, feed boxes (after a look at the well and its proximity to the pen, Skeen refused to drink that water; Djabo knows what's waiting there to claw my gut, she said. The Aggitj agreed with her and went off to look for a cleaner source of water plus some firewood). The ground inside the circle was badly littered, but the klazits and Skeen, Pegwai a little later, shamed into helping by Skeen's example, cleared out the bird dung and rotting leaves and bones and prak manure. By the time the Aggitj returned with huge armloads of roots and short limbs and news of a small stream a short way off, the klazits had disinterred two large tents from the load in the second part and were setting them up.

Skeen carried off a waterskin, scrubbed her hands, and splashed more over her face, then drank a long time. She gasped, spat, slipped the skin's strap over her shoulder, glanced at the sun. A little less than three hours before dark. She looked around. The klazits were tangled in ropes and poles and unwieldy canvas, swearing at the tent while Machimim shouted orders at them, the Aggitj keeping out of the brouha; from the grins on their faces, enjoying it thoroughly. She strolled over to Pegwai who was organizing his measuring and recording instruments into the pockets of a broad bandolier. "We could take a look up there while everyone's still busy," she murmured.

"No need to hurry." He continued with his work. "If you think he'll let us go up there without him, you're dreaming. Here." He gave her two sticks of soft white chalk. "And the this." A pressure lantern. He got to his feet, dusted himself off, put his arm through the sling, eased it over his head, patted it into place. "Ready?"

Hands full of chalk and lantern, waterskin bumping against her thigh, Skeen started up the scrawl of the scratchback, moving rapidly, knowing there was nothing waiting for her, but eager to see that nothing for herself. Pegwai followed more sedately, though his desire was scarcely less than Skeen's. Machimim yelled at them, then came charging out of the fort ring and started up after them, cursing under his breath.

The wrinkle was a broad ledge that stuck out like a pouting lip. Skeen moved to the edge of the lip and stood looking out across the brown landwaves that faded imperceptibly into a dusty yellow-brown sky, pausing to catch her breath and organize her thoughts before she plunged into the Gather. Pegwai stumped up to her, the faint sprinkles of sweat on his face and the redness of his dark skin evidence of his exertions. She smiled at him, lost her smile and looked quickly away. The cut along his jaw had healed, only a faint pinkness left, but it was suffused with blood now and looked like a ragged scarlet crescent; she saw the marks of her teeth with embarrassment and shame, as if she'd been suddenly exposed naked to the gaze of the klazits. She turned away from the empty landscape, pumped up the lamp and lit the mantle, then moved cautiously to the large flat oval opening; sometime in the not too distant past the funnel-shaped hole had been closed by a heavy door, deeply carved in bold curved forms. It was relatively intact, lay flat on the stone. Skeen held the lantern close. Those forms were at once totemic and linguistic—and resembled something she'd seen somewhere. The Stranger's Gate? Of course, but that wasn't it. . . . She hesitated, trying to catch the tail of the memory, then straightened and went on; poking at fugitive memories like that never worked. It'd come later or it wouldn't. Pegwai hastened around her, held a small black instrument to his face, fingers flickering a pattern along the side. When he lowered the imager, she walked on, stepping over other fragments of carved stone torn from the stone of the walls. The sides of the broad entranceway were intensively decorated, panels of wood and stone arranged around glass inserts, some few still intact, the rest shattered to show a tracery of painted metallic lines on the back of the shards and some straggles of fine blackened wire.

The corridor bent through a deep double curve then opened into an immense cavern, a wonderland of glass and metal, rooms like bubbles floating in webs of tarnished silver and blued steel. The vast arching hollow was filled with the sounds of running water, with gentle rustles, with bell chimes from long glass tubes swaying in the breezes that wandered through the spaces. She didn't need the lantern. The Gather was full of light. A system of mirrors, many of them still intact, caught light directed onto them from outside through baffled boreholes, amplified it into a soft silvery glow, enough to illuminate the broken magic of the place. Beside her she heard the whistle of Pegwai's indrawn breath. "What they took," she said, "is trivial compared to what they left." From where she stood she could see a thousand things she'd cut free and haul off if this were a world in her home universe and Picarefy waited outside with the androids set to load her up.

"Hard to know where to start." Pegwai rubbed his hand across his chin. "Lifefire, I could spend a year in this Gather and only begin the survey."

"I suppose we ought to dip into each section and make a rough plan of the way things are arranged." She spoke absently, her mind invaded once again by that flickery uncatchable memory.

Behind them, the guide leaned against the wall with bored indifference. The only secrets that interested him were those in men's heads and between women's legs, not those hidden here, living in these half-shattered artifacts. All this puttering about ruins made him intensely suspicious of the motives of these strangers, though that wasn't his primary reason for being here.

"It would take years to really strip this place," Skeen said, "but it would be worth the time, so much to learn. Is there a chance the Lumat will invest that time?"

Pegwai's eyes caressed the ruins with an avidity equal to hers though not quite the same. "All I can do is gather images," he said finally. "As many images and measurements as we can manage and hope they convince where words wouldn't. Though money's tight. . . ." He sneaked a glance at her, mischief in his eyes.

She caught the gleam and chuckled, then remembered the guide and bit back what she'd been about to say. She pinched his arm. "Let's look about and get some idea how we're going to work this."

They worked for a sennight in the ruined Gather—all that Machimim would allow them—Skeen sketching, noting down dimensions, making charts, Pegwai storing images in the multi-faceted crystals he loaded into the imager. Each night he projected what he'd taken and erased those that were unsatisfactory (delighting the Aggitj who'd never seen such a thing and waking envious desire in Machimim). Skeen took Pegwai aside the morning after the first showing and warned him to keep a tight hold on his equipment, otherwise it might disappear somewhere between the Gather and Atsila Vana.

During the first few days Machimim had followed them about interrupting constantly to ask what they were doing, what was that they were holding, why were they interested in this other bit of debris. Since their answers were I don't know, or it has an interesting look, or this is part of that and I haven't the faintest notion what that is, he got rapidly bored with poking about and left them in peace. On the third day it was one of the klazits who followed them into the Gather; Machimim vanished and didn't return until long after dark. Skeen was coming back from the stream, towel over her shoulder, when he rode in; she ignored him until he strode over, caught her by the arm, and shouted into her face, ''Where have you been?''

She jerked loose. ''Bathing,'' she said. ''Something I don't care to do in male company. Good evening.'' She moved briskly away from him and went into the tent she shared with Pegwai and the Aggitj. Shit, she thought, he's just stupid enough to get caught and then where'll we be.

Pegwai and Skeen worked long hours that sennight, doing their best to get as comprehensive an overview as they could, expecting any moment a horde of angry Chalarosh to descend on them with Machimim's head on a spear, intent on acquiring their heads to parade about. The Ykx had a curiously skewed technology. They were deep into solid state mechanisms, but had almost no transport beside their ability to soar. Their living quarters were primitive, lit by mirrors; simple furniture built, it looked, with hand tools, not even nails but wood dowels and glue—rather odd looking but it had to accommodate those soaring skins that were attached to arm, side, and leg. There were a number of dun-colored blobs about which looked a lot like prak turds until Skeen picked one up. Triggered by the warmth of her hand, perhaps its oils, it changed. Opaline colors glowed and flowed along the mutating forms. She watched, entranced, until she heard the sound of boots behind her; hastily she set the thing down and watched it collapse.

"What you got?" The klazit picked up the dull blob; it didn't wake for him. His pointed ears twitched, his nostrils flared in disgust; he flung it at the wall and snuffled with satisfaction as it shattered and the shards flew all over.

Skeen clasped her hands behind her, fought back the need to fling him after the loveliness he'd destroyed. "Don't know," she said. She tried to keep her voice calm, even, but his eyes narrowed for a moment and he looked dangerous. Deliberately he searched about, found another of the blobs and shattered it also.

Pegwai came round the corner, saw her face, saw the klazit looking around for something else he could break. "What?"

"That cretin is having a glorious time breaking things."

Pegwai exploded. With a flood of elementary Chala, he chased the klazit out of the Gather and shouted him into a huddle on the lip. Breathing hard, he came stumping back to Skeen. "What did he break? Is it completely destroyed or can it be glued together?"

Skeen was on her knees collecting the shards, picking them up, putting them down when they didn't unfold for her. She pushed the hair from her face. "Impossible to tell you, you have to see. . . ." She pointed. "There in the corner, that thing like a turd." She started to rise then sank back on her heels. "Bring it here, will you? I want to see if. . . ."

Pegwai raised both brows, but he went to fetch the blob. When he lifted it from the debris, it began the shift and flow of form and color, this one primarily golden where the first had been keyed to green. Pegwai stopped in the middle of the floor and stared. After a moment, he began stroking the curves and found he could influence the shift with gentle pressure and prods of a finger. With a hiss of indrawn breath he squatted and set the thing down, watched it revert to its inert form. "He saw this and broke it?"

"No. The sculptures didn't come to life for him, just you and me."

"Two gone. Lifefire!"

"Yes. If he picked up another, I'd have cut his stupid throat."

"Just as well you didn't. I'll talk to Machimim tonight. Either they keep their hands off, or the klazits will have to stay outside. Umm, we won't mention these, I think."

"Huh! Peg, if you did, I'd think you'd gone soft in the head."

"Hm. A blanket. Yes, cut into squares and wrapped around them . . . safe from breaking that way. And they won't activate, at least I hope not. If Machimim saw that. . . ."

"Right."

Pegwai spoke to Machimim and Machimim tore a strip off the klazit, but he refused to station the guards outside the cavern. At least they kept their hands to themselves after that. Weren't happy about it. They resented the reprimand from Machimim, were nasty to the Aggitj who knew nothing at all about what happened, took to breathing nasally down Pegwai's neck, watching Pegwai and Skeen every minute, cat at mousehole, waiting for the slightest off-color act. Even when Skeen went for her bath, she had to take the Aggitj along to stand guard. Djabo only knew what those subnorms would try if they got her alone.

Bored with poking about the cavern, ostracized by the klazits, the Aggitj roamed about the slopes, moving for the sake of moving, sometimes hunting coneys and larger game to supplement the interminable dried fish, porridge, and honeyed nuts. Machimim warned them it was dangerous to go wandering about country they didn't know, they might hand their heads to a nomad hunter if they were unlucky. But he put no restrictions on them; he was having trouble enough keeping order in the camp since he was gone most of the day snooping about the countryside.

On the fifth day Skeen noticed a suppressed excitement about the boys. They were up to something. She thought about calling them on it, but there was never an opportunity to speak without Chalarosh ears flicking nearby. The klazits weren't supposed to know Trade-Min, but she was beginning to think they'd played her for a fool and weren't nearly as ignorant as they pretended. That night as she was returning to camp from her bath, she put her hand on Hal's arm and drew him into step with her. "There's an Aggitj settlement in Atsila Vana," she murmured.

The moon was up and bright enough to show her the puzzlement on his face. "Yes?"

"Seems to me a spy's not worth much if he doesn't know the language of the folk he's spying on."

He thought about that a moment, then he grinned and patted her arm. "Gotcha."

She left him at the opening in the circle, stood a moment watching the four boys trotting away. Must be delayed mother instinct. Have to take something for it; get rid of this infection fast or I've got a plague on my hands. Shaking her head, she ducked into the tent and crawled into her blankets. Two more days. She wriggled about trying to find a comfortable position on the hard earth. Djabo bless, I wish we were leaving tomorrow. This is a waste of time, there's nothing here for me. What in Mistommerk will make the Ykx open the Gate for me?

"Rallen," she cried.

"What?" Pegwai came across to her, looked at the small metal plaque she was holding. Waves of a soft pastel blue hardly darker than the material were flowing in interference patterns from her fingers. Dark blue lines flickered in and out of existence, a simply sketched figure of a soaring man. "That's a lovely thing."

She didn't hear him. She was light years gone, sitting in the Roost waiting for the Buzzard to finish with another client. In his workroom because he trusted her and she didn't want company. A pile of artifacts on a table. Playing with them to pass the time. A metal rectangle cold and heavy in her hands. Watching waves of pale blue wash out from her fingertips over glyphs, yes yes, like those on the door and the figure of what she thought then was a winged man. Angel or demon. She closed her eyes, tried to recall what else the table held. Yes yes. I'm sure of it. A dull dun blob. I remember wondering what that was doing with the other things. Why would the Buzzard buy a coprolite? What else, what . . . Djabo, how long has it been? Four years? Five? No, almost seven years. Buzzard came in, saw me playing with the plaque. Rallen work, he said. Rallen? I said. Don't ask me, he said. Kid who sold me the stuff says that's the world name, won't say where it is. What kid? I said. He grinned and asked what I had for him. Rallen. Rallen. Somewhere on the other side, there's a world where Ykx still live. Yes. That wasn't from any ruin, none of it. Rallen. . . .

A band of nomad Chalarosh were hanging about. Late on the sixth day they came up to the fort. The leader talked to nervous klazits while others of the band wandered about poking into everything, kicking at the blankets in the tents, jabbing knives into the sacks padding the cart that carried the foreigners, prying up the tarp over the supply cart, taking the lids off all the waterbarrels. When they were finished looking into every cranny big enough to hold a rat, they went charging up the scratch trail; the klazits grinned at each other and slipped away into the brush, not wanting to be there when the intruders came back by the camp.

The Aggitj watched all that, snorting with disdain as they saw the klazits vanish. When the nomads stomped into the cavern and went crashing about searching for something, the boys followed them looking curious and secretly amused. Skeen watched them and worried. They had it, whatever the nomads were searching for. They knew what it was and they had it squirreled away somewhere. She cursed under her breath, then wrenched her mind away from those beaming idiots and frowned at the panel in front of her. It was in fragments. She'd assembled them, fitting the bits together using the design carved on the front. A complex ideogram. Possibly the Ykx thought in multileveled gestalts that interacted with a complexity that defied translation—like the Hon(ishly-ad)$_{ep\ ideor}^{ap\ onor}$(kohl)noh? The ideograms, if that they were, made

powerful designs with interesting resonances even to her alien eyes. Areas of intense multi-level design. Areas of clearspace or space interrupted with a few simple lines. A visual and tactile people. The designs felt as complex and interesting and pleasurable as they looked.

She'd always liked this part of her profession, the careful measuring and recording of the sites; she never had enough time to satisfy herself, not even as much as she had here. The rest of it was a bore, best done as quickly and efficiently as she could manage, cutting away and packing up those parts of the ruin that seemed most salable, working at top speed, the two or three days at most she could spend there wherever there was. Sometimes she thought she'd like to join a dig and turn academic, spending a decade or two excavating a ruin and studying the people who'd built those structures and lived their lives among them, but that was usually only when she'd struck something especially intriguing and she had to wrench herself away before the local forcers landed on her. Most times she knew very well that such a life would drive her to madness and murder.

She heard crashes too loud to ignore and looked up from her sketch. One of the Chalarosh had thrown a chunk of stone through a glass rectangle and was pulling it out of a wall so he could look into the cavity behind it. The Aggitj were watching with lively interest. Djabo bless, the Chalarosh were still ignoring them. Whatever it is you've got, you cheerful young idiots, be careful. Careful and clever. She sighed. They didn't have a clever bone in their handsome heads.

Seventh day. Departure set for just after the noon meal. Skeen and Pegwai collected all the mobiles they could find, tied them up in bits of blanket and tucked them into their riding cart. Machimim insisted on inspecting the packets, cut open several chosen at random. He stared at the ugly things, nose and ears twitching. "Why take these . . . these unclean objects back to Vana?"

"Because we don't understand them," Pegwai said smoothly. He took the mobile back, being careful not to touch it except through the blanket. "We are going to assay them and do other tests to see why the Ykx kept them lying about."

"Why don't you just find an Ykx and ask?"

"Where? No, it's becoming increasingly clear that there are few if any Ykx left on Mistommerk."

Machimim watched Pegwai bind the bundle shut. "Better you than me," he said.

They spent the morning loading the wagons. Machimim wanted Pegwai's packs put in with the camp gear, but Pegwai was adamant about keeping them close to him. "An oath," he said. "Not something I can trifle with."

The nomad band rode back and forth out in the yellow haze, but didn't come into camp again. In spite of that, they were an ominous presence that affected everyone, even the Aggitj who were jumpy and unhappy and silently stubborn every time Skeen frowned at them.

The dust cloud that marked the nomad presence moved parallel to the carts as they started back the way they'd come, keeping pace with them though the carts moved along hardly faster than a brisk walk.

Every day the dust cloud was there, never closer, never departing.

Skeen had carefully not inquired about what the nomads were looking for, better a bland innocence when the boys lost control of their enterprise, which, unfortunately, they were sure to do.

The fourth day. They started into the foothills. The band set their mounts watching, then one split off from the others and came after the carts. Following. Not trying to overtake.

At camp that night, Skeen pointed this out to Machimim. "What happens if he offs the watch? And then starts cutting throats."

"He won't. Ignore the scruffy rat. Desert tribes, pah. Wouldn't believe you if you told them the sky was up." He yawned. "Always someone plotting against them, or so they believe. Stupid sandheads." He smoothed his hand down the rattail mustaches that dripped from the corners of his mouth. "Nothing for you to worry about. Forget it."

Skeen left him and went prowling in the darkness outside the circle of firelight. He knows what the Aggitj are doing, she thought, and wondered what she should do. What she *could* do. Tell the Aggitj? Pegwai? Pegwai wasn't stupid . . . he didn't need telling. Or want such confidences. He knew quite well it was her that robbed the Poet, but as long as she didn't say the words he didn't have to act on that knowledge. Same here. As long as he could ignore this mess, he would ignore it. The Aggitj wouldn't take her interference as a warning, not them. They'd grin at her and drag her arse-deep in the shit with them. She glared at the guide sitting hunched over by the fire, chewing his cud like a moocow; resentment stirred in her. Gits like him gave her cramps in the soul. Thugs hired by the respectable to maintain the law that pleased them so much until and unless it was applied to them. Most things to do with authority gave her cramps in the soul. She sighed and went to her blankets. When in doubt, do nothing. But keep the eyes open and be ready to jump.

Machimim did nothing, kept himself blandly blind to the maneuverings of the Aggitj, even when they created a minor furor in the lakeside village (skillfully done, she'd give the boys that much), and managed in the midst of it to get a large rustling sack on board with the other gear.

She popped the flap on the darter's holster and clipped the lanyard to the butt, expecting trouble when they reached the Vana shore. Nothing happened. Machimim put them in more carts and they rumbled through farmlands lush with winter crops. The sun went down, plunging them into a thick darkness, the clouds hanging low overhead blocking most of the moonlight, but they went on toward the city; watchfires at the Gemta Telet burning atop the gate towers grew from red points to broad red glows. She tensed as they approached the Gates, expecting some strike from him. Nothing. They rolled into Vana without a sign of a challenge. Machimim could have called on the Gate guards if he was nervous about dealing with them, but he didn't. She watched the guard's faces, what she could see of them (curst veils) as they rolled past. No interest in these late-come travelers, only dull resentment at the duty that kept them from families or other pleasures.

This was going on too long; they were getting away with too much. The longer it went on, the more nervous she got, the gaudier her expectations of disaster. Under her breath she cursed the Aggitj and their plots.

They moved through the silent streets of the Chalarosh city and out again onto the wide roadway that ran round the harbor, finally through the gate into Freeport where the guards were alert and aggressive, demanding assurances and identification before they'd open one leaf of the gate and let the party through.

Machimim took them to a hostel close to the water, saw that their goods (including the Aggitj boys' precious sack) were stowed inside, then he left, taking the klazits with him. Once she'd settled the fee with the Host, Skeen climbed wearily up the long spiral to her room, dropped her pack on the bed, and went to the window. She spotted the watcher as soon as she looked out. Yes. It was almost a relief to see him making expected moves. The other three klazits were no doubt stationed elsewhere about the hostel, watching exits. Machimim brought us here for a reason. No doubt it's a place easy to watch and hard to leave.

She looked at the bed a moment, sighed, and went to see Pegwai.

"Skeen?"

"Need to talk to you." He opened the door wider, she brushed past him and went to the window. "Yes. Come see."

He saw the klazit leaning against a wall. "Aggitj idiots."

"I don't think he'd stop you; follow you, yes. Peg, get out of here fast, before Machimim has time to act. You've got a lot more riding on you than us, so take your tools and go to ground with the Skirrik. Besides, you can do a lot more there to get us out of this trap. See if you can persuade the High Mother to arrange passage for us on the most reliable ship leaving soonest. Before tomorrow morning, if possible. Timka's got the gold. The shipmaster should be one who wouldn't mind having to keep away from here until things calm down, or at least, one who could talk fast enough to keep himself out of trouble. Hm." She thought a minute. "If she can't fix passage, see if she at least can get a list of ships leaving."

Pegwai caught her arm. "Slow down, Skeen, all right, I'll go. In a minute. Tell me first what you're going to do."

Skeen ran her hands through her hair turning it into damp spikes, half dark, half pale. "Djabo bless, I don't know. Shake information out of the Aggitj, yes, then try figuring some way of getting them clear. Get out of this place without cutting any throats, if I can."

Skeen sat in the window watching the klazit wander about in small circles; he was so very bad at this kind of thing she found herself forgetting what a thin edge she balanced on. A gap in time that might be smaller than the space between one breath and the next. She chewed her lips as Pegwai puttered about; he wasn't as slow as he seemed. Not quite. Finally he sighed, gazed regretfully at the pile of discards on the bed, and started for the door.

"Peg," she said.

"I won't say farewell, Skeen."

"No point. Take some advice?"

"If it'll make you feel better."

"Sweet. Don't hurry. Stroll along looking like you haven't a care in the world and don't try losing your tag. And if he stops you, don't argue."

"I have done this before." He made a face at her, shook his head, and left.

Skeen stayed at the window. A few moments later Pegwai walked along the street carrying his pack. He looked calm, his step was unhurried. That's right, make me feel like an idiot. The watcher stayed where he was, but a second klazit stepped from the shadows and moved after Pegwai, ambling behind him with an unhurried stride that matched his. Skeen let out the breath she hadn't known she was holding. Follow without interfering. Whatever it was, it was too big to fit in Pegwai's pack. "Now for the Aggitj."

EVERY QUEST HAS ITS COMPLICATIONS AND THIS ONE IS A HUMMER.

Skeen listened at the boys' door. The laughter inside, the boasting in the young voices made her feel like kicking a few butts. She wondered for a moment if she'd ever been that young and naive and didn't think she had. They had no notion their game was about as secret as a rolling fart. She rubbed her hand across her face (feeling a hundred years old and meaner for every year), made a small annoyed sound, and hammered on the door.

Instant silence inside. Idiots! A confused scurrying. Clothheads! All of it perfectly audible through the flimsy door. Lardbrains!

Hal opened the door and stood in the gap looking uncomfortable.

"Stop that and let me in. Young idiot."

"Skeen?"

"It's not the Doferethapanad. For which you should be grateful. You've made trouble for all of us, you nits. The game stops now."

He frowned, hesitated, then stepped aside.

She marched across the room, pointed at the shutters. "Open them and take a look. No, not all of you, idiots. Hal, you. See that man down by the corner there—he should be walking in silly damn circles. Recognize him?"

"Klaz Inchipit."

Hart brushed past Skeen and looked out. "Sure is. What's he doing there?"

Skeen snorted. "What do you think he's doing there? He's watching this hostel."

"Oh."

"Yes. Oh."

Ders jigged about like a fish on land, went to lean over Hart. "Watching? How come?"

Domi dropped onto the bed. "How come? You know how come. That cursed by Lifefire Machimim. He guessed."

Hal hitched himself up onto the windowsill. "Spy. He didn't guess. He knew."

Hart pushed Ders away and went to sit beside Domi. "So what do we do?"

Skeen clasped her hands behind her. "First thing, my lads. What in Sorn's seven dingy hells is going on?"

"We thought you knew."

"When you told Hal about the spying."

"You didn't ask, so we were sure you know."

"We'd have said if we didn't think you did."

"Hey!" Skeen's yell shut them up; four sets of hazel eyes stared at her. "Stop nattering. Tell me."

The Aggitj looked at each other, then Hal nodded. "Skeen ka, here's how it was. You and the Scholar were in the Gather all the time and Machimim was gone snooping and the klazits turned snarky and they were a lazy bunch, 'd rather sleep by the watertrough than tag after us."

Hart said, "Skeen ka, you know the stream. Well, by the fifth day we'd been most everywhere else so we decided to climb the fall and see what was up there."

Ders nodded. "Another fall, that's what was up there. So we climbed that too. And there was this sort of like cup with a few trees and bushes and grass and a lot of coneys, though they scattered—we made a lot of noise getting over the edge."

Domi said, "And Hal caught whiffs of Chalarosh, he's the best seecher, and then we did, but it seeched weird, not like any of the others we come across. We think it over a sec, then we start looking. And we run down this kid."

"Just a baby, not more'n six or seven. He sets his back against the stone 'n waves this beast at us."

"We haven't seen a beast like it before, but we hear of them. Samchak, we think it is, but it isn't, not a samchak but a mershik which only very special people can have, lot worse any day than a samchak. That's what the boys tells us after."

"Doesn't matter we don't know it's not a samchak, that's bad enough, spitting poison, so we back off."

"Yeah, and the kid has his own mouth open, ready to spit or bite."

"So we decide to play polite and we ask him how come he's up there all by himself. Is he lost, can we take him somewhere? Maybe he wants something to eat, and Hal gets out a sack of honey nuts."

"Right away we see we got a problem. Boy doesn't speak Trade-Min."

"We can back off some more and fall off the cliff or something."

"Kid's hissing like he got a leak, no way we turning our backs on him."

"We decide we better make the boy understand we don't mean him nothing. Isn't that we're looking for him, we just looking."

"So we try talking to him."

"Uh-huh. Takes a while, but that's all right. We don't have much else to do."

"So after a while he calms down some. Hal tosses him the nuts. The kid he's more'n half starved so that makes him feel friendlier."

"This is what we put together from then and after. His father was the To ti Lom of the Sualasual, that's the boy's clan. We get the idea that being To ti Lom means he blows big and swallows little winds."

"The Sualasual and the Kalakal, that's this other clan, they start some damn feud over something, nobody much remembers what."

"Yah, you'd think they're Aggitj."

"Shut up, Domi. This fight kept on for fifty years about, that's what the boy says, he's not sure, but something like that. The Kalakal had more families and were more mean and sly and didn't fight fair, though what Chalarosh mean by fair I'm not sure I know, so they just about wipe out the Sualasual.''

"Yah, since the Boy was born there was just him, his mother and his father the To ti Lom, and a baby sister, and a old aunt. That's it for the Sualasual.''

"The Kalakal smell them out again and again. They kill his father and his mother last winter. Old aunt she slip off with the Boy and the Baby and they get away clean. Which really burns the Kalakal, they stake out the unlucky git that lets the Boy get away.''

"And they go nosing round after the boy, getting closer and closer.''

"And one day the aunt tells him to run one way while she takes Baby and takes off another.''

"That was a couple of months ago. The Boy thinks they are dead now.''

"He thinks that's why the Kalakal are so hot after him now. They want to finish off the feud.''

"He's the Heart of Sualasual, when he's gone, that's it. No more Sualasual.''

Hal dropped onto his knees beside the bed and bent low, slapping his palm against the floor and gabbling a few words of guttural Chala.

A small boy crawled from under the bed and got to his feet with a swift graceful twist of his body.

He was a fragile elf, with the vivid beauty of an imperial kitten, a fresh elegance that survived dirt, spider webs, and rags, a glow about him that made her want to stroke him and cuddle him. He was everything that woke protective instincts to the highest degree in woman. In man too, from the besotted looks on the four Aggitj faces. She'd cultivated a natural resistance to such things, but training and nature were barely strong enough to throw off his appeal. She could understand very easily how the good-natured Aggitj were knocked off their feet, could understand why his family had lost their lives to save his. He was bred for this. Bred for survival, because as long as he survived, the clan existed. The Heart. Djabo's dinky claws, while he lived the Kalakal were a joke to the other clans and while he lived he was poison to anyone who took him in.

Slender, barely wider than a sapling, skin like olive-amber velvet with touches of rose, large mobile pointed ears, pale hair like spidersilk with a soft ivory sheen. Huge blue eyes. A charmer. She sighed. March him out to the watchers and say: here, take this it's all yours? Impossible. She ran her fingers through her hair again, knowing how dopey it made her look. That's how she felt. "No Trade-Min?"

"He learns fast, Skeen ka. Already a few words." Hal grinned at the Boy. "Soon be talking more than Ders."

"What are you planning to do with him?"

"Well. . . ."

"We don't want him killed."

"He'll get killed if he stays here."

"Nobody'll take him, they get killed with him."

"We thought. . . ."

"We thought maybe. . . ."

"Maybe he could come with us?"

Skeen smoothed her hair spikes back down. The absurdity of it all. A Min with murder on her tail. Four brainless but amiable Aggitj extras. A Balayar Scholar with peculiar tastes (no comments about his tastes, old woman, you're involved too deep for judgment). A seasick Skirrik boy with no more sense than the Aggitj. Now a baby Chalarosh with a whole tribe of assassins after him. "Why not," she said. "What's one more?"

"I've got to see Pegwai."

"He's not here?"

"I sent him to the Skirrik Nests so he could look for transport for us. He'd better be told about this. While I'm gone, you busy yourselves thinking out another hiding place for the Boy. Under the bed, hunh!"

In her room, she ran a comb through her hair, squinted at herself in the wavery mirror. It's a haircut for you, old woman, soon as you put foot on a ship's deck. Djabo bless, that'll take away a bit more of that bleach job.

She strolled down the spiral and out the door without attracting any obvious attention—no not-obvious either, as far as she could tell, but before she was three steps on, an inlal of klazits came out of shadow and moved around her. The folk moving along the street (not many, even here in Freeport the streets emptied at night) took one look at the black veils and got out of there as quickly as they could without running. The Abar of the inlal stepped in front of her. "Nakari-chal, the Doferethapanad would speak with you."

Honorific, hey, polite cops, wonder what that means. Well, I won't be eager, which is pretty damn honest, I'm not eager. "I've got things to do," she said.

"The Doferethapanad would speak with you, chal."

So quickly the politeness goes. Ah well. "I hear you."

The Abar nodded, swung round and started off, confident she would follow.

Disciplining a strong urge to take off for elsewhere, she sauntered along behind him, refusing to hurry herself, enjoying his irritation every time he had to wait for her to catch up. Not tactful. There were those who'd say she was ruining any chance of conciliating her captors, but she'd been through this sort of thing often enough to know that those in power did what they wanted whatever the attitude of their victim. She might irritate them into hurting her more severely than they might otherwise, but her self-respect was more than worth the extra pain. And more than once her insolence had actually brought her better treatment.

The Abar led her through the maze of twisty streets to the Gate onto the Bayside Stroll. Some acrimonious argument, then the guards valved open a pedestrian door and let them through.

The long walk to Chalarosh Vana gave her plenty of time to consider escaping. The klazits beside her and behind her were essentially meaningless; if she decided to break loose, there was very little they could do to stop her. She looked ahead to the white peaks that mimicked the curves of desert tents and marked the powercenter of the city. This was the sort of place where her sort of individual tended to vanish without a trace, all those traces scrubbed away by official flunkies kept around for sponging the mud off the official

image. Yes or no? Go or jump? The bay was close enough
and crowded enough so she could lose them in about three
breaths. Be a lot harder to get away once she was in the
Residence. When in doubt, do nothing. She touched the
handgrip of the darter; none of the Chalarosh knew it was a
weapon. When she and the others went before the Cadda
Kana, a klazit questioned her about the darter. She told him it
was a brandy flask and waved it by his ear so he could hear
the water slosh in the reservoir. Right, then, trust yourself,
old woman, things get sticky you can shoot your way out. No
bunch of idiot regressed primitives are going to hold me when
I decide I want to leave. Right. Find out what this is about,
then leave.

They left the Bayside Stroll and moved into Chalatown,
threading through narrow alleys at first then into streets that
grew wider and quieter, moving toward a shimmering white
wall lit at frequent intervals with torches set in the walls of
guard hutches built of the same white stone. They took her
through gates of iron lace (solid iron leaves folded back
against the stone inside the walls) along a winding gravel path
through lush greenery. Enough moonlight oozed through the
clouds to show her wide stretching lawns, flower bed, fountains, clusters of giant reeds, spreading lacy trees. All this
opulence was supposed to impress her with the owner's importance; what it did was wake a deep and bitter antagonism,
a feeling budded in her childhood, blooming full out in her
later years. It was a weakness she had to fight, too easy to let
rage blind her to opportunity. Cool it, old woman, forget all
that. What you've got to do is listen and give nothing away.
Especially the last. Watch your tongue, don't let him jab you
into saying too much. You're not ten any longer, not by a
good many years.

Her escort took her through a high pointed arch in the
center of a cascade of other arches into a tiled area with trees
in huge ceramic tubs, flowering vines dripping from hanging
baskets, a fountain to increase the sense of interpenetration,
outside into inside and the reverse. The klazits walked with a
huddled-together nervousness across the shining immaculate
tiles, glaring at Skeen as her boot heels clattered with careless

noise. Hundreds of small glass and bronze lamps cast a soft glow over the inspace and faint shifting shadows danced around them. Lots of glass about, lots of fine golden bronze with a patina of age and constant polishing. White marble everywhere. The floor an endlessly repeating geometric design in white, blue, green, and flashes of scarlet, tapestry panels large enough to carpet a stadium hanging free on rods, softly swaying walls. The Abar led her on a careful dance through this dangle of carpets, taking her finally into a much smaller inspace with stone walls and doors that shut, sparkling glass windows letting in the diffuse gray light of the shrouded moon, an open skylight above a small round fountain that played water music over a ceramic leaf-form, pale green with darker green lines traced over the surface. Two out of the scatter of lamps were lit, islands of brightness in the shadows, one at the far end of the long narrow space, the other by the man sitting in the room's only chair, a backless thing with arm rests and bowed legs.

The Doferethapanad. Skeen hadn't seen him before; though her interrogators and the Cadda Kana had used his name more than once, he kept his face out of the business. He wore a crisp white robe, had a full head of grayblue hair and heavy brows. Long rattail grayblue mustaches hanging from the corners of a broad, full-lipped mouth. A heavy vertical line between his brows and deep lines carved from large nostrils to the corners of that mouth. His skin had the pinkish pampered look of one who never had to face a harsh wind or too much sun, who was lotioned and massaged, who bathed in perfumed water and slept between silk. Skeen gazed into eyes like opaque brown marbles and decided to ignore the polish. Polite, old woman, that's for you now, no tricks. Keep your mouth shut and your wits sharp.

The Abar went onto his knees and banged his forehead on a cushion at the Doferethapanad's feet. Skeen watched this performance with detached interest. Neither the Doferethapanad nor the Abar seemed to expect her to follow his example, so she stood with hands clasped behind her, feet a little apart, ready to jump if things got sticky.

After a brief set of questions and answers, the Doferethapanad waved the Abar away. He took his silent klazits to one of the glassed-in arches, pushed at a bronze handplate, held the door open while his men filed out, followed them and stationed himself close to the door, out of earshot but able to see everything in the room.

The Doferethapanad beckoned her closer, with a fluid gesture of his hand indicated that she should kneel on the cushion. Skeen sank onto her knees, arranged herself as comfortably as she could and waited for the man to tell her what this was about. He inspected her in silence for some minutes, his long fingers tapping gently at the chair arm.

"This one you see is Massacharamar Machat, the Doferethapanad of Atsila Vana. You are the female being of ambiguous provenance, Skeen of noplace as it were. It has occurred to this one and others that you are newly come to Mistommerk, a green and perhaps dangerous Pass-Through, that you are traveling to places you alone know of for reasons you alone know. This one does not ask if such is the truth, this one would rather not know. There are many things this one would rather not know, because knowing would mean acting and acting could possibly bring either humiliation or danger to the Chalarosh of Atsila Vana and beyond them to this one who sits before you. Not an eventuality to be contemplated with pleasure. Who you are and what you are means nothing to Atsila Vana or the Doferethapanad, unless your actions make it necessary that this one investigate those things, those actions. Which would be most uncomfortable for you and your companions, Skeen of noplace. The Doferethapanad need not elaborate on this theme, this one is sure you understand what is not said. The Doferethapanad does not wish to bestir himself and will not do so unless there is a clear and unavoidable threat to Atsila Vana. No, say nothing. You have not been brought here to speak, but to listen. Your silence is the only thing that will keep your head on your shoulders. Everything the Doferethapanad shall say from this point is speculation, dreams. Were it to be confirmed even in the smallest degree, it would be necessary for the Doferethapanad to act. Such action would be noisy and bloody and most distressing. No. Not a word. Not a sound. Not a smile or a frown or a grimace. The Doferethapanad is certain you understand his necessity.'' He looked down at his long narrow hands, then past her at the water running over the lobes of the twisted leaf fountain. ''The Doferethapanad has already had to act precipitously and remove one who was a favorite cousin but who proved regrettably indiscreet in the messages he carried and the actions he permitted and regrettably unintelligent in his ambitions. It seems a staple of life that every great family must have at least one member of transcendent stupidity. The Doferethapanad requests Skeen of noplace to rise from the cushion and look into the alcove by the lamp then return to her present position. This one hopes it is not necessary to remind her of the need to remain silent and inscrutable.''

Skeen got to her feet, careful to make as little sound as possible, to keep her face in a lifeless mask. Her nerves tingled—there was enormous danger in this room, but it hovered at a distance, held off as long as she danced the Doferethapanad's figures without a mistake. She walked to the end of the room and looked into the alcove.

The guide Machimim lay in a pool of congealing blood, a look of intense surprise on his face. Hm. You thought you were making points, but you only managed to embarrass your relatives.

She walked back to the cushion, knelt, and waited.

The Doferethapanad let a flicker of approval show, then went back to watching the water play over the shiny glazes of the fountain. ''Naturally the Doferethapanad would not listen to the babbling of a fool gone mad from drinking tainted gregra galat. It is to be hoped, Skeen of noplace, that you did not drink from that tainted cruse.'' He paused a long moment, his eyes moving over her carefully impassive face; he returned his gaze to the dripping water. ''The situation between the desert Chalarosh and the settled farmers here on the coast is most complex. Complex and difficult, but at the moment there is a truce of sorts that is profitable to both sides. The difficulties of maintaining that truce are considerable. One of them, perhaps the most serious, is that none of the desert clans can or will speak for any of the others. You will understand that is their greatest strength and also their greatest weakness. There is no way to throw them into confusion by lopping off the head of their common ruler. They have no common ruler. Yet there is also no way for the clans to combine and present a serious threat to the settled Chalarosh. They have recognized the value of Atsila Vana and do not concern themselves with the foreigners living there, at least they have not so concerned themselves during the past century. That could change. The change could mean great trouble to all settled Chalarosh and worse to the foreign enclaves. Rumors have reached into Atsila Vana that such a change is possible, that several clans are on the verge of alliance. Things must be done to counter this danger. This one speaks of such things because this one wishes Skeen of noplace to understand the delicacy of the Doferethapanad's position. There must be no occurrence that would rouse the desert Chalarosh to anger and hasten that alliance. This one is going to pose an absurd impossible event as an example of an occurrence that would be such a spark. It is understood this is only an example and has no relation to reality. If somehow a child from a desert clan involved in a feud were to slip into Atsila Vana and be discovered here, the desert would reverberate with the news. A very special child—the Heart and last of his clan. To protect the child from the feud would rouse all the clans to fury. To hand over this very special child with abject apologies would fill the clans with contempt and greed; they would see the treasures of Atsila Vana as theirs for the taking because they would despise those meant to protect the city. The precarious peace would end. If such a disaster should happen in reality, as of course this is only speculation, those responsible would be put to death in as painful and lingering a fashion as the Doferethapanad could devise. He would not hand over the child. No. He would raise a pile high as the gate towers and impale the child on it for all to see. Then he would close the gates of Atsila Vana and prepare for a century of war. There would be for him one shaky chance of avoiding such an outcome. If the special child passes through Atsila Vana with no one of importance knowing of his presence in time to lay hands on him, if such a child leaves Atsila Vana within hours of his arrival, there would be a minimum of embarrassment and the disaster would be dissipated into an unpleasantness that would pass as the child had passed. If some Aggitj boys too soon out of Boot and Backland to understand the realities of life have laid their folk under such deadly threat, if a cousin of the Doferethapanad drank from a tainted bottle and dreamed mad dreams of power, then out of that madness, ignorance and stupidity, battle, murder and sudden death would flow . . . an unending stream of blood. If, however, a Pass-Through from noplace did such a thing, a Pass-Through with no kin to pay the blood responsibility, then perhaps, ah yes, perhaps a way might be contrived to put the onus on her head alone. A Pass-Through without kin or kind in this world to be harmed. A Pass-Through obeys her imperatives and travels on with no lingering or hesitation. A Pass-Through couldn't be expected to know of the Ravvayad, the assassins whose bite is death and whose spite is endless. If such a Pass-Through had taken the child and sailed with him hidden from all eyes, then the Doferethapanad could proclaim with fervor the patent innocence of all the several parts of Atsila Vana. Were that Pass-Through to take this on her shoulders, she must be content with the virtue of the act; payment would compromise too much. If she has friends in Atsila Vana, perhaps their safety and continued well-being would be something she might consider sufficient payment for her efforts. And more, she would be righting the wrong she had connived in and saving a city from the results that must flow from the acts of those for whom she is responsible. Such an ethical being would not have to be told that should she refuse so necessary a recompense, then she and all her companions will be stripped and beaten, then taken into the desert and left to the whims of the desert clans. The Doferethapanad is certain that the Pass-Through understands the virtue of haste and will be gone from these shores before another day dawns."

"And then he told the Abar to hustle me back here and collect the watchers and they should all go back to their beds and forget the whole thing as it was a madman's dream not worth talking about." Skeen sighed. "I know. Once you

happened on the Boy there was no way you could leave him
there. Doesn't stop me wishing you'd spent your time like the
klazits asleep under a watertrough. Listen carefully. In about
three breaths I'm going to go see Peg and Timmy. Keep your
fingers crossed they've turned up at least one ship heading
out before dawn.'' She untied the sack from her belt, tossed it
to Hal. "See that my things and what Pegwai left are packed
and bring them with you. Hal, you settle with the Host. Don't
let him charge you more than twice what we agreed in
exchange for lost time. Domi, you and Ders make sure the
Boy is well hidden. You don't have to worry about searches—
every klazit or spy will be looking hard somewhere else. Hm.
There's enough for you to carry, makes hiring a handcart
reasonable. Yes, do that. It'll be easier on the boy and that'll
leave most of you with your hands loose just in case. Stay
casual, make jokes if you can; look drunk if you can do that
without exaggerating. Go straight to the wharves and sit out
at the end by the silk merchant's warehouse, so I'll know
where to find you. That's all I can think of. What about you
all? Any questions. Suggestions? You see something I forgot?
No? Good.'' She got to her feet, smoothed her hair down.
"Once we get out past the seawalls I'm going to sleep for a
week.''

Pegwai and Timka were in the garden with the High Mother.
Chulji was crouching in the background, tactfully silent. A
sheet had been stretched between two trees and Pegwai was
showing the images from the Gather. When Skeen came in,
he was explaining a detail of the lighting system. Wanasi
left her standing among the neuters while she went to speak
quietly to the High Mother.

A flurry of orders from Demmirrmar. The neuters fluttered off, collecting the sheet, clearing away the bottles and
plates, diving into bushes, weaving about the High Mother's
private garden, making sure it was clear of sleepers, listeners,
any one or thing that might disturb the privacy of the conference getting set up. A pair of neuters came in with a steaming
teapot and trays of small sandwiches, strips of cheese, and
small tart fruits.

When they were alone under the soft glow of candlelamps, the High Mother filled cups for her guests then settled back with a clacking of her mouth parts and sucked at the straw in her drinking globe. She waited until Skeen had gulped down her tea, refilled her cup. "So. What have those young idiots been up to?"

"You don't really want to know." Skeen cradled the cup between her palms enjoying the heat that passed into her and took a little weariness away. "But I suppose you have to so you can protect yourself. I strongly advise an impenetrable facade of ignorance." Once again she sketched the events of the night. "So you see, if our departure was urgent before, it's imperative now."

"Yes. You are fortunate to find the Chalarosh divided, with tension high, Seeker. Were things a bit more at ease, the Doferathapanad would have gathered in the lot of you and handed you over to the Kalakal." She sucked at the straw, stared out over Skeen's head. "High tide comes in a little over two hours; the night is almost done." She let out a powerful whistling sound that rapidly rose out of Skeen's hearing range.

Wanasi came in a rush, liveliness and brightness like a cloak about her in spite of the late hour. Her carapace was a pale violet shading to cerulean in the shadows; she was sleek and pretty and perky with coltish grace in the flicker of her six segmented legs. She brought a handful of papers with small neat glyphs printed on them, presented these to Demmirrmar with a song phrase that was filled with her pleasure in having completed her task to her satisfaction well within the time given.

Demmirrmar sang a thank-blessing back to her and waited until she left to glance through the sheets. "Three leaving with tide's turn. All Balayar." Her lambent eyes twinkled, she made the bowing sway that was the Skirrik equivalent of laughter. "Tipesh Sco, bound for Mai Semang on Lesket Tjin. Tenglan Mil, bound for Untangka on Ekso Beren. Pipin Kers, bound for Matamashak on Bretel Heran." She flipped through the papers again. "All have cabin space free and have indicated a willingness to carry you all. Not so many

who can afford cabin passage want to leave Atsila Vana,"
she told Skeen, "odd as you might find that."

Skeen turned to Pegwai. "Any preference, anyone you
know among those?"

Pegwai twisted his face into a scowl. "Not Mil. Neither of
us would be happy with a Dih on his ship. The other two I
don't know."

Demmirrmar arched her neck. "Your name was mentioned,
Scholar. Mil said nothing of any unwillingness."

"Tenglan Mil would dice his granny for stew if the price
was right."

"Peg, those destinations. All in the Spray?"

"Yes."

"Which is the largest busiest most important of the ports?"

"No question. Mai Samang."

"Then we'll take Sco's Ship. I don't like the thought of a
clutch of Ravvayad sniffing along an unbroken trail. We'll
change ships in Mai Samang and change again later."

NASTY NEW ENEMIES. THE FIRST FALSE DESTINATION PUT BEHIND HER, SKEEN STARTS SLOGGING ON AGAIN. AS USUAL THERE'S A LOT OF BORING GROUND TO GET ACROSS (IN THIS CASE A LOT OF BORING OCEAN) WHERE NOTHING MUCH HAPPENS BEYOND THE QUESTERS GETTING ON EACH OTHERS' NERVES. SO—CONSIDER THE OCEAN CROSSED. AND TWO DAMP MONTHS CROSSED OFF. NOW OUR QUESTERS ARE VEGETATING IN A CITY CALLED kulchikan, THE MAIN CITY ON AN ISLAND CALLED the sting, ONE OF THE LARGER ISLANDS TRAILING OFF THE END OF A LONG THIN CURVE OF LAND CALLED the tail.

"I never thought to have so eminent a visitor. Like plucking a butter rose off a dungheap, an unexpected pleasure." The dark saturnine face turned from Pegwai to Skeen and she didn't need to be a mindreader to get the message in that dull brown gaze: How I'd love the pleasure of taming you, woman; I am Kral of Kulchikan, everything you see is mine to take if I want. Be glad I'm not a man to break the laws I've made; it means you're safe for the moment, but give me the slightest reason, a hairline of an excuse, and we'll see how long you'll resist me. "You must be careful walking the streets in Kulchikan, Seeker. We do our best, but this is a lawless place."

The Tail was the refuge of rebels, a mix of exiles and outlaws and the incurably restless with representatives from every Wave except the first (no Ykx). Trade here was generally a matter of being a better and often more violent thief than the other thieves. There were a few rules obeyed by everyone who hadn't the power to break them with impunity or wished to stay more than a minute in the settlements and cities along the Tail. Walled towns were truce-grounds, feuds were left outside (the survivors of flare-ups were generally marched beyond the town limits and hung from handy trees); maiming, biting, gouging, anything less than death was a concern only to the individuals involved. Any visitor who shared a meal with residents was safe from attack by those particular residents for exactly three days counted from the first bite of the meal. Services bargained for had to be performed and paid, or the price would be taken from the defaulter's hide—this applied primarily to residents— matters were a lot looser when the transaction occurred between Tailites and visiting traders. Those traders had Truce Havens spread from Sting to Root, guarantees provided by local powers; since these had a habit of skinning or worse those who violated their decrees, the Havens were among the safest spots for travelers, as long as they checked in with the local owners and paid the head tax. Cheating was expected on all deals, the rule of the trade road, but if a trader was fast on his feet, nimble-minded, knew the goods and markets well enough, he could become remarkably wealthy trading along the Tail; among other things, the mountains were rich in gems and metals, especially gold. There were ship-wreckers on the coast, pirates in fleets of small boats (the merchanters had to stay close inshore because of hostile Sea Min), sand bars that shifted with every storm, erratic winds, swarms of wasp-like kirrpitts that could strip the skin from a man between one breath and the next. Land travel was worse. Bands of Mountain Min sniped at miners and swept down on packtrains, though they tended to back off from any guarded by Turlik's rangers; these had a habit of shooting fire shafts and fire was about the only weapon the Min feared. Otherwave bands were generally smaller but just as bloody. No haven in local habitats either. Children were trained in the local ethic from the moment they understood speech. The family is all you have, defend it with body and mind; anyone outside the family is an enemy, attack him or her or whatever without waiting or warning the moment you spot a weakness, guard yourself and back off if he's stronger and knows the land. Attack is always the best defense. The man you kill won't kill you. It's always better to offer a stranger's blood to the gods—that way you increase your chances they won't thirst for yours.

The Kral of Kulchikan moved restlessly in his elaborate chair, looked down at the group kneeling at his feet, turned to the thin dark man standing on the dais beside him. "The tax?"

"Paid, ajja Kral."

"Did the Scholar say why he is traveling in these waters?"

"No, ajja Kral. Till now you have not required me to ask such things."

"Till now we've had traders and scum on the run. No need to ask them why they've come." He waved his long hand and the hangfaced dogrobber moved into the shadow behind the chair. "Scholar, I think you had better explain your presence. We do not want to offend the Tanul Lumat. Someday we might even want to use its services, having an infant daughter with an inquiring mind. But the Lumat is a long way from here and your companions are an odd lot, that you must admit."

Pegwai composed his face into the smiling courtesy of his business persona, laced his fingers together over the bulge of his paunch. "Travelers must go where they can find ships to take them, oh Kral. Our project is the mapping of the north shore of the Halijara Sea including the river systems inland, a task we will not come close to completing ourselves, but the Lumat endures when man succumbs to the frailty of his flesh; we will do our part and pass on the task to others. We are in Kulchikan only to wait for a ship that will take us south. As to the nature of our company, the Aggitj fetch and carry and serve as guards; when we are beyond the amenities of city life, they'll hunt and do camp work. The Skirrik lad earns his wedding jet working for us, serving as translator when necessary, and most important, serving as go-between; everyone knows the Skirrik and how far they can be trusted. The Chalarosh boy we acquired by accident, a long dull story, but he too has proved useful. The Min is the Seeker's friend and companion and also a scout; you will understand the value of having a friendly Min along. We may seem an odd grouping, but it has proved a useful one thus far. Is there more you wish to know, oh Kral?''

"You intend to stay in the Truce Haven?''

"Yes, oh Kral, it seems best. Our stay depends on the arrival of a suitable ship. It might arrive tomorrow, we might be here a month.'' He gave the Kral a broad genial smile.

The Kral looked thoughtfully at him. "Dine with me, Scholar. This evening.'' His eyes flicked briefly to Skeen but he did not include her or any of the others in the invitation.

"Honored, oh Kral.''

"I wish to speak of the Lumat, Scholar, some questions about the young sheltered there. Come prepared to discourse on that.''

"With delight, oh Kral.''

Every night after that Pegwai went to the Kralhus, making a face at Skeen each time the escort came for him, shaking his head at Timka when she laughed at him and wished his tongue two ends.

The Aggitj took the boy with them when they went out during the day to do a little trading and pick up some coin by working at this and that. The Beast was useful more than once, stopping trouble before it started when he opened his mouth and showed his fangs. At night Chulji the Min-Skirrik went with them and the Boy stayed to guard Skeen and Timka, contented with that assignment.

A number of ships arrived and left, many of them Balayar who were interested in the vast Market at the center of Kulchikan, with no wish to venture further along the Tail. A few others wandered in, but they were too small and too scruffy. Not that Skeen demanded Balayar standards, but she wouldn't have trusted any of those shipmasters with a mangy dog.

The ninth day came and passed. The Boy was getting nervous. No Chalarosh had come off any of the ships, but time was beginning to work against him. He began walking the walls at night, peering anxiously down into the streets until Timka or one of the Aggitj came to fetch him. He said nothing about his fears, but Skeen saw them and began worrying in her turn. Pegwai was getting edgy, too; the Kral was looking at him with a speculation he had no trouble reading. The Pallah was wondering whether he'd like having a resident scholar about the place, someone to teach his sons and that daughter he was so proud of. It would be the easiest thing in the world for Pegwai to vanish without a trace into the Kralhus, with the rest of the party slipped into the sea to cut off any chance of bother. Skeen started haunting the wharves, glaring out over the polluted waters of the bay as if she could will the right ship into port. She was getting increasingly irritable in this miserable place where she couldn't even go out and get happily soused in a local tavern and maybe find herself an energetic bedmate or two. No one to talk to—nothing to do but sit and brood. And she was brooding far too much about Tibo; she was about ready to scream and claw at the walls in her need to find him and squeeze out of him why he'd stranded her. The easy answers weren't right. She felt that in her bones when she let herself feel. But I could be wrong, Djabo's bloody claws, I could be wrong, and if I'm wrong, everything I think about myself is wrong, everything I thought I knew. Round and round and round, wearing ruts in the floor, wearing ruts in her brain.

After another frustrating day at the wharves she was pacing back and forth along one of the upper halls, cursing under her breath, filled with bursts of nervous energy she couldn't wear out by working because there wasn't any hard physical labor she could do. Pegwai came trudging up the ramp. She looked at him, turned her back on him, and walked away. He came hesitantly along the hall; his room was two doors from hers. She stood in the doorway watching him. He came even with her. She went into the room and sat on the bed, leaving the door open. He stopped in the doorway. She poured wine from a skin into two mugs and sat waiting. Feet dragging, breathing too fast, he came in, pulling the door shut behind him.

The eleventh day.

A large ship came in. The sleepy wharves came alive—swarms of ladesmen came out of the cracks, shouting her name: Maggí Maggí Maggí. Laughter, elbows working in ribs, the strongest struggling for a place in the front ranks. Maggí Maggí Maggí. Skeen was squashed into a corner, startled, grunting as a foot slammed down on her toes, an elbow caught her on a cracked rib, discouraging a thieving hand with a jab of a sleeve knife.

The ship nudged up to the wharf, a big merchanter looking a bit battered, with new patches on the sails and some char marks and grapple gouges on the rails.

The gangplank slammed down, the Captain came sauntering off her ship. Aggitj. One of the rare female extras. Her not-hair was fine and pale, like limber silver wire, long and mobile, fluttering to a wind of its own. She was long-legged and forceful, taller than the tallest of the Aggitj boys, fleshy but not fat, eyes of dark amber, catching the sunlight with orange glows. Her features were clean-cut but heavy. Her hands had broad palms and long tapering fingers. She took good care of them, kept the skin soft and pliant, the nails short for convenience and buffed to a discreet glow. Her feet had the same generous lines and were given the same sort of care. She wore sandals not boots, wide-legged trousers of a heavy black silk that clung to large but shapely legs. A broad leather belt, stained crimson with several decorative folds, buckled in the back. A heavy white silk shirt over breasts like melon halfs, wide sleeves caught into long narrow cuffs that buttoned from wrist to elbow, flattering slender wrists and long arms. Carbuncles dangled from her ears and flashed red on thumb rings. She walked with the controlled energy of a prowling tiger, the same looseness, the same unconscious arrogance.

She stepped onto the wharf, grinned and waved at the men calling her name, then turned to watch her passengers leave the ship while her armed escort formed up to wait for the men she chose to transfer her personal cargo to the secure storage she kept under permanent lease. All but a few of the passengers pushed through the crowd and disappeared down the alleys between the warehouses, a hard-looking bunch, mostly male; like the ship they'd been through a fight and like the ship they weren't advertising it. The remainder, traders with cargoes in the hold, stood silent beside the Captain as she began calling out names, sending the ladesmen to the one-eyed mate leaning on the rail beside the plank.

As the goods began coming out, the Kral's reps showed up and kept a careful eye on what was being piled on the wharf, ticking items off on long wooden rods with a short-bladed knife, hands moving with swift efficiency, cutting a variety of notches—different depths, different angles, different shapes—making a comprehensive record of what belonged to the Captain and what to each of the several traders hovering over their own piles. Maggí joked with them, laughed, traded quips with the traders and the ladesmen . . . keeping her own record of what emerged, needing no rod or other aid to prod her memory.

When the unlading was finished, the reps left and the wharf cleared swiftly. Leaving the disposal of her goods to the mate, Maggí went back aboard her ship.

Skeen lingered. She liked the look of the woman, her crew, and the ship. Everything done with a minimum of fuss and a maximum of good will. Maggí was well known here and popular. That didn't mean a great deal, but if she cared for her reputation she was that hair more trustworthy than some git who didn't give a damn.

The Captain came off her ship shortly afterward and strode across the wharf. Skeen came out of her corner and walked quietly beside her, feeling towered over, an uncommon sensation for her. Maggí glanced at her, but said nothing, just kept walking.

"Captain," Skeen said after a short while. "Might I speak with you?"

"Why?" Maggí didn't look at her or slow the swing of her stride.

"If you'll be heading back along the Tail and if we can come to terms on price, my companions and I would like to take passage on your ship."

The Captain glanced at her, speculation in her burnt orange eyes. "Terms would include your satisfying me about your reasons to head downtail."

"My companions and I stay at Chaffelu's Inn, the Truce Haven. Perhaps you could join us for the evening meal."

Maggí stopped walking and turned to look down into Skeen's face. "I thought you were Pallah. You're not."

"That's part of the explanation."

"Ah! You read me too well." Quick grin briefly exposing white even teeth, the canines perceptibly longer and more daggerlike than the others. "I'll be there. Hour after sundown." She nodded walked briskly on.

Skeen stood watching her. Maggí needed no bodyguard, at least not in daylight. Several more of the loungers cried greetings to her and she responded with laughter and insults that they took in good part and returned with interest. Well-liked. Whether that spoke for her or against her was difficult to say, this city being what it was.

Captain Maggí stood in the doorway of the private dining room and raised her brows at the mix of people waiting for her, seated on cushions around the low table. A window fan turned lazily, drawing air into the room (the fans were ingenious contraptions, worked by a water screw powered by the tide). The air was damp and reasonably cool. It smelled of the strong incense smoldering on the sill that was meant to cover the odors that made walking through the city something that was never pleasant and only tolerable because the nose grew so quickly numb. Groundwater under the city had been

contaminated long ago and only the poorest drank from wells
and that only when they had no other choice. One of the
items that enabled the Kral to keep his claws on local purses
was the aqueduct bringing pure water down from the precipi-
tous mountains in the interior of the island; only those who
paid were permitted use of that water and the Kral kept a
rigorous patrol of the pipes (all of them above ground so they
were easy to watch). Theft of water was a capital crime. So
the Haven had no open windows—only airshafts that were
connected to chimneys that rose into air that was marginally
cleaner than the miasma that lived in the streets. It also made
the Haven that much safer from night creepers of the two-
legged sort.

Maggí came in warily, settled beside Skeen. "You heard
my name on the wharf but not all of it. I am Maggí Solitaire.
My ship is the Goum Kiskar. We will be leaving in three
days, going downtail."

Skeen started to speak, then smiled and waited as the
servitors came in with laden trays and started spreading bowls
of food along the table; others set down urns of steaming
mulled cider, then scented water in fingerbowls with linen
towel rolls beside them. The servitors worked in silence, left
in silence. When the door was shut again, Skeen introduced
the company—names without accompanying comment, each
individual bowing as his or her name was pronounced. "I am
a recent Pass-Through," she finished, "the others are as you
see." She smiled, a brief wry twist of her mouth, knowing
how Timka and Pegwai would scold her later for what she
was about to say. They didn't understand her, they wouldn't
understand Maggí either. We're a lot alike. She didn't make
the mistake of thinking she knew everything about the Aggitj
woman, but she'd wager all the gold in Duppra Mallat's
chest that the two of them shared a number of common
childhood experiences. Dealing with Maggí with candor and
openness, giving away advantages with open hand, that seemed
folly of the most rampant kind, but she was guessing it
wouldn't be. "Pegwai Dih told the Kral we meant to map the
north shore of the Halijara Sea. That's partly true, but our
goal—well, say my goal since my goal is the driving force—is

to find a Gather of Ykx and talk them into giving me a key to the Stranger's Gate.'' She saw Pegwai roll his eyes up and Timka start tearing a roll to shreds; her mouth twitched again, then spread into a wide grin as she met Maggí's laughing, comprehending gaze. "And there are a number of drawbacks to being anywhere around us. Timka has a sister whose chief goal in life seems to be erasing her from the roll of the living; we dealt with two Min attacks while we were coming along the Spray. Pretty feeble, but that's subject to change as Telka changes agents. The Boy is the sole remnant of his clan with Kalakal Ravvayad hot for his hide. We haven't seen any yet, but the Boy swears they'll come and won't let any trick throw them off his trail. We've been here eleven days, the longest we've sat in one spot since we left Atsila Vana. So if they did follow, they should show up any hour, any minute. And poor old Pegwai—the Kral is starting to think he owns him, wants his own private Court Jester. So you see, there is a certain degree or urgency driving our desire to move on.'' Skeen poured a cup of cider for Maggí then for herself as a signal for the meal to begin. She sipped first, then set her cup down and began filling her plate.

As the meal went on, she was amused by the fascination Maggí held for the Aggitj boys; their interest even seemed to have blunted their awesome appetites. She killed a grin as the thought struck her that the appetites hadn't been killed, merely transformed. Maggí was aware of that interest, how could she not be with four pairs of hazel eyes fixed unwavering on her, but gave no sign she understood, perhaps a slight exaggeration of the grace with which she used her large beautiful hands.

The Boy was watching her too, with an intensity he wasn't aware he was showing, an intensity that told Skeen too clearly for her comfort just how terrified he was. He ate nothing until Domi noticed, clucked his tongue, and began coaxing him to eat. Skeen leaned forward. "Boy," she said softly prouncing each word with considerable force. "They will have to come through me and I don't care how loud the Ravvayad boast, there is not a Chalarosh alive who can manage that.''

He stared at her from a tragic face. But he was only six and more than a little awed by her. He flushed at the attention he was getting, wriggled on his cushion, then began to eat with more enthusiasm.

"Nine," Maggí said. "You're financing this?"

Skeen sighed. "One thing leads to another on this damn world. You make impulsive promises and look what happens. I started with one."

"If you find the key you want, will you be taking them through the Gate?"

"That's a long way off in maybe-never-never. First we catch our rabbit."

"What?"

"Ancient recipe for rabbit stew. Also ancient cliché."

"Ah. The Ykx." She leaned forward, looked around Skeen at Pegwai. "Scholar, you're right to be nervous of the Kral. Some time ago the great grandfather of this Kral imported some talent from the Tanul Lumat to design and build the aqueduct. Word is he never got over his foolishness in letting such talents get away and go back to the Lumat. This Kral knows the story. Do they take girls at the Lumat?"

"Oh yes. The Skirrik insist females be considered. These girls stay in the Nests so our resident Skirrik Scholars can keep an encouraging eye on them. Reassures the parents about them, too; the girls will be well-protected there. Are you interested? There'd be no difficulty about an adult female living there as long as she can pay her way."

"I've got a daughter who shows signs of wanting to be a scholar."

Pegwai chuckled. "You and the Kral. His charming child is just learning to walk." He sobered. "But she is a pretty thing and I should be grateful to her since she's the reason I'm still living here. However, that's for another time. Some children we take without requiring a dowry, if they're unusually brilliant or gifted. Most must help support the Lumat with an initial contribution and a yearly sum whose size depends on the child and the parent and their sponsors. For a girlchild, it's especially needful to find a sponsor among the Skirrik. If I could meet your daughter, talk with her, see how strong her desire seems to be, I might be able to provide such a sponsor.

It's not an easy life, Maggí Solitaire, your daughter will be a long way from home and friends and with strangers however kind; she will need to have a very strong calling to endure the loneliness and the rigor.''

Maggí settled back. ''I thank you Scholar Dih.'' She sipped at her cooling cider. ''The Tanul Lumat knows where to find the Ykx?''

''Rumors and seacaptains' tales, some more reliable than others.''

''Not much to bring you so far.''

''One of the seacaptains is a cousin of mine.''

''Trading in the Halijara? Who is he, perhaps I know him.''

''Perinpar Dih.''

''Perich?'' A burst of laughter. ''Yes, I know him. I was at his off-faring feast a year or two after I came when he retired to Lesket Tjin; he might be your cousin, Scholar, but he's the grandest weaver of tales with the smallest kernels of truth I've ever met.'' She turned to Skeen. ''If you're depending on his report, Skeen ky, you lean on a feeble reed.''

''Even feeble, it's the only reed I've got, Maggí Solitaire. What else should I do with my time? Besides, this is how I earn my living on the other side, sniffing after rumor and long chances.''

Maggí's eyes went vague. ''I have heard tales . . . they say you sail from star to star as easily as I sail from isle to isle.''

''Not so different, no, only in the speeds involved and the distances covered.''

Maggí blinked. ''Where did P'richi locate the Ykx?''

''Lake Sydo.''

''That's Plains Min territory.'' She set the cup down. ''They are as huffy as the Mountain Min here in the Tail about intruders. I've heard nothing about Ykx in there.''

''Been there?''

''No. Too many problems, not enough profit.''

''Well, Peg can do his mapping, so that's no loss, and I can take a look for Ykx. If they're not there, well, I try somewhere else.''

"Where?"

"Haven't the faintest notion. I'll look around, see what I can sniff out. There were still Ykx living south of Atsila Vana only twenty years ago. Bound to be some about somewhere."

"Hm." Maggí said nothing more about the Ykx, but turned to the Aggitj. As she ate, she asked questions about what was happening in Boot and Backland, catching up on things that had happened in the twenty years since she left.

"Yoncal took a second wife," Hal said. "On the knees of Didim because after ten years she was still barren. Blanteri Tugga's daughter. She had a daughter a month before we left."

"Orano's daughter was supposed to marry the Asach Bhessh. She took off leaving a letter saying she didn't propose to be sold like a kova calf and she signed the letter Regi no Maggí. Moh and Kansin, Tohl's sons were called Extra about then, rumor said she went off with them." Domi lifted his cup in a salute to Maggí. "Not the first time that's happened."

Ders giggled. "The Fathers they all stomped hard on the story, about you, I mean, but it was too good to keep. The serfs spread it from Toe to Blade. Lots of girls took heart. Not so bad for Extras either, some of us might get real wives."

Hart laughed. "Not you, davadva, girl Extras are a feisty lot, need a strong hand and lots of patience."

Domi snorted. "You either, nit, if you keep talking like that."

Maggí chuckled. "Listen to him, young Hart; if you want a docile bride, hunt among the Pallah, not young daughters who kicked away their Father's hand. They'll not be looking for another such."

When the meal was over, when the servitors had collected the debris and left a fresh urn of steaming cider, Skeen settled back, smiling contentedly as Pegwai and Timka bargained with Maggí about how far she'd take them and how much it would cost them.

Maggí settled back. "Dawn, day after tomorrow. So far

I've got two other cabin passengers.'' She looked from Timka to the Boy and smiled. ''Don't have to worry about them, they've been on the Tail longer than I have. And I'll have Crew keep an eye on the deckers—any of them make a funny move, he'll go overside.'' Her smile widened to a feral grin. ''The things down there like two-leg meat.'' She turned to the Aggitj. ''Hal, the four of you look capable, but you'd better shop the Market for some arms. Passengers are expected to fight for the ship if we run into pirates or something else.'' She swung back to frown at Timka. ''I said if. When is more apt. Timka ky, do you have a wing form?''

''Yes. You want me to fly scout?''

''You got it. I'll forgo your passage fee . . .'' she raised her brows; Timka looked blandly at her; she went on smoothly, ''. . . and add a fee of ten coppers for every day you fly. Won't likely be more than one day in four.''

''Forgo Chulji's passage also. Two pairs of eyes see more than one. He can fly with me, alternate with me during tight times.''

''I didn't realize there were Min among the Skirrik.''

''Few do. Min Skirrik would like to keep it that way. I'm sure you understand why.''

''If he flies, it'll get out.''

''We're a long way from Istryamozhe and I'm told Tailites don't talk much to outsiders.''

''True enough, but rumors do get around, faster than you think.''

''About Chulji.''

''My weeping coffers.'' A robust laugh, a shake of her head. ''Yes, Chulji's fare is nulled.'' She wriggled back from the table and got to her feet. ''Skeen ky, send the coin round to the ship tomorrow morning; I'm not about to wander about after dark with that much on me.''

A timid knock at her door. At first she wasn't sure she heard it. A scratching sound. Skeen slid out of bed, hesitated a moment, then pulled her robe about her, tied the sash as she padded across to the door.

The Boy. He looked shyly up at her, his fear hovering like

a black beast behind him, the other Beast pressing against his ankles watching Skeen with an unwinking gaze from eyes like filmed-over blueberries.

"Em," he whispered, "may I stay the night?"

"Do the Aggitj know you're here?"

He nodded, looked down at his small bare feet, toes curled under, "I din want to say why," still whispering, "I tell 'm I miss Meme and want some'n to sing me sleepy." He straightened his toes out, curled them up again. "I din want them thinking I don like 'm."

"You can stay," Skeen grimaced at the Beast, "if you don't mind a pallet on the floor. I am not going to sleep with Beast there. I have my limits."

He sniggered and darted inside, scooting past her into the probably illusory safety of her room, the Beast padding along after him, its small dexterous handfeet making no sound on the floor.

She stripped two blankets off the bed, tossed him a pillow. "Ravvayad?"

"Yah, em." He patted the back of his neck. "Feel t' itch here."

"Djabo's weepy eyes."

"Yah, em."

The Aggitj formed a circle about the Boy and marched with swords drawn. Timka and Chulji flew overhead, two great horned owls, eyes and ears alert. Pegwai had his staff (the Aggitj couldn't hide their mirth the first time he did his workouts, tucking up the skirts of his robe and challenging them, counting them all four out with a speed that astonished them and Skeen, too; he was perhaps thrice the age of the oldest and his reach was a good deal shorter, but that length of springy hard wood came to life in his hands). He took point while Skeen followed behind.

It was dark, a thin mist hampered vision after a few meters. The owls flew fairly low, limiting the amount of street they could watch. Sounds had a tendency to boom out or be muffled almost to non-existence. The moon was still up and close to full so there was some light. The Aggitj had wanted to carry torches, but Skeen told them not to be idiots; torches would wipe out their nightsight, probably make trouble for the owls too, and do nothing at all to help them spot ambushers. "Just set us up as easy targets," she said. They hadn't far to go. Much of the Haven was built out over the water; it simplified waste disposal, but the permitted way was narrow and circuitous. It was paved haphazardly, sometimes only muddy ruts, each compound concerning itself only with the stretch of street outside its doors and only doing that minimum of street work because the Kral levied heavy fines on those who let their sections go.

Five minutes—sound of feet, brush of clothing, clinks and rattles and tense breathing, ten minutes—the fog thickened, the owls flew yet lower, their soft-edged feathers making little sound, fifteen minutes—the fog ahead of them acquired a rosy tinge from the torches along the waterfront. The Aggitj relaxed and walked faster, eyes more and more fixed on the glow ahead of them. The owls made a final circuit over the party then swept higher to avoid the danger of banging into sudden towers coming at them through the smoke-darkened fog. Skeen clicked her teeth together and moved up until she was only an arm's length from the boy; her eyes moved constantly side to side, along the wall tops, swift dips to the deep shadows at the base. The sounds from the wharf where the ladesmen were still loading Maggi's ship—laughter, grunts, sharp protests now and then—these came booming at them, telling them they were home free, or almost. . . .

A dark form exploded away from the shadow at the base of a wall, tumbling the two Aggitj aside, driving toward the Boy. Skeen leaped, used her impetus to boot the attacker in the chest and slam him aside; she felt something give under her foot, paid no attention, simply used the resistance to change direction. Behind her an Aggitj swung his sword, separated the assassin's head from his body. Skeen caught up the Boy, wheeled and flung him at the nearest Aggitj. One of the owls plunged down, ripped at the eyes of a second attacker; a moment later an Aggitj sword punched through his chest. Pegwai's staff came whistling out of the fog and thudded into the head of a third, the cracking of the bone loud over the heavy breathing and scuffle of feet in this eerily silent battle. Fast and furious, over in a dozen heartbeats, a cat's cradle of crisscrossing action resolved into a knot of defenders about the Boy, Skeen and Pegwai flanking the circle, the owls dipping and soaring. And three Kalakal Chalarosh dead on the rutted way.

Skeen rubbed her hand along the butt of the darter. Wholly useless in a melee like that, the drug took too long to act— seconds when every millipart of a second might mean death to the Boy. A staff, yes; Pegwai's was certainly effective.

Ders picked up the head of the first assassin. Even in the gloom they could see the pointed ears, pale hair, and rattail mustaches of a Chalarosh. The Boy wriggled in Domi's arms, ran over to Ders as soon as his feet touched ground. "Kalakal Ravvayad," he said, "see the mark on he's brow?"

Skeen rubbed at her chin. "More about?"

The Boy looked around, found the Beast nosing about in the shadows. He whistled a soft questioning phrase. The Beast chirked back at him but returned to his side without hesitation. "Not now."

"But there will be more after us?"

"Yes, emmi, Ravvayad come three, seven, eleven, seventeen and twentyseven. For me, ul send the nine threes."

Ders waggled his tongue at the head, dropped it, kicked it off into the darkness. The Boy watched it bound off; when it vanished, he said (quiet and thoughtful, as if he were talking about something he'd heard about that happened a long time ago), "I's hiding with Tyot Marese and sister with no name when that one and three others not these any of them," he fluttered a hand at the other two bodies, "they jump m' deh and m' meme and kill 'm. I seen it all." He dropped to his knees before Hal, bent until his head touched the dirt, then scrambled to his feet. "You 'venge deh and meme, Hal ach-mina. Chayidach chi. What we say, my life is yours."

Skeen thrust nervous fingers through her hair. "Fine. Now that that's done, let's go. Keep your eyes open. If the other Ravvayad are half-smart, they might think another ambush would take us off guard."

No more trouble.

Skeen watched tensely as they moved onto the broad torch-lit wharf, but if there were more Ravvayad about they contented themselves with observing. She followed her companions on board, nodded to Maggí, but didn't relax until they were settled in their cabins—even the Aggitj (Skeen insisted they ride cabin not decker this time). The cabins having four bunks, the Boy and the Beast slept in with Timka and Skeen, the Aggitj in another, while Pegwai and Chulji shared the third.

The other two passengers were in their cabins already; as Skeen walked past the open doors, she saw them settling in, saw them turn to stare as her companions moved past. She left Timka and the Boy playing a stone and tile game and went back up to watch the ship glide away from the wharf. However many times she saw this, it never got boring . . . the sails snapping up, the sudden difference in the feel of the deck under her feet, the orderly chaos around her, the excitement that rose in her own body, the excitement swirling around her. She leaned on the rail until Maggí saw her and waved her to the quarterdeck, smiled, then went back to watching intently as her crew took care of business with no need of orders from her except once when three deck passengers (Funor muffled in heavy robes) went blundering out of the deckers' well and she sent the Mate to stuff them back.

Skeen enjoyed those first moments of breaking free, refusing to think of anything else until she'd savored them. Then she leaned on the rail and frowned at the deckers. A large number of Funor muffled in their heavy robes among the Balayar, scrubby looking Pallah males, Aggitj extras, and even a few Nagamar females gathered about a crook-legged male. The Funor were split into five distinct groups that kept as far from each other as they could. No way she could tell if they really were Funor. That worried her. And would the Kalakal depend on their Ravvayad? Or would they hire the killing done by someone else, someone Skeen wouldn't know to watch for?

"Hal and Ders had bloody swords."

"Ravvayad after the Boy."

"Well, you warned me. No Chalarosh on board."

"What about those?" Skeen nodded at the passenger well. "The Funor. What says they're really Funor?"

"Not a good idea, claiming to be Funor when you're something else. If you want to check them, have the Boy send the Beast."

"Could cause a panic in your other passengers."

"Not if I'm standing by the Boy when he looses the Beast. Hm. Wait till we're in open water before you try it. I don't want bodies reaching land. I keep my tail clean of feuds and fusses."

The Boy stayed close to Skeen, the Beast scuttling flatly just in front of his feet. They joined Maggí at the edge of the deckers' well; she lifted her hand, the Boy whistled the Beast down into the well. It scuttled through all the groups, nosed with special care at the shrouded Funor, and came trotting back without any sign of alarm. The Boy looked up at Skeen. "Whatever they's, it's not Kalakal."

Maggí hopped from island to island along the Tail, picking up and putting off cargo, spending a day some places, a few hours in others. Losing some deckers, taking on others. The deck passengers had to fend for themselves, cold food and drink, though the ship's cook would sell them mugs of hot grog night and morning when he wasn't busy with his regular work, a little side business Maggí tolerated because he was the best cook on the Tail and could turn the most unpromising ingredients under the most unpromising conditions into a feast a king would relish. Also, unlike other ships Skeen had traveled on, she didn't permit the deckers to light their own braziers. Travel along the Tail was a lot too chancy to have open and unprotected fires about. Chulji went into business with the cook, shifting to a fisheagle and bringing back fresh fish that the cook could turn into stew and sell to the passengers; after all, the Skirrik boy was on this jaunt primarily to earn money for his jet. Maggi was amused at his enterprise and collected a copper a day from him for using her facilities, taking it from his watch-fee when he was officially on duty, from his profits when he was winging out on his own.

* * *

Three weeks out of Kulchikan. Two kirrpitt swarms avoided, thanks to Chulji and Timka; one lurk of pirates had fire dropped on them and lost their appetite for attack along with most of their sails.

Dark of the moon. Cloudy night. Generally clear waters. Chulji was with Pegwai, counting his hoard and sipping at some homebrew Pegwai had acquired at the last port. Skeen was restless and bad company, out prowling the decks, walking off her excess energy. The Boy was asleep, the Beast draped over his hip, snoring a little. Timka spent an hour or so trying to sleep, but Skeen's itchiness had burrowed under her skin. With a last glance at the sleeping child, she left the cabin and climbed to the deck. She saw Skeen sitting on the rail beside some ratlines, staring at the water and playing a mournful music on her flute. For a moment she thought of joining her, but Skeen didn't look like she wanted company. There was a brisk following wind, boring in its steadiness. What crew were on duty lounged about half-asleep, even the helmsman looked bored into a coma. Timka climbed to the quarterdeck, shed her robe, and shifted into hawkform. She wasn't going hunting, just wanted the feel of flight, the intense pleasure in riding the wind.

She flew away from the ship, not wanting spectators to her aerobatics, then plummetted and clawed her way up against worldpull, looped and swooped, soared and drifted until she was pleasantly tired, then started back for the ship.

A form at the rail near the stern, something white and fluttering in its hands. Timka worked higher, faced into the wind enough so that she hovered a steady distance from the ship. The hawkform she'd chosen belonged to a night hunter so she had little difficulty seeing what the man was doing, even from that distance. His hands opened and jerked upward, a small white bird barred with gray went swiftly up; as soon as it had cleared the masts it circled round and headed south. Timka hesitated, torn between getting the man and getting the bird, then called herself birdbrain and took off after the messenger. A few questions would locate the man, no one could hide the presence of a bird (and he likely had more than one) on board a sailing ship, especially since he was almost certain to be a decker. Not Funor, he wasn't wearing the robes, and not Nagamar, the hands were wrong.

The flier was fast but less than half Timka's hawksize; unfortunately it was fresh and she'd just come off a series of exercises meant to exhaust her into a dreamless sleep. She went higher still, moving into a different air so she wouldn't have to tire herself further by fighting a headwind. She'd meant to let the message bird get far enough from the ship so the man wouldn't see its interception, but by the time she caught up with it, she didn't care who saw. She stooped, slammed into it, breaking its neck before it had time to struggle; the sudden weight pulled her lower than she wanted and she had to fight her way up. The boring steady wind that drove the ship was the thing that saved her, lifting her, carrying her along so she hardly had to move a wing. She caught the ship what seemed an eon later but was probably more like half an hour, landed on the quarterdeck with an awkward thunk, almost forgetting to drop her kill first. She shifted to Pallah, pulled her robe about her, then just sat for several minutes looking at the bird, too tired to move but very satisfied with herself. There was a quill tube tied to one of the flier's legs. Whatever that bastard was doing, he was more than likely a dead man now. Unless she was wrong about Maggí and she didn't think she was. Skeen was altogether more easygoing, might even let the man live. Not Maggí; no one who plotted against the safety of her ship or her passengers or both was going to live three breaths after she discovered what he was doing. Timka grinned at the bird. Yes indeed. She stretched, groaned, yawned. Ay, lifefire, I am tired. And no rest yet. She stuffed the bird into a pocket, got to her feet. Pegwai first. Whatever's written here, he's the one who can read it.

Pegwai slit the quill and took out a roll of fine tough paper. He glanced at the dead bird Timka had dropped on the floor. "You'd best get rid of that."

"Later, later. What does it say?"

"Give me a moment to look at the thing." He slid down

the bunk, closer to the lamp, smoothed the crinkled paper on his knee. "If he's used code, this might take a while. Probably not necessary, from what I know of the Tail, not all that many can read anything, let alone a coded message. Ah." Holding the paper close to his eyes, he scanned it first, then went over it more slowly. "Pallah script, no code. Listen. *Ship Goum Kiskar. Made CaConder Point dawn, 3rd Yourchin. Damoun's landing, dawn 4th Yourchin, should be making Cloum by midday 6th Yourchin.*" Pegwai looked up. "Today's the fifth of Yourchin, I'd say he was providing information here about the speed of the Goum Kiskar." He smoothed the paper over his finger and frowned at the tiny neat writing. "*Carrying Trell essences, Atsila silks, metalwork, damask bolts, fine batiks Bretel Heran, plowshares, traps, Funor wines, Pallah brandy, tea Beren, Tjin, Comanso. Also Chalarosh Boy that Kalakal Ravvayad seeking, want much, would pay much for him. Scholar, Lumat might ransom. Two Min on board, flying watch only hotspots, othertimes on deck.* No signature, just a sketch of an eye in a circle. Where's Skeen?"

"Asleep, I suppose. When I came down she was gone from the deck."

"Get her. Chulji, you scoot aloft and watch to see no more of these messages get off. Wait, Timka, did the man see you?"

"I don't know. I was too tired to be careful."

"Better to make no assumptions. Chulji, keep that in mind and don't let anyone see you take off." He rolled the paper into a tight cylinder and slid off the bunk. "I'll wake Maggi; meet me there."

Maggí read the paper for the third time, pinched her lips together; her not-hair whipped about, a writhing silver cloud. She put the paper down with a slow controlled movement of her arm, then slapped her hand on the table. "Uskkikayah! Who?" She spat the last word at Timka.

"Didn't see his face. I thought I'd better get the flier first. Who's in charge of the deckers? He ought to know which of them have birds along. Can't be that many."

Skeen yawned, rubbed her hand across her face. "Any idea who he meant that note for?"

Maggí calmed appreciably as she frowned at the bit of paper, her not-hair settling to its usual fluff about her strong face. "Could be any of three that I know of who'd have the nerve to try me. Wonder if he knows where. . . ."

"Won't," Skeen said. "If you were his runner would you tell him?"

"No. Skeen, Houms has the watch right now. Find him and bring him, will you. Better I don't show my face on deck until I'm ready to act."

Skeen nodded, got to her feet with that wiry ease that was her kind of grace. Her restlessness was gone for the moment and Timka was grateful for that; an edgy Skeen was hard to live around. Pegwai relaxed also when Skeen was gone; his shoulders slumped a little, the tension went out of his hands. What there was between them was their own business, Timka told herself that for the thousandth time, but she couldn't stop her curiosity or the distaste that grew with every manifestation of that relationship. She could tell herself not to judge, but she did. The worst was, she didn't know how much longer she could keep from showing what she felt. Skeen was deft at reading muscle language, picked up on cues that Timka knew she'd have missed nine times out of ten. Well, maybe Skeen was enough like everyone else and wouldn't see what she didn't want to see. So we hope, Timka thought, so we all hope.

The deckers muttered angrily as the Mate stepped over and around them, heading for a stack of wattle crates and the man curled up beside them. The pile of blankets didn't move until the Mate put his boot in, then a tousled head emerged from the ragged nest. "Whaa. . . ." The Pallah rasped his hand along the two-day beard and looked stupid and dazed with sleep. When the Mate reached for him, he wriggled away clumsily, keeping his idiot's gape firmly in place. "I paid, I paid, what're you doing, I paid full deck fare me 'n me birds, wha wha what?"

A long lean beast like a cross between a leopard and a

weasel came padding up, spat the dead flier at the Pallah's feet.

"You're missing a bird," the Mate said softly.

Chulji swooped down, maneuvering deftly about sails and rigging, squawked loudly when he passed over the pile of cages, went swinging up again to circle over the ship.

The Pallah surged onto his feet, clumsiness forgotten. Knife in his left hand, he backed away.

"I don't know where you think you're going," the Mate said. He stood where he was, relaxed, casual, hands clasped behind him.

The Pallah looked quickly about. The decker well was surrounded by Crew, with Skeen, Pegwai, and the Aggitj spread among them. Maggí stood above them on the quarterdeck, a compound bow held ready, arrow nocked, other shafts in a case hooked over the rail. Snarling, the Pallah leaped for the Mate. Without change of expression the Mate caught him in the elbow with one bare foot, sent the knife flying, landed lightly beside him and broke his neck with a second kick.

Maggí lowered the bow but didn't unnock the shaft. "He was sending messages about the ship," she said, her voice carrying over the noises from the deckers, silencing them, "setting us up for attack. If he had friends among you, I hope those misbegotten sons of diseased jakadillos will have the elementary good sense to keep their hands to themselves and get the hell off my ship when we reach Cloum. Mister Houms, have the men take those birds down to Cook. Fowl will be a pleasant change from fish. Any left over from my dinner and Crew Mess, he can sell to the deckers."

A PAIR OF TALES TO KILL TIME TRAVELING DOWN THE TAIL.
or
NOW THAT THE WORD'S OUT ABOUT MAGGÍ'S WARDS, LIFE HAS GOT VERY DULL.

Skeen's tale:

The first time I saw Tibo he was riding luck with spurs on, determined to squeeze every ounce of possibility out of that reluctant lady; he had his own ship, was the slipperiest smuggler and thief in a dozen sectors, boasting he could take anything anywhere and get through the finest mesh of defenses the most paranoid of systems could field. Which was just about true as long as Bona Fortuna rose to his spurs. But the day came when he met her dark sister and Mala Fortuna was the one setting the spurs.

He went for suckerbait and swallowed the hook. No excuse for him except he trusted someone he shouldn't 've, a judas goat sent into a Pit Stop to rope in the top smugglers and lead them blind and willing to the butcher's mallet. Yes, he should have seen the hook, but after years of playing on the edge of the impossible, he'd grown careless. His ship was shot from under him, turned into scrap, but he hadn't earned his reputation on Luck alone and he wriggled loose in an emergency pod, managed to get to ground in the system where he was trapped. More than that, he stayed free and even managed to reach a skipsender and put out the word that he'd gift his stash to anyone able to break him loose. Oh he was a grand little man, that Tibo. He looked *so* inoffensive, he could seem a meek little shadow when he needed to. With his training as tumbler and juggler and bones that bent like gristle or seemed to, and a strength that amazed everyone who tried to thump him, confused by his size, plus a slippery supple mind, he twisted out of trap after trap and stayed loose. A long settled world is a helluva big place to find a sneaky little man in.

There were extravagant rumors about Tibo's stash. He was flamboyant and generous, flung coin about with both hands when he came in to a Pit Stop, but the long ride on Bona Fortuna's back brought him far more than even he could spend. When I heard the offer, I added up some of the things I knew for sure he'd done and the sum was pretty fantastic. And there was something else—what Tibo promised, he did. No sidling and backing off like you sometimes find when folks make promises in trouble that they want out of when the trouble's finished. I wasn't the only one doing those sums. Seven smugglers I knew of went after him. Probably more. None came back.

Heeren Empire. That's what the powers called it. Five neighboring stars plus the Heeren system. A big sucker, that system. Exchange binary. Fifty-nine planets, thirty of them habitable by oxygen breathers, though a couple of those took a bit of transforming before anyone could live there. A lot of debris in-system—gas, half a dozen asteroid belts, two of them canted forty degrees off the plane, something you don't see every day, but you don't see a system that big every day either. The tidal pulls in there were enough to worry even a phlux high on pharish-seven, complicated moving about something fierce. In

lots of ways a smuggler's dream, detecs couldn't cover
... well, never mind, you wouldn't know about those
things. Where was I. Oh yes.

None of the rescuers came back. The prize began to
seem not so enticing. There were even rumors that Tibo
sold out to the Heeren, that the forcers had landed on
him and he bought his life by sending out that call. Folk
who knew Tibo even a little squashed those, but even
they weren't about to try finding him. By the time I got
into Revelation Pit and heard about the offer, the last of
the seven seekers was overdue and she had a meeting
with her ananile shots, what? Oh yes, something like the
fountain of youth in a jector spray, that wasn't something
you walked out on, especially if you've paid for them
already. Expensive, yes. Like I was saying she was late
for her shot, so it was pretty generally assumed she
wasn't in any shape to return. The B-Doc put her money
in escrow, then he sold the shot again. Me, I thought
long and hard, but I've got this weakness, you wave
something impossible in my face, and I've just about got
to have a shot at it. Besides, I liked the little man and it
seemed to me all the types I didn't like would be sneering at us and saying self-righteous blatherings about the
wages of sin. I played a bit at Deiro Dantel's after I sold
what I had left of my cargo; the rest was delivered
directly to a special buyer, but I didn't say anything about
what I was thinking. It seemed to me the forcers had got
ears into some of the Stops. Most of us who hit the Pits
knew each other, at least by sight, but there were always
new hirelings about and new travelers passing through.

One thing I knew without thinking much about it, I
wasn't going to take Picarefy anywhere near that trap.
My ship. I arranged to have some work done on her so
I'd have an excuse to leave her, and I found another
ship, one I could charter, much smaller and just this side
of falling apart. It belonged to a singleton smuggler who
wanted a rest but couldn't afford one; with his Mala
Fortuna, general stupidity, and his crazy jury-rigged ship,
he was just about tapped out so he grabbed at the

chance I offered; he was so tired, he didn't care much even if I wrecked the thing and left him without wings.

I did some juggling, a lot more thinking, got a friend of mine to put in some time on the ship, tightening it up enough so it wouldn't drop to pieces around me, then I was as ready as I'd ever be. I'm sure you know that feeling. When you're stepping off the edge of everything riding half a straw, your belly's tied in knots and your skin is pricking all over and your breath catches in your throat and you think what the blazing hell am I doing here, but at the same time you've never felt more alive, more . . . well, you know the feeling.

I won't go into details about what I went through getting that ship to the Heeren System. You've got some idea if you've ever tried to get somewhere in a leaky rowboat during a hurricane. What with one thing and another, I got where I planned to be some six months later. By then if you offered me a match and a stick of dynamite, I'd have taken you up on the offer and blown that miserable ship into scrap iron.

The thing was, though, the nature of the ship was its best protection. The others had gone after Tibo with everything they could lay hands on. Me, I crept along like a three-legged goat. Forcers out on a smuggler prowl stopped me a dozen times, but I had good papers and a lousy ship; no being in his, her, or its right mind would use that rust farm for anything dangerous. And my looks matched my ship. I looked like a half-molted owl gone senile; I was filthier than the ship and the ship had a stink to it that would choke a buzzard. The forcers who boarded me were extra careful to touch nothing, afraid they'd catch some sort of creeping crud. I'd wager the cost of this ship the ones who had to look at my papers had themselves fumigated as soon as they were back on their ship. Those Empire forcers had a high opinion of their abilities and it was not too greatly exaggerated. Thing was, those clever minds of theirs were also rigid minds—they couldn't think sideways. To consider me or my ship a danger was an insult they couldn't swallow.

The last few times they came across me sputtering along, they just waved me on.

When I nosed into the system, I putted along from world to world, doing a little trading here, a bit more there, paying my fees, getting paper straight, never really sure the ship would get up once it was down, but for all its cantankerous nature and miserable appearance, she was a tough little tub. With a curse or two, a lot of assorted prayers to every god I could remember, and some basic will power, I kept the bucket flying until I got to the world I wanted and got plunked down where I wanted on that world.

I took my time once I was down, doing what I'd done the other six times. I'd spent half a year getting here, another quarter working my way to my goal; you might say I was on my way so long they forgot I was coming. Funny. I made some good finds and better trades; even without Tibo's stash, I came out ahead, but it was so damn tedious. Well, never mind that. I futzed about that world, a gray hag, too feeble to be a danger to anyone— looking, buying, selling—and everywhere I went I left a sign behind, a sign from something I knew about him that very few others did.

He saw the sign and followed me for several days before he came from under and signaled me. We met when we both were reasonably sure no forcers or other snoops were watching. Not any sentimental coming together like the story books tell it, that's for sure, the way I looked and the way he felt, well, never mind. The big problem was getting him onto my ragged old ship. That bucket had hidey holes where no hole could possibly be; the owner told me about most of them, but even he didn't know them all. I spent a lot of that six-months' dip checking them out; whoever thought up some of those had a perverse mind. I wish I knew him; I'd like to spend a year or two listening to him talk. So once Tibo was on board, no forcer was going to find him. We kicked that around a bit. Tibo had managed to keep an eye on the main port, even got onto the apron to do some muscle work heaving crates about, watching how the forcers handled searches. Discouraging. They searched everything, even had some crude sniffers that picked up traces of live cargo. Twice they caught traders trying to smuggle out shalakuza eggs and sinka seedlings. That's what Tibo'd gone in for, Shalakuza Silks. Came from spinnerets on the shalkako larva, an arthropod that lived on the world where we were; it ate a single plant that had to be grown in the special soils of a single narrow valley. The powers wouldn't let any adult specimens of the shalkako, their eggs, or larva leave the world, nor any of the sinka trees. Naturally there was one damn huge bounty for anyone who could get them out, alive or dead. Smugglers were giving the powers fits—which was why they set the trap.

I'd been expecting all that. A year's not a long time to keep this kind of trap working. Would have been easier if we could have waited a couple more years, but the forcers were circling closer every day. He'd got loose a couple times just because he was lucky enough to look the right way at the right time. Just luck. That was all. And he was tired. Worn to skin and bone. Much longer and he'd just wear away to a wisp of nothing. Like I said, I'd been expecting things to be that hairy so I'd set up some habits on other worlds and this. I was a crotchety old hag suspicious of everyone and everything. Whenever I bought or traded for anything, I took delivery on the spot and escorted the goods back to a cubicle I'd rented, getting all papers and official stamps before I moved a step. Tedious and excessively cautious, but that fit my persona and beyond a few grumbles no one made any complaints about my methods; more important, none of the functionaries who processed the papers and the transfers saw me as anything more than a fussy, half-cracked old crone. I'd had enough time already to set the impression deep, so no one would think anything about me traveling about with crates on a jitney, and I had some special crates waiting for the right time. I told Tibo what I had and what I thought and we worked out a plotline that seemed like it just might get him past the sniffers.

Besides the Shalakuza Silks this world produced a cordial wine that was interesting enough to justify its liftcost. I wouldn't make a big profit unless I was lucky enough to hit a fad in cordials, but there was enough in it that no one would wonder why I was bothering with the juice. The cordial was fragile but not really difficult to transport if you took a bit of care. Hard usage would spoil it. I bought a gross of the bottles, had them packed with great care, hanging around and fussing until I nearly drove the packers into murdering me, and left the local inspector yawning. The crate was closed and strapped, the municipal seals slapped on, then the ultimas, then I had the crate shifted to a jitney. I took it to my section of warehouse and was just about as fussy, stowing it where temperatures and humidity were most open. I visited one more city, didn't find anything there, so I came back and wanted to load my ship.

Right away the forcers landed on me. They made me run everything, even officially sealed crates through their sniffer. I grumbled and groused and made as much trouble as I could without driving them too far. Got them hot and bothered and cursing me under their breath. Not aloud, because that would be breaking discipline and get them censured no matter what the provocation. They wanted very badly to catch me doing something illegal, so badly the thought shivered over their heads like heat waves. Of course there was nothing in the first group of crates they ran through the sniffer. Those crates and bundles had in them exactly what the invoices said. About halfway along, there was the crate of cordials. I really got agitated over that one, pointing out that the sniffer might upset the delicate balance of the flavors and leave me with some very expensive vinegar. I got so agitated and adamant about that damn crate, they watched it extra carefully as they put it through the sniffer. And the sniffer registered life present. A very small life, but a positive none the less. They hauled the crate off the rollers, exulting, shaking it up quite a lot, taking pleasure in the roughness. I was near foaming at the mouth, dancing around them, shouting at them. And while just about every forcer in the place clustered around the cordial crate enjoying my performance, the cargo laders for the port were passing the rest of my goods through the sniffer and hauling them over to the ship. I had a pair of android handlers, nothing fancy, but programmed to stow things the way I wanted and they got every crate, bundle, and barrel aboard before the forcers finished with the cordial crate.

I was spitting and twitching, shrieking and cursing in a dozen languages. The hotter I got, the more exultant they got. They pried open the crate and began pulling out those carefully packed bottles and finally came up with what had triggered the sniffer. A half-dead rodent smaller than my fist.

I was howling about suing the lot of them, complaining up their command structure as high as I could reach. The local commander had a couple of his men pick me up, slap some slave wire about my wrists and ankles. They carted me onto the old wreck. Told me to boot the thing out of the system and not show my ugly nose around there again.

Feeling a bit bruised, screeching at them over the com, I did just that; fingers crossed I lifted that bucket off-planet one last time and started booting out of the system.

Apparently the local commander got to thinking after I left, because he had three stingships stop me just short of Teegah's Limit. They searched the ship again, opened crates at random, while I sat fuming and calling every plague in the catalogue down on them and all their ancestors and all their descendants, legitimate or otherwise. Then he sent me off with another warning not to return that sounded as futile and stupid as he had to feel.

How'd I work it? I'm sure you guessed. Tibo was in a shielded crate two down after the cordial box. When he was working at the port, he noticed how the forcers sometimes let the remainder of a cargo be processed through the sniffers while they dealt with the suspicious boxes or bales. On busy days they didn't want to hold up legitimate traders and travelers. So we picked the busiest time of the busiest day, and I proceeded to irritate and distract them. If they were as good as they thought, they would have ignored me and stopped everything while they searched. They didn't. Well, that convinced me of one thing. They certainly had noses in the Pits. They were waiting for those they knew were coming, but not for me, because I kept my mouth shut. Not for a grotty old woman in a ratty-tatty ship. As for the second search, well, didn't I tell you about the hidey holes? Tibo rode to the Limit in one of the larger holes; the dismantled crate rode in another. After that if it looked like we were about to be fished out of skip, he popped back in the hole and sat out the search. It was a long slow trip back to Revelation Pit and we got to know each other a lot better.

Oh. Something else. Tibo's stash. He didn't send the call. Someone up in the powers did that, had a bright idea of extending the trap and getting rid of the smugglers that were giving them fits. Tibo's stash turned out to be mainly illusion. He sent a lot of coin to his huge family and he lived high. He hadn't the price of a tramp's bone when I busted him loose, so I was pleased to manage a small profit off my trading. He did know where I could find some Achelarian ruins, hadn't done anything about them because he wasn't a Rooner; we formed a partnership, him providing the site and a strong back, me the ship and the expertise. That worked out so well, we stayed together for the next five years.

(Skeen stopped short of telling Maggí about Tibo's betrayal; he was hers to curse, no one else had a right.)

Maggí's tale:

When I was a child I ran with my brothers. Our father was a scholar of sorts; given the choice he'd have been happy to spend his life at the Tanul Lumat, but he was Asach har Aloz and had no choice. He left the running of the stead to his wives. My blood mum, his third wife, died when I was born and he almost had me killed, but the other two mums wouldn't let him. I was the first girl. If he didn't want trouble marrying off his sons, if he wanted to keep them from being cast out as extras, he needed trading clout. After a long interval he married again and I had two new sisters. Took the pressure off me and kept the other mums busy. They didn't exactly forget about me, but limited their interest to seeing I was kept clean and fed. The twins, who were two years older, took over for them once I was let out of the nursery and adopted me as an honorary boy. As much, I suppose, because all three of us were in our way blotches on the family book of lives. Boy twins. A double birth was a curse, an evil omen, besides meaning two extra mouths the Father could never marry off onto some other family. And Me, I was a mother killer, a big baby coming near a month late. Ucsi, Ishri, and me. After a few years they managed to talk the older boys into accepting me. I learned everything they learned from reading and writing, to tracking kisbyas that had attacked the herds. Eldest Brother the Heir Yoncal made me a bow and was as proud as a rooster with a flock of sleek hens the day I matched him shaft for shaft. By the time I'd reached my fourteenth year I was brown and rough and had a tongue like a dungviper when I was attacked. And if my tongue didn't back the serf off, I could fight hard and dirty.

Time caught up with me. My courses started. I knew pretty well what was happening—the mums had got that much through to me, though I wouldn't learn the other things they tried to teach me. My sewing was knots and gaps. Dance and deportment, ah well, just say I was most times out riding with the herds. Cooking, yes, the boys made me learn enough for me to be camp cook so they wouldn't have to. I complained because I thought it wasn't fair, but they reminded me I was just a girl and if I didn't want to do the cooking and cleaning up, I could stay home where I belonged. Ah well. I tried messing up a few times, burning things, but Yoncal wasn't stupid; he spanked my behind pink and I didn't try that again.

Time. You want to hold it back, you want to stop the changes, but you can't. My body betrayed me. I hid what was happening as long as I could. I knew my freedom was gone the moment the mums found out.

How right I was. One of the serving maids saw the bloodrag before I could hide it and told the mums. My life changed totally. They kept me in the house until I was nearly crazy. They scrubbed me and buffed me and bleached me until the tan and calluses were gone. I looked in a mirror and didn't know myself and didn't like what I saw. I was watched constantly, never had a moment alone. Every fussy little woman's skill I'd run out of learning was crammed down my throat. Everything I valued about myself was viewed with loathing and forbidden to me. I tried to hold on, to cling to what I knew was good and right, but even my brothers abandoned me; it was as if I'd caught some disease that they were afraid would rub off on them. I was confused and miserable. My body was stretching and reshuffling itself. For some reason I started growing again and shot up nearly three spans that year and turned skinny as a stripped sapling. That was bad enough but my breasts grew, too, and my hips broadened and I thought I looked grotesque. My sisters sneered at me and the mums were angry at me all the time and Father was shut up with his books. He didn't care a snap of his fingers about any of his children. He didn't know anything about his sons; he talked to them on the holy days, asked the required questions in a voice without interest or energy; otherwise he never came near any of us. Ah well, I can't even remember what he looked like, he doesn't matter at all. The ones I knew were the mums and my brothers and sisters. And they all tried to make me into the thing women were supposed to be. I hated it, I hated everything, myself included. But I didn't know the words for what I was feeling, I didn't know any arguments I could use to convince anyone that what they all were doing was wrong. For me it was wrong. After a short rebellion that got nowhere, I gave up. No one understood what I was trying to say, at least that's what they told me. They told me all this was for my good and the good of the family.

My fifteenth year passed. I never saw my brothers any more except now and then passing through the halls and the critical looks they gave me, well, the ground dissolved under my feet. Nothing was solid. Nothing was real. I gave in. And because I couldn't be half-hearted about anything, I made the mistake of trying to be small and dainty and feminine. But I was large and clumsy and my temper was uncertain those days, and even more uncertain when I finally understood that no matter how much I wanted it, I couldn't be the charmer they were trying to make me. Couldn't. All my life till then there'd been nothing I really wanted to do I hadn't been able to learn and do. I could ride anything I could mount, pull a bow almost as strong as Yoncal's, track a kisbya over solid rock. I could braid ropes, throw a bull kova by twisting his tail, well, I needn't go on with that, you get the idea. I tried, but deep down I didn't understand what they wanted, I couldn't feel it. My sisters, young as they were, seemed like they were born knowing what I couldn't learn. That made everything worse. I ignored them when I was running with the boys, let them see how much I despised what they did. Now, well, they were just getting back at me for all that. I was in their world now and I was no good. They made me feel it, oh yes.

My sixteenth year passed. My body settled down and rounded off. I was much too tall, but I got some meat on my bones and even turned a bit pretty, though I still had a very insecure grasp on what feminity was all about, at least as it was defined in Boot and Backland.

The mums started carting me around the Rudssas, sort of semi-auctions where nubile daughters were shown off to potential husbands. The other Ashanku sent their sons or came themselves if they were looking to add new wives to their steads.

If I kept my mouth shut, and the mums made sure I knew what a hell I'd have at home if I didn't—if I kept my eyes modest, laughed delicately and daintily at Asach jokes, and murmured idiocies that the mums made me memorize along with the appropriate situations to use them—if I did all these things, the mums thought they could settle me with some degree of credit. I wasn't sure exactly what I wanted. I thought if I could attract someone like Father who'd more or less ignore me and let me go my own way, I wouldn't mind that so much. And I was curious about sex. I knew about animals, I'd helped in the breeding chutes though the mums were outraged later when they found out about that. There were one or two Ashanku who seemed interesting and others who seemed cold enough for me as they looked over the girls like buyers inspecting kova heifers at an auction. Which really wasn't all that different, if you thought about it, from what our mums and other mums were doing with their daughters. But none of the likely ones paid any attention to me. I was too tall, too sullen, I looked and felt stupid. They didn't want intelligence, at least not girls that let it show, but liveliness and a degree of wit were necessary to attract them. I had neither and I wasn't pretty enough to make the lack unimportant.

We went from Rudssa to Rudssa and my constant failure corroded my soul until I felt—ah, even thinking about it now twists my gut. Yes, even now when I know quite well how stupid it all was, how cruel and distorted it was. Even now I remember and I ache for that child. What other standards did she have to measure herself against? The lessons of your youth sink deep. These days when some fool says *look at that fat cow trying to be a man, pitiful isn't it,* the rage rises in me—the words are an insult to everything I am, takes a while to pull myself together and get things into perspective and recognize the envy and spite and inadequacy behind those words. I want to stop reacting to things like that, but it still hurts, Skeen, that child is still inside somewhere aching because she failed and failed and failed again to fit herself into their idea of her. Enough of that. Brandy does that to me, I get sentimental and soggy. Where was I? Ah! Toward the end of summer, when the mums were beginning to despair, the Asach Keesh began sniffing around me. He wasn't exactly ugly, just old; that didn't bother me too much, it was the things that oozed from his eyes and tainted his touch that turned my stomach. I didn't understand what I was seeing, but it made me want to run away and hide. He sat by me at one Rudssa, touching me fairly chastely when he was in the light, but the thing in his eyes, the wetness at the corners of his tiny mouth made even the properest touch an obscenity. He was at the next Rudssa and took me into the dances where he mauled me as much as he could without making himself too obvious. By the end of that Rudssa I was as close to fainting as I've ever been because I knew for sure he was going to ask for me. I didn't know what to do. I tried to tell myself that I was worth more than fifth wife to an ancient smelly wreck, but he was a wealthy, touchy, important man. Even if he wanted to, even if he cared about me, Father wouldn't dare offend Keesh. And he didn't care; to disturb him with my fears and loathings would be useless. Worse than useless, it would only make my sale that much surer. By the time we got back to our hold I had a high fever and was shaking with chills and vomiting even after there was nothing left in my stomach. I gave the mums and the maids a hard time, though that wasn't deliberate. It just happened.

In the morning I was called to my Father's public room and he told me what I was expecting to hear. I knew it wouldn't do any good, but I tried to say no, I tried to say listen to me, I'll die before I let him touch me. My Father closed his ears to my voice; he left the room, untroubled, unmoved, forgetting about me as soon as the door was shut. The mums wrestled me away and later had me beaten and locked up and fed a meal a day of bread and water until I was dizzy with hunger and fear. They went at me every day. I had to do this for the family, they said, for your brothers, for all of us. If we broke off now, the Asach would declare feud on us and start a war that would wipe the family out. Keesh was rich and powerful, with many serfs and younger sons married to his daughters and his acres stretched ten times the breadth of the har Aloz lands, and they were in the rich lowlands not up here in the niggardly hills. I tried to tell them how I felt, but they wouldn't hear me any more than my father would. I could get used to him if I tried, I could get used to anything if I really tried; it was woman's fate to suffer, nothing I could do would change that, no point in thinking it would. I was going to Asach Keesh har Tosso. I could make it easy on myself by submitting or I could fight and find out how weak and helpless I was, how futile I was. How stupid. You're not stupid, the mums told me; use your head, learn how to fool him and get what you want that way. I told them he made my skin crawl, but they just kept saying you can get used to anything. They wouldn't look at me when they said it, and I understood finally and completely that they were helpless and every word I said hurt them and the only defense they had was to deny the hurt and invoke the image of the suffering silent woman who was nonetheless extremely powerful through coaxing and manipulation. I stopped arguing. I recognized the futility of depending on anyone for help. I tried to reconcile myself to what had to be. And vomited everything I ate for the next week. For two days I had raged, for seven days I tried to conform, for two more days I racked my brain for some way out. By then I knew I couldn't do it, I simply could not endure that man's touch. There was no one who would listen to me or take my part in all of Boot and Backland. I would have to leave Boot and Backland. At first the thought terrified me. I had no money, no knowledge of the world outside Aggitj holds. I did know how to ride and hunt and live off the land. But winter was coming soon and before the fist snows I'd be shut into Keesh's hold. I thought about killing myself, but I didn't want to die. I thought about killing Keesh, but I'd heard far too many stories about what happened to self-made widows. I wanted to live. But how? Har Aloz steading was high on the slopes of the Spine, but Asach's lands were down close to the coast. Somehow I had to break free of my guards when I was being hauled to my lovely bridegroom, get to a port, and use my bride gifts to bribe my way onto a ship. And try to keep from being raped and collared. I had no illusions about pretending to be a boy. I'd lost a lot of weight, and I hadn't done any physical training for almost two years. My muscles were soft as butter and about as responsive. And in spite of the past weeks of misery my breasts and hips hadn't reduced their obtrusiveness one hair. I stayed up all night plotting and in the morning I looked so weary, so dull and dispirited, it was easy to convince the mums that I was ready to accept my fate.

They watched me still, not trusting my meekness, but I was free to go where I wanted as long as I stayed in the women's quarters. They tested me, let me go outside, let me ride—as long as I kept a guard of three serfs with me. I continued to show listless and exhausted and finally they relaxed. Everyone relaxed. Yoncal patted my shoulder and told me I'd have a splendid time, Keesh's stables were famous from Toe to Tip. Titur began teasing me about being a fine lady, wagered I'd be running the women's quarters and making the other wives hop before the winter was out. My sisters fingered my wedding robes and were nearly slain with envy. Everyone acted like this was the finest event since lifefire was a rushlight.

Except the Twins. Ucsi and Ishri were destined to be called Extra however well all their sisters married. They had followed Yoncal's lead at first and treated me like he did. But they'd ridden as escort with the mums and me to too many Rudssas to have any illusions about how happy I was going to be. That was a sly move to see if the boys could attract dowered daughters in spite of their being twins. Apart they were beautiful boys, far prettier than me. Together they were a wonder to behold. But even that extraordinary beauty couldn't overcome their bad

luck in being twins. Single births ate enough of the
Father's substance and the taking of multiple wives generally meant far too many mouths around even though
only one woman in three was fertile and only one woman
in five could produce as many as three living children.
Because twins were apt to produce more doubles they
were always called as Extras and driven beyond the
borders. They'd seen my misery and weren't blinded by
family needs; they'd held my head and helped the mums
clean me up after that last Rudssa.

On the day before the Asach's escort came to fetch
me, Ucsi came to my room. I was locked in, but he didn't
bother with the door; he came down the side of the
house and in my window. I always had a window open at
night if it wasn't raining or snowing or freezing cold and
this was a mesru-summer night, one of those in late
autumn that are warm and pleasant breaks just before
the snows when only the fallen leaves told you that
summer was gone.

I wasn't asleep. My trunks were in my rooms, all
packed and corded for transport. I was emptying out the
smallest, the one I planned to keep in the caros with me.
In place of the fripperies and cosmetics I was stowing
my bow and all the shafts I'd managed to steal, male
garb I'd taken from Yoncal's winter gear, rope and knives
and a frying pan, needles and thread, and everything I
could think of I might need on the run. I was trying to fit it
all in when Ucsi swung in and stood laughing at me.

"I might have known," he whispered. He hugged me
and sighed with relief. "Ishri and me," he said, keeping
his voice low, "we're due to be called Extra, he wants us
out before winter comes. So we talked him into letting us
represent the family at the Presentation of the Bride.
Soon as that's over, we told him, you can declare us
Extra and we'll be right on the coast. That way Keesh
will have to pay our expenses, not you. He thought it
was a good notion and found it hard to believe we'd
managed to make that much sense. So we're going with
you. We'll have our severance purses. He grumbled but

came up with twenty gold each, so we've got that. I came to see if you were really so cowed as you looked and if you weren't, to say you can come with us if you want. Might have known you'd have your own plans. You don't have to go with us, but it'd be nice to be together a bit longer and we can take care of you, too." He grinned at me. "Besides, you know what sort of cook Ishri is and I'm worse. You aren't much, but you're stads ahead of us." I nearly swallowed my fist to keep the laughter in. I wanted to laugh and sing and shout my joy to the lifefire, but I got over that fast enough. Ucsi helped me finish packing, then we sat on the bed and planned until the dawn was red outside. He went out the window and climbed back up to Ishri who was curled up and sleeping, Ucsi told me later, calm as a mouse in his nest. I went to bed and tried to sleep. I didn't expect to, but my body fooled me. It said enough was enough, and plunged me deep almost before my head touched the pillow.

The escort arrived a little before noon with a huge ornate caros drawn by a matched team of biroun, black as the jet the Skirrik p2ize, their hooves and horns polished till they gleamed, the points on the horns filed so sharp they looked like they could split a thought. The Rossam bowed low and called me Lady. The Teybibi minced out and got creakily to her knees, long time since that one had bowed to anybody, knocked her head on the dirt by my toes and stayed there crouched like a great black toad until I said the words that let her labor to her feet. Honors. Hah! I didn't need anyone to tell me just how little those honors meant. All this poshness, all this ritual were meant to show off his possessions and his rank. I was a part of those possessions now, or as good as, and took on the glow of their glory. The mums pulled the traveling biseh over my head, a kind of roomy sack with eyeholes, then all of them hugged me. I could feel them shaking, and hear from their breathing that they were crying. Well, they were the only family I had, so I hugged them back and whispered not to worry, I was all right, look how well he treats me already. They said nothing, knowing as well as I did how little all that meant. But they patted me and got me settled in the caros and produced the ritual howls of grief as the caros started moving.

The caros was a closed one, so I started to pull off the biseh; the mums used to let me do that when we were going to the Rudssas because if I had to wear it all the way, I'd arrive half out of my mind, sweaty and crying. I hated being bound up, and the biseh made me feel like a netted chicken. With the gauze curtains tied down we could get light and air and no one could see in. The Teybibi, the Asach's widowed elder sister sent to be my chaperone, screeched at me to stop that; she caught my hands and pulled them into my lap. She was strong as a bull kova. When I protested, she slapped me, the biseh muffling the blow only a little. She told me to shut my mouth and behave myself if I knew how. There was anger and jealousy in her voice and hard intent. She meant to break me into obedience before we reached the Asach's hold. I'd never met anyone like her before, I knew that by the time the day was over. She was harder than stone, more vicious than a rabid kisbya. She hurt me whenever I displeased her and she was determined to be displeased. If I was silent, she said I was sullen and stupid; if I answered her no matter how mildly, she said I was insolent. And so it went. I said she hurt me, not that she beat me, because she didn't beat me, just pinched and slapped and twisted until I was nearly driven wild by the pain she knew how to inflict without leaving signs of her actions. She didn't even bruise me. I got a moment alone when I bathed and looked at my body because I couldn't believe I could hurt so much with nothing to show it, only a few reddish spots that were already fading. The Teybibi would have forbid the bath if she could, but Ucsi and Ishri had ridden ahead and bespoke it for me along with a good meal and a pot of mulled wine. And she didn't torment me after I was in bed. If she feared any living being, it was her brother so she wasn't going to bring me to him limp with exhaustion. When I thought of that, I turned colder than an ice-storm wind and tried not to think of it again. If the Teybibi was afraid of him, what must he be like? What. . . .

We were to be on the road five days, spending the last half of the last day in an Inn near Yezram freeport. This, so the next morning I could be brought in procession to my husband-soon, clad in fine raiment, riding a milk white biro mare with obsidian horns and hooves. Keesh's boast that a man of his years was still vigorous enough to cover a girl younger than his youngest daughter. See her and envy me.

We reached the Inn an hour before sundown on the fifth day. Ucsi went into Yezram while Ishri stayed behind to get their traps ready and keep the Teybibi off my back.

Late that night I clunked her on the head, tied her up, and gagged her. I felt like cutting the viper's throat, but miserable as they were, I still had family. Bad enough to run. Father could handle that, disown us, declare all of us exile and Extra. He was planning to do that anyway to the boys, no trouble to curse me and disown me, too. But blood meant more blood. Blood without end. Much as I wanted to pay her back for five days of torment when I didn't dare fight back because that could ruin the escape, as much as I wanted to shame and humiliate her and bleed the acid from her veins, I could not. So I bound her into a cocoon of quilts and stuffed a dirty stocking into her mouth. Then I packed my gear in a back-carry bundle, doubled the rope around a bedpost, and climbed out the window.

Soon as I was down Ucsi reeled in the rope and Isrhi brought round three mounts, the rest of our gear roped behind their saddles. "Your escort is sound asleep and I do mean sound; you should hear the snoring." He grinned at me. "Uyus in their beer."

We rode off at a smart trot, not hurrying, we didn't want any snoop still about to get the idea we were running from anything. The wharves were a little over a stad off. We rode through that cool quiet night, the split hooves loud on the shells put down to lay the dust; I don't know what the others were feeling, we never got to talk about it much, but I was scared and excited and. . . . You talked about that leap-into-the-dark feeling, you know what was in me.

Ucsi had bargained with the owner of a small coast-leaper that was leaving with the tide for Atsila Vana. The wiry little Balayar took the mounts as passage payment, quite aware who they belonged to; he got them on board with a speed and efficiency that started Ishri giggling, though he contrived to keep his amusement soundless. Less than an hour later we were on our way.

I found out later that no one discovered the Teybibi until nearly noon when someone came from the Asach to see what was holding things up. The escort was still snoring; the Teybibi was stiff as a board and so furious it was a while before she could talk, then a while when she only sputtered her rage. It was the Rossam who saw that I was gone and slapped her into coherence. And it was the Rossam who sent men galloping into Yezram to hunt for me. They found no trace of the twins and me. Those who knew anything, knew better than to say it; those who knew nothing voiced their ignorance with loud indignation. They didn't work too hard at it, too much time had passed. Keesh raged at the Teybibi and nearly had her strangled, but did not; he didn't quite dare take on the name of kinslayer and the curse of kinblood. He sent her into the hills to live alone in a tiny hut. His wives and daughters must have cried blessing on me for that at least. He had the escort beaten and set to work as field hands for his meanest krav-serf. He was going to cry feud with my father, but let himself be talked into waiting and when he heard my father had named us Exile and Extra, he was pacified enough to drop his war-talk. And next year he got his bride from an older but poorer family. She was small and dainty and clever enough to seem docile and rumor reached me that she led him a dance of fools before she died in childbirth. A twisted smile. As for us, our plans went awry faster than we'd

imagined. The shipmaster made a good living out of the
Extras he enticed onto his ship; before the land dropped
below the horizon Ucsi, Ishri, and I were in a drugged
sleep. Like with those Extras before us, he got our gear,
our severance purses, and he sold us to slavers in the
freeport at Atsila Vana. I woke in the hold of a slave ship
bound for Oruda. My brothers went somewhere else. I
never saw them again. A sigh.

"Ah well, a quick and effective lesson in the way of the
world. That was twenty years ago, Skeen. As you see, I've
come a long way from Boot and Backland, long in every
sense of the word.

A BRUSH WITH DEATH HERE, A BRUSH WITH DEATH THERE, IT'S GOOD FOR YOUR CIRCULATION.

They moved south along the Tail through brisk weather
that drove the ship at spanking speeds from port to port. The
flying Min twice more brought back news of ambushes; once
they burned out the hopeful pirates, once the band was too
big and Maggí circled wide about them; it lost her some time,
but she could well afford the delay. She was delighted with
the Min. So were her sailors and the passengers whether deck
or cabin. The Crew had part shares in her cargo besides bits
and pieces of their own; while they were more than compe-
tent fighters, they saw no urgent need to prove their skills.

Chulji preened for the crew and showed off his forms with pride and delight. He was very young after all. With thoughts about promoting an alliance between him and Timka that would give the little Min a place to settle with a reasonable degree of security (and take Timka off her hands), Skeen questioned Chulji about his age and discovered he was not quite fifteen, probably about half Timka's age. Nothing there. Timka was *born* older than that. Promises, promises. Why don't you keep your mouth shut, old woman, you'll be gnawing on your kneebones soon if you don't watch it.

The ports were all different and all much the same, raucous, smelly, dangerous. Some were mostly Pallah, some mostly Balayar, some Chalarosh, some Funor. Aggitj Extras in all of them and a scatter of Nagamar hiding out from shaman curses and a lacing of Skirrik earning their jet. Even a few Skirrik mining jet up in the mountains of the long curving peninsula that was the base of the Tail.

Latun. Pallah-run. One hour after they went ashore, a Ravvayad triad struck. A spear thrown low and hard. Pegwai's staff caught it and sent it at a wall where it hit sideways and clattered to the ground. The Ravvayad melted into the tangle of streets so fast that Chulji lost them almost immediately, though he fluttered about for several minutes trying to catch sight of them again. Two hawks larger than he came darting down from the low clouds and went after him until they saw Timka in the street. They plunged at her, but Skeen darted both as soon as they were in range and they crashed onto the cobblestones; with a hiss of rage, Timka snatched Skeen's bootknife, bent over them and with a complicated twisting cut, dispatched them. She stood back with a look of intense satisfaction as they melted into a sort of speckled gray jelly and oozed away into the cracks between the cobble. Skeen looked from the spear to the smear on the pavement. "Shit."

Pegwai laughed. "Yes" he said. To Timka, he said, "Are they working together?"

"Yes. No. What do you expect me to say?" Timka looked at the knife, wiped it on her skirt and held it out to Skeen. "Once, it's coincidence. If it happens again, you don't need me to tell you what that means."

Tevel. Chalarosh council, large Balayar minority. The Company remained on board while Maggí and the rest went ashore to do their trading. Timka was nervous, water Min swimming about the ship kept her in a continual turmoil, a mixture of fear and fury that kept her pacing round and round the rail like a claustrophobic in a closet he can't escape. Maggí came back on board in a foul mood. She'd refused to take any Chalarosh as deckers and the touchy Chala had turned nasty about things like permits and dock fees. She left an hour later, some of the passengers having to scramble to make the boat. The water Min followed a short distance, but dropped away when the Goum Kiskar reached open water. Timka emerged from her sour mood and went to the bow to let the wind blow over her and the sun warm her.

Two nights later half a dozen fisheagles swooped at her as she stood at the rail watching dark water slide past. She was alone, the Company was below, the Crew was busy elsewhere, the deckers were wrapped in their blankets asleep. The eagles came out of the cloud scatter, riding the brisk wind, moving at speed, giving her almost no warning before they struck. A few months back they might have got her, but she'd learned a thing or two about self-defense since she'd been traveling with Skeen. An instant was all she needed. She flung herself to one side, rolled under the shrouds where the ropes would keep the eagles off her and shouted for help. Mister Houms the Mate snatched up one of the short javelins kept ready on the quarterdeck and skewered one of the eagles, had another javelin ready, but the attackers wheeled away while the one fallen to the deck was starting to melt. Timka cought hold of the javelin's shaft, swung the dead Min up and shook him off the point into the ocean. "Thanks," she said when Houms came to reclaim the weapon.

"No sweat," he said; he scowled at the slime on the blade and called one of the crew to take it below and scrub it clean. "That going to happen again?"

"I doubt it. Min don't like dying."

"Who does."

So it went, Min and Kalakal Ravvayad attacking in turns or together, attacking and dying. Aggitj and Min, Scholar and

Thief, Skirrik boy and Chalarosh child . . . those encounters
shaped them, made them a formidable fighting band. And as
the days passed, what the Aggitj and Chulji and even Pegwai
had joined in a spirit in a spirit of careless adventure, the search
for the Ykx and the opening of the Stranger's Gate became
something taken very seriously indeed. Otherwise Timka and
the Boy had no future at all. Even Skeen who had never quite
believed in this business, but started on the trek because she
had to do something or go crazy sitting around and stagnating,
even Skeen found her attitude changing; the Key to the Gate
was just about her only way of sloughing the responsibilities
she'd collected. And Tibo, Tibo, where are you? What are you
doing now? Who are you with? Where, where is Picarefy?

Port to port to port. Round the curve of the Tail peninsula.
The ports gradually changed, turning orderly and more open,
the people in them colonists rather than outcasts, families and
clans of the impatient and the landless. At the first of these
towns Maggí called the Crew together and warned them to
remember what happened the last time they hit this place, and
any fines she had to pay would come out of their hides.

Port to port to port along the north coast of the Halijara sea
until they reached Karolsey at the mouth of the Vraditio
River. Lake Sydo was a huge irregular body of water in the
geographical center of the Suur Yarrik; a number of rivers
wound south from that lake, one of them Shemu (the river
Perinpar Dih traveled up when he took his rescued Ykx
home). The Vraditio was much shorter, but it was a cranky
river with a lot of low falls and boulder strewn rapids and it
curved around a vast coastal swamp filled with hostile Nagamar.
The Company planned to ride up the Vraditio River to the
Lake and talk the Ykx into sending them down the Shemu to
Cida Fennakin.

IT'S WINDING DOWN, THE TRAVELING IS ALMOST DONE, THE QUESTION WAITS ITS ANSWER.
or
DON'T TALK TO ME, I BITE.

Maggí took Skeen and Pegwai through Karolsey to the sparsely settled North Hills section and pulled the bell rope at a large compound; over the clangor of the bell they heard children's laughter, shouts, a name called over and over. A wicket opened in one leaf of a massive double gate, showing the side of a man's head as he yelled over his shoulder for silence. He faced around (there was a slight diminution of the noise behind him) presenting a smiling Balayar face. The smile broadened to a beaming grin. "Maggí Solitaire! A moment, a moment." The wicket slammed shut and a moment later the gate opened enough to emit a short rotund man. He bounced over to Maggí, hugged her, bounced back, moved his eyes from Skeen to Pegwai, raised his brows.

Maggí chuckled. "May we come in, Sogan?"

"Oh. Yes, yes, don't mind the children; Zenica's at the market yet with Mai and Lanco." He backed through the gate, gesturing for them to follow.

The enclosure burgeoned, teemed, swelled with life; trees, shrubs, flowers, small furry animals, almost as many birds as there were leaves, and children everywhere. They followed

Sogan, wading through waves of vigorous life, as he led them into the house and out again into a smaller sparer garden. He got them seated on benches and offered them wine cider tea fruitade herb tisane until Maggí stopped the flow of hospitality with a lifted hand. "Later, friend," she said, "there's plenty of time for that. Now is the time for listening."

She introduced Skeen and Pegwai and rapidly sketched out their quest, the dangers they brought with them and what they were going to need to continue their journey. "So," she finished, "What do you say, my friend? Can you help them?"

"Magí, Maggí, you never could make much of a story. What a story this is. Ho, what a story, I have to know it all, every nuance." He leaned forward, focusing all his intensity on Pegwai. "You must, you must tell me the end, oh Scholar, so Nanojan can sing the whole." He bubbled over with laughter at the blank astonishment on Pegwai's face. "Nanojan Sogan is who you see, my dear, Nanojan the ancient and decrepit, dependent on the charity of children and the joyous strength of Zenica the Pallah dancer. You will tell me, say you will."

Pegwai opened and closed his mouth but no sound came forth; awkward in a way he'd never been before, he came all anyhow to his feet, stumbled across the short space between the benches and fell to his knees in front of the startled old Balayar. He dipped his head to the tiles then straightened. "I have read . . . I have read everything the Lumat has of yours, oh Master. I have . . . I had never hoped . . . no one said . . . ." He swallowed and after a moment achieved coherence. "I would be honored, oh Master; whatever happens, I will try to see you have my notes and if I reach the Lumat safe, I'll send you everything from here to there." He got to his feet, his natural ease returned, and laughed a laugh to match Sogan's. "Nanojan the Singer. I begin to think young Chulji is wiser than he knows; he said when he joined us that poets would sing about our quest." He settled himself back on his bench. "Maggí, we can't. . . ."

"Endanger the ancient poet?" Sogan made his soft bubbling chuckle. "Oh Scholar, oh Pegwai Dih. No no, I will not have it. I will talk to you all, especially the Boy. The children will love him, yes yes. Two? Yes, two are Chalarosh also, orphans out of the Tail. He's a nice boy? He won't bite? Then that's settled, you'll stay here until your gear is ready and Zenica can find you a proper guide.''

Maggí cleared her throat. ''Perhaps we'd better wait for Zenica, old friend; she might not want a handful of strays landed on her without warning.''

Sogan sighed and shook his head. ''Oh Maggí Solitaire, oh Solitaire, you miss too much.''

''Now, Sogan, who're you trying to push on me this time? Give it up, my friend. What I miss, I don't miss, if you see my meaning. And to return to more apposite topics, it's not only the old poet who'd risk danger. What about the children? Ravvayad out to kill a six year old would hardly spare another.''

He made a tossing gesture with both hands. ''Lifefire burns as well as blesses; if it be, so be it.''

Maggí got to her feet. ''Well, old friend, we will spend the night on my ship and come again tomorrow this time. Think over what you've heard and talk this over with Zenica. We want your aid in finding a guide and outfitting the Company, but there's no need to do more unless you are sure you know what you are doing.''

MARCHING ON TO APODOSIS.
or
OH MY ACHING SADDLE SORES.

Dinner in Maggí's quarters. Maggí and Skeen making last minute plots. The others are elsewhere eating at Ship's Table with the half dozen traders now occupying the other cabins.

''Cida Fennakan,'' Maggí murmured. ''I've never made it

that far west. Not a good place, Skeen, you want to watch yourself. Funor run it. Rogue males." She looked thoughtfully at her glass. "Might make a new market. I don't know. Couldn't be much worse than Kulchikan. The thing is, I've got no contacts there. Not yet." She smiled at Skeen. "Friendship is friendship, but I've got a ship to consider. So, same price to meet you there as to bring you here."

Skeen tapped her fingers on the tabletop. "Why not. I'll have to work anyway once we get there."

"It's more than the ship, Skeen." Maggí gazed at the wall, eyes unfocused. "I've got a place," she said softy, "a beautiful green valley where no one comes but me. Where my daughters live. I've got a flock of children there. Like Sogan and Zenica. And two of them are daughters of my body, got because I wanted them; their fathers know nothing about them. They depend on me, the children and the quiet folk I found to live there and take care of them." She blinked, sat straighter. "I know I don't need to ask you not to say anything." She sighed. "There are times when I want desperately to lay all this down," she waved her hand in an including circle, "when one more fight is that fight too many, especially when it's something stupid like some man trying to tromp me just because I'm a woman. Ah well, that feeling doesn't last long. Soon as I've had a good night's sleep, a hot meal, and the hangover has settled to a dull throb, I know very well I'd last maybe six months before I had to get out and do something."

Next afternoon, before she left the Company at Sogan's house, Maggí took Chulji aside. "Come along with me, young Min, join the Crew and work for shares as well as five coppers a day flying fee. This is the smoothest trip we've had down the Tail, and the most profitable. And I know Hammorianet who's High Mother of the Nest at the jet mine. With a little maneuvering there's a good possibility I can get you a discount on the jet she produces."

Chulji's antennas fluttered and his mouth parts clicked together; he jittered around, watched the Boy and the Beast for a moment, swung back. "I really wish . . ." he started, reached out and touched Maggí's arm very gently. "I can't come with you now, Captain." He clicked his mouth parts in frustration. "I can't leave until I know whether the Ykx will give Skeen the Key to the Gate. The Boy. . . ."

Maggí took his gripper and smiled at him. "Loyalty isn't something to be ashamed of. We'll be glad to have you soon as you're free." Her smile widened to a grin. "Not a surplus of Min about willing to run around with a mixed bunch like my crew. We aren't exactly respectable, young friend."

With Nanojan's reservoir of good will and Zenica's energetic efforts and Skeen's bag of gold (rapidly depleting), the Company collected supplies and mounts for the trip upriver and in two days were ready to leave—except for the guide. Few on the coast had much idea what lay inland. The Plains Min were up there somewhere and did not welcome visitors; in the fringe lands of the Hill Country between Min and coast colonies were outcasts, hunters and trappers, hermits and mountain men, and bands of raiders who swept down on outlying farmsteads and mining settlements. And on the far side of the river was the Great Swamp; everyone but Nagamar who tried passing through there went down with fever or died from the bites of the poisonous leggy serpents, or had their flesh stripped from their bones by any of a hundred variations of the kirrpitts that were such a menace along the Tail, or had eggs laid deep in their muscle by bore-worms and were eaten alive by the larva that hatched from these. Not a place to explore for the pleasure of it. In spite of the dangers of Swamp and Hill Country, there were men in Karolsey who'd go anywhere there was a promise of trouble, excitement, and profit.

On the third day Zenica produced a possible guide. He'd been to the Lakelands before, he was one of the semi-wild wanderers moving from wilderness to town and back, trading for furs with trappers who couldn't get into town for some reason, touching the fringes of Plains Min territory and trading with them, now and then wheedling something out of the Ykx. He confirmed the existence of a filled Gather on the eastern shore of Lake Sydo (Pegwai nearly flew out of his skin with the news, but Skeen was more ambivalent). The man was irritated that someone else knew about the Ykx, but was reconciled to it when Pegwai informed him that the Tanul Lumat know about that Gather before he arrived in this world. Zenica sent him to the Quiet Garden to talk with Skeen and settle the terms of his employment.

He came in silent and stiffly hostile, a small man covered with honey-amber fur that darkened in a mask about his eyes and over his ears; he stared at her from behind the blue foil eyes of a high bred cat. Another singling Pass-Through. There were more of them about this place than Skeen had expected. She wondered why the Honjiukum didn't realize there was something funny about that valley . . . hunh! Maybe they did. Maybe I really did manage to fox them with the hijjik stampede and they headed for the valley just in case. She looked up as the man stopped in front of her. "Sujippyo?"

His expression didn't change. "Torska?"

Skeen smiled. "Now that we've got that settled, what're you going to cost me?"

"Maybe nothing."

"True. We wouldn't have to pay the river and it'll take us where we want to go. But a river's got no tongue to tell us about snags ahead. It'd be worth something to know about those. Not all that much, we've got two Min to fly scout for us. And a scholar for strategy and me for all round meanness. This Pass-Through plans to pass back, sujippyo, and she'd tromp flat anyone who tries to stop her." She stopped talking and let him think it over. Silence stretched between them. After a few minutes he got to his feet and started toward the door into the house. At the door, he turned halfway back to her as if to say something, but without warning he flipped something at her.

She plucked from the air a slender sleeve knife, meant to hit her hilt on. She'd caught the hilt. She held it up, raised a brow. "Well?"

His smile was a slight tightening of his lips, a rippling of fur over his bold cheekbones. He crossed to her and took back the knife. "You read muscle damn well."

"Because I caught the hilt instead of the blade?"

"That, yeah. Zenica didn't name you."

"Skeen."

"Ship Picarefy? The Rooner?"

"Got it."

"When?"

"Tomorrow morning just before dawn."

"Got it. You providing the mounts?"

"Karynxes. One extra available for a guide."

"Ten gold. Now."

She laughed. "Why not. That's what Zenica said to give you and I expect if you ran out on us life would get uncomfortable for you here. Maggí and I are excellent friends." She bent to one side, caught up a small pouch and handed it to him.

"Meet here?"

"No. The Esher Gate. If the Ravvayad follow precedent, they'll hit us between here and the gate. They've failed every time they've tried that, so I suspect a double attack this time. You might take a look about the gate for anything that smells suspicious. Be careful. . . ." She broke off, shook her head. "Sorry about that, I've been around the Aggitj too long. By the way, you want to tell me your name? Or do we just call you guide."

"Britt'll do. It's enough."

"Britt it is. Tomorrow, Yes."

"Yes."

The attack came half a stad before they reached the gate—four naked twisting forms. Pegwai cracked one skull, Skeen broke a kneecap with the staff she'd taken to carrying, the Beast bit the downed man and leaped away, Hart's spear skewered a third, and the last started backing off, mouth gaping, poison glands swollen ready to spit the corrosive deadly fluid at anyone who got too close. Skeen darted him, the Beast scurried over and bit the Ravvayad in the face, then curled up in the Boy's arms. The housefolk from Zenica and Sogan who were leading the karynxes some distance behind the Company came up with them, handed the leadropes to Skeen, calmly ignoring the bodies splayed out on the street. "Lifefire tend your journey with Bona Fortuna," the taller man said; he inclined his head, then walked off with his associate who hadn't said a word the whole time.

"Well." Skeen made a face at Pegwai when she saw his

silent laughter. "Were they afraid we were going to ask them to come along?"

Pegwai poked at one of the corpses with the end of his staff. "They don't approve of the company we keep, that's all."

Britt was waiting just inside the gate. "I took a short walk along the road," he said. "Nothing obvious, but just this side of the crescent bend I saw a flock of gurdjis fly up from one copse and settle in another."

Skeen nodded. "Chul, see what you can see without being obvious about it." As the Min-Skirrik boy fluttered off, a soft gray mourning owl, she swung round, scowled at the karynxes. The Aggitj, Timka, and probably the Boy were expert riders, though karynxes might be strange to them, but she was merely adequate and Pegwai not even so good as that; his legs were too short and plump to get much purchase. "Ders, take care of my karynx, will you. I'm walking for the first bit. Peg?"

"I'd rather have solid ground under me if I have to swing this." He banged his staff against the dirt.

Chulji came fluttering back, shifted to Skirrik. "Three of them," he said. "And three on the other side of the road."

"Djabo's bleary eyes. How far from the road?"

"On the left, two karynx's length, a little closer on the right."

"Bows or spears?"

"Both."

Skeen rubbed her chin. "Boy, you know their constraints. Will they sit in the trees and try to skewer us long distance?"

"Yah, em. They's room out here. If they can't get me, ul try fo's many a you's they can get."

"I see. Hm." She turned to Britt. "Two choices. Fight or go round. Me, I'd rather go round. Can we?"

"Roundabout and a lot of time, that's all; easy to find riding room down here."

Skeen ran her fingers through her hair (hair that was mostly dark brown now, with only the tips pale and stiff). "If there were just the three," she said, "I think I'd try taking them out. Six, though. . . . I don't know. I'm not happy at the prospect of them creeping up on us some night when we're deep in the mountains."

Pegwai leaned on his staff. "Forgetting whether it's six or three, if you were alone without us on your mind, what would you do?"

"Go round now and take them out one by one when they followed."

"Well?"

Skeen slapped her hip. "All right, why not. Britt knows the land and they don't. Let them sit and sweat." She smoothed her hair down, moved the few steps to Ders and took the leadrope from him. "Seems I ride after all. Let's go."

THE ADVANTAGE OF THE HIGH GROUND.
or
WHAT A HANDY THING IT IS TO HAVE WINGS.

Because he didn't have a Pallah form yet and might never have one (which made riding a karynx decidedly awkward), Chulji volunteered to fly watch over Ravvayad, flitting back at intervals to let Skeen know what was happening. The Kalakal assassins sat patiently in their copses until half the morning had passed, then they filed into the middle of the road and stood arguing for a while; eventually they walked back toward Karolsey until they reached the place where Skeen and the others had stood waiting for Chulji's scouting report. Three kept on going, vanishing through the gate. One dropped to his hands and knees and moved his head in circling darts, sniffing out their trail. He followed it a short way, got to his feet and came back. The three stood silent in the road and waited until one of the others came through the Esher Gate riding a karynx and leading three more. Then with three mounted and one tracking, changing the tracker every hour, they started after the Companions.

By the time the four Ravvayad circled back to the road it was almost sundown. They rode hard until their mounts were stumbling with fatigue, then made camp, graining and watering and rubbing down the karynxes before fixing themselves a cold meal. Chulji left them chewing stolidly on dried meat and hard biscuits, washing these down with drafts of water they fetched from the river.

In the other camp, some twenty stads ahead of the Kalakal, the Aggitj divided the night into four watches and drew straws to determine who would sleep when. After introducing a very nervous Britt as a friend, the Boy set the Beast to prowling the trees around them.

There was no disturbance of any kind that night.

Bright clear dawning, turning to a warm rather windy day. They rode past rich farmland. There were few houses visible yet they were seldom alone in the landscape—drovers watching herds, women washing clothes beside the river, and men, women, and children working in the fields. Most straightened (glad of the excuse to rest weary backs) to wave at the travelers and call out greetings.

Toward the end of the day they passed from croplands to grazing lands, low rounded swells covered with a short succulent grass. The road began to tilt upward and lose its identity as a road. By the time they camped for the night (having made another forty stads; the karynx lope was effortless and slightly faster than a similar gait in a horse), they had gained ground on the Kalakal because their pursuers had to let their mounts rest and recover from the hard work of the first day; part of every hour they slid from the saddle and walked beside the karynxes.

Another quiet night.

By midday they were deep into the foothills, taking a lesson from the Chalarosh and trotting part of the time at the

stirrup so the karynxes would have the energy for a run if that
was needed. Chulji reported that the followers were making
up time because they were still on a relatively flat stretch of
road while the Company was dealing with steep rises and
sudden drops and a pathway that was so unused that only
Britt knew exactly where it was. Some distance below them
the river whispered noisily about the rocks in its bed and on
the other bank mists and clouds of insects rose from the
swamplands stretching out to the horizon without many breaks
in the low wide-spreading trees, with only the occasional
glint of water among the cottony green. The land seemed
empty, but Britt was much more alert now; Timka shifted
also and scouted the land ahead of them while Chulji kept a
close watch on the Kalakal. Timka flew back to report she'd
seen five other persons moving on the mountain slopes ahead,
widely scattered, none of them anywhere near the river.
"Trappers," Britt said. "Maybe miners. Maybe just some
wilders out hunting for their next meal."

When they stopped to camp, Pegwai was exhausted and
had knots in his muscles that kept him sitting still and silent
for his pride's sake. If he moved too suddenly, he'd groan
and give way. Skeen watched him sweat for a few minutes,
then shook her head and got to her feet. "Whenever Tibo
visited some of his family, he came back like that," she said.
"Friend of mine, trained as a tumbler and juggler when he
was a boy; tried to be a boy again, showing off for the
family. On your stomach, Scholar." She bent over him,
squeezed his shoulder. "Only therapeutic, I promise," she
murmured. "Company manners."

That night Skeen was restless, very tired. Too tired to
sleep, she told herself—both of us, she told herself when she
heard Pegwai shifting about too often. Thinking about Tibo
was a mistake, she told herself, and this time it was true.
Thinking about Tibo fed the ache of need in her and the pain.
That and the nearness of the event that would free her from
this world or keep her here forever. What she'd told Pegwai
about searching further, if there were no Ykx at Lake Sydo or
if those Ykx proved uncooperative, that was moon-dreaming,
talking to keep her spirits from sagging so low she couldn't

get out of bed or eat or do anything but sleep or gloom. Fifteen days Britt said. Three gone. Small creaks and rustles as Pegwai turned over again. Sleep, old friend, you need it. Take your own advice, Skeen, another night like this and you'll be a rag. Peg. Peg. Peg. She wanted him and didn't want, was afraid of wanting. More terrified than she'd been the first time she'd slipped alone into a warehouse going after empty flakes and domp boards, a combination of terror and desire that churned her insides to mush that threatened to run out her toes.

An hour or so before dawn Ravvayad came creeping around the camp, trying to get close enough for a clean shot at the Boy. This wasn't the desert they knew, this land was too lush for them. They weren't accustomed to working through slender shivering trees and crackly brush, they had sloughed their robes, wore only weapon harness and loincloth; but even so their clothing snagged on branches, their feet seemed to seek out small dry branches and crunch them with crackles loud enough to wake the dead. They didn't make one quarter the noise they thought, but it was enough. Domi heard the rustles, his not-hair picked up their body heat. He turned slowly trying to locate them. Out in the darkness the Beast hissed and spat. Domi gave a shout, loosed a quarrel from his crossbow into the center of the loudest sound, clawed the bowstring back and shot again. Then the guard was beside him, holding out his bow. Domi took it, shot a third time while the guard laid in another quarrel. He held the bow out, but Domi shook his head. "Gone," he said, then pointed as the Beast came trotting into the small dell, smugness dripping off his small body. They watched him snuggle up against the Boy.

The moment the alarm sounded, Pegwai and the other Aggitj rolled from their blankets and leaped to stand in a circle about the Boy, Skeen on her feet, darter out. They all relaxed as the Beast sighed and flattened himself against the Boy's side. Timka shifted from her cat-weasel form, spoke softly to Chulji, who took to the air a moment later, a night-owl on silent wings. She pulled on the loose robe she was wearing on this leg of the trip (it made quick shifts simpler) and belted it about her. "Chulji's up," she said. "He'll watch them back to where they're stopping."

*   *   *

Dawn, pink in gray; breakfast fire, coals more black than
red. Skeen emptied her mug, handed it to Ders for washing.
"Britt, tell me about the land ahead. It's time I started
working on the Ravvayad."

"No!" Timka leaned over the fire, hand out, reaching
toward Skeen. "No. You stay with us."

Skeen looked startled. "What?"

Timka folded her hands in her lap. "It's easy. I've been
thinking about this. Ji and I can put them on foot. Spook the
karynxes from under them. We have to get close, but we can
do it under cover, where there are trees—tall ones, get away
while they're picking themselves up. It's not so dangerous
that way. Besides, the Beast and Domi took out one of them
and Domi scratched another and they spent most of the night
catching up with us. Without karynxes they won't have a
hope of catching us. It's not so dangerous, don't you see?"

Skeen smoothed a finger across her lips, frowned at the
fire. Pegwai watched them both, saying nothing. The guide
was back among the trees, detached from all this, watching
with cool interest. The Aggitj and the Boy bustled about
getting the breakfast things washed, the gear packed and
loaded on the karynxes, leaving the planning and all the
arguing to the others. Skeen watched the fire die a while
longer, then she looked up. "It won't stop them," she said.
"They'll find other mounts."

"Where?"

"I don't know."

"Neither will they."

"Don't discount luck. Bona Fortuna is a capricious dame,
she can conjure life out of stone for them if she chooses."

"Whatever happens, we'll slow them down. Do it again if
Bona Fortuna kisses them. They can't stop us. Even if they
suspect us, they can't shoot down every bird in the sky and we
can stay out of bowshot while we're watching them, get away
quick once we've hit them, hit them any time we want as
long as we're careful."

Skeen gazed at her, gave her a long slow smile. "Point
taken." She got to her feet. "Hal?"

"Saddled up, gear stowed, ready to go, Skeen ka."

Pegwai grunted onto his feet. "Do you realize how sharp that backbone is? Comes right through the leather." He sighed. "I'm ready, I suppose. No use putting it off any longer."

"Timmy?"

"If you must, Skeen, will you please please make it Ti? I'm flying today, I'll see you come the noon halt." She stepped out of her robe, shifted to hawk and swept up out of the dell.

Skeen frowned after her, a look both speculative and amused, then she swung into the saddle. "Let's go."

Noon halt. "They crawled back to their camp," Chulji said, speaking through a mouthful of cheese and raisins and the contortions of his mouthparts that were the Min-Skirrik equivalent of a broad grin. "A nush or two later, one of them goes riding back toward Karolsey. All hunched over he was. You plunked him good, Domi, shoulder or back. The other two ate and then they rolled up in their blankets and took a nap; they woke up about an hour ago and started coming after us. They're way way back and not coming fast."

"How long before they catch us again?"

"Well, hard to say. Unless we waste an awful lot of time, not before dawn, even if they ride all night, um, probably even if they really pushed the karynxes. I'll watch them some more, but I don't think they're going to try."

Skeen turned to Timka. "Then I say wait. Leave them alone for a while. Two reasons. We're setting up a pattern—we ride and try to increase the distance between the two parties, defend ourselves if attacked, but we don't go after them. That way they will be the more surprised when you hit them; your job will be easier, safer. And, though they don't know it, they're acting like rear guards back there, keeping the locals off our backs." She flicked the end of her nose, laughed. "I wonder if they realize that."

"I'll keep watching them, Skeen." Chulji rose and fluttered away.

"And I'll keep hunting out ambush points." Timka rose, dropped her robe, and fluttered away.

"Min," Skeen said. "I thought I was getting used to them."

Pegwai walked beside her to her mount. "Timka is very different now."

She turned to look at him, her eyes blank. "I was thinking that this morning. I'm not sure any more. Maybe she knows." She swung into the saddle, gazed down at him. "More knots?"

"Not so far, Lifefire be blessed." He stroked his hand along her leg, smiled up at her. "I suppose it's as well we stick to company manners."

"Damn you, Peg." Half-irritated, half-laughing, she clucked the karynx into a walk.

On the fifth day out, the pair of Ravvayad were still trailing over a dozen stads behind and showing no real interest in catching up.

Two hours before sundown, Timka came darting back, dropped to the ground in front of Skeen and melted to the naked form of the woman they knew. Skeen threw her the robe and she slipped into it. "Trouble ahead," Timka said. She tied the belt with a sharp jerk of the ends. "Waiting for us, about half a stad. Nemin—a general mix, wearing rags and leather, long shaggy hair; those with hair, beards, about two-thirds are Pallah. No Chalarosh, some Nagamar males, one Aggitj, the rest are Balayar and rogue Funor. Two with longbows, otherwise spears and knives. One has something that looks like a saber. I think but can't be sure others have slings and whips. About a score of men all told. But there was a lot of growth around, trees and brush, so I'm not really sure about numbers. Place seems to be molded for ambushes. Steep slope left side, cranky going, ravines, scree that looks unstable, lot of brush with thorns. Right side, sort of leaning cliff. The only clear path lies along a narrow stone lip that hangs over the river. If we want to keep following the river, we have to take that lip."

Britt nodded. "I know that place, more blood spilled there than on a butcher's ground. At least twenty?"

"Yes. Spread along about two hundred paces."

"Standard tactics—they mean to let us pass, then close both ends of the lip, spook the karynxes over the edge, cut the throats of any left alive." He brought a leg up, crossed it over the saddle in front of him. One hand on his thigh, the thumb of the other hooked over his belt, he frowned at the sky and chewed on the smooth black flesh of his lower lip. "We can't go round, just back. You won't go back. Don't need to tell me that. Happen to catch sight of a one-eyed man, black hair halfway down his back, wide as he is tall and that's saying some?"

"I saw mostly shadows and bits."

"That many, though, sounds like Naels the Eye. Runs about with three or four, picks up strays when he needs them."

Skeen looked quickly around at the others. Eyes on her waiting for what she'd say. "What about fording the river, going by on the far side?"

"Nope. Nagamar have been burned too many times by hillmen. These days they kill whoever sets foot on their side of the river. And this side, if you take a look down there, you'll see there's a brake too thick to force through mounted. Might do it if you're on foot and desperate and didn't give a shit about your hide."

"Lovely. How far are you in this?"

"How exactly do you mean that?"

"Only that you're hired to guide, not fight."

"Come up with something reasonable, I'll do my part."

Skeen grimaced. The Aggitj grinned at her, waiting; they'd grown up a lot on this trip, there was an assurance about them that showed, but they still waited for her to point the way. The Boy waited, quiet and resigned, with the Beast in his arms; can he remember anything but fighting? Pegwai smiled at her with the kind of confidence that irritated her; he was too old and too artful to be acting like that, like he was another Aggitj. She smiled down at Timka. "You and me?"

Timka didn't bother answering; she pulled off the robe, tossed it to Skeen who draped it across the saddle in front of her, blurred into that snaky powerful cat-weasel, gray and tan fur mottled like a clouded leopard's pelt, long limber neck,

large furred pads that made less sound than a feather moving
over difficult ground, gray horn claws, ripping teeth that
showed fearsomely when she opened her mouth in a soundless snarl that needed no translation.

Skeen nodded, turned to the guide. "Britt, hold up here
about an hour, shouldn't take more than that to clear the road
or get ourselves killed. That happens, you get everyone back
to Karolsey."

Pegwai started to protest, then shut his mouth.

She smiled at him, slid off the karynx and moved over to
Timka-cat. "Hal, you and the others, you take care of the
Boy." She clipped the lanyard to the darter's butt, did a body
flutter to loosen her muscles. "You know the land, Ti-cat.
Take us around behind them."

They clambered across a pair of ravines, slipped like shadows through a thin scatter of trees, glided round impassable
clumps of dry thorny brush, picked a careful path through a
mutter of dry grasses, leaves, and small twigs. Skeen had
learned silentwalk on litter-scummed warehouse floors where
noise alarms would have nailed her if she faltered. Not so
different from this. Ti-cat was a hunter by nature and instinct,
padding over scruff and scree, soundless as a ghost on a foam
mattress, a ripple in the air, barely visible even when Skeen
was looking directly at her.

Naels' men were getting restive. The Company was due,
but they weren't suspicious yet and paid little attention to
what was behind them. Not used to being hit from behind,
Skeen thought; they do all the hitting. She grinned at Ti-cat,
got a fearsome grin back from her. They crept to within a
man-length of the ambushers; Skeen eased the holster flap
back and brought out the darter.

She started down the line, darter set on spray, its almost
inaudible clicks merging with the rustle of the leaves; she
shot whatever bits she could see, legs, arms until one man
shouted alarm when he saw the next over topple from a low
branch. After that Skeen didn't bother about noise, but ran
full out, the darter spitting its bursts until the reservoir ran
dry. Before that happened, she managed to take out close to a
dozen of the ambushers.

Ti-cat hit them as they began to wake to danger and start for Skeen, hamstringing the runners with a slash of her claws, sometimes taking the time to tear out a throat as they went down.

One man had a longbow, but it was awkward in close work. He tried to get the distance he needed and managed to get off one shaft. Timka flashed away, her flank misting so the point went harmlessly past her. Before he could try again, Skeen was on him with her boot knife. Slash through the bowstring, foot hooked behind his heel. As he toppled, Ti-cat flashed her bloodied claws across his throat. Another exchange of grins, and they went after the rest, working together as if they'd practiced it for years. A stone grazed Skeen's head, Ti-cat rushed in low and fast, a flow of tan and gray, raked the legs from under the slinger, flicked her claws across his throat. A bobtail lance sent Ti-cat scrambling and shifting into the misty half-state. A huge man hefted another, ready to throw the moment she solidified. Skeen came in behind him, put a knife in his kidneys then across his throat. And so it went until they'd cleaned out the trees and brush, until all the wilders were down from the darts, or dead.

They walked out onto the stone lip, settled to wait for the others. Skeen took the small leather-covered waterbottle from her belt, refilled the darter's reservoir, slipped in a new capsule of paragee, uncovered the charge plate, and laid the weapon on the stone to catch the long rays of the setting sun. Better if it were noon light, but every little bit helped.

Timka curled her paws beneath her and stretched out in shade. After a minute she began licking the blood off her paws and washing her muzzle with a lazy contentment, almost purring. Skeen watched her a while, then laughed. Ti looked around, purred louder.

A large bird swooped low, screeched, went darting away. "Chulji?" Skeen said. Ti-cat nodded.

Ten minutes later Britt rode his karynx onto the lip.

Skeen caught up the darter, slid the cover over the charter and holstered the weapon, got to her feet, and looked past him. "The others?"

"Five minutes back. Better to be sure." He ran his eyes over the shadowy slopes, the gently rustling trees. "The wilders?"

"About a dozen drugged, some others hamstrung or otherwise wounded, the rest dead. Why was Chulji here? What about the Kalakal Ravvayad?"

"Following as before about five stads back. Chulji came to report. The Scholar sent him here to see what was happening. Your Aggitj are annoyed at missing the fight."

"Wasn't a fight. More like a trap shoot."

"Naels One-eye there?"

"If he's a big man with black hair twisted into a single braid, a beard that parts in the middle, huge hands, and a way with a bob-tail lance, then he's one of the dead. Ti-cat treed him and I slit his throat."

Britt's nose twitched and his ears flattened against his skull, then he tried a tentative smile. "Remind me not to irritate the pair of you." He glanced at Ti-cat, looked quickly away when she gave him a cat-grin filled with curving yellow fangs.

Chulji flew over again. A moment later the rest of the company rode onto the lip. Skeen swung into the saddle and tossed Timka her robe as she shifted to her Pallah form. The Aggitj came swarming around her, throwing questions at her, interrupting each other, their karynxes sidling and dipping their horns, infected by the boys' excitement. "Hey, calm down," she was yelling so she could be heard over their noise, "or you'll have us all in the river. Listen, you'll hear it all once we're in camp. I don't want to hang around here," she glanced toward Timka, saw she was mounted and ready to go, "the tale will tell better over a hot cup of tea."

The guide stood at the edge of a long bare slope of scree looking down at the river that was all black glides and silver foam in the light of the waxing moon. Skeen went to stand beside him. "How far is the lake?"

"We should reach the Bend country this time tomorrow. Five to seven days after that, depending on what meets us and how the going has changed since I was last there. North of

the Bend is Min country, though they don't come into the
canyons much. I'm not sure how they'll take strange Min in
their skies.'' He glanced south along the river. ''They won't
like us pulling that pair after us. Nor will the Ykx. Ykx and
Chalarosh mix like oil and fire. Maybe you can fiddle bringing the Boy; he's a cub and the Ykx think high of cubs. That
pair's different. Ravvayad killers.''

''Hm. What's the leeway with the Ykx?''

''They'll be watching four, five days out; the Min will let
them know someone's coming and who it is.''

''Right. The Ravvayad are staying back; I get the feeling
they're following until they can get reinforcements, maybe
some new leadership. What they've got hasn't worked out
that great for them this far. Canyon country coming up. Hm.
Give them two more days, Ti can scout out the ground, then
we take them out.''

He said nothing, she was talking to herself and he knew it.

They rounded the bend of the river and started moving
almost due west through increasingly stony canyon lands, a
maze of steep-walled cuts with the Plain rising farther and
farther above them. Barren arroyos cut the walls; most of
them had streams of varying depths and ferocity dashing
down them to merge with the river—streams they had to
ford, as many as a dozen in a day.

On the middle of the second day in the canyons, when the
sun was striking down on stone and water with dazzling force
and the world was half dissolved in light, Skeen and Timka
went crawling over scree and scruff into a hollow among
huge boulders near where another arroyo stream tumbled
down to the river. Skeen poured water on a towel, wrapped it
about her head and settled into the meager shade, Timka
dropped her robe and took wing, spiraling into the wind to
ride the thermals over the canyon, a golden bird dissolving
into the hot gold glare. Skeen blinked up at her. ''Min! Life
is not fair, not at all.'' She wiped her hands on the eddersil of
her tunic, drew her arm across her brow to wipe away sweat
that kept getting into her eyes. She sighed with envy, added a
bit more water to the sodden towel, then she eased back and

drifted into a light doze, stirring now and then to glance at Timka.

An hour passed. She stirred, looked up. Timka broke her circling, dropped down, rose quickly, flew toward the arroyo and dropped again. Skeen pulled off the towel, rose onto her knees and eased across the hollow to a place where wind had blown dried weed into a crotch between two of the larger boulders.

The Kalakal were relaxed, their karynxes ambling along. Though they still wore their robes, their veils were untied, blowing back from their faces; those faces were flushed and coated with sweat. They reached the turbulent arroyo stream and started across, eyes on the treacherous footing. Skeen set the darter for bursts, rose to her feet and put a burst in each of them, part of the burst hitting them in the faces. The water caught hold of them, tugged them out into the river where their sodden robes dragged them under. The karynxes would have bolted, but Timka came bounding down the arroyo, a sure-footed cat-weasel, and locked their feet with her Min control of ordinary beasts.

Skeen scrambled down, stripped the gear off the beasts, went through the saddle pouches, dumping everything but their store of coin into the river. She left the pouches and the rest of the gear on the scatter of boulders for anyone who might want them. She looked at her hands, swiped at the sweat on her face. "Why not," she said aloud. She stripped, tossed her gear onto the same rocks, and waded into the shallow eddy where the spray of boulders swept into the river.

While she scrubbed at herself with the handfuls of grit, Ti-cat stretched, yawned, and laid her long body out in a boneless pile of fur atop one of the flatter boulders, yellow-bronze eyes fixed on Skeen. A moment later she yawned again, shifted to her Pallah form, and slid into the water. Laughing and agile, she jumped about splashing water over Skeen, startling her into laughter and retaliation.

When they tired of playing, they sat side by side in the swirling water, enjoying a cool clean feeling, comfortably weary, wholly relaxed. Skeen turned her head, looked lazily at Timka. "We make one helluva fighting team."

"Naels One-eye wouldn't argue with you if he could still talk."

"Pegwai thinks you've changed a lot."

"You?"

"Probably not as much as it seems from the outside. You think you've changed?"

Timka fluttered her hands in the water, watched them distort as they wiggled. "More in the past months than in all my life before. My home folk are ignorant because they don't want to know. They don't know about the Min living with the Skirrik, living in harmony—both kinds valued. They don't know about Plains Min because nobody messes with Plains Min, no Min slaves in the coastlands. They don't even know what Pallah are really like and Pallah are right there. If they don't know, how can they want more than what they've got? I want, Skeen. I want to do . . . to see . . ." she spread her hands, "everything."

"A lot of that everything is pretty grungy. Don't expect wonders."

"Skeen."

"Sorry."

A large hawk came spiraling down, landed on a boulder, and screeched at them.

Skeen sighed, got to her feet. "Go away, Chulji, tell them we're coming."

Three days later a great dark form rode the thermals above them.

"Ykx?" Skeen said.

"Yes. One of the outriders."

They watched as the Ykx circled above them a last time and drifted away toward the west.

"The herald flies before us."

"Yes."

The lake stretched to the horizon; its blue glittered glass-hard in the hammering sunlight. Pale and distant, half lost in heat haze, the heart island Perinpar Dih had mentioned shimmered like a mirage under a swarm of soaring forms. Skeen couldn't see the lake's far shore, but this one was spectacular with fold after vertical fold of hard gray granite and cliffs rising a hundred meters above the gentle slope of the sandy shore.

The guide led them along the grassy dunes near the foot of one of the folded cliffs, out around a bulge and into a narrow crack in the cliffs that led into a miniature valley with woods, meadows, a gossamer streak of waterfall at the back and about five hundred meters away, a small bubbly stream with a single deep pool. There were some huts among the trees, rough stone walls and what looked like ax-cut shakes on the roof, a pole corral with water trough and a broad shallow manger. Skeen went into one of the huts, looked around. Two beds, a chair, and a table. A box on the wall with a hinged lid that held a number of candles and some neatly turned candlesticks. She came back out. "Not fancy, but it'll keep the wind off and the rain out. Ti, you want to have this one with me? Good. The rest of you suit yourselves."

When the karynxes were in the coral, feed box and water trough filled, Skeen went hunting for the guide and found him up near the mouth of the valley, sitting on a flat round stone about a meter thick and five meters wide. He'd stripped off everything but a flimsy pair of underpants; still, sweat was beading on the skin that showed and his fur was already damp in blotches. The sun was almost directly overhead, hot, bright; there was no movement in the air, the steep sides of the valley shutting out any wind. "You do this every time you're here?"

"What you have to do," he said. "Sit and wait until they decide to come calling."

"Night, too?"

"No. No thermals, downdrafts instead. They don't walk unless they have to."

"Want to set up watches? The rest of us can broil an hour or two and give you a break."

"Better not, might scare them off. They're touchy. Took me almost a month to get anyone to come near me the first time I was here. But I would appreciate some cold water and towels now and then."

"I'll tell the Aggitj; they're good about things like that. What are they like? Hard bargainers? How long before they show?"

"They know me, so the waiting and watching should be shorter. Might not be, depends on the mood they're in." He glanced at her, looked away. "What you get depends on what you've got to trade."

He rubbed thumb against forefinger as if he were rolling his thoughts into small neat balls. "Why do you want to go back there? From what I've seen, you'd do well here."

"Questions, Britt, questions I can't answer this side."

"Family?"

"No. Just questions. Ones I'll have no rest from until I get answers I can accept."

"Sounds like the kind of questions no one finds answers for. Why waste your time?"

"It's my time."

"True. And mine, you're paying for." He looked up. "They're watching now." Three dark forms sailed across and across the narrow jagged slash of sky. "There'll be more tomorrow."

She closed her hands into fists, scowled down at them, beat them suddenly, once, against the stone, then backed away. "Waiting," she said, "the last stretch, that's the worst. I'll send Ders with water in half an hour, that all right?"

"Yes." He lifted a string of wooden worry beads from the stone beside his knee and began running them through his fingers, eyes closed, lips moving, some kind of meditation, a way of passing the time. She watched a moment, happy it was he who had to do that sitting. I'd bite my nails off up to the elbows. She sighed and started back for the camp.

At noon the next day, Skeen took food and water out to Britt. "You were right. Swarms of them out today." She set the bread, cheese, and fruit on the stone, added a pot of tea and some mugs. "Would they get agitated if I joined you there for a while?"

"You think I know? Give it a try and find out. If you feel like it."

She tilted her head back, stood with hands on hips watch
the Ykx drifting about overhead like autumn leaves blown
ing along by a gentle autumn wind. "Come down," she
called to them, but they neither heard nor obeyed. "What's
another day." She climbed up beside Britt and poured herself
a cup of tea. "You ever think of going back?"

"No. And I'm not thinking of it now either. I'm a lot
better off here."

"Some good people here, folk I'll miss if I don't see them
again." She bit into a plum and brooded over this while she
chewed, tossed the seed into the bucket she'd used to carry
the food. "But I'll say this, being stuck on one world (don't
tell me how interesting it is) gives me claustrophobia. And
don't sing me those songs about the beauty of Nature with a
fuckin' capital N, I've had altogether too much of that. Bugs
and snakes and no hot water for a bath unless someone hauls
it for you, wearing the same understuff until you're itching it
instead of your skin." She tapped the waybread to chase the
gnats away, looked at it with disgust. "Fight the bugs for
every mouthful. Huh." She dripped the bread into her tea,
worried off a bite, and sat chewing at it. Britt laughed at her,
began telling her about the year he spent as a slave on a
Pallah estate some distance north of Dum Besar.

Two more days passed.
Noon the third day; Skeen hauled Britt his midday meal
and joined him on the stone.
The Ykx came spiraling down through the hot gold noon
air, wrapped in a shimmering sphere twisted from the sunlight. He hovered before the stone, covered in fur like the
guide, a short plush shading from a pale amber hardly darker
than day-old cream (over his chest and the fronts of his upper
arms) to a darkish gold-brown about the color of a dark bay
horse. His flight skins draped like a cloak along his sides,
cream on the front, bay on the back. He wore a vee-shaped
harness passing from groin to shoulders with horizontal straps,
the leather elaborately inlaid with metal and gemstones, joining the two slants of the vee. All light and airy and elegant
(her fingers twitched with a quiet greed), yet the mechanism

that worked the lift bubble was concealed there, and probably several weapons that could do disastrous things to flesh and bone.

He touched down on the stone; the bubble dissolved and he stood looking from one to the other with deepset amber-crystal eyes.

All doubt flashed away. "Raaal lennn." The word came out in a drawl of vowels and an en that was a quivering hum.

The Ykx heard her, lost his calm for a fragment of an instant. "What does that mean to you?" He struggled to keep his voice even, but didn't quite manage it, a beautiful fluting voice that couldn't help playing with the syllables of Trade-Min until they were barely comprehensible.

"I am a thief," she said.

"You admit it so casually?"

"You asked me to explain. Will you listen or lecture me?"

Britt stared from one to the other, saw they'd forgotten him. He'd said to her, what you get depends on what you have to trade. She had something to trade all right and from the look of it, the Ykx would sell his firstborn to get it.

"I will listen."

"In the course of playing my trade I had acquired certain objects." She gazed blankly at the Ykx, memories suddenly vivid. Buzzard's storeroom, wandering about too restless to sit, still fuming at Duncan; she'd kicked him off Picarefy to Picarefy's delight, then fought with him half across Revelation. What am I, garbage dealer? All his fault, that wart, that. . . . It had been a miserable trip, that one. Low-grade artifacts, her timing off, her nose half-ruined by a frag with Duncan because he messed up her deal with the locals, almost getting them both caught. One of those locals was a hulk who decided he wanted a hack at a foreign woman and challenged Duncan for her. The shithead wouldn't let her deal with that walking gonad—no, he had to show off his muscles and his training. "While gold can be spent anywhere, other things need a specialist to handle them. In the shop where this person did his business I saw quite by chance a number of objects the dealer had just acquired. Among them was a plaque with a low-relief carving of a being much like you; and there are objects with lines and forms much like those on your harness. I found them interesting and asked about them. Rallen work, the dealer said. He'd purchased them from a young man only an hour before; that's why he remembered the name, but he knew nothing of the world where the young man had acquired the objects, nor did anyone else I spoke to."

"Were they old or perhaps recently made?"

"Recent. It is true. This is my profession. Old things bring higher prices. Several of the objects were cast in bronze; you know the patina that age brings to bronze. It can be faked, I don't deny that; there was no question of faking, that bronze was new, almost raw. Why would a man however young and inexperienced destroy half the value of such pieces by removing that patina? To say nothing of the work required. I can't see any reason for that, perhaps you can."

"Noooo. . . ." The word was a long shivery sigh. "What do you want?"

"To go back. The Gate is closed. Open it for me."

The folds of the Ykx's flight skins shifted and stiffened, dark blood running in veins that had been pale before. He blinked slowly, made a complex gesture she couldn't read. "You have been candid, sinsa, let me be equally candid. This is the last Gather on Mistommerk and it is beginning to die." He went silent again, battered by a hope he was afraid to host. "What you bring . . ." he said finally, "if we can believe . . . don't be offended, please, we dare not believe too easily." His hands moved over his harness. "I must, I must confer. You'll wait? Ah, my mind rots. Of course you will wait. I will return. Tomorrow. Yes. Tomorrow." The glow thickened about him and he rose in a graceful sweep toward the top of the cliffs, flattening on the air when he was high enough, soaring swiftly away.

Britt frowned at her. "That was real?"

"Yes."

"You're pretty damn sure about those things you saw."

"That's my business and I'm pretty damn good at it."

"So I heard. Also that you're slippery as half-melted ice but you keep your word once you give it." He slid off the stone. "You've bought your Key. They'll back and fill a bit, but they're hooked. Bona Fortuna kissed you today."

"About time." Skeen strolled beside him toward the camp.
"I was getting to know the dark twin a bit too well."

The sky was thick with dark flakes the moment the sun was
high enough to wake the thermals. Skeen came from her
cabin with her bucket of bath water, saw them, and laughed.
"Word's out." Britt's voice. She looked around, saw him
leaning against the wall of his hut.
"Looks like," she said. "What now?"
"Go sit, both of us. Until they decide to talk."
"Djabo's overbite!"

Shortly after noon the next day three Ykx came drifting
down to the bargain stone.
They questioned Skeen intensively, probing as far as she
would let them into her background (they didn't know the
right questions and she could lead them round and round
without appearing to evade whenever she didn't want to
answer), taking her over and over the incident at the Buzzard's, squeezing everything they could out of her memory,
detailed descriptions of the things she saw, the reasons she
connected them to the Ykx, why couldn't she remember
more, who was the youth who sold the things, where did he get
them, how could she possibly find him after seven years with
so much room to disappear in? All that and more, over and
over.
Skeen answered calmly, patiently; she could be very patient
when she was tracking down rumors of new ruins or when
she was in a Pit exchange doing the other part of her business, bargaining for the best prices on her goods. She was
selling now, a dream and its context, her price a way home.
And by the time the Ykx finished with her, she knew the
terms they'd ask and how far she could push them.

THE BARGAIN IS CONCLUDED.

"We will send an emissary with you."

"Give me a choice. If we aren't reasonably compatible, we could get killed arguing at the wrong time. Let me talk to them, just a chat, You know, see if they can relax with me."

"That is reasonable."

"you know your people better than I; choose those who are able to adjust quickly to strange situations and use them, those able to learn languages and absorb non-verbal information."

"That is most reasonable."

"And don't humor me, it makes me irritable; if I'm teaching fliers how to soar, tell me."

"We hear and obey."

"Are you laughing? I certainly hope so."

"You are a strange person, Skeen myo."

"I refuse to take anything too seriously; if you find that strange, how sad."

"I am afraid, Skeen myo, that we have lost our laughter at least in part; if you succeed in bringing Rallenyo to us, we'll find it again."

"I sit rebuked, my friends. Send on the candidates."

Lipitero was a silent scarred refugee from the Coraish Gather, one of the few survivors. She was older, beyond her fertile years, had a gnarled competence that Skeen found more acceptable than the enthusiasm of the other candidates. Lipitero had seen her children slaughtered by invading

Chalarosh, was nearly killed herself, had dragged herself from under a pile of dead once the Chalarosh were gone, done some crude bandaging on her wounds, and cast herself into the air—soaring out over the desert not caring much whether she lived or died. With a little help along the way and a lot of luck, she reached the Sydo Gather still alive. In the years since, she'd recovered from that horror and developed a wry pleasure in being alive; though she'd never really found a place in the Sydo Gather, she'd made herself useful and been content. The Chalarosh Boy bothered her, but she could bear his presence because she wanted so passionately to bring the Rallenyo back; in a way those ghost figures were replacements for the children she'd lost.

THE KEY SEEKS THE GATE. TELKA WAITS FOR HER REVENGE, BROODING ON THE MOUNTAIN. THE CHALAROSH REGROUP AND ACQUIRE A NEW LEADER. ON THE FAR SIDE OF THE GATE, TIBO IS SOMEWHERE, DOING SOMETHING. or THIS QUEST ISN'T OVER YET.

Skeen strolled out of the valley and stood bare-footed on the sand, lake water lapping close to her toes, water that got darker and softer as the sun dipped lower behind her. A few clouds drifted above her, tinted salmon and gold, heralds announcing the sunset. She kicked at the damp sand and thought of Lipitero. The Key. Odd sort of Key. Too bad it doesn't come equipped with a magic carpet. She thought about that and chuckled. Well, it does. More or less and restricted to one person's use. Lipitero, magic key, magic carpet. Ride the winds almost as well as the Min. I'm getting silly. Must be tired.

She went back into the valley to help eat the supper Pegwai had ready for them. Tomorrow was soon enough to think about all the things she had to do before she could walk back through the Stranger's Gate.